The Lies We Trade

Tyndale House Publishers
Carol Stream, Illinois

Praise for The Lies We Trade

The Lies We Trade is a dynamite debut! Kristine Delano expertly blends domestic suspense with a fascinating behind-the-scenes look at the high-stakes, high-drama life of a Wall Street power player.

RICK ACKER, bestselling coauthor of the Tupelo Grove series

An exciting debut from Wall Street insider Kristine Delano, *The Lies We Trade* is a taut, smart, and suspenseful page-turner full of mystery, betrayal, and hope. I look forward to more Kristine Delano!

TOSCA LEE, *New York Times* bestselling author

The Lies We Trade by Kristine Delano took me deep into the high-stakes world of Wall Street glamour and family secrets. . . . Fans of edge-of-your-seat suspense will be captivated by this masterful blend of corporate intrigue and deeply personal stakes with a wonderful, hopeful ending.

COLLEEN COBLE, *Publishers Weekly* and *USA Today* bestselling author of *Ambush*

A first-class corporate thriller . . . [and] a deeply emotional domestic suspense story, with a fragile family having to withstand nearly unbearable pressures—coming from both within and outside of the home. Delano strikes a wonderful tone with her strong but flawed protagonist Meredith Hansel, making us root for her as her world crashes down. An impressive and timely debut, *The Lies We Trade* will surely find a large audience eager for a multilayered, emotion-forward thriller.

CARTER WILSON, *USA Today* and *Publishers Weekly* bestselling author of *Tell Me What You Did*

Meet your new go-to author for tense, clever psychological thrillers! In *The Lies We Trade*, Delano takes readers on a twisty thrill ride that will keep you guessing until the very end. Highly recommend.

CONNIE MANN, author of *The Crown Conspiracy*

Kristine Delano

THE LIES WE TRADE

Visit Tyndale online at tyndale.com.

Visit Kristine Delano online at kristinedelano.com.

The Lies We Trade

Cover design by Dean H. Renninger

Interior design by Cathy Miller

Edited by Sarah Mason Rische

Published in association with the literary agency of The Steve Laube Agency.

For information about special discounts for bulk purchases, please contact Tyndale House Publishers at csresponse@tyndale.com, or call 1-855-277-9400.

Library of Congress Cataloging-in-Publication Data

A catalog record for this book is available from the Library of Congress.

ISBN 979-8-4005-0492-1

Printed in the United States of America

32 31 30 29 28 27 26
7 6 5 4 3 2 1B

To my husband, Chris—because you're you, I didn't have any firsthand experience to draw upon when writing about a marriage on the brink. So really, all those hours of research are your fault . . . I forgive you.

1

ONE WEEK BEFORE

I always watch for the pivot—I sense it before I see it and I notice it before the crowd. The unusual hire, the buried earnings report, the hitch in the speaker's voice that covers a lie. We each have our own unique superpower. It won't be until much later that I'll realize I've misplaced mine.

"So, Meredith." The host's British accent is gustier than when we spoke off-air. "A lot of investors are wondering—did anyone see this market correction coming? Were you caught napping like the rest?"

My smile tightens. "Markets are unpredictable by nature. The goal is never to predict every move. It's to manage risk appropriately."

"Right, right. But your mid-cap funds were still overweight in tech last quarter, weren't they?" He arches a brow. "Any regrets?"

"Selective overweighting," I correct him and speak to the green light above the camera lens. "These mutual funds are new to my portfolio, but we're confident in our allocations."

His smirk twitches, as if I sidestepped a premeditated trap. "Some might argue that sticking with tech at all was risky. Wouldn't a more conservative approach have protected your investors better?"

There it is. He's been waiting all segment to imply that I've been reckless. That, perhaps, I'm not quite up to the job. I ignore the drip of sweat careening down the back of my neck. "Markets reward conviction, not hesitation. If I'd shifted entirely, I assume you'd be asking why I missed the upside?"

A flicker of irritation crosses his face. "Fair point," he concedes, though clearly he doesn't think so. "Let's talk liability. How did you convince your firm to risk their reputation on a wager?"

The recording light blinks yellow, signaling the interview is nearly over. With everything in me, I need off this stool. I speak into the camera, careful not to scowl. "As you know, Garman Straub is a powerhouse on Wall Street, but we're also a trusted asset manager. We invest in individuals and institutions, from high-tech companies to innovators drilling wells in remote communities. We drive innovation." Straightening my spine, I shift my gaze back to the host. "We don't wager. Why did we launch two exchange-traded funds, called ETFs? Because our clients' financial success is our priority, and our track record speaks for itself."

The host plasters on his broadcast smile. "Well, I suppose we'll find out if your strategy holds. Meredith Hansel, portfolio manager from Garman Straub, it's been a pleasure."

"Likewise. Thank you for having me."

A shrill bell pierces the air of the New York Stock Exchange. "That's a wrap. Great job, everyone," a voice booms from behind me.

I take my first full breath in twenty minutes. Hardwin could have warned me. Our chief legal counsel set this up through his contacts in London. Ever the statesman, he'd never admit motive, but he likely wanted this interview to remind me of my place—dependent on guys like him who've been at this far longer and have paid all their dues.

Flashing an untroubled smile, I shake the hand of my smooth-talking host, and then peel the wires from around my right ear. My hair snarls. Definitely too much spray. The more I pull, the bigger the tangle. I glance over my shoulder. The host smirks. Never fails, at some point I lose my poise.

As I stand at the sound booth teasing out single strands of hair from the earpiece, Betsey marches toward me.

"That was outstanding, Meredith. They want you to stay on." She yanks a folder from her bag, her heavily made-up eyes shining with unshed tears.

"Not a chance. This one's yours." I shove her notes back at her.

"But that producer said—"

"We don't care what any producer says, Betsey. You're up next, and you get the friendlies." I tighten my shoulder blades, willing her to match my posture. "You're ready. You know our funds as well as you know the warm-up at your kickboxing gym."

"Probably better. I do want to do this." She bites her bottom lip, painted a pretty coral, and then lowers her voice. "But Meredith, do you think *they* want me to do this?"

"Of course they do." But I know who she's talking about. It's not the producers or the teams here. Although she's helped me raise a billion in assets, I had to use an undue amount of political capital to get her here. If she missteps, it's a hammer to both our reputations.

"Not everyone wants us to succeed," she whispers.

A sense, almost like a vibration, pulses in my temples. I flick my hair behind my ear. "Of course they don't." I lean in, lowering my voice. "We work in an industry predicated on greed and self-promotion. Not everyone's a bad guy, but they sure don't want us to succeed at their expense." Hardwin's casual mention of this interview comes to mind—a fluff piece, it was not.

"I know." She drops her gaze to the floor. "I just have this feeling . . . like . . . like we might not have the full picture of our sales."

As if I've been sucker punched, air leaves my lungs. Scanning the faces around us, I drag her away from the microphones and cameras. "Betsey," I hiss. "You report to me as a *sales* manager. What do you mean you don't have a full picture of our *sales*?"

The unshed tears return. "I'm sorry. I didn't mean to alarm you. I just—"

The vibration in my temples transforms into sharp jabs. "You can't throw statements around like that. We review the numbers every day. Are you telling me we have a problem?"

"No. No. We're good."

"Hear me, Betsey." I try to keep the annoyance out of my tone but utterly fail. "If you come at me with innuendo, I cannot help you."

"I understand, Meredith. Nerves just got to me." Her chin, as white as a porcelain doll's, trembles.

"You're on the road this week?" I soften my glare as she nods, urging her to regain her composure. "We'll talk when you're back. But right now, I have to run. You got this next interview?" I expect only one answer, because I can't stay. I simply can't.

"I'm ready." A smile inches up through the worry still etching her face.

"I know you are. I'll check in with you later." I snatch my phone out of my leather satchel. "And hey, we'll be right back here in a week. We get to ring that closing bell." I hook my thumb at the white-marble balcony on the other side of the New York Stock Exchange. "Remember, you've a lot to be proud of."

A young producer with a purple bow tie and slicked-back hair marches toward me. I catch his eye and point at Betsey. It's her interview. He scowls but shifts direction.

On my phone, a confirmation for my next meeting appears. Although I'm expecting every single word, my mouth goes dry. Not only must we watch our backs, but we all have secrets we're forced to keep.

I drop my phone back in my bag and look toward Betsey, now standing in the midst of the hair and makeup team. With her shoulder-length auburn tresses swept up into a chignon, she looks regal—a completely different woman from only a moment ago.

She is the woman I've come to rely on.

As I whip toward the exit, my left stiletto twists under me. I stagger forward and grab the edge of a trading booth. Somehow, I remain upright. Running my palms down the silken wool of my pencil skirt, I plant a smile and glance backward.

Betsey, her lips now painted a blood red, silently mouths, *Be careful.*

2

MONDAY

They want me to ruin Betsey's life. They've compiled their case, down to this last career-crushing document, but they need me to land the final blow.

I can't do it. This is Betsey we're talking about. She's a colleague, a friend. Years ago, I plucked her from Columbia's applicant pool. I've been her champion ever since.

Alternative ideas leapfrog through my mind. I could simply march from the office, only to be tracked down. I could insist on hiring my own lawyer, only to delay the inevitable. I could fake a heart attack.

My head throbs.

Though I'm often lauded for my strategic savvy, the only thing looping through my head right now is how to convincingly slump to the broadloom carpet without wedging my hips between chair legs. And is the pain supposed to radiate down the left or right arm?

Hardwin clears his throat. "The last line."

He slides the forms across his mirror-polished desk, the pages almost hidden under his massive hand.

As I lean forward, my sharp kneecaps press up against the front panel of his ornate mahogany desk. Our seating arrangement is not lost on me. Instead of taking my place across from him at the conference table, I sit like a schoolgirl receiving a remedial math lesson from my elder.

This is all a mistake. I refuse to be strong-armed into signing anything. This is not an annoying interview he's proposing—it's a restraining order.

Hardwin knows our record-breaking sales have a lot to do with Betsey's efforts. We're not only fracturing her career; we're wrenching our ability to keep pace with the demand we've created with our new funds. A sharp jabbing pain between my ribs forces me to take a shallower breath. "Maybe we all just need a cooling off?" My voice is astonishingly strong.

Hardwin reclines in his tufted leather chair. The back of his shiny, freckled head grazes the dusty law volumes behind him. Even during sticky legal inquiries, I've never seen any of these ancient books referenced or even moved. His office is all for show.

"This is for your own protection, Meredith."

I bristle. Since when do I need my colleagues to protect me? Not having made my mark, I lay my pen down. "I want to take a beat. I think she might have gotten—"

"Meredith, this is the course of action we've all agreed is in everyone's best interest." Hardwin is a man who listens more than he speaks. So, when I try to make my case another way, I'm shocked when he speaks over me. "She came to your home and paced your lawn. We had to send security. It got ugly. She threatened our staff. Completely unacceptable." Hardwin shifts his considerable weight, and his chair snaps back to upright. His white-herringbone-clad belly spills around the lip of his desktop. "You need to think of your family."

I bite back a laugh. He's telling me to think of my family. That's rich coming from the man who expects his team to be in the office hours before the opening bell and to stay well past when commuter traffic has waned.

"When she was at the house yesterday, my family wasn't even home. I'd promised my husband an uninterrupted hiking day. I'd even left my phone behind. I missed her calls. Maybe, if I could speak with her now . . ." My voice squeaks out from between my painted lips, my whole mouth sticky.

I'm hating this version of myself. The decision to sign is both complicated and draining. Garman Straub espouses a no-tolerance approach to harassment, and yet this is a professional, talented woman we're talking about. And the legal action I'm being asked to sanction—I flip through the pages again—is aggressively career-ending.

This situation has gotten out of hand, but I know why they assume I'll fall in line. I've been groomed. They've taught me, and most of my colleagues, to swallow their machinations and taste leadership. I must admit, sometimes I applaud their tactics. But sometimes, they flaunt their obsessive need to control, like when business casual Friday came with a dozen pages of charts on sleeve lengths and fabric weaves.

That was absurd. This is appalling.

As Hardwin sits taller in his chair, he grabs the mother-of-pearl buttons on the front of his shirt and yanks against his girth. "It's simply a first step. Just the application. At any point we can drop the filing, but we have to send this message."

I open my mouth.

He continues. "Letting her go is no longer sufficient. You know they wanted her gone almost a week ago."

I swallow a snort. Why would he feel the need to soft-pedal his authority in this situation?

Hardwin is *they*.

At the sharp knock on the door, my shoulder blades tighten.

A dough-faced young man, wearing what looks like his father's old suit, pushes into the opening. Although I can't place him, the eager look in his eyes must mean he's one of Hardwin's guys. "She, uh . . . Betsey trashed Meredith's office."

A heat blooms in my chest.

"Alyssa had to call Maintenance. It's a mess." His words continue to slam into me.

I try to rise from my chair. My knees scrape against the mahogany apron of the desk. I'm wedged in way too close. Betsey trashed my office? Violated my space?

I twist and free my legs. My muscles tense. I'm ready to shove this chair, this desk, this ridiculous young man, out of my way. I stagger to my feet.

Two sets of eyes watch me, waiting for me to lose it.

3

I FORCE MYSELF TO SIT BACK IN MY CHAIR and breathe like the professional I imagine myself to be. The concern on Hardwin's face is tinged with something else, something hopeful. Maybe if I too become erratic, he can justify proceeding on his own, bypassing me entirely.

I stare down at the document in front of me.

How dare she.

I haven't spoken to Betsey since she did her first broadcast interview a week ago. There wasn't a hint of trouble in the video segment, but a day later, while in Cincinnati, she got into a shouting match with a financial advisor. Even that could be explained away. But then she never showed for her main-stage presentation at the Impact Conference. I've left a dozen messages.

But the train wreck was yesterday, Sunday, when she was fired. Now this. And how did she even get in the building?

"Is Betsey here? I thought we asked her to come in this afternoon and sign the separation agreement." My voice is not as shaky as I feared.

The law associate, still in the doorway, bumps into the office. His lips curl as if he wants to add shade to the edges of his gossip.

Hardwin's massive hand slices through the air like a dorsal fin through the surf. He is done with these theatrics. Erratic aggression and office trashings don't happen at this *global financial institution with over one hundred and fifty years of prosperity and integrity*. I parrot from the elegant Garman Straub brass plaque on his desk.

"Thank you," Hardwin booms, expressing anything but gratitude.

As the young man retreats, the door clicks shut. He will spread his news, and all the teams will soon be in a lather.

"She was here. Her badge was still active. I take responsibility. Apparently, she had more to say to you." Hardwin's arm is still suspended in the air as if he's planted his flag. To his left, a sepia-hued image of him hangs on the wall. He's barreling across the Harvard turf with a football tucked in his elbow. His other arm extends out like a battering ram. His hands and what they signal are legendary.

This space is his kingdom.

My office is my refuge.

Even with the guidance of executive coaches, I've struggled to establish a personal brand, which is the hallmark of other Wall Street darlings. They have a voice and a style that attracts followers, like short sellers to a bear market. Much to the exasperation of my hired guns, I'm not a lone-wolf portfolio manager. Every day, we make investment decisions within the funds to achieve our clients' investment goals. From stock selection to tax-efficient trading, we do it as a team. I've never felt comfortable owning any trademark, especially my own.

But my office has been my sanctuary. I knew the moment I stepped foot into the glass-walled space how I'd redesign the layout and choose fabrics to breathe peace and creativity into the sterility. I curated a place for high-performing teams.

Betsey has landed her shot.

“Blue, or would you prefer black ink?” Hardwin cocks his round head at me. He has likely watched the anger on my face settle into conviction. In these last moments, my mask has slipped.

Even without a mirror, I can see myself in Hardwin’s relieved reflection. Above high cheekbones, my light-brown eyes, fringed by thick dark lashes, are shining with constrained fury. In grade school, clever playground chants immortalized the size of my mouth. It’s now my strongest feature. I release all the tension in my face and plant a look of serenity. I’ve come to learn—even a hint of a smile on my full lips can be contagious.

“This is all so unnecessary.” But as I say the words, I break contact with his heavily lined gray eyes and pick up the pen.

I scrawl *Meredith Hansel* on the crisp, uncompromising line.

Assured I’ll get a copy of the restraining order when it’s filed, I head to my office—recently turned last straw—and try to ignore the guilt flowing like acid through my veins.

Behind me, the click of heels on the marble hall slows to a skid. “Good morning, Meredith. You got another request.”

I glance over my shoulder and a zap of nerve pain radiates up my neck. I dig my fingers into my trapezius muscle. Over the past year, my local members-only Pilates studio has seen nothing of me, but they’ve been faithful to exercise my on-file credit card every month. I whisper a silent plea to my neglected joints. If they can get me through the next two days, time for self-care lies ahead.

Alyssa hands me a printed email. Her large eyes, the color of well-lit jade, blink behind her black-rimmed glasses. She’s beautiful in a way guaranteed by perfect bone structure, but she takes pains to conceal it. She's a discerning young woman who's likely borne the weight of being too pretty.

"You know our response." My inbox bulges with messages identical to this one. All ask for the same favor—to squeeze one more body onto the narrow balcony of the NYSE.

"But it's the CEO of our index provider."

Another worthy invite. In fact, the entire lineup over at our index is outstanding. They supply the low-cost backbone of popular stocks for our funds. Leaving us time to manage a list of disruptive companies that win. They are kind of like the designer of the perfect black dress, but it's our accessories that make the statement. And their CEO is clever and engaging.

I swallow against the tightness. "Alyssa, I can't manufacture space."

She lowers her gaze to the floor. "But I thought—"

I internally groan. "You're right." The distraction of this morning has me in a brain fog. She's already determined that we have one more spot on the balcony for the bell ringing. By market close, my freshly fired sales manager will not be allowed within a hundred yards of the New York Stock Exchange. Most folks on my team would've taken at least a moment of satisfaction in signaling my mistake, but Alyssa almost appears embarrassed for me. Somehow this feels much worse. "Please extend the invite—Wait. No, don't."

She glances up. No sign of puzzlement. Perhaps she assumes I will redeem myself, or at least wants me to believe in her confidence. Alyssa is good at managing up. So was Betsey. The loss of her leadership and ingenuity on my sales team is almost inconceivable. How can I even begin to replace her?

A burning sensation rips across the back of my eyes. I did this. I knew Betsey was trying to tell me something at the NYSE before her interview. She practically begged me to listen. Instead, I baited her to go off on her own and find evidence. But of what?

I shake my head. I missed the pivot.

I can continue to scold myself but, right now, I've got a bell ringing to pull off. There is one more ceremonial spot, one more string. I feel like the piñata we bought for all the kids at Reid's tenth birthday. Ruthless little faces gathered beneath the colorful dangling ribbons, every yank made with an aspiration. I mentally sift through the pile of favors I've already gathered.

Maybe it's not one of my strings that ought to be pulled. I could ask Hardwin. He had a few ideas when we first brainstormed the list but robustly declined his spot. Tight, elevated spaces are not his places of comfort.

I slowly nod as a better idea occurs to me. "Ask Terrence who he'd like to extend the invitation to."

Alyssa's eyebrows rise to right above her rims at the mention of our chief compliance officer's name.

I hand the email back to her. Terrence loves the legacy of the firm. He's our unofficial historian and will appreciate the opportunity to rack up another favor. Maybe with someone who we'd all enjoy meeting. Terrence transacts in the currency of remarkable stories.

Alyssa nods. "Maintenance finished up in your office. Also, Candace stopped by. She wants to check in with you about protection."

That word again. A growl grows in my chest. I swallow. "I'll connect with her later. Thanks." I don't need a chaperone. I need to get back to work.

Alyssa turns toward Terrence's office. I watch as heads crane from around screens to greet her. She's not my chief of staff but she plays one most days. In the beginning, people underestimated her, then ignored her, and now, as lead analyst, she's the one they observe to gauge the tone of the room.

I tug on my suit jacket and continue toward my wing.

With all that's in me I hope that *trashed* was an overstatement.

I open my door, and my attention immediately goes to my Oma's Queen Anne sofa. Newly reupholstered in sand-colored crushed velvet, it lounges spryly undisturbed under my Matisse lithograph. I close my eyes and sigh.

The sofa could've been repaired, but its butchering would signify more than I want to contemplate. I glance in the large rolling trash bin by the door. Shards of glass blink up from the refuse. My eyes narrow as I scan the room.

The family picture from my desk is missing, but overall, the space looks the same. Do I want to know what the Maintenance team tackled?

I slide open my top drawer, the only one I keep unlocked. In a cracked silver frame, our four goofy faces yuck it up in the wind off Penobscot Bay. This makes no sense. I stand the mangled picture, missing its glass, on my blond oak desk. Betsey had no reason to attack my office and shove me off the edge. From what I know, things got heated with security, but her hard work was more responsible for our success than anyone else on my team. If I'd just taken the time to follow up after the interview like I said I would. Did she really feel like someone was working against us, or was she on the precipice of a breakdown, and I refused to see the signs?

I suck in my lips and attempt to *let it go*—the sentiment Hardwin gently barked as I left his office.

My eyes close against a rush of tears. As effective as I've been at shoving away my emotions, in this moment of solitude, I leak. I tip my nose to the ceiling and take a huge breath. It should be a day of celebration, and instead I've become untethered.

I sit at my desk and tell myself, in no uncertain terms, to get a grip. Clicking my laptop into the docking station, I run my fingers through a long sequence of passcode digits. I bypass my inbox. After today, it'll all calm down. I've got no more favors to bequeath. We can squeeze no more bodies, no matter how prominent, onto the balcony.

I switch tabs on my computer and briefly review the plans for tomorrow's town hall. I've sprung for the spicy salmon rolls from Hari and a mashed potato bar with slices of filet. We call it a town hall, but it's an office party. No television cameras or New York Stock Exchange confetti for the teams of professionals who spent many, many nights at their desks making sure performance algorithms tracked the global markets.

Guilt pricks me.

Have I done enough to appreciate the analysts, lawyers, data scientists, marketers, and sales professionals who contributed to the success of our ETFs? Maybe we can get some of those wicked cookies everyone loves?

I pick up my cell phone.

An assault of missed calls from an unknown number peppers my screen. Betsey hasn't stopped. After Candace tracked me down yesterday, I followed her instructions and blocked Betsey's contact. I thought the warning coming from our head of security would be enough, but at around nine last night an unknown number began to call my phone. This one is new. Last night when I spoke to Candace, I should've insisted on speaking to Betsey but now, after signing the order, there can be no contact.

I quickly swipe away from my phone's home screen and raise our family calendar, noting it's already late morning. Shoot. Reid's at his weeklong robotics camp and I forgot to say goodbye. He tried to talk us out of making him go. Not because he doesn't love robotics, but because his best friend is spending his fall break on a camping trip out west. Our twelve-year-old takes time warming up to new people.

I open the tracking app. One of my favorite things, especially when I fiercely miss my people, is seeing all my dots where they're meant to be.

I freeze.

Reid's dot is in downtown Scarsdale, stacked on top of my husband's. Why did Clint allow our son to talk him out of camp? Not only am I away too often, but Clint relies on me to be the heavy.

Bitterness coats the back of my throat as I press my husband's contact.

Scratching noises and then I hear Clint's voice. "Meredith?"

"Where's Reid?" My voice catches.

"Uh, in his bedroom. What's wrong?" Clint's tone shifts, an urgency in his words.

"He's supposed to be at camp. Why did you let him stay home? We discussed this before I left. I thought—"

"Slow down. What are you talking about? It's ten o'clock in the morning, Mer." A door slams. I start to speak, but Clint continues. "I take him in a few hours."

My fingers wiggle my mouse and refresh my calendar. Camp check-in isn't until 1 p.m. today. I sink back into my chair. "It's been a day already. I started looking at Tuesday's plans for the—anyway, I guess I got my timing screwed up."

"And you needed to micromanage me from thirty miles away." His voice is quiet but brutal.

I straighten. "I was concerned Reid wasn't at camp. I'm not micromanaging."

"Right, because you never make mistakes."

My breath stutters. No, I certainly do make mistakes. "Maybe this is too much." I slowly close the lid of my computer.

"You think?" He clears his throat. "Look, Meredith. For now, it is what it is. If we can't solve it with a counselor, we're not going to solve it on the phone."

"You're right." I pinch the bridge of my nose.

"Can I get back to putting away the unused hiking gear?" The emphasis on *unused* is unmistakable. I am not done paying for my choice yesterday.

"Sorry to interrupt." I end the call and lower my damp face into my hands.

How do we protect our marriage from us?

4

AT TEN MINUTES TO FOUR, fourteen of us pile onto the slender balcony overlooking the trading floor of the New York Stock Exchange. Well-lit backdrops for investment shows and advertisers are interspersed between booths that still shelter the floor brokers who manage some of the large custom orders for their firms. But many of the seasoned specialists who used to shout and gesture while amassing their company's fortunes have been replaced by automated algorithms operating from New Jersey.

An electricity crackles in the air as I press toward the left of the podium. Everyone jostles for space, and an outstretched arm inadvertently grazes my nose. I rock back on my slender red-bottomed shoes. Even with my added height, Dave and Terrence create a suited wall separating me from the front of the balcony.

I swallow a growl. Dave is Terrence's pulled string. If I had known Terrence was going to waste my favor on an insider, I would have confirmed Alyssa's plan and invited our index provider's CEO and not our head of sales.

I shuffle to my right. Our placement is scripted, and as the creator and portfolio manager, I earned my place at the front. These are my team's highly innovative, active ETFs we're celebrating. I conceived of them, and my team has made them a go-to investment for discerning client portfolios. With everything else happening today, is it too much to ask for everyone to stand where they're meant to be?

Suddenly, Dave throws back his head and I stumble into the wall. He roars with laughter as he finishes a lewd joke about a topless flight attendant. I've heard it, and others, countless times before. Certainly not a remarkable story. Why does Terrence even want him here? Dave's sales teams have barely participated in our success, and he's made it clear from the beginning that I'm peddling a second-rate solution that will never compete with the so-called *proven strategies*. Although he's been having a hard time arguing with my sustained results.

Shifting to my left, I try to scrape by the guys, but the balcony is now full. My family and friends are watching CNBC to see me, and all I see are blue suits.

"Hey, Dave. Terrence." I raise my voice, but either our head of sales and chief compliance officer don't hear me or choose to ignore me.

I could make a scene. But from their higher rungs, they could make every other day difficult. After the actual bell ringing, photographers will take pictures of us at the podium below. I'll get my moment. A television spot does not define my worth. I'm a master of the long game, which serves as both my advantage and, apparently, my Achilles' heel. I started my career in finance as a financial advisor. I loved the idea of helping moms and pops amass the fortunes they would need to send their kids to college and retire comfortably. I learned it was a prioritization game. The more successful your advice, the more affluent clients you gained, and therefore the more you were told to slough off the ones with few assets and unprofitable referrals.

My third Christmas at a boutique Kennebunkport practice, I was strongly encouraged to drop ten languishing accounts—send a letter, provide a referral, and focus on the A-list clients crowding the top of my daily to-do list. Instead, during our shuttered week before New Year's, I stacked my calendar with living-room meetings and extended phone calls. Bob and Vera O'Shausenny told me of their plans for a bunk room renovation enabling them to host their many grandchildren in Maine. Although their meager savings might afford them such a plan, their ability to retire remained many years away. No matter that I was making almost no revenue on their accounts, their gratitude for my financial management of their precious dreams made it impossible for me to move them off my list.

Two weeks later, while sitting with my boss, trying to convince him of my plan to keep all my clients, an urgent call was forwarded to his phone. Bob and Vera had won the Maine State Lottery. Big money. Big fees. We never addressed my client list again.

Now I create the investments that financial advisors sell to the moms and pops and to the top of their list. I still play to win, but always with the long game.

"Meredith." Phil Langford angles his shoulder between the wall of suits. "What are you doing back there?" His fuzzy white eyebrows have journeyed up his lined forehead. Relief twitches my glossed lips. His brow hairs, which often look as though they are attempting to escape his face, have been moderately tamed.

"Making my way to the front." I jostle past Terrence. He has the good grace to slide his gaze away. If our boss hadn't pulled me forward, these guys would have boxed me out. I imagine stomping on their insteps with my Louboutins, but of course I do no such thing.

"Good. Good. I'll press the bell button first and then you. Good?" Phil positions himself at the center of the podium.

"Yes." I step closer to Phil and look down at the three buttons and gavel. We were instructed to continuously press the primary controller to simulate strikes of the brass bell below.

"Are you good?" Phil asks. He's a gifted CEO, but when he's nervous, *good* becomes his go-to word. Dave, as annoying as he is, does an uncanny impression.

About fifteen feet below, photographers and video cameras prepare for the shot. I need to remember to thank Phil's wife for the well-timed face grooming.

"We start our celebration early," the liaison from the NYSE explains from my left. "When they cut to our stream, you'll be in full cheer. On my signal, we're clapping and we're cheering. Everyone set? All right, here we go. Five, four, three, two, one." Like well-trained seals, we slap our hands together.

On the confidence monitor, I watch the seconds tick down.

"Markets closed! We're striking the bell," the liaison announces.

Phil presses the button, and a shrill ringing fills my ears. Continuing to clap enthusiastically, I then wave at the various cameras directed at us. Trading on the stock exchange has finished for the day.

As my boss takes a slight step back, I slide my hand over the controller. Years of planning, persuading, and performing numerous trading cycles to ensure we get it just right have led to this moment. My cheeks ache at the size of my smile. As my gaze sweeps across the trading floor, gratitude swells within me.

Then my breath catches. It can't be.

Betsey tips her round chin in my direction, never losing eye contact. Her features look as if they're etched in stone.

A chill prickles along my hairline. How did she get past security?

The bell bleats as my finger continues to pump the controller. I twist toward Phil. He wears a huge grin. Even if he did spot her, he'd probably not recognize the woman we fired. The woman who compelled a restraining order. The woman who attacked the last joyful photograph taken of my family.

My gaze darts down and to the left as I scan through the people below. I see Candace's salt-and-pepper bob. She stands at the ready. I never connected with her today, but I know our entire security team was briefed. Always in the background but looking as if her internal coil is one tick from releasing, Candace immediately notices my shifted focus.

When Phil hired Candace, sidebars from his almost all-male executive team poked fun at an older woman being hired to manage security. That levity was quickly extinguished when her special intelligence record in Iraq and her jujitsu championships were revealed.

I nod slightly at our head of security. Her countenance stiffens. I drag my gaze back to the trading floor. Candace marches forward.

I scour the area around the Cygna booth, where Betsey was just standing.

Phil elbows me to stop pressing the button. He then bangs the gavel hard on the sounding block.

A tremor courses through my body.

The woman who's not permitted within a hundred yards of me has vanished.

5

PHIL PRESSES ANOTHER GLASS of champagne at me. My hand is remarkably steady. Following the initial escalation as we left the balcony, no sign of Betsey was found. Because of security questions, I missed the opportunity to autograph the wall and instead listened from the bottom of the stairs to the muted whispers between Dave and Terrence. They probably speculated that my overwrought brain imagined the unhinged woman. Security is tight at NYSE.

It's inconceivable no one else saw her, but they're not questioning my report. Instead, teams are checking the admission list and the cameras. It's not lost on me that she was standing in the exact spot where we spoke one week ago.

I assume she's long gone.

Thankfully, the guys keep any musings to themselves, and Candace assures us no one who is not on the list will step foot into the reception room. I'm conflicted. As much as I don't want to derail our long-awaited celebration, I'd like to wrestle Betsey to the ground. Has she completely lost her mind?

It's barely 4:30. I shouldn't even sip at the flute sparkling between my fingers. Two glasses of bubbly or wine over dinner are no problem. During the day, half a glass starts to make everything slightly warm and fuzzy. Apparently, it also gives me a tendency to exaggerate my own might. Given the time Betsey spends in her kickboxing gym, wrestling her to the ground seems unlikely. And although I grate at any indication that I'm overwrought, I am operating on only a couple hours of sleep. Again. As well as a definite lack of strength training.

"Did you see Lucas from Meymack is here?" Phil leans in and stage-whispers.

"I invited him." A confidence straightens my spine as I hear the solid ease of my words.

"Of course you did." Phil chuckles. "Enjoy this, Meredith, but don't rest too long. I want you back planning our next headline." He strides away.

I pivot and deposit my glass onto a bussing tray and ask for some water. Concealing a deep breath, I glance up at the incredible stained glass ceiling. Like a gold and crystal crown embracing the gilded room, it's been covered for a century, since a bomb scare in 1920. I pause and then catch a snippet of our fund promotional video on one of the discreetly fitted LED screens between two of the baroque columns. I've seen the media clip countless times, but it raises a trembling inside me to see the inspiring testimonies heralded inside this gorgeous NYSE boardroom.

My stomach shyly grumbles. I notice a charcuterie along the wall. Perhaps I can nab a canapé or a cheese and cracker. They must have something that won't leave little flakes all over my buff wool suit.

I take a swallow from my iced tumbler and head across the room.

Dave approaches with his garnished Bloody Mary held high. "Nice party." He stops short of clinking my water glass as he scowls at my humble liquid. Day drinking is always a group sport.

"Thank you. Glad you could make it." I try to slip around him, but he nonchalantly shifts his weight, blocking my breakaway. He then glances around the room as if he didn't notice.

Dave always has thoughts, whether about topless flight attendants or creative sales strategies. He's always prepared to fill the space between other people's sentences. But he's also talented, runs a successful sales team, and never lets anyone forget how valuable he is.

"Yeah, well, I had enough time to block my calendar. What, like, sixteen months since we launched the funds?" Dave gulps his drink. Droplets of tomato juice pepper his trim mustache above his thin pale lips.

He either doesn't realize I know his invitation was procured this morning by Terrence or doesn't care. He made his excuse to skip this reception until the spot on the balcony opened. The lure of television cameras was not to be missed.

As head of sales, Dave could have pushed in on the balcony a month ago when he first saw the proposed list without his name, but instead he feigned disinterest. He likely assumed the bell ringing was going to be a B-list event. We worked hard to assemble strong supporters of the funds as well as those we'd like to bring on board. Most importantly, instead of requesting a bell ringing when we launched, we waited until we had success to celebrate.

I'm still surprised Terrence used his invite on Dave.

Does he need Dave's support on a project, for a vote? Or perhaps Terrence also plays the long game. I file the alliance away.

Dave is only here because Betsey is not. Unease at seeing her earlier still sits in my gut. How dare she show up today after causing such a scene at my home and office? While I scan the room and spy

Candace still stalking the perimeter, Dave drones on about how bell ringings have become almost commonplace. As if all that I've planned is not unique or good enough. Besides, in his world, truth need not be true—it can merely be a confidently created narrative dispersed through the mill.

I nod. "Excuse me, Dave, I see someone I invited. Enjoy yourself."

Dave snatches my arm.

I clamp my lips down on my gasp.

Each of his fingers presses through my autumn-weight wool suit and into my scrawny bicep.

A heat builds through me. This time I will make a scene. He knows better than to touch me. We are likely being watched, which harms us both—predator and prey.

Abruptly, he releases me as he steps closer. "Don't get too big for your britches, Meredith. You are only a portfolio manager."

I slowly raise my eyes to his, every muscle in my face taut with what I hope conveys irritation, but I suspect also appears as distress. I despise the part of me that still looks to this man for validation. My words hang between us as I spout them. "I'm a portfolio manager who has raised a billion dollars in just over a year with funds which now trade on three of the four major wirehouse platforms. A portfolio manager who leads a winning team."

"Your team? Where are they?" he hisses, but he doesn't need to search the room.

The heat in my chest turns to ice. I loathe this man.

From the beginning, Dave was the vocal challenger to inviting anyone but my second-in-command, even to this reception, where we have more capacity. In fact, his opposition has been keen from the moment my idea for the funds was floated. If it's not his idea, he's not interested. He opposed me utilizing his mutual-fund sales team, requiring me to build a small but mighty ETF sales group focused only on the new funds. And they have hit it out of the park. The only reason they aren't here is because guys like Dave insist on taking their places at high-profile events, like bell ringings, that according to him are growing as stale as low-coupon bonds.

"What do you want, Dave?" My tone is neutral. The long game unfurls itself before me. I'm not willing to let anything go sour today.

"What I want—Hey, Lucas, nice to see you," Dave darts back. The head of Wealth Management at Meymack steps beside him. His financial advisors were early adopters of our funds. Since Meymack is arguably the largest broker-dealer on the street, their trendsetting has helped fuel the demand.

"Just the person I wanted to see." Lucas disentangles himself from Dave's enthusiastic shoulder slaps and reaches for my palm. "Meredith." My name is almost a sigh on his lips.

I want to pull away. Intensely. I need a moment.

But I remain still.

A huge benign smile parts Lucas's full lips. "Thanks for the invite. Phil said I owe you."

"Glad you could make it." My hand slips from his and hangs unnaturally inert against the wool of my skirt. I force myself not to wipe the dampness from my fingers.

"Of course. Folks can't stop talking about your fund wizardry. And getting them on the Meymack platform in less than a year . . . You're the woman to watch."

I clamp down on a grimace and hope it looks enough like a grin. *Woman to watch.* My mother would bristle at those words. She wouldn't let them go unexamined and certainly wouldn't be smiling with anything but sarcasm. Her voice echoes in my head. *Would Dave be "the man to watch" if he'd come up with the innovation?* I brush aside my mother's transplanted annoyance and appreciate the sentiment.

Lucas was one of the many executives who spoke up in support of getting our ETFs on the Meymack platform. It can take years.

His voice is persuasive.

"While I have you, wondering if we might set up some time to have your team come out to visit the Cherry Hill office. Maybe help them craft their customer presentations to be more engaging." Lucas slides his phone out of an inner suit pocket.

Dave barks out a cough. "Cherry Hill—one of your largest branches. They haven't been out to see them yet?" His concerned tone only barely masks his glee at discovering my team's failure.

"Of course they have." Lucas swats his long tapered fingers through the air as if dismissing a fly. "Meredith, you might remember, last time you came out, they only assembled their senior staff. I'd like to get the entire office involved. If you're busy, I understand. I know you've got those training videos out there . . ." Lucas's upper lip curls as if he's sucking on something sour.

"We'd be happy to come back out." I bite the inside of my cheek and take a hungry glance at Dave's reddening face. The online lessons were Dave's brainchild. Betsey thought they were too simple and didn't cover the type of questions our team was getting from the field. The videos were highlighted on the website anyway.

I wipe the smugness from my face and have pulled out my phone to quote a few possible times when I notice three missed calls from Erika.

My stomach clenches.

I already exchanged congratulatory texts with her after the bell ringing. She watched it with her AP Microeconomics class. Erika is a typical teenager. She can have moments focused on others, even impulsive pride in her mother's appearance on television, but she quickly ricochets back to herself. Pretty sure these calls don't have anything to do with me. And Erika is allergic to actually speaking on a phone, always preferring her fingers flitting across the tiny letters on her screen.

I lift my face from my phone. This interruption is also my means of escape. "My team will get back to you on timing, Lucas. I need to return a call."

"No rush. We can do this all by email." Lucas's words drip less enthusiasm. Men like him are not used to being left in a conversation by others on lower rungs. He turns to Dave and asks his take on the greens in Vegas for the upcoming Shriners Children's Open—my prompt to slip away. Golf is not my game.

My phone pressed against my ear, I pretend to be already engaged as I shuffle through the crowd to the door. I wait until I push out into the hallway and find a small glass-doored nook, created for just the thing I need—a quiet place to phone my daughter.

"Mom." Her voice is barely a whisper.

"Hi, sweetheart. Is everything all right?"

"I, um . . . I, uh . . ." Soft sobbing fills my ear.

"Honey, it's going to be okay. Tell me what's wrong." I glance at my watch. Erika's go-to response when things get messy is tears. I want to be patient, but I have a roomful of people waiting. I should've called Clint first. He could tell me what event she'd not been invited to, or which friend snubbed her in the hall. All valid concerns. All concerns I would gladly commiserate through, but I need to fast-track the story today.

The sobbing is not abating. I can picture her tucked into a bathroom stall at the high school. As a junior in good standing, no one seems to pay attention to her whereabouts, assuming she's in class or where she needs to be. I've questioned Clint on the wisdom of such freedom with anxiety rates so high.

"Erika, honey, how can I help?"

"You can't," she chokes out.

"Fair enough. Want to give me one word? One hint on what you're upset about?"

I pinch the bridge of my nose as I wait for a response and then silently count to twenty, fighting my constant urge to fill the vacuum. Our couple's counselor has been working with both Clint and me on listening—not pretending to attend, only to then offer our perspective when the other takes a breath. I add five more seconds to my countdown for good measure.

"Erika. How about one word? It will help if you say it. I don't need details. We'll share the weight."

The sound of a distant door closing and then a big sniff come over the line.

I hold my breath. *Just say something, sweetheart.*

"Trapped."

6

FOR THE NEXT EIGHT MINUTES on the phone, I don't get anything more out of Erika. I assure her she isn't trapped. She always has options. I offer to call her dad or a couple different friends who are teachers at the school to connect with her. She declines all offers.

In an effort to distract her, I recount Dave's air of superiority, including the pitch of his sharp nose when his videos were insulted. Last week, Erika interviewed a few members of his sales team for a class project. On the train ride home, she declared his videos boldly primitive, which at the time made me laugh. This time she gives me a couple gratifying snorts.

I refrain from telling her about the small oval bruises likely blooming on my arm as we speak.

She finally stops crying and agrees to do school from home. The plan to leave seems to regulate her shallow breathing. I get a momentary twinge. This is remote micromanaging. Did Clint already tell her she had to stay at school? I'll have to call him next.

"Love you, sweet girl."

"When are you coming home?" That's the longest string of words she's pulled together over this entire call.

"End of the week." I cringe. "Unless you need me." As I say the words, I utter a silent plea she won't ask. As convenient as being in the city is this week, my extended stay is all about Clint's desire for space. As things were unraveling on Sunday, while packing the truck, I'd agreed to take up residence at the hotel until Friday—and then instantly regretted it. But I also don't have the standing to overturn my promise.

After telling my daughter goodbye, I call Clint.

"Erika's pretty upset. She called me a few times. I told her she could do school from home." I slam out the words and then brace for his rebuttal.

"Fine. I'm here, planning the lumber delivery for that kitchen remodel."

What kitchen remodel? I thought he was screening in that massive deck over in Greenville.

His voice softens. "You looked good, by the way."

A tear that pooled while on the phone with Erika streams down my cheek. He hasn't complimented me in weeks. Maybe longer. "Thanks. It's been a crazy day, and I'm actually supposed to be at the reception for—"

"Go. I'm not keeping you." His tone hardens.

"I didn't mean—"

The line goes dead, and I pinch the bridge of my nose, hard.

Opening the door, I resist the urge to sag against the jamb. Our relationship, our marriage, has never been like this. We met by accident. I first saw Clint's hazel eyes peering out from under the brim of his ball cap, emblazoned with the Maine Warden Service logo. I couldn't look away. He was asking me details about my life and my family while holding my wet, frozen foot between his warm hands. Up until recently, his touch has chased away the chill, not invited it.

"Excuse me. Meredith Hansel?" A young man steps in front of me as I reach the doors to the reception. "Something was delivered for you."

I scowl at the squat, thin envelope he shoves toward me. My hands remain at my sides.

"Don't worry. We have everything scanned coming into the building."

I wince as I take the envelope. I wasn't worried it was something that could harm me until he mentioned scanners. My only thought had been event logistics. I don't want to bother with any administration right now. I turn the manila envelope over. Only my name on the front. No other indicators. We all got our commemorative silver coins before the bell ringing, and a few others and I had gotten Lucite plaques back at the office.

"Thanks." I glance toward the elevators, but Phil is probably missing me. Similar to every CEO I've ever met, he gets edgy when left unattended too long. Instead of heading downstairs to the manned coat closet to store the envelope, I walk back into the room, straight to Phil.

"There she is." Only a moderate amount of annoyance tinges his words. "Meredith, can I introduce you to the head of research at UBS?"

I shake hands and greet the next dozen people as the envelope grows warm in my left hand. At one point I actually feel the package with my other fingers to ensure it isn't heating up.

I finally excuse myself for the restroom, my curiosity eating away my desire to be the perfect hostess.

I rip open the seal and pull out a handwritten note.

A chill runs up my spine. I know this loopy writing. I quickly glance under each of the stall doors. No feet, but it's like I can feel

Betsey's presence in the white granite room with me. I secure myself behind the last door and think of Erika locked away and feeling trapped.

I stare down at the single sheet of paper.

On the drive is the data. Verify it.

No innuendo. Only facts.

I scrubbed the names, but the rest is as I found it. I recommend you keep this to yourself, as what you hold will threaten others. But I've lost my voice with you, so I at least encourage you to be careful with whom you trust.

I hope you agree this has all gotten a bit ridiculous, but based on the stakes, we probably shouldn't be surprised. I will always cherish our meetings at the Rotterdam Room. The confidences we shared over sips of oaky Chardonnays for you and two olive martinis for me—the stories are like snapshots in my mind. You can continue to trust me to keep your confidences.

I'm "calling safety." Lending you research. After all, success is the result of the right steps taken day after day.

You have until Friday. I'll be in touch.

The page quivers in my shaking hand. I read it three times before shoving the note back into the envelope.

Betsey and I've never been to the Rotterdam Room.

But Lucas and I have.

7

BESIDES THE NOTE, the only other thing in the envelope is a bubble-wrapped thumb drive. My laptop is in my workbag back at the hotel, but it would do me no good. The USB ports are all blocked on our corporate devices. A safety measure to ensure sensitive data can't be stolen and the machine can't be compromised. I check the contents of the envelope again and then shove the note and the drive back inside.

It's clear Betsey is giving me some kind of data and she has pictures of me and Lucas at the Rotterdam Room. The threat is clear too. She will tell if I don't deliver by Friday, but deliver what? She makes no demand. Only that I verify.

What about the line about "calling safety"? Makes no sense. She must be sending me some message. Perhaps the line is for me to decipher? Nothing immediately comes to mind. My head throbs with annoyance. Criminal threats and police reports are not what this day is supposed to be about.

She is right about one thing. I won't keep this obvious attempt at manipulation to myself. I'll bring it to the office tomorrow, report it to our compliance department, and hand it off to our IT guys for safekeeping. They can assess the risk and determine what to do. But not today.

First, I have to speak to my husband.

I return to the party and shake a few more hearty hands. We only have the room for another twenty minutes. My ankles wobble, and I'm thankful I brought a pair of wedge sandals for the dinner tonight. My feet are surviving, but there's a limit to their patience with my fashion choices.

But will I even be at the dinner tonight?

I can't just call Clint. This is a conversation we need to have in person. I have to go home.

"Meredith. Was hoping to have a word." A man with slicked black hair and kind brown eyes steps in front of me.

"Hello, Aarav." His name only occurs to me because I studied the guest list again as I freshened up at the hotel. I reach for his hand. We've met a few times at conferences. I'm genuinely glad he came, but I need to make my exit.

"Thank you for the gracious invite. Your success is apparent." He glances around the room. His face is devoid of the smile common among the attendees who are enjoying a leisurely afternoon with top-shelf cocktails.

"We've worked hard," I say. Maybe I can ask Clint to meet me in the Bronx in half an hour? Or not. I forgot, I'm not in Midtown. From Lower Manhattan it could take me twenty minutes just to get to the Harlem Line at Grand Central.

"Yes. And as you know, we run a principled office." His stillness makes me aware of my own fidgets.

My brow knits together. What are we talking about?

"A good advisor makes the best investment choices for their clients based on their specific needs, not because of aggressive sales strategies," he says, placing emphasis on no particular word.

I try to relax my face. *Aggressive sales strategies?* What is he referencing? I consider sharing a story about when I was a financial advisor to help him understand how similar we are. I decide instead to stay focused on him. "Aarav, my team and I have always respected offices, like yours, that take diligent care of their clients. We would never try to hard sell you."

His lips seem to disappear inside his mouth as if he's chewing on his next words.

I wait, harnessing the technique our counselor has used when Clint and I clam up. Although based on my failure to share anything of real substance during our sessions, I cringe when I leverage any of her techniques.

"Perhaps we can speak another time." His eyes stay leveled on mine.

"We can certainly follow up, but if there's something I need to know?" I keep my arms loose by my sides and resist the urge to fuss with my necklace. My kids often call me on my telltale nervous habit.

He glances over my shoulder. "You should enjoy your party." Shifting his gaze back to mine, he lowers his voice. "Are you taking the right steps to ensure your ultimate success?"

My breath catches. Those are eerily similar words to those written in Betsey's hand at the end of the note. The entire envelope again radiates an unnatural heat in my left hand.

I step closer to Aarav. "I'm sorry, I think I've missed something—"

"Meredith," Phil's voice booms from my right. "Can you join me at the door? A few people want to say goodbye."

"Yes, of course. Just need one moment." I turn back, but Aarav has stepped away.

I reach out to him, brushing my fingertips against his dark suit.

"Wait. Please. Tell me what you meant." *Are you a part of this? Did Betsey get to you too?*

"Meredith." He sighs. "You will be a success, but I encourage you to not push your team too hard. Their visit last week had a tone of, well . . . urgency or worse."

Last week? Worse than urgency? What does that even mean and how does this relate to the words on the note?

"For me, it's always about doing right by my clients and my staff. We'll talk soon." He gives me a tight smile and then raises his stiff hand toward Phil as if ushering me toward him. Although I'm not looking, I can feel Phil radiating frustration from his sentry spot by the doors.

"I'll be in touch." I force a smile and then stride toward my CEO, whose left hand taps a blustery beat against his thigh.

Nothing Aarav said makes any sense.

My team has never visited his office. We've been intentional with offices that appreciate educational materials ahead of any sales meeting. That was the reason I invited Aarav to this reception. I wanted him to see our success and have a reason to follow up. But if Aarav shares that our ETFs have even a whiff of desperation, stakes are much higher than growing our sales. Mass sell-offs have been ignited by less.

Betsey, have you deliberately sabotaged our success?

8

THE DING FROM ABOVE the smudged paneled door announces my arrival. Late-afternoon sun casts bright geometric shapes on a filthy low-nap black carpet. The air hangs heavy with the mingling scents of stale sweat, decaying food, and the sharp tang of pine disinfectant. Stifling a sneeze, I dig my nose into the shoulder of my gray pullover. A faint hum radiates from the shop's fluorescent lights, punctuated by the occasional beep or chirp from an electronic device. Navigating past two long counters encased in chrome edges, I see an array of tech gadgets lined up like an army of weary cyborgs awaiting their next command. Small note cards display cryptic descriptions but conspicuously lack any visible prices.

Behind the counters, shelves groan under the weight of boxes, manuals, and spare parts, creating a labyrinth of pedagogical chaos.

"Do for you?" A thin balding man with an elaborate neck tattoo crosses his arms over his ribbed T-shirt and sucks his teeth at me. His accent sounds Eastern European, and his tone implies he owns the air I'm breathing.

I approach the display case. "I have a thumb drive. Are you able to help me retrieve the contents?"

My inquiry hangs between us. He doesn't immediately speak. Instead, his hooded eyes assess me, as if weighing whether I'm vermin to devour or simply a plaything to bat around for his own amusement.

I stopped by the hotel on the way here, changed into jeans, and shoved my previously styled hair up into a Yankees baseball cap. Not that I'm trying to be completely incognito, but I don't need to advertise who I am. Based on the fine layer of sweat spreading across my chest, I probably should've stayed closer to Broadway. On the off chance I bumped into someone I knew, I tore up over a dozen blocks into a nondescript area of the Meatpacking District.

"You have the drive. Let me look." The man inches his palm toward me, his sinewy fingers beginning to curl as if they can already feel my device in their clutches.

But my thumb drive rests in the bottom of my cross-body leather satchel. My plan to wait until tomorrow to turn it over to security shattered when Aarav told me someone on my team visited him last week. Impossible. Except he runs one of the most respected offices at Meymack. In fact, I had my team wait to visit him because I wanted to get the educational presentation exactly right. Aarav hates to be sold to.

Beside me, a shadow falls across the counter, dulling the chrome edges. I glance toward the front of the store.

A massive man consumes the entry. His presence seems to swallow all the light streaming in through the glass. Obscured by the brim of his cap, his face points straight ahead, while his legs, the width of pylons, straddle the space in front of the door.

I do believe I'll be spending money in this place before I leave.

"I'll need to get the drive." I address the much smaller man behind the counter. "How much?"

He purses his chapped lips. "Depends on effort to extract files. Give me. I'll look."

I glance down and see a dated laptop for probably not much more than I'll end up shelling out to this guy. I also don't want to be maneuvering through one potential extortion situation while gaining myself another. Who knows what's on the drive? Could be paranoid sales projections that show the funds losing assets, or could be dirt on people Betsey thinks have wronged her.

Whatever it is, it certainly won't be good news.

"How about if I buy that laptop now, and then I'll come back with the drive if I can't get to the files?" I point at the display case.

"This one." He pulls out a silver Dell computer. "You need a power cord?"

"Yes." I pick up the white card he places on the counter.

He quotes me a price almost double the tagged number on the back of the brief specifications.

Annoyance ripples through me. Not at the obvious gouging, but because I ever thought coming here was a good idea. "Does it have a regular USB slot?"

He turns the machine over in his hands. "Couple of 'em."

I pull out the cash and hand it to him.

He tosses the laptop and cord into a plastic bag. "You come back if you can't get those files."

I nod and turn. The mountain of a man remains planted as if I've not quite concluded my visit.

Trapped.

Erika's word echoes in my head.

I phoned her twice when I got back to the hotel. The rock that formed in the pit of my stomach as my calls went to voicemail grows heavier as I watch the massive man's dull eyes rake over me. He picks at something in his front teeth with his long yellowing thumbnail.

If I've learned nothing else in my fifteen years in and around Wall Street, it is to never project fear. I casually roll back my shoulders and nick my head to the side. *Move. I'm leaving.*

The man swags his broad chin at me, his eyes narrowing, but he then steps back and opens the door behind him.

I steer my way around his bulk and squint into the glare reflecting off the steel building across the empty street.

My running shoes scuff the pockmarked concrete sidewalk as I stumble toward the hotel. The sensation of being trapped has not left me.

9

I PULL MY SPINE AWAY from the hotel chair as the telltale sounds of the laptop booting up fill the space around me. I probably should have asked the neck tattoo guy to turn on the computer and prove the technology actually worked. Ridiculous to buy something without any indication it was functional. Does it even have an operating system?

I glance over at the embossed card on the desk explaining the hotel's Wi-Fi. I may need to download a Microsoft package to get started. I scrub my face with my hands. I'm getting way too embedded in this seriously flawed plan.

A deep-purple background appears on the laptop's display and a dozen different application icons line the bottom toolbar. The laptop has Microsoft Office installed as well as a few different browsers. Labels pop up and disappear as I run the mouse pointer over all of them. I'm in awe as I open File Explorer. An empty Documents folder displays on the screen. Small mercies, as I certainly don't want to inherit anyone else's junk.

I poke at the small gray thumb drive and then turn it over. *DatCore. Data at the core of your business.* Betsey must have picked it up at a conference, one of the plentiful tchotchkes available at the booths. I probably have one just like it tucked in my desk.

Do I really want to do this?

A much wiser course of action is to wait until tomorrow and get Compliance involved. It's their job to assess and mitigate corporate risk. Risk that I should not be assuming.

I slide the small device toward the lamp and study Betsey's note again, quickly skipping over her revelation about Lucas and focusing on the next line.

I'm "calling safety." Lending you research.

Perhaps those words in quotes will appear somewhere on the drive, but then anyone who sees it will have the same information. No. It must be meant only for me. I say the words out loud and then again. I google *calling safety* and see references to the game of pool as well as football, neither of which has any relevance to me or my relationship with Betsey. I say it again and something nicks at me. But the phrasing is wrong. When we were pulling long hours getting the funds up and running, we'd sometimes shout, "Calling Security" when someone had a wicked good idea. It was a joke that made us both laugh like the nerds we were.

I poke at the sentence again, swapping *safety* for *security* and then frowning at the next awkward three-word sentence. My breath catches. When I modify the punctuation, I now see *Security lending. You research.*

I rub the note flat against the desk as if the paper itself might confirm if I've solved the puzzle. Security lending has been a fundamental but prosaic element of operations, mirroring what we do for the mutual funds. Although it's one of the thinnest revenue lines, we have made a point to lend out assets that are in demand. Kind of like

Airbnbing your unique beach bungalow before you sell it to buy a place in Vail. Is Betsey telling me to examine our lending practices as a firm? Why? We've had the same guys with the same goals since before I joined.

I fist the small drive, closing my fingers completely over the device. The metal is cool against my warm, damp palm. There's a good reason our work laptops are locked down. All those training videos on regulations and firm protection swim through my adrenaline-soaked mind. I can see myself being filmed right now, sitting in this very hotel room holding this unknown device with bold text hanging over my head.

Should Meredith insert the thumb drive she received from an ex-employee into a laptop she bought at a sketchy technology shop in Manhattan? Yes or no?

In order to pass the required training session, the answer is clear.

I insert the silver end of the drive into a USB port.

Wrong move. Restart this training module.

On the desk beside me, my phone shimmies. I startle. The sense of cameras trained on me feels real, like I'm actually being filmed.

On my phone, Erika's name and sweet picture from her fourteenth birthday appear. I slap closed the laptop screen and shoot up from my chair.

"Hey, sweetheart. Thanks for calling me back."

"Hi, Mom."

"Feeling any better?" I ask.

"Sure." Her voice is so small. She sounds eight instead of her usual twenty-five.

Clint used to ride me about Erika's dated contact picture. I'd shrug as if I had no idea why I kept it, but I knew. That was the last day I remember feeling like I had a grasp on what I was doing as Erika's mom. It was a beautiful April day and we took Erika and three of her besties to an extravagant ropes course. Erika cheered as I was the first to throw my body from the top of the pole to the spider net across a three-story drop. Even snug in our harnesses, it was exhilarating to transverse the obstacles, moving higher and higher, as we laughed and applauded each other. Over two years ago, I had no idea my pedestal was so precarious.

"Tell me what's wrong. I want to help." A tinge of orange begins to frame the glass and steel building outside my window.

"You can't," she whispers, her voice barely audible over the line.

"I'm pretty good at solving problems, you know," I say, injecting some levity into my voice. "I was quite a nerd in high school."

"Seen the pictures." A tiny laugh knits her words, and for a moment it feels like we're back to our old banter.

"See, not all bad. Having friend trouble?" Those girls must create drama to give themselves something to do.

"Maybe. I gotta go."

"Not yet. Honey, it will feel better to talk about it. I promise."

Erika's sobs fill the silence, and my own heart aches in response.

"Oh, sweetheart. I wish I was there." Nothing truer, and at the very heart of what Clint and I can't resolve.

The crying continues over the phone but at least she hasn't hung up.

"One word," I whisper, trying the same tactic as before. I wish I could be more creative, but I instead double down on my only past success. "Just one."

I wait through the whimpers. My heart squeezes in my chest. I should be there.

The sounds change and the phone goes silent for a moment before a tiny voice says, "Text."

"You want to text, sweetheart?" I take a deep breath, hoping she will too. "Or did someone send you a bad text?"

The soft crying returns and then the call ends.

I close my eyes and picture my sweet girl huddled on her bed, her silky blonde hair fanning over her face and pillow. I long to hold her close, to shield her from the pain of growing up in a world that seems intent on breaking her spirit. Wishing I could transfer all my available strength and confidence into her battle to make it through high school, I imagine crawling in next to her and hugging her stiff body to mine. This junior year has been rough.

I call her back, but my call goes immediately to her default voicemail. I send Clint a text that Erika needs him. As the sun sets the sky and the buildings ablaze, the weight of my inadequacy burns me from the inside.

I pace back to my desk.

The thumb drive glares green.

10

AS I REACH FOR THE LID to wake the computer, I see a text from Erika.

I'm fine. I have a precalc quiz tomorrow. Have to study.

I immediately respond, but she declines my offer to come home. We make plans to connect again after my dinner.

I sit unmoving in the desk chair. I should go home anyway. Two calls from my teen in one day. Something is obviously the matter. Something more than the usual skirmish. But I know what will happen if I leave now. I'll miss the dinner in my honor—well, in honor of our successful funds—and I'll show up at home to mother a daughter who won't talk. She'll eventually open her door, remind me she has a hard quiz to study for, and say it's no big deal. She's just feeling emotional. *And hey, stop taking things so serious all the time.*

This wouldn't be the first time I've left everything hanging at work to return to a normal teenage household. The last time was about a failed Snapchat streak. Thankfully, Betsey covered for me without a hitch.

Tonight, I have no backup.

And Clint certainly doesn't want me home.

I rub the track pad to find the pointer on the screen. If my husband returns my texts with anything approaching a change of heart, I'll be on the first train. Until then, I'll respect his wishes. Regardless of my justifications, the clock is ticking on me telling him. There is also the matter of what he deserves to know.

I open the File application. A temporary drive appears in my list of options down the left side of the window. My highlight moves toward the labeled drive.

I again feel the cameras. I see myself in a cameo appearance on another video with a question cloud hanging over my head.

Will she or won't she?

I open the drive and flunk the module.

Only one file appears in the navigation window. I press the touch pad.

An Excel spreadsheet with dozens of columns of numbers opens on my screen. It looks like coded sales by lots, much more detailed than I've ever seen. Since ETFs are traded on the open market, it's almost impossible to attribute sales to specific investors. Mutual funds have that advantage: We know exactly where they are being bought and by whom. ETFs offer a level of privacy for investors, but it's also much harder for us to target our sales. Our wildly successful ETFs have been growing despite our inability to know who's buying them. This spreadsheet looks as if someone has gotten their hands on very sensitive data. But how?

Some of the wirehouses and even a few intermediaries have started selling summarized sales data but nothing this detailed, and besides, we made an early decision not to spend capital on that kind of information. We would produce high-value funds and foster relationships with financial advisors to explain their benefits. Thus far, this has been a successful strategy.

Impossible to argue against this kind of data being valuable. But also, very troubling to consider how it was produced. Since we haven't purchased even the basic data, the only way to assemble this kind of detail would be to convince someone to steal it.

The hotel phone rings. I pick up the handset.

"Evening, Meredith." Phil's jovial tone fills the line. "We have a couple cars meeting us out front in thirty minutes. Suit your timing?"

A question that's not a question. My CEO's timing is always my timing. But Phil called me himself. Might be a first.

"Of course. See you in the lobby."

I quickly copy the file onto the laptop and then slide the laptop between the mattress and box spring of my bed. I take the thumb drive to the personal safe in the closet and lock it inside.

As I step into the shower, my daughter's delicate face comes to mind. Would it help her to know her mother feels exactly the same way as her? Trapped. And this time getting out is going to take a lot more than moving aside one massive man.

11

A SHARPLY DRESSED DINING HOST opens the heavy door. Carved into the ebony wood, open-mouthed dragons breathe fire into the valley village below. I drag my gaze away. The smell of sizzling meat, roasted onions, and yeasty bread assails me. This is a dinner for victors, hearkening back to nomadic tribes who slaughtered wild beasts. Not a big carnivore myself, I'll still order a steak the size of my head, but what I've been looking forward to is the metaphorical breaking of bread. We have a unique opportunity to sit together, brag on our families instead of ourselves, and find common interests.

Minutes after I've been ushered into our private wine cellar room, Dave struts through the open door. Not everyone has the same perspective. I imagine some of us anticipate the fun of instigating others to say what they normally wouldn't. They give themselves permission to openly prod and taunt.

As I take my seat beside Terrence, I imagine asking him why he used his one favor on Dave. Perhaps Dave was in his office when Alyssa stopped by, and Terrence was forced to extend the invitation? I can see Terrence being diplomatic. Or perhaps Terrence failed to realize the external demand for the last spot on the balcony. On the other end of our long table, Dave pulls out the empty chair beside Phil. A grinding tension in my neck bleeds away. I won't have to suffer through his smug presence tonight.

The restaurant used to be a bank, and the eight-foot-diameter vault door we walked through to get to our private table is an impressive relic. Chandeliers drip crystals from the ceiling and bottles of wine line the top of the wall.

After dinner orders are taken, Phil shares his enthusiasm for the day and holds up a glass to his senior staff. The wine is excellent, as usual, and I engage my colleagues around me, determined to stay in the present. I won't allow my thoughts to wander across the dark avenues, back to the trouble awaiting me in my hotel room.

With no clients to impress or vendors to schmooze, everyone appears relaxed, but that is too simple a read on the table. Dave was not wrong. I am only a portfolio manager. The title can come with great notoriety if the funds you oversee are a success, but I don't run a large division and I'm not a member of the C-suite. My inclusion, as an outsider—but also the source of our evening's celebration—is causing a rift in the stasis. It's evident in the stolen glances across the tops of highballs and long-stemmed wineglasses. I report to the CEO, but my place in the pecking order has not been formally established. Having been grafted into the pack, my team has not had to contend for our position in any power play.

With the inclusion of all of Phil's direct reports, a reevaluation of the hierarchy is in order. Dave, who heads up the entire sales division for Garman Straub, doesn't look away when I catch him staring at me from four positions down. To his advantage, I am not up for the fight tonight. The delivery of the thumb drive exposed my underbelly—pink and weak.

And the impression of his fingers has grown dark on my arm.

As I scrape the last bits of my delightful key lime cheesecake from my dessert plate, I continue to try to probe Candace, who sits across from me, about her time in Iraq. Since the basic information shared during her introduction about eighteen months ago, little more has circulated. She's always kept a professional distance. So, I'm torn. With everything going on, I don't need any more attention, but I'm also fascinated by what I've heard about the work she did. Besides a distant cousin on my mom's side, I've not had the chance to talk to anyone who saw active duty in the Middle East.

"Come on, Candace. Throw us a bone. We're here for it. We love stories." Terrence knocks my elbow with his.

I can't help but grin. Our chief compliance officer has partnered with me in my quest to get Candace to talk. He's legendary for getting people to spill their guts.

"This dinner is not about me. Meredith, how did you come up with the idea of the funds?" Candace asks.

I hesitate.

"Not so fast. She asked you first. Why don't you tell her about how you got the DFC." Terrence takes a heavy gulp of his brown liquor.

Tiny lines grow deeper around Candace's eyes as she shifts her gaze to him.

"What's a DFC?" I ask.

Terrence slides his dessert plate away. Like me, he could stand to eat a second one. "Only the highest award for extraordinary aerial achievement that the Air Force bestows. The Distinguished Flying Creed . . . or maybe Code." Something about his tone leads me to believe he knows exactly what it stands for.

"Cross," Candace says.

"Of course, Distinguished Flying Cross." He makes his neat brown eyebrows dance on his face. He got her to talk. "I'm a bit of an air combat groupie. Especially around this one." Terrence laughs but I can hear the undertone of something much more serious. "So, tell us."

"I don't think Meredith is interested in—"

"But I am. Was the award for your overall service or a specific mission?" I ask.

Candace sighs. "The whole crew was awarded." She glances down the table, perhaps to see if Phil is ready to leave, saving her from talking about herself.

"It's all right, Candace. I think I've pried enough. Thank you for your service."

Candace nods and then surprisingly does throw us that bone. "It's what we were trained to do. While on mission to evacuate the US embassy in Baghdad, we came into some trouble and had to scramble, but we got those guys to safety. They made a deal of it, and I got the DFC."

"Skimming the surface." The ice tinkles as Terrence deposits his lowball on the pressed white tablecloth.

"What kind of trouble?" I ask softly across the table.

"We were conducting our preflight duties." Candace relaxes into her words, suddenly willing to talk. "A firefight erupted on a ramp one hundred meters from our Draco—our, uh, U-28A single-engine Pilatus. Iraqi security forces opened fire and attempted to commandeer the aircraft. They wanted to leave country."

"Incredible. How did you escape?" I ask.

"There was no discussion of escape. We knew what would happen if we aborted our mission. As a crew, being able to help those taking the most risk, getting those Marines out, was the best part of the job."

"You got them out."

"Of course she did. They stayed until every one of those grunts made it out." Terrence beams at Candace across the table.

"Not so cut-and-dry. We took on tracer fire and landed on a non-existent airfield. The next day—" Candace immediately stops talking and rises, her eyes on the end of the table. Phil has pushed back his chair and is leaning over to grab his reading glasses. Candace is never off duty.

"One more thing, Meredith." Candace tucks her chair squarely under the table as if she is securing a military vehicle into a base lot.

I stand, sliding my purse strap over my shoulder, and wait for her to continue with some words of wisdom about always keeping the mission in mind while under fire.

"You got a package delivered today."

I freeze. Why did I think she wouldn't know about the delivery? I toted the envelope during most of the reception. "Yes. I meant to tell you about it."

"I'm sure you did."

"In all the craziness today, I was only able to peek inside. Just a thumb drive."

Surprise flashes across her face, so fast I wonder if I actually saw it. First time I've ever seen Candace with a tell. As interesting as it might be, I know she's unhappy. I've likely lost any goodwill we were beginning to build. I should have casually mentioned it as soon as I saw her. I'll be handing it over and will have a target on my chest, but at least not my back, as I'm sure she is someone who hits head-on.

"Who was it from?" Terrence bumps out of his seat. He has definitely overindulged.

"I think Betsey. My best guess."

"You got a drive from the woman we fired, and you filed a restraining order against—and you're telling me now." Candace breaks eye contact and nods at Phil as he moves toward the door.

"Figured it could wait. I can't access the drive from my computer, and I'll be back in the office tomorrow to turn it in to Compliance. To Terrence." I glance to my left.

Terrence is absorbed in his phone, seemingly having lost interest in our conversation.

"That's the procedure, right?" I ask. Better to appear nonchalant than guilt-ridden. My mind is checking in with each of my major body parts to ensure they aren't fidgeting, flushing, or featuring the unruly emotions swirling inside me.

"Why do you think it's from Betsey?" Any trace of friendliness has left her face.

Not sure when I decided not to mention the note, but I need more time with it before anyone starts digging. "My name scrawled on the front—I think I recognize the handwriting. Besides, all of her desperate communications . . . I just assumed."

"Logical." Candace walks around the table to stand directly in front of me. "Based on the events of the day, I think we both know it would have been wise to hand it over to me right away."

I shrug as if I agree but also question if the timing makes any difference.

As Candace marches toward Phil, a bead of sweat trips down my spine.

12

TUESDAY

Gray light filters through the partially shut blinds. I shift restlessly, punching the pillow before curling deeper into the nest I've created within the downy comforter and warm bedsheets. Last night's silence from both Clint and Erika reverberates loudly in my head. By the time I got back to the hotel, it'd been too late to call, and neither of them responded to my good-night texts. For an extended moment, I stood over my rollerboard imagining shoving everything I could into it, calling a car, and going home. I would speak my secrets and then urge Erika to speak hers.

Instead, I eventually curled into the plush wingback chair by the window and idly scrolled through social media while keeping one eye on the envelope lying on the desk. Just after two in the morning, I tossed a navy sweater over the unnerving package and slipped between the cool, crisp sheets.

The weight of the day that has barely dawned presses down on all sides. The envelope needs to be handed over. By me. I need to tell them what I know and then wash my hands of Betsey. As I rehearse the words I will use when I walk into Terrence's office, disappointment curls its merciless tentacles around me. I really thought I'd assembled my dream team at Garman Straub.

I flop onto my back and press my finger into my right temple to try to relieve the growing tension. Over the past who knows how many weeks, sleep has become so elusive. Same thing happened right before I switched careers. I'd been living my calling, or so I thought. Constructing financial plans and sharing in the dreams of my clients, I was content. And then I literally fell into becoming a portfolio manager. Two of my clients from Kennebunkport were snowbirding in Key Biscayne. I combined a mini vacay with meeting them and, at the last minute, decided to spend a day at a conference about exchange-traded funds. Running late for the keynote session, my heel snagged on the carpet, and I went down. Hard. Always a klutz growing up, my knees have taken a beating over the years, but it was the mortification of tossing my hot coffee down the aisle and sprawling face down among hundreds of seated guests that hurt the most. The guy onstage even stopped speaking. I remember glancing up and feeling his mortification on my behalf. I did the only thing I could do. I shot to my feet, took a bow, and scooped my now-empty paper cup from the floor. A light applause turned enthusiastic as the speaker made a joke about making an entrance. I darted down a row and took an empty seat.

After the keynote, during the break, I discovered I'd become a minor celebrity. A few people even asked if it was staged. My entrance and awkward flight through the air had come just as the speaker was remarking about the power of mistakes and the privilege of your sequel.

The people I met because of my moment of humiliation became

the people who changed my career trajectory. These new funds called ETFs wiggled their way into my brain and then bore down deep.

After I spent a few nights tossing and turning at the prospect of blowing up the easy rhythms of our lives, Clint didn't even flinch when I told him five years ago I wanted to make the move from producer to creator and take a job with Garman Straub. It took many late evenings and stolen moments between meetings to come up with solid plans for new investment strategies. Then, three years ago, I presented my idea for a highly innovative family of ETFs.

The reception to my ideas was mixed.

In the end, if your idea has value, the naysayers don't matter. You only need a ripe market and at least one voice that is willing to shout in the darkness alongside yours. Especially effective is if the voice belongs to the CEO of a successful Wall Street firm.

I press my face back into the pillow. This playback is a distraction, because it's not my career, the funds, or the dinner that is gnawing at me. It's not even the file I have yet to fully examine or the note with the veiled threat and no demand. It's something else. Something weighing on my heart. I stare up at the white ceiling.

Is Erika looking up at her ceiling right now, or is she sleeping her usual sleep of the anesthetized? I'm convinced that the best sleep of your life is when you're a teen.

I sit straight up in the bed. What did she say during our second phone conversation yesterday? Even the fact that there was a second call has every alarm bell clanging. I assumed she said *text*. Her phone is a constant source of angst in our house. Either she's on it too often texting her friends or she's been shut out of a group text created by some friend one day, enemy the next. What have we done to this generation of children growing up with these identity-crashing devices?

But what if she didn't say *text*? She'd been crying and it had almost sounded like her three-year-old lisp had returned, because the word had sounded a lot more like *sext*.

Hoping there is a less-terrible slang definition, I slide my phone from my bedside table and google the word. *Sending or receiving sexually explicit or suggestive images, messages, or videos on electronic devices.* Nope, as bad as I thought. My baby couldn't possibly have meant that. She hadn't even started talking about dating. Teen friendships took all her energy. And ours.

Without hesitation I make the call.

A low grunt greets me.

"Sorry, honey. Were you sleeping?"

"Was I sleeping at four a.m.?" Clint's voice sounds as if gravel pelts every word.

"I'm worried about Erika."

"Okay." The bed creaks. "What's happened?"

"How was she last night?"

"Fine, I think. I was late getting some updated trail maps sent to the printer after dropping Reid off. I ordered our favorite pizza from D'Ellies."

My skin prickles in the cool air, and I tuck the sheet around my waist. He's a talented cartographer and a very good dad. "Thanks for doing that. Did she talk at dinner?"

"Rob came over."

I close my eyes. Clint's Appalachian Trail buddy with a round face and a mop of brown curls appears behind my lids. He's always throwing back his head and laughing his strange can't-quite-get-the-old-roadster-engine-to-turn-over laugh. It used to make me giggle, but lately it just makes me tired. "What time did she get to bed?"

"What's eating you, Mer?" He asks the question as if my answer is the last thing he wants to know.

"Something she said yesterday. She was pretty upset. Do you think there's a guy?"

"What? What guy? No. I don't think there's a guy." His tone shifts and he's almost talking over himself.

"Fine." I raise my open palm as if in surrender. "You're right. I'm probably reading too much into it. Hard to tell over the phone."

"So, she hasn't mentioned a guy?"

"Not specifically." I decide not to tell him the word she used and save him from the experience of acid sloshing through his stomach too. "I'm not there, so I don't really know what she meant."

He puffs into the phone. "That what this is?" His voice lowers. "Some kind of smoke screen to get back here? To get your own way?"

As if I've been physically slapped, my hand flies to my cheek and my eyes fill. My own way? None of this is my own way.

I lower the phone and watch as my finger ends the call.

Silence pulses in my ears like crashing waves.

I hung up on my husband. But how dare he think I'd create an issue with our daughter to manipulate him. She's our priority over any infuriating marriage issues. I need to know our baby, our first-born, is all right. And, of course, the one place in this world I want to be is the only place I can't go. Home.

I move my trembling fingers over my screen and click on the Messages app. I send Erika a good-morning text and ask her to call me when she gets a chance. I remind her how much I love her.

She won't get the message for another few hours until she retrieves her phone from our family docking station. I hope she's sleeping soundly, the friend drama has resolved, and that she simply said the word *text*.

I place my quiet phone back onto the bedside table and slide out of bed.

I don't call Clint. And he doesn't call me.

13

MY HAND HOVERS above my office handset. Before I left the hotel, I examined the file again. It contains some incredible information if I can crack the code. No names, either of investors or advisors, are listed, but a great deal of information about the specific trading. If we had this information, it would be a game changer in how we think about sales. Right now, shares of our ETFs, like all ETFs, are bought on the open market. We don't know who. We don't know why. Kind of like consigning your clothes to a thrift store. You get the revenue but no idea of who is wearing your lime-green miniskirt or if they may also want that fringed purse your Aunt Nellie gave you for Christmas last year. From this thumb drive data, we could see patterns and target our sales. If the data is real.

But Betsey's game seems half-baked. She has my attention but with no demand. If she's going to use the Rotterdam Room—though I can't bring myself to believe that she has anything of substance there—what does she want from me?

I arch forward in my seat and my arm bumps my Starbucks. I right the cup and jump from my black leather chair in case the dark roast blooms toward me. Again, a klutz. Pale-brown liquid has gurgled onto my desktop and seeped like mold onto the printout of my team's monthly sales itinerary. I grab a few tissues from the box I always keep tucked on my photo-laden credenza. After years of clients sharing their retirement dreams, suffering through deaths, and shouting at their siblings about ownership of their mother's ugly Christmas pendant, I continue to be prepared. My office, with its brocade pillows and comfortable chairs, also hides a litany of emotional-support devices, including a stash of coloring books for that rare wee visitor. Our walls are hardly family-friendly, but I love it when someone on my team brings in their wide-eyed munchkin for an afternoon.

I mop up the spill and then sit hard back into my seat.

Betsey had to know I'd hand over that thumb drive. Otherwise, she would have found a way to get it to me that didn't risk our entire executive staff seeing her, while she was under a restraining order, no less.

I lift the handset. It's not quite eight, but I'm hoping to catch Aarav before his day gets too busy. I need to know if Betsey was in his office. Did his words at the reception, matching Betsey's from the note, mean more than a face-value platitude on success?

The phone rings and eventually dumps me into voicemail. I ask for him to call me back at his convenience.

I then pick up the envelope with the thumb drive and head to our chief compliance officer's office.

"Good morning, Meredith. Great day yesterday." Terrence strides from around his desk and extends his hand. His tailored charcoal suit hangs meticulously from his athletic frame. A silk tie with pinprick blue flowers, knotted in a loose Windsor, adds a bit of whimsy to his otherwise austere appearance.

"Thanks for your support." I slide my hand into his.

He motions for me to take a seat in the club chair closest to me, in front of his massive window overlooking the sun-drenched Chrysler Building, across to Third Avenue, and then a peekaboo view of the Queensboro Bridge. Erika declared this view her favorite of all the offices she visited last week. I clutch at my bag, anxious to see if she's left any response.

"Hear you have a town hall and reception planned for all the teams this afternoon. Thanks for including Compliance." He crosses his ankle over his knee, exposing gray socks subtly printed with a variety of silver spoons. Only Terrence dares to have both his socks and his tie be overtly playful, something I habitually admire.

"Naturally. They were invaluable in helping us structure the various materials." I shift and try to resettle in my chair. My tweed seat base is lower than his, and I'm forced to look up slightly at Terrence. I wonder if he even realizes.

"You mean my team banned you from communicating what you really wanted to." He chuckles.

"Not at all. They're creative and exceeded my expectations. I thought they'd only find ways to say no, but instead they gave us alternative ways to describe our funds, sometimes considerably better than the original wording." Maybe I exaggerate, but his team was helpful in crafting the marketing materials. I'd been warned that the Compliance team would be all about protecting the firm from regulators, so I was surprised by how much I enjoyed their partnership.

He throws back his head. "I'm just busting their chops. My team is like family to me, but don't let them know I have a soft spot."

I nod.

"What can I do for you, Meredith?"

I watch my hand tremble as I reach into my bag. I force myself to take three small cleansing breaths through my nose so as not to appear as flustered as I am.

I pull out the mailer and lay it on the wide arm of my chair. My handwritten name blaring up from the burnt-gold padded envelope.

"Is that it?" He doesn't lean forward and barely glances down as if I've become an unexpected liability.

"As I mentioned, it was delivered yesterday at the Exchange. It's—I believe it's from the woman we fired on Sunday." I hand him the envelope.

He raises an eyebrow as he places it on the small round table between us. "Betsey? The woman you saw on the Exchange floor?"

"Yes. Inside is a thumb drive. It's troubling."

"After the restraining order, she gave it to you?" He hooks his head toward the envelope but keeps his eyes trained on my face.

"Well, a stock exchange employee actually handed it to me." It's unnerving the way he's looking at me instead of the envelope. "He said they had it scanned. It's just a thumb drive."

Terrence nods but continues to watch me.

"I need you to know that I've accessed the drive. On my personal laptop. Nothing about the packaging indicated it was about the firm." The lie rolls easily from my tongue. So many years of being taught the power of leverage. I need them to know that I know what's on the drive. Last night with Candace I indicated I hadn't accessed it, so if asked I'll just have to say I needed to ensure it was even related to the firm before I handed it over.

"Why wouldn't you think it was about the firm if it was from a woman who was let go?"

"I know Betsey—we've become, uh, friends. It could've been personal."

"But it wasn't personal?" He cocks his head at me as if seeing me for the first time. I've never been one to cause trouble. Frankly, there is rarely any trouble to be had. Our culture is one of judicious professionalism. The things that go on overtly at other Wall Street firms are hidden here.

"No, not personal. So, I'm leaving it with you."

He stares at the envelope as if it might be a bomb.

14

OUR CEO'S FACE REDDENS as he stands and knocks his fist onto the polished black table. "This conversation has gone on too long. I'm not going to let some"—Phil glances at Hardwin sitting to his right—"some woman blackmail her way back into this firm. What are our other options?"

Hardwin straightens and reiterates that the numbers in the file look authentic. That Betsey Comarsh has apparently been calling and visiting some friendly advisors to gather their sales information. These offices went on record to indicate they were trading in the new ETFs. The theory is that she was able to marry that data with overall sales data and create a remarkably accurate sales inventory. By having this data, she holds power. Not only is this valuable to us, but our competitors would definitely benefit.

As Hardwin continues talking with more legalese than substance, the table learns nothing new. He is simply rehashing what we've already discussed.

"What makes us think she wants back into the firm?" A voice from a chair positioned along the brocade-papered wall cuts in.

The ten of us at the table glance over at the well-upholstered young man in a suit a couple sizes too big in the shoulders. He's the same associate who told me about the trashing of my office. I now know he works for Terrence in Compliance, not Legal.

"I mean, if it is her, she's not asking for anything, right? She just handed it over. Why?"

Phil's bushy eyebrows twitch. The wall seats are for observers only, and most of them are empty for this meeting. The young man was invited to answer questions about his initial review of the data, not to ask questions of his own.

I roll my shoulders back and rehearse responses in case I'm asked to address his annoyingly astute questions. Perhaps Betsey didn't compile it and is simply trying to warn us that the data exists. Or perhaps she wants to demonstrate her proficiency, in case anyone is willing to offer her a post–restraining order recommendation. Both of these answers are complete rubbish, but I've backed myself into a corner with what I can tell them.

"I think the solution is obvious." Dave ignores the posed questions. "Hardwin tells this Betsey to cease and desist. It doesn't matter what she's done here with the sales data or what she wants. We've wasted too much time on this already."

This stirs up commentary around the table, with factions shaping up around either going after her legally to shut her up or bringing her in to see how she compiled so much data so accurately. I'm not in either camp. I like Betsey. A mix of sugar and vinegar, she has a way with clients, enabling her to achieve remarkable sales. But lately, with her behavior so erratic, even threatening? Not a hill I'll die on.

"Second thing." Dave speaks over the ruckus. "Betsey needs to be charged with stealing company property. She should not have this proprietary data."

I might want to claim my hill after all. Someone needs to talk to Betsey before authorities are called. How would involving law enforcement, again, serve the company or anyone around the table? Especially me?

A few questions fly at Hardwin, who stutters through legal definitions and older precedent cases. It appears he is stalling until he can huddle with his team about what they really can do.

Finally, Terrence coughs. "Beyond what Ms. Comarsh can be charged with, what are you, Dave, as head of sales for the firm, going to do with the information we've been given?"

"I assume you'll tell me." Dave lifts his chin. There is a visible tension in the way they're speaking to each other. So different from the camaraderie on the balcony. Maybe they're not the strongest alliance around the table.

The wall dweller speaks up again. "Why don't we have this kind of data? Dave, you have sales data like this for the mutual funds. Why have we elected not to purchase from the largest wires or an intermediary?"

Dave's eyes skitter over the men around him and land on the table in front of his clenched hands. "It was decided based on cost—"

"But the ETFs have been so successful. Did you not at some point consider it?" The young man looks completely unaffected, but the awkwardness of this exchange prompts the guy across from me to sputter into his tight fist. His cheeks quiver, likely constraining a giggle that would be perilous to release.

To disarm the attention he is gathering, I cough gingerly into my shoulder.

Dave swings his body toward me but doesn't make eye contact. "There's one more person we haven't addressed."

My skin goes cold.

Phil rhythmically clicks the top of his pen.

"I offer the floor to our portfolio manager to explain what she knows about how this sales data came to be. Perhaps she has insights into Betsey's motivation, how she came by this data, or what she truly wants to get out of handing it over to us."

The clicking stops. No one says a word.

Phil trains his eyes on me. "Meredith, is there anything else you haven't shared?"

I remain completely still and imagine myself whipping out Betsey's handwritten note. *Oh, this? Did you want to see everything from the envelope? My bad.*

The door opens. Perhaps it's Candace and her security team coming to haul me away.

Phil's administrative assistant enters, her voice ringing like a tide bell on a vacant, foggy shore. "Sorry to interrupt. Meredith, you're needed on the phone."

I shift my gaze back to Phil.

Phil scowls. "Right now?" Something seems to pass between Phil and the woman who has been coordinating his business life for decades. Phil nods at me and extends his hand to the door.

As I walk past Dave's chair, I hear him mutter something about my leaving being for the best.

15

NONIE POINTS TO THE PHONE on the glass and chrome conference table in Phil's office, offering privacy after obvious urgency. My heart flutters in my chest. Can't be Betsey. They continue to screen all my calls.

"Hello." I speak softly into the receiver as if warding off any more conversations I don't want to have.

"Meredith, it's me." Clint speaks with haste. "Look, someone at Reid's camp saw me taking pictures of the drop-off and the first event. I-I got a call this morning asking if I'd be willing to share some of the photos—"

"I'm sorry." Although my tone indicates the opposite. He's interrupting me to talk about sharing pictures he took? "I'm kind of in the middle of something. I'm going to need to call you back."

Clint huffs. "You want in or out?" His words sound bitten off and like it cost him something to say them.

My fingers throttle the phone. He's using another therapist

maneuver. Although I'm not sure his delivery was what she had in mind.

I give him credit, though. He remembered to ask the question.

And I get the message.

One night last year, I came home late to the kids and Clint already at the table. I shoot for two family dinners during the school week, but I'd missed my train. As I stepped into the kitchen, Dr Pepper shot out of Reid's freckled nose. Erika laughed so hard the legs of her chair slipped to the side and she ended up on the floor. I started giggling just at the sight of my family having such fun. But when I tried to get them to tell me what had them in stitches, I got overlapping incomplete fragments. No one could explain what had created such an uproar. Later, alone with Clint, I tried to make him understand how much I wanted to feel a part of their tribe. This was a story I retold with our therapist. We established that it would take effort on both our parts.

If I wanted to be on the inside, I had to take time when I was on the outside. I couldn't fall too far away while I was at work and then expect to be caught up later.

"I want in. Always," I say into the phone. My fingers ache as I clamp down on the one thing connecting me to my family.

He breathes deeply. "So, I was pulling down the shots from our cloud and there was this, um, picture."

A tingling sensation breaks out across my scalp, as if my body knows what he is going to say before I do. I turn toward the original Ansel Adams print of California redwoods on Phil's wall—the rough trunks, the feathery leaves, and the stark contrast between the light and shadows. The image surrounds me.

I hear an almost strangling sound through the phone as if Clint is trying to swallow a too-big bite of my Mississippi pot roast.

"Did Erika take an inappropriate picture?" I whisper.

"How did you know?" Clint's dull voice is devoid of its usual frustration with me.

"Oh, my baby." I shut my eyes against the monochromatic forest pushing in.

"She wouldn't tell me what's going on." Acid has leaked back into his tone.

"Do you know if she sent the picture?" I imagine her before she called me last night, sitting alone in her room, being harassed to send it. Did she send the photo and then call me, or did I fail as a mother to say the thing that would have stopped her? I should have skipped dinner. I should be home now. I glance toward Phil's open office door and see myself marching past the conference and out of the building.

"I called her at school. She answered her phone but wouldn't even acknowledge me and then . . ." Clint sucks in a large amount of air but says nothing more.

"And then what?" I sag against the table. The chrome edge bites into my upper thigh.

"Meredith, I don't know what to tell you. I heard other teens yakking it up in the background. It just sounded wrong. Frenzied almost. Something was off."

We sit in silence for what feels like minutes as I try to piece together Erika's calls, her relief in coming home yesterday, but then our quiet, studious daughter being surrounded while on the phone with Clint. None of this sounded like Erika.

I glance toward the conference room. The men in that room will not only decide what to do about Betsey's thumb drive, they will decide the future of my funds, and they will decide what to do about me.

"Delete the photo. I'm coming home."

16

I STRIDE BACK INTO THE CONFERENCE ROOM and the table goes silent. I remain standing and look at Phil. "I'd like to say something."

"Of course." He nods. "The floor is yours."

"I agree with Dave." A few short inhales and mumbles emanate from the suits. "I should be able to explain how this data came into being." I glance over to the wall dweller. "We have looked at purchasing such data to help our sales strategy, but even if we had, it never would have given as complete a picture as what we have in that file."

Dave opens his mouth to respond, but I speak over him. "I know a few of you knew Betsey. And a few of you and your teams had issues with her approach. She is smart and diligent but has some rough edges. Things seem to have gone off the rails this last week." I glance at Hardwin. "That's on me. I want to be part of the solution, but I can't tell you where this data came from."

Out of the corner of my eye, I see Dave making a sour face and nodding as if my poor judgment speaks for itself. But I also notice he is not leaning over to Terrence to share his ever-present thoughts. He does this with predictable regularity. Never when Phil or Hardwin are speaking—Dave knows his reach—but he plays confidence-wrecking games with others. Instead, he continues to watch me.

Perhaps he assumes I'm digging my own trap. Perhaps his silence is worse.

I pull my shoulder blades back. I only have myself to offer. "As to your other recommendation, Dave, I think we should carefully consider whether we take legal action. Maybe Betsey has done us a favor. We needed to know this data was out there and find out if this was an isolated situation orchestrated by her or if we have a bigger problem of data breaches across the company."

A few of the guys murmur to each other. Did they not discuss if this might only be the tip of the iceberg? What if other unexplainable data files exist? I glance around the table. Who would benefit from data such as this?

If I asked that question out loud, everyone would point to where I stand, my knees locked in solidarity with my rigid shoulders.

I take a measured breath. "As for me, these funds were my idea, my execution, and I want to continue to manage the amazing teams who have supported our success. That being said, my husband was on the phone. We have an urgent situation back at home. I hope you can understand. I have to go."

I walk toward Phil and extend my arm.

He stands. His thick white eyebrows crash together as he shakes my hand. "Whatever we can do for you and your family. You let us know."

"I will." I turn back to the table, finally recognizing the unease that has settled in my chest like rubble from a battle that continues to wage. "I trust you all will make the best decision for the firm and everyone that relies on our integrity. Thanks for letting me speak. I'll be in touch."

17

TEN MINUTES BEFORE MY TRAIN, I head to the single restroom behind the pretzel vendor, which is always clean but rarely occupied, and push open the door. I'll travel the length of Grand Central to avoid the public stalls.

Inside, as I reach to twist the lock, the steel door crashes in toward me.

I yelp and jump away.

Before I can push back, Betsey stands before me.

"What are you doing?" My anxious words come unbidden from my mouth. It's obvious she followed me, but was she waiting outside the building on the slim chance I left early, or did someone tip her off?

Her usually full auburn hair is flat and tucked behind her ears. Her dark cobalt eyes appear almost royal against her sallow skin. She looks faintly ill but also intensely alert, like perhaps she's not getting enough sleep either.

My immediate impulse is to reach out to her to ask if she's okay, but I don't. I've been warned, but that is not what stops me. This woman has upended my life. She is not safe.

I shift my weight back toward the sink and grip the leather strap of the heavy bag that holds my laptop and at least a ream of folders and unread articles.

"Did you analyze it?" Her voice sounds remarkably clear.

I hold up a hand like a shield as I try to pivot around her. She blew her chance with me and many others. With my other hand, I dig inside my bag for my phone.

"Stop!" Her shrill tone cracks the air around us. "I need you to stop." She swallows furiously, almost as if she is choking on her own anxiety.

I glare at the woman who has at best ruined her own career and at worst put an entire firm at risk. "How did you know to find me here? Are you following me or—"

"You showed them." She purses her lips. The disappointment obvious but also inevitable.

"Of course I showed them. We filed a restraining order. I can have you arrested." I lift my hand still clutching my phone.

"This is so past any restraining order." She slowly shakes her head like she's dealing with a toddler who's spilled her Cheerios. The only fissure in her now-controlled demeanor is the slight tremor in her hands. Her mauve-painted fingernails look like they've been gnawed. "We have to work together. Like we started." She takes a step toward me.

My heel stutters on the slick tile and I brace myself against a rolled ankle. At a minimum I need to remain upright. "Betsey. I don't understand you. You missed a conference. You've been visiting offices not on the schedule." I take a quick breath. "You stalked my home. You trashed—"

"No. You don't understand. We have to talk."

"I'm not talking to you. I can't. I signed a restraining order. I'm under strict instruction. Not just by the firm but by the police." I sigh. "You need to figure yourself out, before you lose everything." I shift again to try to get around her. "I urge you to talk to someone. Call Terrence or Hardwin. I think they'd be open to helping you."

"When was the last time you looked at the custodian contract?" She raises her eyebrows and waits. "You haven't since before we launched, have you?"

"Betsey, the data you created—they're talking legal action." Whether or not they're still considering it, I have no idea, but I need her to back off. "You don't know what you're doing."

"Me?" She puffs out a laugh and then lunges toward me.

The lip of the sink bites into my spine. "Step back. Now."

She raises her hands and turns toward the door.

My thigh muscles tense. As soon as she opens that door, I'll be at full sprint.

She suddenly spins, her eyes mere slants. "Is it you? Tell me it's not you!" Her shrill tone bounces off the dull wall tiles.

"I'm calling 911." I raise my phone.

"Wait." Her white dress shirt flutters under her suit jacket as she takes a deep breath. "You've always trusted me."

"I always trusted you, but I think we're a bit past that." Now it's as if I'm the one speaking to a child.

"You think I chose this? You just don't see."

"I see plenty." Whatever is going on with Betsey, she needs help. Trashing my office, threatening my marriage, and now cornering me in a bathroom is not the way to get mine. "Do you need a doctor? Someone you can talk to?"

She shakes her head, more in exasperation than denial. "I know what you're thinking. I haven't been sleeping. But neither have you."

I recoil.

"The dark smudges under your eyes." She points her now-trembling finger at me. "But it's not about that. I need you to give me the latest securities lending agreement. I can help you. We can help each other."

I was right about the note—that she was pointing me toward the agreement—but it hardly matters. I speak slowly and with an edge. "I'm not giving you anything." But why in the world would she want the securities lending agreement? It's a standard contract we have with our custodial bank.

"Don't say that. I don't want to hurt you. But—"

"Enough." I raise my phone and dial. "Let me out."

"Fine. You can go, but let me give you something." She fishes around in the slate-blue purse hanging on her shoulder and pulls out a small white envelope. "Take this."

I glance at my screen. *Call failed.* I have no signal. "Yes, my name is Meredith Hansel," I say into my phone, with a slight tremor in my voice.

"Don't make me ruin you," Betsey whispers.

My chest tightens with a feeling of déjà vu. "I'm having a situation at Grand Central," I stutter into the phone.

"There's a number. On the back. Call it. Ask for me. But either way, I'll see you or your husband on Friday." Betsey thrusts the envelope at me.

Both my hands flatten my phone against my ear as I speak to Betsey. "I'm not taking that."

"You've made this so much harder than it needed to be. Unless, of course, you already know." She continues to hold out the envelope.

"I'm trying to leave the restroom behind Flava's Pretzels," I say into my phone as I twist past her and reach for the door handle.

"Time is ticking," Betsey hisses behind me and grabs my hand. Her fingers are icy. "And it's not my clock."

I yank away from her as she shoves the stiff envelope into my fist.

"Friday!" she yells after me.

18

AFTER BEING BUZZED INTO BUTLER HIGH SCHOOL, I pull open the glass-paneled door to the administrative offices. A pungent smell hits me first. I'm used to a wide variety of olfactory experiences on the streets of Manhattan, but this sweet, musky burn must be the Axe body spray Erika complains the boys spray liberally in lieu of showering. I suck in my lips before parting them to take a breath.

A large wooden desk structure, a relic of decades-old architecture, dominates the space. Stacks of papers, folders, and old notices about spring formals and choral concerts cover most surfaces. Positioned in each quadrant of the large built-in desk, three older women and one young man sit doing the business of teen education. None of them look up when I walk in.

We toyed with the idea of sending the kids to private schools, but being in one of the most affluent school districts, Clint and I both thought a public education the best way to prepare them for the world they will inherit. At the start of every new school semester, I plan to join the PTA.

"Excuse me. My name is Meredith Hansel. I'm here for a meeting with . . ." The principal's name escapes me. *Oh, Clint, why are we here? We should be talking to her at home.*

The young man points to the door behind him. "Erika's grandfather is already here. You can go right in."

Hitching my breath, I glance toward the office. Clint is looking right at me. The room is loud with phone calls, kids goofing off on the bench behind me, and a low rumble from some air-handling unit in the far corner. Maybe he didn't hear what the guy said.

Clint's eyes close slowly, and he turns away.

Not the way I wanted to start this. I don't bother correcting the oblivious young man, who has already picked up his telephone handset. I used to. I'd snuggle up to Clint and try for a joke or talk about his incredible sense of direction or the way he can fix just about anything. How proud I am to be his wife. Never worked. My verbosity only dug me in deeper.

I've learned to wait him out.

I slide in behind my husband, who has yet to look at me again, and then lay a quick hand on Erika's shoulder. As I settle into the last of the three chairs, a man in a blue button-down and tie but no jacket strides in after me and takes his seat behind the desk.

"Thanks for joining us. I'm Dr. Amit Singh." The principal's voice has a hint of a lilting accent. His thin lips smile briefly as he knits his fingers together and lays his clasped hands on the desk. Piles of multicolored folders and papers line the left and right of him, but nothing inhibits our view of his steady gaze. Even the brass plate engraved with his name is shoved to the side.

"I'll dispense with the nonessentials. There was a substitute teacher in Erika's Honors English class today. Mr. Doward is new to our school. He was provoked and filmed. As you might imagine . . ." Dr. Singh continues to convey his disappointment, but I barely listen to his words. My heart bangs in my chest. Why are we starting with this story about a substitute?

I stare at our daughter slouched between us. Erika's head is bowed. Her pale-blonde hair, which is just starting to darken, curtains her face with a silky fringe. She hasn't spoken. Erika is compassionate. She's a tutor for kids struggling in math and an advocate for neurodivergent learning environments. Since she was a baby, she has been sweet and compliant. Beyond the normal surliness, mostly to me, and the too-frequent tears, she's a good girl.

I glance up when I realize the room has gone quiet. No one is speaking. I sit perched on the edge of my seat. I'd like to scoot back but fear the movement might indicate my desire to contribute to this conversation. Clint made it clear through texts during my ride north that he wants to be the one to begin.

I wait but no one says anything.

Finally, I wiggle back in my wooden chair. Perhaps the movement will prompt Clint to begin.

The silence stretches.

"Do either of you have any questions?" The principal widens his dark eyes in an obvious effort to prompt us.

I steal a glance over at Clint. He looks a bit green and is staring down at his lap. Perhaps talking about the picture is a lot harder than he imagined. Is he going to be sick? I've never asked that question of my husband before. He is the man you want when the night closes in. I scan the room for a trash can and see the lid peeking from behind the steel side of the desk. Should I grab it just in case?

"What's the punishment?" Erika's voice is stronger than her posture.

My head whips around. "Wait, I don't think I understand." My gaze shoots to Clint, who has the same shocked expression on his face as I likely have on mine.

"That's why we're here. Right? To punish me." Erika tucks her hair behind one of her ears.

I startle. Her upper cartilage has two thin gold loops.

When did she do that?

About a month ago, we talked about her getting another piercing. I said it was unnecessary, and I thought she agreed. Apparently, one was not enough.

I squeeze my own platinum stud, skewering the rear post into the pad of my thumb. The sting of pain dulls the anger working its way through my stomach and up through my chest. One issue at a time. Frankly, we're not even here to listen to some messy business about a substitute teacher. We're here to talk about the picture. Clint hasn't been able to get more than a few words from Erika. He pushed to set up this meeting with her principal just to get her to open up, and she called his bluff. I didn't agree to the plan and wanted him to wait until I got home. She shouldn't be forced to talk, but I have lost my voice with Clint lately.

"Who pressured you?" Dr. Singh's words are slow and cautious.

Erika shakes her head.

"I know you. You're a National Honor Society student. You're respected by the faculty here. I know you didn't do this on your own." Dr. Singh leans farther over his desk. "I want names."

"You don't have to answer that." Clint's arm shoots over the back of Erika's chair. His hand grips her opposite shoulder. He's regained his bearings. "I'm sorry, sweetheart. I should not have insisted on this meeting. I apologize for wasting your time, Dr. Singh. We need to let Erika share with us what's been happening with her and, uh, her friends. I let my frustration get the best of me." He starts to rise.

"I did get your call, Mr. Hansel, about wanting to meet, but that is not why we're here." Dr. Singh shifts his focus. "Erika, I don't want to punish you."

"Punish her?" Clint barks.

"No, Daddy." She hasn't called him that since American Girl dolls claimed a prominent corner in her room. "I did this. I called out the substitute and shared the video."

Video? The story Dr. Singh shared with us was about Erika? I blink back the tears in my eyes. Frustration is the worst emotion. There's a purity to fear or rage. Not pleasant, but easier to parse and then lean into. Frustration is anger, confusion, and the inability to understand my daughter all rolled up into a soggy mass inside me that is now threatening to drip down my face. I plunge my hand into my bag and scramble for the small pack of tissues I always keep tucked inside, but Dr. Singh beats me to it. He slides a previously hidden box toward us.

"Erika, why don't you tell us what happened in your own words." He gives our daughter a small smile.

"It's as you said. I wasn't thinking." She retreats back into her curved spine.

"But I think you were. You had something very specific in mind when you lashed out like that. What was going through your head when you taunted him?"

Taunted him? Our daughter may throw teasing jabs at Reid and vice versa, but we're not a family that ridicules or hassles one another, even in jest. In fact, we're more likely to say nothing at all.

A lump settles in my throat. Do I even know who we are as a family anymore?

Erika raises her face to Dr. Singh. "I'm not—I'll never be . . ." Her voice is barely above a whisper. Then she shrugs, like none of it matters.

"Never be what?" he prompts. At least he's no longer demanding names. Maybe he has a legitimate chance to get her to open up.

"Beautiful." A single sob escapes her lips. "I don't know. I mean, I don't need to be beautiful. I just want to be . . . normal."

My heart breaks at Erika's inability to see herself the way I can. She is beautiful. There is no doubt, but her maturing body feels like a betrayal to her. She's a soccer, track, and lacrosse girl. A curvy figure is an albatross. I've seen her wear two sports bras to try to look more like her friends who have retained their athletic shapes. Is that why she took the picture? Some attempt to make peace with her own body?

"I don't see the connection," says the principal.

"It doesn't matter." She grabs the back of her neck. Her fingertips whiten as she presses in.

"It does. It does matter." Clint lowers his arm so he can shift in his seat to look at her.

"He lied, okay?" She snorts. "He told me. He said I was beautiful." Her spine straightens, and she sets her features in icy detachment.

I begin to see the girl who could do the things Dr. Singh described.

"Who?" Dr. Singh's brows furrow and he flattens back in his chair as if he doesn't want to know her answer.

"Danny. Danny Doward."

"Doward? The substitute teacher?" Dr. Singh shuffles through a folder on his desk.

Erika grabs two tissues and presses them against her face. Clint leans over and whispers something to her I can't hear.

"It's okay, I can do this."

Yes, yes you can, I want to shout.

Erika looks straight ahead, addressing her principal, whose eyes are still scanning the paperwork in front of him. "A month ago, I went to a par—a gathering after the first football game against Essex."

I bite the inside of my cheek. What party? We all went to that game, the season opener. Erika had gone home with Cicely, her friend since third grade.

She continues. “I met Danny. We hung out. He was older. He was talking to a bunch of the seniors.” Suddenly, she whips around in her seat and faces me. “I know what you’re thinking. It was nothing. At first, I just thought he was interesting.”

I gingerly lay my hand on her arm and, against my better judgment, nod for her to continue.

She faces forward again. “He wasn’t a nice guy. He bullied some of the less confident underclassmen and . . . Never mind.”

“This is one of your substitute teachers?” Clint barks.

“I don’t know anything about this. This was his first day here and evidently his last.” Dr. Singh shuffles some papers on his desk, unwilling to make the easy eye contact he’s made through most of our meeting.

“I saw him this morning in the hall. He walked by me and whispered I was beautiful. The way he said it creeped me out.”

“What do you mean? Is he the reason you took that picture?” My confusion is starting to lift. He must have played on her insecurities.

“No!” she shouts.

“What picture?” Dr. Singh straightens and stares at Erika. This narrative—where she’s in the wrong—he seems much more comfortable addressing.

“There is no picture. Just the video. My mother’s confused,” Erika says sharply, leaning toward her dad before continuing. “I did what I did to stop Danny. I was upset, and then he used that same bullying tone with Ethan. I just snapped. Ethan’s brilliant, but he struggles getting his ideas out. Danny was riding him and making him stutter. I had to make him stop . . . I don’t know. Let’s just get this over with. What’s my punishment?” Erika purses her lips as if she is clamping down on words she dares not say.

Clint stands. “We’re leaving.” His navy-blue T-shirt ripples over his shoulders. "Dr. Singh here needs to clean house. And we need to take our daughter home. I'll be in touch."

Dr. Singh is the only other person who stands. "I think we should continue—"

"I said we're leaving." Clint's voice is soft but has the power to lift both Erika and me from our chairs.

19

CLINT AND I FLANK OUR DAUGHTER as we walk back to the car. My body feels like I overdid it at the gym and then got beat up as I left the locker room.

Erika's gaze doesn't stray from the concrete in front of her shoes.

"Anyone up for a Blizzard?" Clint asks. The first words spoken since we left the principal's office.

"Ice cream?" The incredulous words fly out of my mouth before I can consider. My throat clenches. This is the tone that constantly gets me in trouble. What is wrong with me?

"I could eat junk food." Erika's voice is light, almost like it once knew how to laugh.

"Meredith, want to live on the wild side?" Clint cranes his neck to glance at me.

His levity makes me trip.

We drive to Dairy Queen. At just after 1 p.m., the parking lot is not empty. Clint drives to the back of the squat building and finds a place.

As we walk into the fast-food restaurant, the stench of grease and freshly mopped floors assails me. I spy the restrooms to the rear. "Maybe get me just a plain dish."

I use my shoulder to push open the door and walk up to the mirror. My makeup is gone. I don't even see streaks of leftover mascara. I'm certain I put some on this morning. My brown eyes with golden streaks radiating out from the pupils stare unblinkingly back at me.

This is all my fault.

How could I not know about this guy? This man? There has to be more to this story. The picture has to be related.

Honestly, is it really a surprise? I've been so distracted. So focused on myself. Not to mention my job. A job I could be losing as we eat mass-produced ice cream. There's a meeting right now that will decide my fate, and this is the first time I'm even giving it a thought. Maybe I don't care what they decide. I can't do it all. I can't be present here and know the right things to say to my kids and husband at just the right time and also be on top of all the firm alliances while coming up with their next big thing. It's just too much. Even without the ridiculousness with Betsey.

Oh, Betsey.

The small white envelope smolders in the bottom of my bag. After sprinting to catch my train and find a seat, I almost tore into it, but then Clint's texts started, and of course the emails from the rest of my sales team, who've lost their leader. I haven't had a spare moment to give yet another person power over me.

I wiggle my index finger under the seal and rip along the fold. A jagged piece of the flap flutters to the damp tile floor. The envelope is ready to spill its guts. Even before I pull out the picture, I know what it will be. Who it will be.

How did she know to follow me? Or did she just happen upon us, taking a picture in case she wanted to blackmail me?

The image is not what I expected. There are no faces. No way to know definitively that it is us. But she knows I know. That's enough. Lucas's hand hovers over my lower back as he escorts me from the Rotterdam Room. I squint down at the image. He wasn't touching me, but you can't tell from the angle. The picture was taken from within the bar. How had I not seen her?

The restroom door opens and a preschooler in pigtails runs in chanting about sprinkles and whipped cream. A young woman in impossibly short shorts comes laughing in behind her.

I slide the picture back into the eviscerated envelope and wave my hand under the paper towel dispenser. Ripping off a long sheet, I place it under the tap and then pat my cheeks, forehead, and neck. The coolness tingles against my hot skin.

My whole body aches with what I need to tell Clint and what Erika will tell us next.

I return to the table. They sit slumped on the same side of the booth. Erika's head rests on her dad's broad shoulder.

Clint glances up at me. "I didn't get you any ice cream."

I awkwardly bump in on the other side of the table. "Fine. Wasn't really hungry."

Clint grins down at the top of Erika's head. She looks so young cuddled up to him. "That's the thing. We decided we were. We ordered burgers and fries. Blizzards will come later. We weren't sure what you were up for."

"Burgers?" There is the tone again, but the thought of food makes me want to vomit.

"Yeah, burgers." As he looks at me, his face loses its mirth.

A blue-clad employee pushes two trays onto the table and then grabs the plastic numbered tent.

My stomach lurches at the smell of grease. But instead of wanting to empty itself, it moans with hunger. I had a nice dinner last night and don't often eat breakfast, so I shouldn't feel as ravenous as I suddenly do.

"Here you go." Erika empties half her fry sleeve onto a napkin and pushes it over to me.

"Thanks." I pop a warm, salty fry in my mouth. My stomach growls. I follow up with two more. Wow. Delicious. I glance at the registers.

"You want to go order?" Clint asks.

A couple large families with wound-up preschoolers tumble into the lobby. "In a minute."

Clint shifts his focus. "Erika, your mom and I are out of our depth here. You've got to tell us what's going on." He takes a bite of his burger, oozing with ketchup, and uses his thumb to keep the lettuce from sliding out. His jaws appear to be wrestling with the food instead of eating it. This all must be a brilliant ruse to keep it casual without the pressure of school or home.

"I'd just had enough. I didn't plan it. He just needed to be stopped." Erika takes a bite of her burger. The apparent ease with which she's now speaking gives me whiplash. It's as if she's decided this part of the story, this part of her life, she'll allow us to see. "Full disclosure, I wasn't the one who filmed it. You can tell by the angle. But I did share it." Her eyebrows race to her hairline as if she's daring us to accuse her.

"Can we see it?" I ask. Either she can show us now or Clint and I will find it later.

She seems to come to the same conclusion and places the phone in the middle of the table. The video starts with a shaky frame—the shoulder of Erika's light-pink fleece and a few strands of blonde hair drift into view. A young man with close-cropped black hair and a heavy jaw comes into focus. Has to be Danny Doward. He stands rigid in front of a student desk, his broad frame looming over a skinny teen slumped low in his chair. The classroom is quiet at first, the audio too low to catch the words, but then the voice—sharp, female—is unmistakably Erika's. There's a sudden swell of noise—students jeering, chairs scraping. Danny's posture shifts, his stance morphing from aggression to shock to something sharper. Anger. His eyes lock on the camera. He stomps forward, his face twisting. His massive hand blurs as it shoots forward. Suddenly we're looking at the scuffed linoleum and the toe of a white sneaker—then the screen cuts to black.

I fall back into my seat. Had Dr. Singh even watched the video?

"I couldn't hear. What were you saying?" Clint blinks a few times as if trying to clear the video from his eyes.

"I, uh, it wasn't clean. You don't get all of it in the video, but I swore at him and called him a bully. And then at that point, you can't really hear everything I say, but I accused him of being a predator."

"A predator?" Clint says the word slowly.

"Yeah. The video stops because he tries to grab it and then it's just footage of the floor."

"Why a predator?" I ask, not really wanting the answer. Calling her beautiful in the hallway was creepy; I can't stomach thinking it could be more than that.

"He seemed the type, but honestly, he looked confused when I said it. I don't know."

Clint wipes his mouth. "So, you were protecting another kid. I appreciate that." He glances at me. "We appreciate that. You met this man at a party?"

"I knew you'd make the party a big deal. It was nothing." She sweeps a couple fries through a mountain of ketchup.

"All evidence to the contrary." Clint's words are sharp, and Erika drops her next bite onto her tray and shoves her hands in her lap.

"So, you met him." I try to put a smile into my words before we lose her. "Maybe you didn't know how old he was? Did he look young? Did he know how old you were?" My tone, which began normal, has developed a bit of a shrill.

Clint's eyes flash to mine as if he'd expect me to focus on the age gap.

I swallow. *This is our daughter with a grown man. Get over yourself.*

"No. I don't know. You're missing the point. The party was after the football game. There were lots of people, college-aged and probably beyond. I don't know. He upset me this morning and I've just—never mind. I have learned my lesson." Erika's shoulders slump as she pushes away her tray. "I'll go back to being me."

Clint picks up his burger but just holds it in front of him, his eyes still trained on me.

Are we missing the point? Probably. I feel like I'm way too close to an impressionist painting made of colored dots. I know I need to step back to see the bigger picture, but my nose keeps getting pressed toward the canvas. "What else were you going to say?"

"Nothing. I'm done. Are you guys almost ready?" Erika grabs her tray.

"You've only taken one bite." I gesture to her burger.

"Tell us why you took the picture." Clint lays his hand on the table and loops a pinkie finger over Erika's tray, keeping it on the table.

Erika slumps against the ribbed red-vinyl cushions of the booth.

"Honey, we just want to talk about it." I look away from Clint's nail turning white as he bears down on the molded plastic of her tray. "We're not mad. We only want—"

"I know you want to talk about it. You want to talk about everything." Erika furtively glances around as if she realizes how loud she's gotten. The place is busy. Three tables of little kids with their families surround us. No one is paying attention.

Clint takes another bite of his burger. One I am sure he has to choke down. My stomach has lost all appetite, again. No way do I want to eat a fry. I pop one in my mouth anyway. We both seem to know it is our turn to be quiet and appear patient.

"The picture was nothing. I'm sorry I took it. I don't know why. I can't believe you saw it." She crosses her arms in front of her chest.

"Did you send it to anyone?" I ask as quietly and as neutrally as I can.

Erika yanks the tray from the table and lurches from the booth. "No."

20

AS WE ARE PILING BACK INTO THE CAR, my phone pings with a message from Terrence. Another executive meeting to discuss the thumb drive just finished. My fingers hover over my screen. I don't know where I should be. I just need someone to tell me what to do. As a parent, as a portfolio manager, as a wife who's caught in something ugly . . . there are too many catastrophes, too many directions to run.

"You should head down there." Clint keeps his gaze on the rearview as he pulls the car out of our space.

My heart swells. He read my mind. I glance over at him. He nods, but his eyes don't leave the road. A warmth spreads through my chest. It's something.

I twist in my seat. "Erika, I can stay?"

"I'm done talking." She looks out the window.

"We'll keep you home from school for a few days."

"I'd already decided that," Erika snaps from the back seat.

"No. We decide these things as a family." Clint's eyes flash at the rearview.

"Family," she huffs.

I whip around. "What? Tell us what is wrong with you." The anger in my voice surprises even me, but I dig in. "In fact, give me your phone."

Erika squints at me like I'm something stuck to the bottom of her shoe.

Clint starts to say something, but I speak over him. "I'm not calling it a punishment. I just think you need a break from your phone and posting anything." I push my hand toward her.

The car slows and pulls over to the side of our road.

"No. You don't need to stop. Let's get home," I say over my shoulder to Clint.

He shakes his head, but I hear the blinker click and we start moving again.

"Now, Erika." I speak low and slow.

She slaps her peach phone with a flowered PopSocket onto my palm.

I spin around and stare out the windshield.

As the car barely rolls to a stop, Erika is out the door. We both watch as she barrels across the flagstone pavers and into the house.

"Maybe I should stay," I mumble.

"She's said all she's going to say for now. Especially without her phone." Clint's cheeks, covered in the faintest gray stubble, puff out as if other words, harder words, are being held at bay.

I probably don't want to hear them. "I didn't plan to take her phone. I'd just had enough."

"We both had."

I nod. "I'm going to grab a few things inside. Maybe I should come home tonight?"

Clint unfolds himself from the driver's seat. "I can drive you to the station."

Twenty minutes later, we are back in the car. I click my seat belt and then shift my shoulders toward the door so I can more fully face my husband. "You didn't answer my question."

Clint's chest rises and falls as he pulls up to the stop sign at the end of our block. "Of course you should plan on being home tonight. This stuff with Erika needs both of us."

My heart chugs behind my rib cage. I desperately want to ask him if he's also willing to work on us. Is he in or is he out? Instead, I shift my hip so I sit straight in my seat.

"I don't know, Meredith," Clint whispers.

The bridge of my nose burns as tears threaten to flood my eyes. This is the second time today. He used to be able to read my mind all the time. Sometime between our move to Scarsdale and the dredging of permanent ridgelines between his eyes, he lost the ability or perhaps the interest to read me. I stay silent. He's like those mussels we peeled off the seaweed-strewn rocks off the cost of Blue Hill, Maine, last summer. One little nudge and they shut up tight.

The bulges in his shoulder and down in his forearms slide and pulse as he maneuvers the car through town. How anyone can think he's my father or Erika's grandfather is a mystery to me, no matter our age difference. He's the sexiest man I know.

I should tell him about Lucas. This thing with Betsey could go sideways fast. If he doesn't hear it from me, we could be in real trouble, but how can I lay it all on him now?

I smooth the folds in my light wool skirt. As a tire hits a pothole, my bony knees bump against each other. I've gotten too thin. I used to struggle to keep my weight down. In high school, I often believed, as Erika does, that my curves were fat. Have I told her that? I haven't wanted to give her ridiculous notions any credit, but maybe it would help. I tug at my hem. Would she believe me? I could show her pictures. She used to love laughing at all the grunge-inspired fashions and big-wave hairstyles.

I'd hate for her to compare herself to me now. I may be on the runway-fashionable side of my weight, but I've lost all muscle tone. I'm nothing to aspire to.

Clint slides the car gear into park. "Don't miss your train."

My hand hovers over the door handle. Gutless. I missed my opportunity to say anything of value, or perhaps that was my plan all along.

I'll be home tonight. We'll talk then.

I look back at my husband. His usually carefree features droop on his face.

My heart thuds silently. "I love you." I open the door.

His hand catches my left arm, pressing into my bruised flesh.

I wince and whirl around, too quickly.

He drops my arm as if he's been burned.

"It's just that—"

"See you tonight." The light in his chestnut eyes fades and he turns away.

21

ALL THE WAY BACK TO THE OFFICE, I expect Betsey to appear from around every corner. My hand fumbles around in my purse until I finger the bent corner of the torn envelope. There's no way she understands what she witnessed.

All is quiet as I walk to my office. Before locking my purse and bag in my wardrobe, I check the time. Three minutes after five. The town hall has just begun.

As soon as the elevator doors open on the thirty-ninth floor, a sea of sound washes over me. Conversations, laughter, and the tinkling of dishes emanate from the Bull and Bear conference room about twenty yards away.

I grab a mocktail with a sprig of spruce from the silver tray just inside the door. There's beer, wine, and an open bar ready to make a wide variety of cocktails, but I'm loving the trend toward interesting flavors without the spirits. I take a sip of the woodsy tonic and find myself surrounded by traders, analysts, and marketing folks clinking glasses to the success of our funds. While praising each one of their contributions, I also scan the room for Hardwin or Terrence. Although I'd love to simply ask my boss what they decided to do with Betsey's data, there is deference to be shown by allowing one of Phil's other direct reports to deliver the news. Also, Phil is the CEO. I tread lightly with what I ask of him.

Best to start with our chief legal counsel. Actually, best to start with one of his trusted lawyers. Get the inside scoop so I know how to show up when they come for me. Because they will come.

Unless . . . Maybe they determined the data is fake and we can move on from this nightmare. Maybe Betsey was just joking about confronting my husband on Friday. And maybe I'm trapped in a stage production produced by brilliant twentysomethings exploring the ludicrous notion of work-life balance. Maybe I'm going insane.

I excuse myself from the group as I spy one of the lawyers who helped with the filings when we first launched the ETFs. Months of late nights to get the paperwork to the point where the SEC would have no reason to deny us. We learned each other's favorite take-out restaurants and the intramurals we played in college. I'm taking another sip of my delicious drink when a large hand pats my shoulder.

"Meredith, nice event."

Sometimes I forget how tall Hardwin is until I am standing next to him. Across a desk or in a conference room, he seems less of a mountain.

"Thanks. Was looking for you and your team. They were instrumental in getting us launched on time and without incident."

"As is expected," he says flippantly. "Look, we need to talk."

"Of course. I'm scheduled to go up and say a few words, and then maybe after—"

"Phil's going to go up. It'll be good to have him give his thanks.

Everyone knows how you feel." He scrunches his nose like I'm an endearing little thing.

Do they? I doubt anyone around here ever knows how I'm feeling. We don't transact in feelings. And right now, I'm feeling very rattled, as if I'm standing in the station, everyone rushing by to catch their train, and I have no idea where my track is or even where I'm going. Hardwin doesn't seem to notice. Or perhaps he doesn't care.

"Let's head to my office." He swings his arm around to guide me but stops just short of touching me.

"Hardwin." Dave strides up, blocking our progress to the door.

"If it can wait, I need to catch a word with Meredith." Hardwin indicates the door.

"Phil needs you."

Hardwin grumbles and then takes a small step back. He's surprisingly light on his feet and seems to always be spatially aware. After all this is over, I should ask him more about his years playing ball.

"Meredith, I'm sorry. Our conversation will need to wait." He almost bows in sincerity.

"I understand. Do you want to find me when—"

"I'll talk to her." Dave lifts his chin to Hardwin. Inches taller than me, Dave still needs to look up to make eye contact with our chief legal counsel.

Hardwin hesitates.

"I was in the room. I know what needs to happen." There's a constrained energy emanating from Dave. He almost vibrates with it.

"I'm happy to wait." I take a step back, pulling alongside Hardwin. On this day, of all days, I have no desire to be alone with Dave. And he looks way too eager to deliver his news.

"No." Hardwin nods. "Dave's right. I'll catch up with you later." He turns and strides away.

Catch up with who later? Will I be around later to be caught up with? I scold myself for thinking this way. Besides this hiccup with Betsey, I've orchestrated the most successful fund launch Garman Straub has ever seen. I need to keep all things in perspective, but I can't seem to help fixating on the worst case—a public firing with tragic headlines in the *Wall Street Journal*. Somehow stoking the terrible image is like an antidote to the panic threatening to pummel me.

As we walk in silence to Dave's office, I realize I don't have my phone on me—I left it in my bag. I've moved mountains trying to get time on this man's calendar. In fact, I'm convinced he's created trips to advisors' offices and wholesaler summits to avoid discussing sales with me. A chill runs down my spine as we take the last corner. I don't want to be here. Everyone who has a workstation in the small bullpen outside his office is at the town hall.

I enter a land of tchotchkes.

Dave's office never fails to both irritate and impress me. He has collected, sometimes modified, and then even created a few scenes from competitors' brand material. Like two columns of stuffed animals in shirts from competing firms clipped into thin leather traces pulling a sled with a man in a suit. I squint down at the display. Is the Ken doll meant to be Dave? I can't help the smile that curves my lips. How much time does this man have on his hands?

I walk toward the small corner conference table, and a familiar image on the wall catches my eye, a map of the New York portion of the Appalachian Trail. I breathe in heavily through my nose and raise my hand like I might touch the glass. I'm no stranger to AT maps. My husband is obsessed. After growing up in Maine and then through his years as an EMT in Fannin County, Georgia, he intimately learned both ends of the iconic backpacking adventure and has collected and recently created many trail schematics. Clint would love this version. Maybe I can ask Dave about it. Maybe it's a sign that I'm going to be all right. An intricately wound letter *T* rests proudly in the lower-right corner of the framed map. Interesting logo.

Dave has removed his suit jacket and laid it on the back of his desk chair. His body is still vibrating with a strange energy.

Perhaps the map is a sign to find my way out of here. Now.

I choose a chair closest to the still-open door and settle at his conference table.

Dave cocks his head at me. Likely he wanted me to pull up to his desk. *Not today, buddy.*

Dave strides from around his desk, yanks back one of the other black leather chairs, and plants himself at the table. His nostrils flare above his trim mustache and beard.

Good to be starting this nice and friendly. My Jimmy Choo–clad toes press into the beige carpet. I'm a breath away from bolting.

Dave stares out his large window, with a flyover view of the New York Public Library on to the art deco crown of the Empire State Building. "You'll be happy to hear, as we were, that the data is fake. A good fake, but a fake all the same." He shifts his gaze back to me. "While we were meeting, teams from fund accounting and legal were able to track lots and determine the report was manufactured."

I blow out a breath. "That is a relief." How could Betsey not realize we would verify the data? Ridiculous I even suspected she could get her hands on it.

"It's a good forgery. I'll give her that." He throws out his arms. His shirtsleeves ride up, and silver-toned cuff links embossed with what looks like antique compasses sparkle in the fluorescent light. "I have to say, this has all been disappointing."

"Yes." I decide to employ the rule of improv and try for agreement in order to move the scene forward. I want to get back to the teams and maybe grab one of those decadent cookies. "This whole business with Betsey has felt a bit tarnishing on a couple days that should have been only celebratory."

"Will be good to put this behind us." He's being remarkably evenhanded.

I pinch the base of my gold cross necklace until the bite of pain in my thumb unhitches the tension growing in my chest. I know how to handle arrogant Dave. Affable Dave, I have little experience with. I take a few small breaths.

Dave smiles with all teeth. "Meredith, we don't want to waste any more time. Phil, and all of us, have expectations. As I tried to tell you yesterday at the reception, this is not your pedestal. You're not playing to a crowd. We work as a team. The board meeting is on Monday. I understand you've sent Phil some ideas."

I stiffen. Why is he asking me about this? He and Hardwin pulled me out of my own celebration to deliver news that didn't require any action, and now he's reminding me of something I know. Something he knows I know. Phil already has my draft. I'm waiting for him to give me his comments on our new product plans.

"Yes," I say.

Dave tugs on one of his sleeves. If I didn't know him better, I'd think he was nervous, but that makes no sense. "However you're pulling these funds together, you seem to have a touch. These things can run their course, so use it while you've got it." He bumps back from the table and stands. "Thanks for coming."

I get to my feet and shove my chair under the table. This has to be one of the more bizarre meetings I've experienced. But I don't want to spend another minute outside of the town hall. Besides all the people I have to thank, I've got a mashed potato bar to hit and a few more mocktails to sample.

"Thank you, Dave," I call over my shoulder as I reach his door.

"Oh. One more thing." He swings his suit jacket over his arm. "What else was in the envelope?"

"Sorry?" My heart stutters.

"Besides the thumb drive. Any correspondence?"

"No. No context at all." The lie flows without a hitch.

"Very strange." His voice lowers a tad as if talking mostly to himself. "With the data being a fake, I can't quite figure what she's after. Maybe just to throw you off your game. Especially this week." He takes a few steps toward me. "And she hasn't reached out since you received the package. She was desperate to get ahold of you and now nothing?" He shakes his head as if his kid just told him their dog messed in the kitchen.

"Perhaps she'll be in touch soon?" Not quite a lie but certainly one of omission. I should have come clean about her cornering me at Grand Central. That was stupid not to, but I need to get my head straight on what these guys can be told.

It's all about having a plan. I've built a career on multitasking and being present in the space I occupy.

The next time I see Betsey, I swear I'll call the authorities and then Hardwin, perhaps in reverse order.

And now I need to find the courage to speak to my husband. I glance over at the trail map. Our whole family needs to learn to communicate. This difficulty with Erika is making everything else feel superfluous.

My heart is beginning to slow its gallop. I pretend to scratch my cheek. Thankfully, my face doesn't feel hot. I open my mouth to finally ask about the map, but he speaks first.

"You let us know when she contacts you. Because she will."

He's not wrong.

"Of course," I say as I stride from Dave's office with my shoulders pulled back and my chin a tad higher than necessary. I need not telegraph any weakness, which would only prolong this meeting. It's time to put an end to any distraction, but in order to do that, I have to tell Clint about Lucas.

22

FIGHTING A SHIVER, I step back into the bustling town hall. The cacophony of conversation and the clinking of glasses surround me. This atmosphere is so rousing—the vitality of ambitious professionals using this celebration to seek their next opportunity, their next big break. Phil must have already spoken. He can put a charge through his people like no one else.

My steps falter. That was their plan—to get me out of the room, to keep me from being the one talking to the teams, to separate my leadership from this success. They must not know what to do with me yet. But so far, if Dave is to be believed, I'm still included in Monday's board meeting. Hope swells inside me. I shackle myself to its warmth.

Through suits, I spy a deep dish of lobster on the mashed potato bar and head in that direction. As I get to the delicious display, Terrence's animated voice catches me. As if the words of his story are arrows shooting through the room, I try to catch a few midflight. *Sydney Opera House* and *water cannons* fall into my quiver. Must be his classic tale of when the Asia-Pacific mutual fund launched and not only was his luggage lost when he got to Australia, but he was detained by immigration and missed most of the meetings, arriving in the city just in time for a water salute as part of a WWII commemorative festival. I've always loved how he talks about gazing out at the water sprays and knowing their mutual funds would find success.

I've had the same sense about our ETFs. Only I'm data-driven and hate to ever check luggage.

While imagining the boats in Sydney Harbour, I smile and walk toward Terrence, exuding confidence to mask a fragility that lingers inside me. The data has been manufactured, but that doesn't change that Betsey believes she has leverage over me to give her what she wants by Friday. Suddenly, I wonder if I'm the only one who knows this.

As I make my way through the sea of faces, I pause for only moments to make a greeting or give my thanks. Terrence catches my eye, but then Hardwin appears next to him and whispers something in his ear. They both stride in the opposite direction.

I pause. He doesn't want to talk. At least not here. It's as if they're all in the same huddle, poised to trot back to the line of scrimmage, and I'm on the sidelines with the band, unable to read my own sheet music.

Perhaps the worst-case scenario is not the terrible headlines of my firing but receiving no mention at all.

Amid the clatter of laughter and swish of a few cheap polyester suits, I hear a snippet of conversation from one of Dave's sales guys.

". . . showed up at the Everson office. Although he's always gracious, you could tell he wanted to drop-kick her from the room. She was spouting some weirdness to him about investor due diligence. I interrupted her talking to one of the admins who was setting up lunch in the conference room. We'd ordered from that incredible—"

"Good afternoon, gentlemen." I set my shoulder into their tight circle. "Thanks for coming." So, not only did Betsey visit Aarav's office but also Everson. I channel my anger at my sales manager into determining how to manage this conversation.

Bryan's Adam's apple bobbles a few times before he responds. "Thank you, Meredith. Great party."

"Good to know Betsey made it to Everson and was able to speak to Hal." The first name of the office's managing director pops onto my tongue right on cue. It pays off as their gazes stay fixed on me. "I'd wondered, as I hadn't gotten her notes."

"You knew she'd be there?" another of Dave's guys asks.

"She's one of my most successful technical sales leads," I say with authority but without answering.

"Of course, I only meant that we often coordinate before, and this time, she didn't have a presentation. She just seemed to be prompting private conversations." Bryan seems to realize he's maybe said too much. He shrugs. "You know how Hal is about procedure."

I nod. We all know about Hal's need for control. What was Betsey thinking? "It wasn't her first time there. She thought individual conversations would be more helpful than the formal dog and pony."

"Makes sense. Just kind of wondered why she was meeting with the support staff." A pink flush rises up Bryan's neck.

The guy to his left speaks up. "She'd cornered one of the admins and was asking odd questions about trade submissions."

I take a sip of my drink and nod my head. "What really upset you both?"

"This was my appointment." Bryan's voice has grown louder. "It made us look bad to not know she was coming, and when she got there, we looked unprepared when we didn't know what she was doing."

"I get that. With Betsey gone, I'll be doing some restructuring with my sales and support teams. We should all sit down and make sure you're not caught in any more weirdness going forward." Weaving my gaze through their eager expressions, I raise my glass at Dave, who, by the sour look on his face, has noticed his team holding court. "In fact, let's be creative in this next quarter."

"Creative?" asks one of the guys, with a well-groomed mustache.

"Sure." I lower my voice. They all lean in. "Did you see that article in *FA* magazine about layering client experiences with continuing education?"

The guys glance furtively at each other before a woman with a pixie haircut and dark-rimmed glasses speaks up. "Didn't they rave about the trends toward extreme sports?"

"Yes. Exactly. Instead of boring meetings, mixing it up. You all would have to tell me if the ideas in the article were decent or maybe you have other thoughts?"

Like I pulled my finger from a fissure in the dam, their creativity starts rolling.

I never look back up, but I can feel the weight of Dave's irritation, and shame on me, it gives me strength.

23

I CHECK MY PHONE. It's ten minutes after six. If I leave now, I can make the 7:10 train and be home in time for kitchen cleanup. Maybe they've even set aside a plate from family dinner. Well, it can't be called *family dinner* without Reid. I miss the little guy. He's got to be having the time of his life at robotics camp. I wish they'd post pictures online like they do at summer camp. On the train home, I want to go through what Clint took at drop-off.

A queasiness suddenly gnaws at my stomach. Perhaps I've looked at enough images for a while.

Leaving now, I'll be a tad earlier than expected. I'll take the win. As I'm shoving my laptop and notebook into my bag, my phone buzzes. A text from Hardwin's admin requests I jump on a conference call with him and Terrence. Phil wants them to share his thoughts and their edits on my board pitch.

I sit heavily in my chair and pull my computer back out. I never should have celebrated early. This happens way too often. But in this case, perhaps I can get their notes, work on revisions on the train, and at least be home before Erika plugs her phone in for the night.

I let out a slow sigh, remembering that I have her phone. Which she's probably still snarling about. I need to get home and talk to her before she goes to bed.

I open up the slides on my computer. Hardwin and I never did catch up at the town hall. I'm still not sure if the message Dave conveyed was what Hardwin, or even Phil for that matter, had in mind. Perhaps I'll find out.

My desk phone rings, and I put it on speaker.

"Nice town hall, Meredith. You set a new standard on how to show our appreciation. I told some of the guys to take note." Terrence's voice is strong over obvious road noise.

"Thank you. I heard Phil did a great job speaking to the troops. His words meant a lot to everyone." Especially since I was stripped of my opportunity.

"Hats off to Phil, but I think your spicy dragon rolls were the real star of the party." Terrence laughs.

"No doubt," Hardwin cuts in. "In case we have service issues, we're in the car. Peter's driving us to the west side of Philly. Early morning with Vanguard's team." He mumbles something about a sun visor.

"Right. Hope it goes well." My finger taps rhythmically on the desktop. "I also wanted to touch base with you, Hardwin. I spoke to Dave but just wanted to check in with you as well."

"He said he told you about the data." Hardwin speaks deliberately.

"Yes. What a relief. He—"

"That's what he confirmed. Moving forward, we just had a few notes on your pitch." Hardwin dives in, and for the next forty-five minutes, he and Terrence talk through my three short pages and handful of slides. Initially, I make furious notes on their comments but soon realize it's mostly stream of consciousness. Phil might have shared some initial thoughts with them, but this is obviously the first time either of them has more than skimmed the pitch. They want to hear from me more than they have insights on what I put together.

After they'd agree on a point, I'd think we had an edit, but after circling the new idea, we'd land right back on what was in the document. Eighteen months ago, I'd have volunteered to ride on the roof of their black Escalade for the opportunity to witness these two debate and discuss my ideas. But now, I just want them to be done. I realize after about twenty minutes of banter that I am the entertainment for their drive. I won't be let go until they finish their fun.

After another half hour, in which I miss the train that would've gotten me home before Erika usually goes to bed, Hardwin finally starts to wrap.

"Meredith, do you think you have what you need to put the finishing touches on this?"

"Yes." I glance over my scribbled pages with many more cross-outs than legible directives and then wiggle my mouse to peer at my document. "I'll add another sentence of context to our penetration numbers . . . and . . . I'll . . ." I search for something else of note to change.

"And the word *distinguish* in that paragraph about competitors, you'll maybe come up with something more, I don't know, something with gravitas," Terrence says.

"Right, yes, I'll—"

"You know, reading it again, I think it's fine as is. I hope we've been helpful, Meredith?" Hardwin asks.

"Very." I drop the marked-up document into the recycling bin under my desk. "I appreciate this window into your thoughts."

"Well, we better draw our curtains." Terrence laughs. "Wouldn't want you to get too good a look at the levers and pulleys."

Both Hardwin and I join in the obligatory chuckling.

"We'll see you in the office on Thursday," Hardwin says.

"Yes, have a good evening, gentlemen." As I reach for my phone's disconnect button a Teams message flashes on my screen with a picture of two of my traders holding tablespoons of wasabi, ready to feed each other. Both of their mouths hang wide open. I jerk back in my seat at the thought of that much horseradish paste hitting anyone's tongue or gut. They probably laid bets. With equity traders, everything is a wager—from pastry deliveries to pedestrian crossings.

I squint into the image and see the glass corner overlooking the paneled concrete facade of the Met Life building. They're in our conference room. Those brilliant morons did this at the town hall. I certainly hope they didn't take their madness on the road. *The party's over, boys.*

"You think she's ready for the boardroom?" Hardwin's voice suddenly booms from my speakerphone.

My hand freezes directly above the disconnect button.

"Hardwin, this is not her first rodeo." Terrence's voice sounds muffled.

"But her first time presenting. She's solid at thinking on her feet, but do you really think she should be the one to deliver the pitch?"

"This is her work. It's not like it touches our core business of mutual funds." Terrence's voice is markedly slowed, as if he's considering what Hardwin is saying.

Hardwin often guards his words, leading others to make a conclusion he has likely already come to, but he's being recklessly transparent now.

He's saying I'm not ready.

Perhaps Hardwin wants to be the one to deliver. His lawyers have been the ones managing all the fund filings with the SEC. Also, the board just hired its first woman. Most of the men have been on the board for decades. Hardwin probably wants to pull the experience card—everyone will feel more comfortable with someone with his years at the firm. But this concept of experience cuts both ways. If they don't grant opportunities, unproven leaders never get to be proven.

"It's not only her. It's her team's work, as she clearly pointed out." Hardwin's voice is almost too casual. "She didn't do any of this alone."

A small snort escapes my lips. I suck in my breath.

There's silence over the speakerphone. Did they hear me? Perhaps I should tap the mute button. Will they hear that? It's late, but someone might come to my door.

"When do we do anything alone? What's your biggest concern?" Terrence's voice is low, as if he's moved farther away from the phone.

"This latest data business. I feel like she might be holding back. Perhaps she knows more than she's saying."

My chest starts to burn. I'm still holding my breath. I gently peel apart my pressed lips and take tiny sips of air.

Terrence doesn't respond but must make some gesture as Hardwin continues talking. "I'm not sure. Seems so strange there was nothing with the data. No note. No communication."

"We've been over this. I see no reason for her to lie. She came forward, and as you know, Candace has been on it." A beat of silence. "If Meredith did get herself entangled, we'll know."

"Maybe . . . maybe it's that she accepted it all too fast," Hardwin says.

Terrence muffles a cough. "You didn't mention that before."

"Just playing back what Dave told me. He said it all felt a bit awkward."

Of course it was awkward. They insisted I leave my own town hall and miss thanking everyone from the podium.

"Don't you think if she had something to do with the data and knew it was legit, that Dave, of all people, would have seen it in her reaction? I mean, you pulled her from her own party."

Exactly. My own party. Thank you, Terrence.

Wait.

If I knew it was legit? The data is legit?

"Yeah, he didn't sense she disagreed."

"So, there you go." Terrence's voice has regained its confidence. He wants to move on from this conversation.

"Maybe." Hardwin matches Terrence's tone and then speaks softer. "Maybe she didn't question it because she's going to look into it herself."

My mouth drops open. He's giving me more credit than I deserve. I haven't considered verifying their declaration, but now they better believe I'm digging in.

"I don't see it. She's too busy anyway. You know that—"

"Excuse me, Mr. Donovan." Peter's voice interrupts. "We've arrived at the hotel."

"Thank you, Peter . . . Hey!" Hardwin's voice booms. "Are we still—"

The line goes dead.

24

MY FINGER AUTOMATICALLY LANDS on the disconnect button, although the men are gone. They've left my phone, my office, and my swirling head. My ears ring with the silence, like the faint high-pitched screeching of a bird of prey circling with its talons out, ready to strike.

The data is real.

My boss's legal advisor doesn't trust me.

The data is real.

Hardwin was right. I was so desperate to believe Betsey wasn't a threat, I didn't ask a single question about how they'd gone about debunking the file.

The data is real.

I pull up a blank document on my laptop. My fingers fly over my keyboard. I started in this firm as an analyst until I earned my spot as portfolio manager. I'm good at breaking it down and then building it back up into something that matters.

What else do I know?

Betsey wants the securities lending agreement.

I log in to the share drive and see how far I can get. I start with documentation on the funds themselves. There are folders for prospectus, marketing, sales, performance, and so many others. I open up the Foundations folder and read a document I wrote in the early days to fire up the troops. The funds have evolved, but the fundamentals are consistent. We'd use the exchange-traded structure to house a thematic investment opportunity fueled by active management with an option overlay on a negatively correlated index. It was like preparing the perfect farm-to-table meal tuned to the anticipated tastes of your guests but also spending a bit of the budget on a few jars of tomato sauce and dried pasta in case of a kitchen disaster. Both Hardwin and Dave had thought it a fringe concept. I even remember the exact wording Dave used to dismiss the idea. "No one is arguing our need to enter the ETF space. Our mutual fund strategies have given this firm a long, successful legacy. Exchange-traded funds may support our future. But this . . ." Dave had raised my pitch portfolio at the conference table. "This is a novelty. We need a Tesla, and this is a . . . a dune buggy."

It had taken me a month to walk back his impact. Being late to the ETF game, we'd never break in with basic portfolios that were in their own race to no fees, only making a profit based on their huge scale. While everyone was content to be chum in shark-infested bloody waters, we needed a blue ocean of investors. We had to solve a problem we could articulate, and we had to be first.

Even after the green light, I barely allowed myself to believe it. I threw everything and every hour at ensuring our success. Looking back now, not everyone could keep up, and I didn't slow down to make sure they stayed on board. I left a few bodies in that channel as we motored into open water.

But Betsey was not one of them. She was in the boat with me, from almost day one.

I open another folder and flip through. At the bottom, I find what looks like a template for the lending of securities. The agreement is straightforward. If our ETFs hold a security that a financial institution wants to borrow, our lending agent will manage the loan. There's a lot of detailed policy but nothing about investors or advisors. They're at the entirely opposite end of our food chain. How can the contract be related to Betsey's investment data?

Maybe it's not. I navigate back out to the root drive and look for one of the partners' working folders. Maybe Betsey is simply testing me to give her leverage. And maybe the securities lending agreement is only the beginning.

I let my back fall against my chair's cushion. I should have given Terrence the note and washed my hands of this whole mess from the beginning. They're going to find out.

Betsey picked a perfect time to blow this all up. I'd been so wrapped up in our celebration. If I'd handed the whole thing over, I could have gone home immediately. Clint deserves to hear it from his wife. A fat tear squeezes out from the corner of my eye and careens down my cheek.

There's a quick double knock on my door and then a woman in a dark-blue polo and chinos walks into my office with her head down.

I scrape my shoulder against my cheek and then silently berate myself. I have a box of tissues an arm's length away. Old makeup likely streaks my gray suit.

"Good evening. How's the night going?" I smile with what I hope is friendliness and not despondency.

The middle-aged woman replaces the corner bin, which is likely empty, and turns toward me. Her eyes round for a moment before she speaks. "Fine, miss. Are you going to be much longer? On Tuesdays

I usually . . . but I can come back." The woman's eyes scan the office. Must be a deep-cleaning night.

"No need for anything tonight. I had a . . . an incident with . . . Never mind. You can skip my office this week. I probably have a lot of late nights ahead of me. Anyway, all set in here." Why am I stumbling so hard to ask the woman to go?

"I understand." She returns her blue window cleaner to her cart. "I will note for the morning crew to do a quick pass."

"Thank you." I tuck in behind my computer screen.

The cart whooshes across my carpet with a slight hitch in the wheels and then stops.

"Not my business . . ."

My head pops back around the screen.

"Maybe go home." The woman sucks in her full top lip. Her face is devoid of makeup, and her hair is scraped back into a long thin ponytail. "Maybe they take enough."

My eyes flick to the clock on my computer, five minutes after ten. I didn't make it home. I nod and try to smile at the kind woman, who probably knows way more about me than I realize. My hand flattens against my face. I shove my laptop into my bag for the dozenth time today and then turn to my phone. I'm calling the car service. The train schedules at night are sketchy at best.

The ringing of my desktop phone startles me.

"So, you are still there?" Clint's voice, wrapped in a heavy sigh, expels out of my speaker.

"Yeah, I'm sorry. It's been a crazy night. I—"

"I knew inviting you home would have the opposite effect."

I watch the little hairs on my left forearm rise. The warmth of the room has evaporated. I am so tired of being manipulated by the people closest to me. I've made it too easy. I'm a target with multiple bull's-eyes. He invited me back into my own home and I let him. No, worse than that. I asked to be invited back. And on top of isolation, he's shaming me with the prediction I would let him down.

I grab my suit jacket from my chair and punch my arm through one of the sleeves. "You're right. It must have been your invitation that skewered me to my office chair dealing with stressors I shield you and everyone else from."

"Meredith, I've never asked you to be some sort of superhero. In fact, the opposite—I asked you to share your life."

I lean over and talk directly into the phone's speaker. "You have no idea what you ask of me."

"Yeah, my mistake. My mistake to think that on a day like this my wife would want to be home with her family." The line clicks off.

Anger rages inside me.

I immediately press the line and dial the number I know by heart. "I need a car to the Midtown Hilton."

25

THE SOFT GLOW OF LOWER MANHATTAN'S CITY LIGHTS seeps through the drawn curtains, casting a delicate luminance across the otherwise sterile hotel room. I stretch and arch away from the unyielding embrace of my hard-backed chair. My body is exhausted, but my mind hums with a tension that won't let me sleep.

I pull up another meeting note. Over the past year, Betsey and the rest of the team have been fastidious about keeping their plans and results updated in our contact management system. In the beginning, I was great about reading them every week. Every word. We'd meet on Mondays and talk about what was working and how to best explain our brand-new funds to advisors and their offices. The notes were thorough and insightful.

The notes are now a collection of back-of-the-envelope mutterings.

I'm to blame.

No accountability, no quality. I run my hands through my limp hair and then twist it into a messy bun, shoving an old UBS pen through the knot to hold it. We stopped meeting a few months ago, but not all at once. I check the calendar. First it was Dave's sales meeting. We'd warranted an invite, probably at Phil's insistence. After that, two weeks later, a holiday. Then over the next six weeks, we only met twice. Then the final nail in the meeting coffin had been a rescheduling to Wednesday that had somehow cancelled our recurring reminder, and I'd never put it back. That was two months ago. It wasn't like I didn't see these people all the time, but the routine of reporting and meeting had provided a rudder, keeping everyone tacking into the wind. Had losing that been my fatal mistake with Betsey?

Over the past six weeks, Betsey's notes have become sporadic at best. Definitely distracted. But our sales only rose. It was easy for me to find other areas to apply the gas. Whatever she was doing had been hidden in the success. I'd even stopped checking in with her on travel plans, hence the unexpected trips to both Aarav's and Hal's offices. None of the other sales guys had spoken up, but if I surveyed all Dave's external wholesalers, I bet I'd find others who'd been surprised by her appearance.

I search for Hal's office on Betsey's calendar and see two visits back in the early months of our field visits. Nothing recent. But she must have submitted an expense reimbursement. In order to get your costs covered, the meeting must be logged in your calendar. I shift again in my seat. I wish I'd gotten the date of the visit from the guys at the town hall. Betsey probably visited a nearby office and tacked this one on. I could search, but without notes, I'm not sure of the point.

A sharp knock makes me jump in my seat. It's ten minutes before two in the morning. Only one person could be here. *Please let it be him, with an overnight bag and ready smile.* I fly up from my chair as someone pounds on the locked door.

Then I freeze.

A manila envelope peeks from under the jamb.

"Ma'am, I'm sorry to disturb. The woman said it was a family emergency." His muffled voice continues to apologize as more of the envelope slithers into my room. As if it might strike, I move no closer. I have to tell Hardwin and then the police.

"Ma'am?" his voice pleads. "Your phone line is on do not disturb, but she said it was an emergency. Something about your husband? If there is any help you need . . ."

She must have paid him handsomely to deliver this to my door in the middle of the night. I suppose I'm thankful he didn't tell her my room number. I should have reported her at the train station. What if she's not working alone? I do have Hardwin's serviceable restraining order, which has remained untouched.

My breath sticks in my throat. I'm playing right into her hands by living in fear.

Striding to the door, I snatch the envelope from the carpet and then bang once on the still-locked door. "You can go now. No more deliveries."

I don't consider my options. I pinch the clasp of the envelope and glare into the yawning opening. Inside is a single item that looks like another picture. I slide it out.

This one leaves no doubt.

Lucas and I sit at the booth in the Rotterdam Room. His arm drapes the back of the corner booth. My hand grasps the stem of my wineglass while my face tilts toward him. My cheeks are flushed, and my mouth is slightly open as if I've been caught midlaugh. Lucas is looking toward the ceiling, a huge grin on his handsome face.

A sticky heat crawls up my back. I remember this moment. As my hand trembles, the picture begins to blur. This had to be our third time together. He'd been letting me understand him and had just finished telling me a story about a time when his little brother punched him in the face. When Lucas was in middle school, his mom would blow a whistle on summer nights when it was time to come home. His younger brother was still in grade school, so his whistle came much earlier.

One night, the neighborhood kids planned to play manhunt. He explained the game was like hide and seek in reverse: each person who is found joins the seekers. This had been Lucas's favorite game. But the previous week, he'd gotten in trouble for moving some boards under a neighbor's shed to find the perfect hiding spot. So, before they started the game, they'd reassessed the boundaries based on who was playing and whose mom would kill them if they traipsed through a flower bed or woke a baby. Just as they chose the seeker, the first whistle blew.

Lucas hadn't noticed his little brother was even in the group of kids waiting to play until his head recoiled and he heard the slam of skin against skin. Pain exploded under his eye. Through wet eyes, he saw someone hopping and howling like their spaniel after the trash truck. Lucas was ready to punch back until laughter overtook him. His scrawny little brother had injured his knuckles on Lucas's face.

All the little guy had wanted to do was play the game, and his older brother, his rock star, had taken too long organizing it.

At first it seemed a bitter story to me, and I told Lucas so. But Lucas chuckled and said, "I love the memory because I saw the kind of man my brother would be."

"Violent?" I asked.

"No. No. Passionate and brave. He'd learn to control the impulse, but he'd been a tagalong before then. That night, I saw him as someone I wanted to stay out with me until the second whistle." Lucas was almost snorting with laughter at this point.

"Because he punched you in the face?" I started to laugh because I couldn't help it.

"Yeah, because he stood up to the absurd. We were a bunch of ninnies wagging on about rules and not playing." Lucas threw back his head, and it must have been at this point that the picture was taken.

I flick the snapshot over. Scrawled in blue ink are the words *You have until Friday.*

Shaking my head, I speak to the silent room, "Oh, Betsey, you don't even know who you're threatening with these pictures."

26

WEDNESDAY

I can't move my arms. My panting resembles early labor. Like I did then, I focus on the filling and emptying of my lungs. My left bicep roars as I try to unpin it from my side. I've overdone both arms, but an old tendon tear really punishes me. The hotel gym has some of the best cable and rowing machines in Midtown, at least according to me, someone who hasn't done anything athletic in ages but used to know my way around a gym. I started working out in high school when what was known about coping with anxiety was limited to peer-reviewed articles in medical journals. I worked out my emotions on the weight machines. The more I hurt, the less I felt.

Based on my crazy schedule and believing in the importance of strength and flexibility, I turned to early morning Pilates a couple of years ago. I haven't darkened the doors of any gym in ages. Last night, moving my body against the stacks and pulleys helped work off the stress of Betsey's latest communication. But right now, my desperate need for sanity has created a liability against clean hair.

I tuck my chin into my neck and round my back. While whimpering, I slap shampoo through my sopping strands. The cleansing of my hair and body takes all my concentration and for that, I'm grateful.

Minutes later, I step out of the shower and into the foggy bathroom. I stand in front of the opaque mirror, unwilling to wipe it. I imagine the dark circles under my eyes, more like bruises than simply lack of sleep.

Keeping my elbows bent, I tuck the corner of the towel under my arm as I stand dripping on the white tiled floor. My right arm is not nearly as bad as my left, but I loathe the idea of holding a hair dryer. Instead, I bend at the waist, haphazardly wrap and shove another towel around my head, and then shuffle into the bedroom. I settle into the smattering of pillows against the cream upholstered headboard. The other side of the king-size bed is strewn with papers, my laptop, and notebook. After the gym, I probably got an hour of sleep in between the research and the worry. My mother always taught me that worry was for those who lacked the discipline to see the problem through. It wasn't until Clint that I gave voice to my fears and was offered the grace to sometimes worry. Last night I let the confusion and anxiety win. I have to start fighting back.

I fight with information.

When I slide my laptop onto my crossed knees, the battery icon shines red. I should get up and plug in the beast, but the thought of moving is too painful. My computer has been without power all night, and I likely have another forty-five minutes before it shuts off. I ought not wager my typing speed against the battery's draining life, but the urgency is motivating. It's time to bring in some reinforcements, or better yet, go on offense.

This tangled mess with the legitimacy of the data, Betsey's Friday deadline, and the pictures with Lucas demand I know who can be trusted.

Desperation claws at me as I open a blank email message, compose my thoughts, and begin to write.

[DRAFT]
From: Meredith Hansel (Meredith.Hansel@garmanstraub.com)
To: Phil Langford (Phil.Langford@garmanstraub.com)

Dear Phil,

I want to thank you—not just for encouraging us to celebrate this week but for being a steady presence these past few years. You lead with conviction, and you bring out the best in your teams. I've never told you how close I came to never meeting you. How I almost threw away my shot.

I was waiting for our appointment when my phone rang. My mother's thin voice carried the words I couldn't comprehend—Dad was gone. I told her I'd come right away. Nothing else mattered.

Then I saw you, striding into the room. I didn't want to talk about you, your company, or any job. I wanted to talk to my father—the man who carved the Thanksgiving turkey doing his best Swedish Chef impression.

But leaving meant surrendering to the truth. If I stepped out that door, my mother's words would harden into reality. A world without my dad would begin. I wasn't ready.

You smiled as you saw me. I don't know what my face did in response, but instead of greeting me, you pulled out your phone and scowled—not in frustration, but something deeper. Something that nearly uncoiled the knot inside me.

Gripping your phone in one hand, you extended the other. “Good of you to come, Meredith. I just need thirty seconds to talk to my wife.” Your eyes glistened.

I nodded, swallowing hard against the burn in my throat.

To keep from unraveling, I did what I do best—I analyzed. I searched my memory for what I knew about your family. First, she was an ex-wife, and in an industry that trades up trophies, you'd never remarried. Second, a grainy newspaper photo surfaced in my mind: you, your wife, and Annabelle in front of a towering Christmas tree. Tiny Annabelle, in a frilly dress, perched on your lap—not your wife's. Your arm draped over the back of her chair, her hand wrapped around your knee. A twenty-six-year-old article—part news story, part eulogy. But how do you eulogize a toddler?

You sniffed slightly, tucking your phone away. Then you turned to me and said something I'll never forget.

Do you remember?

[DRAFT]
From: Meredith Hansel (Meredith.Hansel@garmanstraub.com)
To: Phil Langford (Phil.Langford@garmanstraub.com)

Dear Phil,

Thank you for supporting the celebration of the funds today. When we planned the launch of our ETFs, we were in a blue ocean of opportunity. Now we race ahead in a very different environment. The sharks are coming. Our water is turning bloody. Many are coming after us for the piece of the market we represent. We need to control our costs and ensure we have a path for fee modulation that protects us from being priced out of the market

[DRAFT]
From: Meredith Hansel (Meredith.Hansel@garmanstraub.com)
To: Phil Langford (Phil.Langford@garmanstraub.com)

Dear Phil,

Thanks again for this week. It's come to my attention that there are aspects of the funds I designed and launched that I'm not fully read in on. Specifically in the area of securities lending. I am starting a task force to look into all aspects of the funds. Please advise if

[DRAFT]
From: Meredith Hansel (Meredith.Hansel@garmanstraub.com)
To: Phil Langford (Phil.Langford@garmanstraub.com)

Dear Phil,

Betsey is coming after our contracts, and I have reason to believe the investment data is real. None of this is good

[SENT]
From: Meredith Hansel (Meredith.Hansel@garmanstraub.com)
To: Phil Langford (Phil.Langford@garmanstraub.com)

Dear Phil,

I've always remembered what you said the first time we met: *Time is the valued currency of a wise life.*

I thank you for your willingness to spend your time celebrating the success of the ETFs this week.

While pressing forward with our new pitch on Monday, we also need to watch our flank. Please let me know if you have any issue with me assembling a task force to thoroughly examine our ETF contracts and policies. We need to understand our structural strengths and weaknesses as we plan for the new funds. I will ask for a few volunteers to ensure we have fresh thinking and report back to you on our progress.

Best,
Meredith

After pressing Send, I delete all the other drafted messages. The battery alert flashes in the upper left corner of my screen. Putting my laptop to sleep, I slide it off my knees and yelp as I catch my falling towel.

As I stretch my aching arms, I imagine Phil reading my email. If he is the source of the data or the reason why they lied about it—a burn of acid reaches up into my chest—he's likely to tell me to leave the flank-watching to him. I walk to the closet, refusing to consider what it means if he doesn't let me move forward.

27

"I DO NOT HAVE ACCESS to all of the fund folders on the share drive." One of my analysts who works on the mutual funds I inherited last quarter walks into my office, most of his face hidden behind his laptop screen.

I glance back down at my open email.

"What can I do for you, Temor?" I stress the sharp edge in my voice. My door is, mostly, always open, but there is a bit more formality to the office than just barging in when someone is obviously working, or, rather, trying to remote-mother.

"I apologize, but I do not believe I have the right permissions." There is almost a musicality to Temor's slight East Asian accent. He combs his unusually long fingers through his dark hair. The casualness of his appearance is in direct contrast to the proper cadence of his speech pattern. He's new and either has not learned the adage about dressing for the job you want or has chosen to ignore it. I don't know him well enough yet to gauge the wisdom of his choice.

"Have you put in a request to Compliance?" I ask.

"I can get him set up." Alyssa walks into my office with two coffees. She raises the mugs above her head, almost spinning entirely around to get past Temor. As I've witnessed countless times with others, I watch for his eyes to graze over her body, but he neither moves out of the way nor appraises her.

She sets one mug on my desk. "I'll run by in a few minutes." She pauses and then raises her hand and shuffles it at him. "Scoot."

He bobs his head and scampers out the door.

"He's brilliant," she says.

"Really?" I lift the warm mug to my lips and breathe in the freshly roasted beans. I used to stop for an overpriced nonfat latte on my way in every morning, but the company recently got these amazing machines that grind and brew beans to order. I miss my frothed milk but appreciate a creamy shot of coconut milk from the dispenser—and that the coffee is always available and saves me from squeezing through the line to get to the pickup corral. I savor my first sip.

"Really." She widens her eyes. "Like, beyond all the regular geniuses."

Maybe he can be more helpful than he knows. "Thanks for the delivery." I raise my mug. "Anything weird about that securities lending agreement?"

"You just emailed me the link ten minutes ago," she deadpans.

I raise an eyebrow and take another sip.

"No." One side of her smile turns up because of course she's already looked at it. "On first glance it's pretty standard. No strange contingencies. Exit language looks reasonable. Is there something I should be seeing?"

"Maybe not."

Alyssa cocks her head. "But maybe."

"Take more time with it."

I can almost see the gears turning in her head, and I'm instantly hit by a not-so-esoteric concern. Alyssa, if not given more responsibility, is going to leave.

"No problem. I'll let you know soon." She double-takes at the sight of the mangled frame on my desk. "Hey, what happened here?"

"Betsey's redecorating."

"Betsey?"

"Remember on Monday when she trashed my office?" How could she forget? She was the one who told me Maintenance had finished.

"Betsey wasn't in your office on Monday." She talks slowly like she can't believe she's explaining this to me.

"Are you sure?" I stammer.

"No, but I am sure that the maintenance guys were here about something in the HVAC system, and it got a bit messy, so the custodians came in to clean up."

"No one trashed my office?" A screech grows in pitch as I take hungry glances around my office. Betsey didn't attack my refuge. She didn't shove me over the edge.

"Of course not. I can't believe you thought that. Why would you assume . . . ?"

Wasn't it the wall dweller in Hardwin's office who said Betsey trashed my office? What did he actually say? Had he used her name, or had I assumed? I shake my head, dismissing Alyssa's question. Doesn't matter. Betsey's threats about Lucas are real. "Then what happened to my frame?" I say with a lot more fervor than I feel.

"I have no idea, but it wasn't because anyone trashed your office." She moves toward the door.

"One more thing," I sputter, still trying to reassemble the narrative in my head.

As she turns, Alyssa straightens the silver mirror by the door.

When she pulls her hand away, something flutters to the floor. She picks it up and hands it to me, her eyes wide. She probably recognizes Betsey's loopy handwriting as well as I do, but all that's written on the folded paper is my name.

My heart quickens as I shove the paper under my opened notebook, as if hiding it will make it like it doesn't exist.

Alyssa's eyes snap back to mine as I clear my throat.

"The thing is . . ." I lay my hand on my notebook and then move it to my lap. I'm way overthinking this. I had planned to ask her about her ambition, her willingness to take on a larger role, but if I ask her that now, it may look like I'm tying it to her silence. Or maybe not. A note simply fell to the floor. Odd but not worth a career boost. But now that I've delayed speaking, it looks worse.

I inwardly groan. "Could you work a bit with Temor? See how we might use him more effectively on the ETFs. Perhaps he can explore possible cost savings as competitors enter the field." Yes, that sounds reasonable and gives Alyssa opportunity to begin to create her own team.

I'm applauding my quick thinking when she says, "Sure. And I'll keep quiet about secret notes falling from hidden places."

I wait until she's gone to get up and close the door.

Tucked into the corner of my velvet couch, I lay my head along the soft rise of the curved back. As close to an embrace from my buxom grandmother as I can get now. She was quick with prayers, hugs, and swats. Right now, I feel like I need all three, and she would know that. My body slackens against the plush cloth as I stare down at the folded paper. Was this placed by someone else in the building working with Betsey? Is this some kind of coup to overthrow Phil's leadership? Or does Phil know more than he's letting on?

I pick up the note and read.

Hey—

They're coming for me. I thought we'd have more time.

Came by your house yesterday, and suddenly Candace and her goons showed up. You won't answer your phone, and if you're reading this, I've likely been escorted from the building. I kick myself for not connecting you in earlier.

Meet me on the corner of Nassau and Cedar at 3 p.m. I have something for you.

Betsey

I'm starting to feel like one of those poor women in a Netflix suspense miniseries. I rub at my still-sore arms and grunt. I am not weak. So, maybe it's time to be the heroine who learns to hide duffel bags under stair treads, procure fake passports, or at the very least start to see patterns in the deliberate acts of those around me.

I return to my desk and start making a list of what I know versus what I have been told. I know I was handed an envelope at the NYSE event. I know it came from Betsey based on the note and her follow-up at Grand Central. I was told she trashed my office. I know I signed a restraining order.

As I continue to categorize my thoughts, I start adding people to my list. Hardwin and Terrence both believe the data is legitimate but want me to think otherwise. Remembering the Word document I've already started with notes about the data, I decide to get organized. I open a new Excel spreadsheet and label the columns to categorize who knows what information. I realize I have no idea what Dave actually believes. The investment information on the thumb drive against the demand for the securities lending agreement still makes no sense. There has to be a relationship I'm missing. Maybe there's something hidden in the data itself?

An hour later, I'm head down scouring the thumb drive spreadsheet for secret codes or patterns of trading. I thought perhaps someone was buying up shares, indicating prior market knowledge, but none of the pivot tables I've run found any significant relationship between sales and share price.

A staccato knock on my door.

"Come in." My neck crackles. I raise my arms to press into my muscle, and they both scream at me. I drop them quickly to my sides.

Candace's stillness exudes a sense of constrained potential energy that makes me want to fidget. Like at any moment she could fly across the room and flatten me.

"Bit sore. I laid into the machines yesterday," I say.

"All right. Is this something you're concerned about?" Candace strides into my office.

"No. I'm sorry. I thought you saw me, and I wanted you to know."

"Saw you where?" she asks.

"Never mind." Like a round of *who's on first.* I shake my head and push up from my chair.

"All right." She neither smiles nor scowls. "Do you have a minute?"

We awkwardly stand looking at each other, my desk separating us. I haven't asked her to take a seat, but I just stood. It's as if I'm suddenly new at my job.

"Certainly. Please take a seat." I indicate one of the chairs in front of my desk, and I sit back down. Suddenly, I become very aware of what's on my computer screen. The data I let her assume I didn't have. I quickly put my computer to sleep.

We both sit in silence for what feels like minutes but is likely only a few seconds.

"I mentioned I wanted to hear from you if Betsey got in touch." She keeps her gaze leveled at me.

"Yes," I say.

"So, has she?"

"Actually, sorry, yes." I reach into my bag to retrieve the note. Betsey called Candace's team goons. That's on her.

Candace flips open the folded paper, her face placid. "How did you get this?"

"Less than an hour ago, found it behind the mirror." I don't indicate who found it. Alyssa doesn't need this kind of attention.

"This mirror?" Candace gingerly removes it from the wall and examines the back side before flicking her eyes to me. "Perhaps this explains why there was no note with the data. She had planned to give it to you in person."

I take a page from her playbook and keep my mouth shut.

"Nothing else?" She glances around my office, maybe wondering as I did if other notes are shoved away in hiding.

"No. I think she's waiting for me to look into the data."

Candace just nods.

"Which of course doesn't make any sense, since the data is fraudulent," I stumble. "So maybe she'll be in touch soon." I need to either continue to not offer conjecture or get better at improvisation, and fast.

She's quiet again.

Finally, I break. "Is there anything else?"

"Yes. I was just meeting with Hardwin. He mentioned some additional stress you've been under with home and getting ready for the board meeting on Monday."

"He did?" I try to keep my voice neutral, but this is so annoying. People telling me I'm under stress or not sleeping well or having some anxiety. It crosses the line in an intimate way. I'll choose when to share about my mental health or my sleep patterns. In this case and in most cases, I'm open to feedback on my work product and conduct, not my personal life.

"He wanted me to give you something." She pulls out an envelope from an inner suit pocket and hands it to me.

I draw back, my body protecting me from one more message.

"Take it, Meredith."

I trap the word *no* behind my teeth as I force my hand to grip the creamy linen envelope, the weight of a formal invitation. Am I being invited to a party? By Candace and Hardwin? It wouldn't be Candace and her husband. My fingers twitch.

Did she notice?

I slide a gilded gift certificate out of the envelope.

"It's apparently to a nice place in Scarsdale." Her voice lacks its usual staccato charm. I can't quite read the tone. Sarcasm or maybe bewilderment? She never lets the security mask slip, especially with me.

I study the card—certainly is a nice place. Provisions is one of the top farm-to-table restaurants in the area. Clint and I used to make it a point to get there once a season but haven't been there in years. Reservations take months to procure.

"You have a reservation for two at seven thirty tonight and—"

"A dinner reservation tonight?" I flip the thick card stock over, looking for the catch.

She rounds her eyes at me as if saying, *Yes, that's what I just said.* "Also, you've been emailed details about a booking for a cottage Thursday night through Sunday in the Poconos. A thank-you for all the hard work."

"I'm sorry." I want to ask her to repeat herself but sense her growing frustration with me. I'm being rewarded? "You're sending me on vacation to the mountains."

"The company is." Candace nods curtly. "Your hours have likely put strain on your family, and this is our way of supporting you."

A chill runs up my arm holding the card—like they're all reading out of the same playbook. Is it Hardwin's idea to get me away from here, and from Betsey, until after her deadline?

"Time is a limited currency. Wouldn't want you to waste it," she says.

I swallow the stone lodged in my throat. Phil must have shared my email.

As if Candace can read my mind, her eyebrows slightly raise as if saying, *Of course this is their way to get you away from your mess. Be thankful this is the direction the company is choosing to go.*

"Maybe I can take some time next week? After the board meeting? I have a lot going on for the next few days." I indicate all the folders and my computer on my desk.

My cell phone rings. It's Clint. I expect Candace to excuse herself, but instead she remains completely at ease, as if the call is for both of us.

"Give me a minute," I say.

She nods but doesn't budge.

I press my lips against a sigh and answer the phone, but I'm suddenly unsure how to. We haven't spoken since he accused me of purposefully not coming home. I blurt out the highly imaginative "Hi."

"How are you?" Clint asks.

Not what I was expecting. He hasn't asked that question in ages. Part of our counseling is to inquire and share specific information about ourselves, and not use platitudes or open-ended nonsense.

"I'm fine." I can break the rules as well.

"Erika and I are leaving for her dentist appointment soon."

"How is she?" It's like we're roommates talking about when our puppy needs to go out.

"On her phone."

"What?" I spin around to face my couch and lower my voice. "But I have her phone."

"She has a burner." Now I hear it in his voice. He's holding himself tight like he may erupt if left unchecked.

"A burn—" I twist to my left, and my eyes catch Candace's. If she won't leave, I will. I shoot up from my desk and my chair rolls back, slamming into my credenza. I leave it and walk out my door.

"Are you still there?" Clint's voice takes an edge.

"Yes. Sorry. I had to get out of my office. She has a burner phone?"

"Had." He lets out a heavy breath into the phone. "I had to wrestle it out of her hands."

"Oh, Clint." Makes sense now why she gave up her phone relatively easily yesterday.

"I know."

I look through the glass doors to the central elevator bank. If Hardwin and Candace want me gone, maybe it's time I just agree. My family has to come first. "I'll meet you at the dentist."

"Appreciate it. Question is, can I get her there? She's locked herself in her room. I've decided to give her a minute, although we need to leave in forty-five if we're going to make it."

"Can I share an idea?"

"All ears." If there is sarcasm in his tone, I don't hear it.

"Remind her of the fifty-dollar cancellation fee. If she misses the appointment, it's coming out of her account."

"Not a bad idea."

I glance back down the hallway toward my office. "I'll meet you there."

"You really will?" This time, maybe a tad of sarcasm.

I ignore the bait. "Yeah, maybe I'll take a couple days off. Perhaps we can all get away to somewhere nice."

"Who are you, and what have you done with my wife?" He chuckles without any pointy little edges. A sound I haven't heard in far too long.

When I return to my office, Candace hasn't moved.

"I'm heading home. Well, to the dentist first and then home. Please thank everyone who had a part in these gifts. We will enjoy them."

"Good to hear." Candace walks to the door and then turns right before leaving. "One more thing."

I finish reentering my password to wake my computer and then look up.

"The fake customer data on the thumb drive. You didn't make a copy?"

I glance down at my laptop and then back up at her. "My computer doesn't allow outside USB drives."

Candace remains staring at me.

"I pulled it up on my personal computer before handing it over. I needed to know if it was about work. It was just a thumb drive."

She turns and glances in the small silver mirror, but she's not looking at her own reflection.

"Copies?"

"I gave what I was given to Terrence."

I hold my breath as I open my inbox to find an email about the cottage reservation. Access to the data is my leverage. I have a handful of copies stashed. My stomach rolls with acid. I need to get out of here.

I'm turning into someone I don't recognize.

Her retreating footfalls echo in my ears.

28

OUTSIDE THE DENTIST'S OFFICE, I sit on a wrought iron bench under a large willow tree. Blades of grass dance in the light filtering through the hanging leaves. I breathe in the heady scent of nature. Two years ago, there were lengthy discussions about perfuming our office air. The lobby of the building had been doing it for years. It was subtle, but it was supposed to encourage both loyalty and pride in our workplace. They decided instead to upgrade our air scrubbers to improve air quality. I close my eyes. The authentic, vibrant sweetness in the tender breeze speaks to something deep inside me.

"Meredith," Clint calls out to me.

I blink into the bright rays reflecting off a van's windshield. He shifts to his left, and his broad shoulder casts me in shadow. I smile at the man who shows courtesy even when I don't always appreciate it.

I shift my focus to the parking lot. Where's Erika? Clint texted me that the late cancellation fee had done the trick, and they were on their way. I open my mouth to ask when I see a shuffling body in an oversized hoodie take shape behind him. She must be sweltering in this unseasonable heat but gives no indication.

I stand, and we walk into the office as if we're a normal family, not one on the brink.

After Erika's no-cavity appointment, we decide to walk a quarter of a mile to a food truck park. Erika says she's not hungry and besides her teeth feel weird after the fluoride. Clint says she can eat after thirty minutes and that the feeling will fade. Erika shrugs but slumps along behind us. Clint and I talk only of inconsequential things, like the Japanese maple in our side yard at home that needs to come down. Clint worked hard to save it after a strange beetle infestation, but the damage was too great. The tree is not huge, but it's close to the house. I offer to call someone, knowing full well Clint will take care of it.

"By the way, I got a call from Rob this morning. He, uh, wanted to give me an update on a grant he found."

"He's looking into grants?" I ask. Rob has ideas that usually require others to work. I immediately rebuke my skepticism. Rob did build and sell a successful outdoor business, but, in my opinion, on the backs of his employees.

"Yeah, I've been meaning to tell you about Wilson. They've taken an interest—"

"Can I have money?" Erika has wrapped her hoodie around her waist and is wearing an oversized T-shirt with the picture of some rapper I've never heard of. Although being in the dark about the man with a mouth full of shiny metal and a dragon scalp tattoo is not surprising, I didn't think Erika liked rap music. I've never seen her wear a shirt like this, and it's huge on her. One shoulder threatens to spill through the stretched neckhole. I decide not to go for the obvious and instead be relieved she won't be passing out from heatstroke. The temperature has to be reaching into the high eighties.

"Sure." Clint raises his eyebrows as he hands her a twenty.

I haven't seen Erika ask for cash in forever. She always uses that online payment app, Hippa, with a request to Clint or me after the fact. It's how she gets paid for all her tutoring. Maybe the trucks only take cash?

"Meet us at the picnic benches over there." Clint points toward a grove of elms with a smattering of tables.

Clint and I scan the trucks. There's an Indian Flame truck to our right that makes my mouth water. Maybe they have a spicy mango chicken or lamb korma. Even a plate of fried pakora with tamarind and mint chutneys.

I love food, but I don't always have time to enjoy it. While my mother has always been a small eater and a small woman, my dad ate with gusto. Whether it be a prime rib on Thursday nights at Oakey's or a panko-crusted fish sandwich at The Shore, he was the man everyone wanted to eat with and cook for. He'd comment on the cinnamon added to a great rib rub or the fresh mint in a Greek salad. I inherited his discerning palate. Never as good as him when I was young, my sophistication grew as I started taking clients to new and different restaurants. When I came home and we'd play our culinary version of Name That Tune, I began to stack the deck with strains of coriander and charnushka. He'd howl with delight when I'd stump him.

Clint loved my dad. Clint grew up Maine conservative. The most exotic dish from his mom's kitchen was "chop suey," a mixed pot of macaroni, hamburger, and tomato sauce. But always up for an adventure, Clint encouraged Dad to school him on marinades, fermented stocks, and dishes from far and wide. In his last year, Dad was overjoyed when Clint cooked him a pad Thai that rivaled any we'd had before.

"I'm thinking Tomato Tomatoh. A nice cup of soup with grilled cheese sounds delicious." Clint points toward the bright-red truck beside us with only a couple people in line. The logo and images on the side panel are as bland and uninspired as it gets.

It likely makes no difference where I get my food, but I have a craving far beyond lunch. I want to stay close to my husband, feel his warm, solid body next to me as we order and wait for our food—my arm stroking his back and his fingers tucking my loose hair behind my ear.

"Sounds yummy. Let's do it." I squint toward the menu on the side of the truck.

"Seriously?"

"Sure." I shrug.

He slides his warm hand into mine and tugs me forward. My feet forget to move, and I stumble. He tucks my arm against him, and I lay my head briefly against his shoulder as we get in line behind the one person ordering. Who are we?

"What do you want?" he asks as he scours the menu written in white chalk on the side of the truck.

"Whatever you're having," I say, content to watch a big guy in a grubby white apron liberally buttering a stack of thick white bread.

"No, really. What do you want? I'm getting the pesto tomato cheese with a side of gazpacho."

I whip my head up at the menu. That does not sound like greasy grilled cheese and overpriced Campbell's soup. "Perfect. I'll do that too."

"You're acting strange. Don't you want to get something different so we can sample each other's?" He pushes slightly away from me to peer down into my face.

I go up on tiptoe in my flats and peck him on his juicy lips.

He hesitates a moment and then tugs me into him. "I like it."

We carry our bounty along to a picnic table where our daughter already sits, tearing donut holes and dunking them into one of three gooey sauces. If I glance over at Clint, I know his eyes will tell me not to comment. She's doing it to deflect. If we argue about her lunch, we won't have energy left to address the bigger issues.

"That looks healthy," Clint deadpans as he climbs over the bench and settles his lunch in front of him.

Erika shrugs.

"You have my change?" Clint asks as he breaks off a corner of his grilled pesto strip and pops it in his mouth.

Why is he trying to antagonize her? He's always the parent pleading for peace and taking fifteen thousand breaths before we say anything. Maybe he's reached the end of his rope too.

"I might get something else. This is really sweet." She pushes the thick wax-paper bundle a few inches away over the grooved wood surface but stays tucked on her side of the table.

The park is pleasantly full for a Wednesday. Enough people to keep the trucks making fresh lunch options but not so many that people are forced to eat too close together. A man with his phone clamped between his shoulder and his ear walks by with some sort of curry wrap. A delicious blend of cumin and coriander invades my senses. I glance down at my untouched lunch trying to remember my bigger purpose.

"Why don't you just say it, Mom?" Erika's voice is full of glass shards.

For a moment, I think she's asking me to admit that I lied about what I wanted for lunch, but when I raise my gaze to hers, I know she's thinking of herself.

"I mean, you've come all the way here. It's not like you even like grilled cheese." Her mouth hangs slightly open, and she shakes her head at my food.

I take a bite of my pesto panini strip. The flavors are good, but the heavy-handedness of the butter makes my stomach acids go on high alert.

I pat my mouth with my napkin. "You're right, I came all the way here for you. I'm worried about you."

She closes her mouth and raises her chin at me like how dare I worry.

"Well, first, I want to know about the picture." As I say the words, my mind briefly flashes to the two pictures taken of Lucas and me, and I stupidly say, "The one your dad found."

Her head tilts as if she's mentally weighing my words. I don't dare glance at Clint. I mean, what other picture could I be referring to?

I plow ahead. "Did you take it for yourself or . . . maybe for someone else you haven't told us about?"

Something like confusion or even fear flashes in her eyes but is then immediately replaced by a look of part disgust and part detachment. "It was nothing."

"But it wasn't nothing." Clint speaks up, half his lunch gone.

"It was. Gross that you found it." She shivers. "But it was nothing."

"And this phone your dad found?" I ask.

Her back straightens, and her eyes light with fire. I see my mistake right away. This is the fight she was expecting and has geared up for.

"You took my phone," she spews. "What did you expect me to do? I have appointments with students who need help. You act like you have it all together, but you have no idea."

She knows just how to press me, always has. We only win if I can keep my cool. I reach across the pitted table, but her arm is just out of my grasp. "Then tell me."

She shakes her head. "I need to get back. I've got a lot of work." She balls up her crinkly paper and pushes up.

Clint lays his splayed fingers on her hand clutching her wadded-up "lunch."

"What?" Erika keeps her gaze toward the parking lot.

"Watch your tone. And are you going to eat that?"

She dramatically releases her hold. "I'll be at the car."

"Wow," I mutter as she marches away. "I barely recognize her. What is happening?"

After digging into the wreckage, Clint dips a sugared hole in what looks like a creamy caramel sauce. "Seriously good." He taps on the paper under my sandwich strips. "Don't let her get to you. I guarantee this has nothing to do with us. Eat up. Little greasy but really good."

Although I want to rush to our daughter and demand the answers she refuses to share, I take another bite and then another. The tomatoes are fresh, and although I haven't yet sampled the soup, I'm enjoying my lunch.

"I got something today," I say with a playful tone.

"Hmm." Clint swirls another hole in what looks like vanilla.

"Garman Straub is sending us on a vacation." I wrinkle my forehead in exaggerated confusion.

"You're kidding." He shifts toward me on the bench.

"No. They booked us a family cottage in the Poconos starting tomorrow night and . . . well, what do you think?" I stop myself from telling him about the dinner reservation for just us for tonight. I'm not sure why. Maybe see if we can make it through this afternoon's truce.

While pulling one leg over the bench, he twists more fully around so he can look right at me. "I'm confused."

"I know." I chuckle while screwing up my face. "It's almost like they're trying to get rid of me." Because of course they are. But at this point, I'm relieved to not be playing amateur detective, and maybe if we can pick up Reid and get away with Erika, we can all find our way back. And I'll tell Clint about Lucas. This time I really will.

"That's not what I'm confused about."

I nab one of the last two donut holes and dunk it in the dark chocolate sauce. My throat makes a little mewl sound.

"Why did your face look pained when you told me about the cottage? Is the thought of going away with me a chore?"

I stop breathing. What just happened?

"I see it. All I have to do is look at you and I know."

"Know what?"

"Exactly. All I get are whispers of disgust on your face and distracted moments."

"Unfair." I shake my head. "You're the one who wanted a break. You're the one who wanted space." I slam down the sugary mess without taking a bite and then grab the stack of napkins.

"Meredith—"

"No, I'm out of ideas. You're punishing me for something you're feeling. I can't . . ." I swallow hard against my lunch threatening to come up.

"Finish your thought, Meredith." Clint's jaw clenches shut, probably as tightly as his mind.

"I can't keep beating my head up against your brick wall." I scour my hands with a handful of napkins.

Clint grabs his lunch. "We've found something to agree on." Without looking at me, he rises from the picnic table.

I slump and lower my head into my balled-up fists.

For the first time, I honestly question if Clint and I will make it.

29

AS WE WALK BACK TO THE CAR, a library of unsaid words stacks up between us. My phone pings with a text from Alyssa, who almost always emails.

Temor and I have something. Are you in the office this afternoon?

I glance over at Clint, who seems to not be paying me any mind.

Wasn't planning to be. Might be taking a few days. Something important?

The dots dance for a bit before her response appears.

We can talk by phone but better in person.

Even without knowing what they've found, I somehow know this is the pivot. A weight settles across my stooped shoulders. This is when I either embrace Betsey's extortion or I stop. I turn to Clint here and now and tell him. I let him rail. Maybe only one of us goes to the cottage. But I take away Betsey's power. If the data is legitimate and it points to something illegal with our investors, I can quit. I can manage the collateral career damage, and we can survive the quake.

Or I can plow headfirst and confront Betsey with the truth.

"Honey." My voice breaks.

He stops and turns, looking not at me but at the park.

I wait for him to choose me. He doesn't.

"Just go," he says with a shrug.

"What?" I step forward, careful not to spook him.

"It's work, right? They need you to come, and I need you to go. I need you to figure out whatever has you stuck." At last he focuses his clear hazel eyes on mine and swipes his thumb over my shoulder with almost a tenderness. Almost.

With all my heart, I want to lean in, but I keep myself rigid. He misconstrues even my weekend invitations. I need to hear what he has to say.

"And then come back and be excited to go away with your family. Whether it be to this blasted cottage or somewhere else."

I wither under his hand. "But, Clint, I—"

"Don't. Just go. Erika needs time to cool off." He pulls me against his hard chest. "This is a huge week for you. I keep forgetting. Own it, and then let's figure us out."

I nod into his chest, unsure if I'm being a good wife by listening to my husband's needs or simply doing what I know, way deep down, under the wreckage, I want to do. Fearing the latter, I breathe in the rustic woody scent of him.

He's the first to step back.

^ ^ ^

An hour later, I'm approaching the address of the coffee shop Alyssa texted me, only to see a septic van parked up on the curb and men in overalls walking in and out of the propped door. We won't be going anywhere near here. I dig for my phone and see a five-minute-old text from her telling me of a sewer pipe issue at the café and saying they're heading around the corner to the Rotterdam Room.

I rock back on my pony heels. I could text her back and divert us, but what reason would I give?

Alyssa and Temor smile up at me as I enter the restaurant. Part café, part bar, it has the vibe of a members-only club but is open to all. I've never seen an advertisement. The dark lighting, lack of Wi-Fi, and small tables make it an unusual spot for our kind of business. I keep my gaze directly on them, and pull my thoughts and my eyes from scampering toward the red velour corner booth. I take a deep breath and shove back my shoulders.

"Thanks for the field trip, boss. Nice to get out of the office." Alyssa unfolds a hook under the table and hangs her bag on it.

I blink. Did she just happen to find that handy gadget? I never knew the tables had those. Always just plopped my bag on our booth. I still refuse to look in that direction.

Temor glances around. "This is a cool place. No idea it was here."

That was always the point.

"I've been here a few times." Alyssa looks directly at me.

The hairs on the back of my neck twitch.

Her unlined face appears relaxed, but is there something odd in her tone?

"How about you, Meredith?" Temor asks as he picks up the beverage list in the center of the table.

I smile. "Why don't we get something to drink, maybe a snack, and you guys can let me know what you found."

After our seltzers with splashes of various fruit juices are placed in front of us, Alyssa takes a tiny sip and then clears her throat. "Temor and I combed through the agreement. The terms were clear, very straightforward."

Temor continues when Alyssa raises her napkin to her lips.

Probably covering a little burp. That's the thing about seltzer drinks. "We also reviewed the indemnities, guarantees, and exit strategies. It would probably have been better to have a lawyer with us—"

"Don't let him fool you." Alyssa jumps in. "He may not be a lawyer, but he can certainly play one on TV. He knows the phrasing, can parse the references, and could even anticipate future clauses."

I grin at this obvious pairing. I should have teamed them up ages ago. "Strong praise. So, what did you find?"

Alyssa and Temor look at each other. "Nothing."

My shoulders deflate. "Nothing? Why are we here?"

Alyssa nods at Temor, prompting him to speak. "The point is why the contract exists at all. Our ETFs are listed but with no obvious counterparty."

"Wait. The counterparty has to be our custodian. Isn't it part of the package?" U.S. Bank holds all our lending arrangements across our funds. We didn't color outside the lines. What was good for our mutual funds was good for our ETFs.

"No." Alyssa and Temor steal glances at each other.

"But that would mean . . ." I recognize the curiosity on both their faces. They figured out this agreement might be juicy. If this agreement was executed with anyone else, it could be quite bad for Garman Straub and specifically our investors. I freeze, my hand halfway to my drink.

"What else did you just figure out?" Alyssa leans toward me.

Temor begins to respond, but Alyssa speaks over him. "No, not you. Give Meredith a minute. She sees something else."

They both wait for me, but I'm not ready to share. "I'm going to need more than a minute."

Alyssa bites on her bottom lip, likely the only way she'll telegraph her disappointment in me. I was right, Alyssa needs more challenges. She's too good for her day job.

"Was this just an oversight? Like someone drafted it but never intended to use it?" Temor asks.

"Maybe. When we pitched the idea of the funds to the board almost three years ago, I explained that the revenue we could make on lending out our more unusual assets could offset their expense. Our teams always look for opportunities. Makes no sense to lend Apple stock, for example, as it's easy to source. But some of our securities are difficult. Easier to borrow from us than to try to purchase." The existence of this contract could imply an illegal arrangement. Why would someone risk it? The most obvious answer is money. But that might be too simple, as loaning out our securities is not exactly going to bring in major financing revenue.

"Excuse me if I ask a question I should know the answer to." Temor clears his throat. "Our custodian manages the bulk of the lending, but we have these additional contracts for deals we see as lucrative?" He studies the small platter the waitress lays in the center of our table.

"No. All lending runs through our custodian." I stop talking as Alyssa catches my eye. We both have been in the business long enough and know where this could end. It's kind of like that beach bungalow, if we had an exclusive deal with Airbnb to manage all its rentals but went rogue to rent it on our own. Of course, Airbnb allows that for real estate. But our policies and prospectus require we only rent through our version of Airbnb and with precise policies in place. The SEC demands it. Any arrangement outside of our custodian looks like fraud.

"Where do you want us to take it from here?" Alyssa pops an olive from the Mediterranean appetizer plate into her mouth.

From the way Temor is attacking the rolled grape leaves, I probably should've ordered something more substantial. They probably skipped lunch.

Where do I want them to take it from here? Easy question. It'd be great to have their sharp minds dig into the investment data on the thumb drive—confirm it's real and how Betsey could've created it or gotten her hands on it. Was that what she was doing on those unscheduled office visits? Creating or simply verifying the data she'd found?

Temor is running a piece of pita bread through the oil-slicked hummus. Alyssa seems to have given up on the plate and is instead watching as two more couples are seated next to us.

We can't stay here, and I'm not going back to the office. I need somewhere with privacy. And they need food.

"On the train here, I sent you a brief summary of the board pitch idea. I'd like you to shift gears and look at my presentation for Monday." I go on to explain about the premise for the new funds.

Both Alyssa and Temor take notes, but I sense an edgy frustration from Alyssa in the way she grips her pen. She knows most of this already and therefore knows exactly what I'm doing.

After a bit more explanation, I rise to leave.

"Are you sure this is all you need?" Alyssa unhooks her bag from under the table and then looks directly at the booth I've been avoiding for the last hour. Her gaze swings slowly back to me. "We want to be most helpful."

The steeliness in her eyes so matches Betsey's, my breath catches. I would swear they're working together, but if that was the case, Betsey wouldn't need me. Alyssa could hand over the agreement and anything else Betsey wants. Alyssa can't be involved.

But she sure thinks she knows something.

It's starting to feel like everyone knows something they shouldn't.

I force my shoulders to relax. "Reviewing my presentation is the way to be helpful. I'll arrange for some food to be delivered to the office. This can hardly qualify as lunch." I wait until they both stand

and collect their bags. I then point to the table and lower my voice. "As for the matter we just discussed. I'm confident there's something we're not seeing or agreements we're not privy to. So, leave it with me. I'll circle back, but for now, you'll both move on."

I make a mental note to remove their permissions from the fundamental share drive folders.

For the sake of their own promising futures, I need to be in this alone.

30

AFTER A COUPLE HOURS holed up in a coffee shop across from Bryant Park, I slink off the elevator and make a beeline for my office. Hardwin, and maybe Phil, are expecting me to be at home getting ready for my date night. I'm sure whoever is behind the data and stand-alone contract wants my prying eyes many miles away from here. But it's too late; I can't unsee what I've seen. If they bypassed our custodian, it's been happening since launch. Come to think of it, I'm pretty sure someone in Legal gave an update to the board on the status of the custodial arrangements a good two months before the seed capital was released, which was right before launch.

I need to find those meeting minutes.

As I'm blocking Alyssa's and Temor's access, I recognize that the same could happen to me at any moment. I need all the files on my laptop. Regulations about emailing corporate documents to personal accounts are strictly enforced. Maybe hard copies are best.

I pull up the files I need, noticing that I'm still able to navigate the share drive freely. I batch send to the personal printer I have installed under the longer L wing of my desk. I usually just use it for quick working documents as it's quite a bit slower than the commercial Xerox beast we have down the hall, but in this case it's worth the extra minutes.

I also print out the pitch deck for Monday and then assemble a thick file folder with the board presentation on top.

In the hall on my way back to the elevator, I hear my name.

I turn.

Hardwin's dark eyebrows are pulled together, his jaw tight.

I want badly to slip through the thready seams of the marble floor. "Hi, Hardwin. On my way out."

"Thought you'd left for the day." And I thought he'd still be at Vanguard with Terrence. Why is he back so soon? Do I want to know? He strides toward me. Nothing menacing in his posture, but I feel my body vacillating between fight or flight.

"I did. And am leaving now again." I force myself to chuckle. "Clint loved the gift of the cottage. I assume you had a big part in that."

He waits a beat before responding. "We thought you deserved a break. Sometimes it's hard to decide to take proper rest on our own. Always another thing screwing us to our seats. I'm glad we could lend a hand."

Did he overemphasize the word *lend*, as in securities lending?

I keep my breaths regular even as my heart knocks around inside my chest. "True. Thank you. Well, I'll be on my way. See you on Monday."

"Wait." His eyes aren't on my face but instead on my bag.

Does he know what I'm carrying? What I plan to do?

"Since you're still here, can I steal you for a quick meeting?" He turns, not waiting for a reply.

I certainly feel stolen.

Hardwin opens the door of a conference room, where two of his lawyers are already seated. I take a seat in the chair closest to the door, but I'm still able to look out the glass wall to the hallway.

The two guys continue their banter about the latest regulatory updates with the SEC. I have nothing to offer. During the discussion, I take furtive glances at Hardwin, but he never looks at me. Just as I'm about to excuse myself, Hardwin lobs a question at me.

"Have you got any insight, Meredith, on any distinctions in the fiduciary responsibilities of the independent fund trustees of a traditional mutual fund and an exchange-traded fund?"

What an odd question. The responsibility of the trustees is to provide independent oversight for all funds. They operate impartially from the fund company. Both ETF and mutual fund trustees have the same responsibility to investors—to ensure that the firm's profits and goals are not put before investor interests. I can think of a few reasons he could be asking me this question in front of these guys, but the most concerning one is that he knows I've been looking into our fiduciary responsibility to our investors and am questioning whether he broke that trust by authoring the contract Alyssa and Temor analyzed.

I stay relaxed in my seat. "Obviously, trustees of both mutual funds and ETFs have the same tenet of mandated responsibility as laid out in the Investment Company Act of 1940." My tone is casual, maybe even a bit bored. "But perhaps what you are pressing on is that trustees who have sat on only mutual fund boards might not have the same experience with ETFs and therefore can be at risk for missing investor protections. For example, the role of capital market structure." I keep my gaze leveled at Hardwin. "I can assure you our independent fund trustees are strong in the mechanics of both funds, and we have invested in their continuing education. I am confident our investors are well protected."

"Good to hear." His eyes slide away from mine, and I get a quick glance of Candace walking by in the hallway.

The sharks are circling, but are they also inside the cage with me?

"Anything else you think Meredith might find interesting in the world of regulatory updates?"

The guys make confused faces at the papers in front of them. Likely assuming I requested to hear their latest thoughts.

"Well, Meredith, unless you have any questions for us, I'll see you on Monday."

I press up too quickly, and my chair races back and hits the window ledge behind me. Second time today. I take a quick breath and position my chair under the table, remembering Candace's cool presence at dinner.

I speak over Hardwin, who has just begun to ask for a FINRA update. "I do have a question." All eyes shoot to me, but I have nothing. I gamble that something will come to me as I lift my bag from the floor. When I straighten, the words trip from my mouth. "Have there been any recent cases against firms? Perhaps trustees bringing action against their asset managers?"

Hardwin nods his head slightly.

I might not be someone to discount or control so easily.

"Anything, gentlemen?" Hardwin asks.

The guys look at each other and then down at the papers in front of them.

"Good question, Meredith." His steady gaze slips back to the table. "The team will get back to you."

^ ^ ^

I've chosen a new hotel, and after struggling only twice with my key card, I push open the spring-loaded room door with my shoulder and step inside. The air is cool with a faint scent of fresh linen. Sunlight streams in through the sheer curtains, casting geometric tiles of gold across the paisley carpet. My tricep hollers at me as I toss my suit jacket on the white-sheeted king-size bed. Massaging my upper arms, I check the time, twenty-two minutes after six. My stomach gurgles. I've sat in front of two delicious plates of food today and barely eaten anything.

As I was ordering food for the team earlier, I cancelled the reservation for tonight. Clint is right: I need to resolve this madness at work, and then I must focus on him and the kids. But right this moment, I'm ready for a bed picnic. I call down for a Caesar salad with blackened salmon and a bowl of berries with fresh cream.

While I wait for room service, I change into a pair of worn-out leggings and a sweatshirt. Laying out a large towel on the bed, I then arrange a few of the dozen pillows against the headboard. As I bend over to reach into my bag, my eyes snap to the gap between the bottom of the door and the floor. I stop. My breath sticks in my throat. I march back to the bathroom and grab another towel to shove across the sill. I'll have to replace it after my dinner is delivered but better than eyeing the opening, or it eyeing me.

Betsey will have to find another way to dispatch her missives.

An hour later, all the succulent fish is gone as well as most of the salad. I was much hungrier than I expected. As I tear into my linen-wrapped yeast roll, I once again scowl at Betsey's investor data. How can I verify its authenticity? Before we launched, the team from fund accounting provided a way for employees to get approval to purchase shares of the ETFs through a trade reporting portal. Due to some issues with tech as the funds went live, I got a number of complaints from employees who wanted to purchase. All those trades were run through the same advisor code.

Details about those trades could be on the list—if it goes back that far.

I run my bread through the pat of creamy butter, in similar eagerness to Temor and his plate of hummus.

Perhaps the people who complained never ended up buying, because I don't find any entries that resemble my notes. I also don't see any advisor codes that even have the same pattern as the one we used at launch.

I don't see anything resembling my trading record either. The last time I purchased shares was over six months ago. Perhaps this data is fake after all? But then a zip code catches my eye. I know that number. Aarav's deep-brown eyes come into focus. I haven't heard back from him since I left my voicemail yesterday.

I sort and find more than a dozen entries, then look up the zip code. Yes, Westport, Connecticut. His town.

Aarav's Meymack office is called the The Fides Group. He has great Google reviews. The fourth name, who gave him five stars, has me tossing the heel of my roll back on my plate. Charles Boldir talks about the personal service, portfolio management, and conversations about the latest investment opportunity that is both less expensive and more tax efficient.

The headboard quakes as I sit back hard against the pillows. I know Charles. My Kennebunkport office managed his late father's assets. We'd tried to woo him to Garman Straub, but he was happy where he was. I read his comment again. Perhaps the latest investment opportunity is our funds.

I find his address and date of birth in the investor spreadsheet. My stomach twists. The personal information looks legit; he's around sixty, and something about Greens Farms Road sounds familiar, but I don't know if he actually purchased the shares that are listed next to his information.

Remembering the words in Betsey's note and Aarav's comment about steps to success, I wonder, *Was Betsey trying to point me toward his office?* I flip back to the Meymack web pages that highlight The Fides Group. There it is. *We take the right steps to ensure your future.* Can't be a coincidence. Was this her way of telling me the data is legitimate?

I decide to go about this another way. I copy and paste the entire column of zip codes, nothing else, and create a quick pivot table to determine those locales that have more than one investor on the list. Tiny dots of perspiration bleed from my hairline as I start to match the zip codes to known Meymack offices.

There are too many to be a coincidence.

This is not just sales data; this is highly sensitive personal data by investor, provided by or stolen from Meymack. I sit back and stare at the screen, my heart pounding in my chest. The realization hits me like the gavel coming down again and again at the closing bell, sending shivers down my spine. Someone within Meymack is leaking confidential information, and it's not just a few isolated cases—it's systematic. And someone at Garman Straub is receiving it. But why?

I glance around my dimly lit hotel room; the air feels thick, each breath I take labored. With surprisingly steady hands, I reach for my phone. My fingers hover over the screen. This discovery is too volatile, too dangerous to ignore. I need to confront this truth head-on. But as I contemplate who to call, a sense of dread wells up inside me. Whoever is behind this is playing a dangerous game, and I'm about to step right into the trap. If I admit I know, someone else will have everything they need to snare me.

I place my phone aside and settle back into my pillows. Everyone has a reason to see me flounder. Perhaps Phil has gotten greedy and is willing to risk an assortment of side deals to line his own pockets. Hardwin could be using his contracts team to create any number of ways to defraud investors. Terrence could be so focused on legacy that he's not keeping his eyes on what's going on right in front of him. And

Dave, he's got the most to gain in all this. If he gets rid of me, he has dominion over all the funds Garman Straub produces. Because if you are going to defraud investors and line your pockets, lending out a few select securities is not the straightforward way to go about it, but it does set me up quite effectively to take the fall.

Side glances and snippets of conversations over the past year crowd my mind. Evidently, I've missed something fundamental in the management of my ETFs to allow anyone to steal revenue from our funds by compromising the securities lending. I didn't list Betsey among those with reason. Maybe I'm unwilling to admit such a breach of discernment. How could someone so close to me play me for a fool? Trying to be objective, I press into the memories of working, laughing, and sharing my stash of breath mints with Betsey. Not until those moments before her interview with the friendlies did she ever make me question her. Was she so effectively careful? But I've come to realize, every dirty little secret is a prison to the one who keeps it.

I lay my head back and begin to catalogue where I might have missed evidence of fraud, with so much time spent in meetings and looking at data over the past months to years. Whispers and furtive glances crowd my mind.

Shrill ringing jolts me awake. Disoriented, I flail my arm about my head before soreness pins my elbow back to my side. Scooting up into my pillows, I tentatively grope around me. In the dim light, my fingers fumble across the nightstand. Clutching my phone, I sweep a stack of papers and send my laptop teetering to the edge of the bed. I drag it to the other side of me, gritting against the tightness in my body. It lands on an open folder. What a mess.

I glance at the screen as my finger swipes to answer the call. I bite down on a groan as I read my neighbor's name a moment too late. "Good morning, Mrs. Varnella."

"Oh, Meredith, dear, I hope I'm not disturbing you." Her voice, as always, is tinged with urgency.

I sit straighter in bed, kicking a pillow onto the floor. How could I possibly have fallen asleep in such disarray last night? "No, not at all. Are you all right?"

"I'm fine, you sweet one. A bit of pain in my hip, you know how hard—now shush, Napoleon." A yappy bark continues as Mrs. Varnella both yells at and soothes her dog. "What was I saying? Oh right, my silly hip. They're talking about replacement again. I don't know why they think this time I'll agree to getting gutted like a fish. And you know the trouble I've been having with my weeping eye. Such a nuisance, but yes, I'm fine. That's not why I'm calling."

As I gather the strewn papers around me, I scratch my left cheek and come away with a soggy bit of lettuce. Gross. I tumble out of bed, suddenly desperate for a hot shower.

"It's your garage, dear. It's a blight on our neighborhood." Mrs. Ruby Varnella has thoughts on all aspects of our home. She's hated everything we've done to try to modernize and has pointed issues with the flowers that "crowd" the beds along our new patio.

I step out of my leggings. Maybe this time when she gets going on whatever complaint she's gotten herself riled up about, I'll interrupt and plead my apologies later.

"Someone's gone and spray-painted all over it!" Her words rush out in a flurry. "It's dreadful. Absolutely terrible."

"Spray paint? I'm not following."

"Your garage," she says, stressing every syllable.

"Someone spray-painted our garage? Are you sure?" Did Clint do some repairs to the siding, and she's just overreacting?

"I'm standing right here in front of it, dear. You know how Napoleon likes to take his morning constitutional as the sun rises. Now shush, you," Mrs. Varnella baby-talks to the dog.

"I'm sorry, Mrs. Varnella." I speak over her. "You're standing in front of my garage, and someone has spray-painted what exactly?"

"Well, I'd rather not say the word . . ."

Someone spray-painted an actual word on our garage! I take a deep breath. "Do you see anyone? Anyone on the street that shouldn't be there?"

"No, but I understand your meaning." Her tone has shifted. "I think we should head home."

"Take care. I'll deal with it. Thank you." I try to pull the phone away when I hear her talk again. I bang my head lightly on the bathroom door.

"Of course, dear. What are good neighbors for?" Her voice lowers. "I can tell you this: the word rhymes with *rich* and, um—"

"Yes, thank you. I know the word." I promise to keep her updated and do my best to cover my garage as quickly as possible. I agree, not a good look for the neighborhood. Talking over her, I tell her goodbye a few times before she lets me go.

I make two calls, which go much quicker. Clint will follow up with the police.

After a ninety-second shower, I rake my hair up into a ponytail and sniff at my sweatshirt. My train buddies will need to be okay with a faint stench of old Caesar dressing. For just such fashion emergencies, I grab a Mets cap from my bag and pull the bill low. I cram both computers and all the paperwork into my leather bag and quickly pack up my Tumi.

In twenty minutes, I'm on the next train home.

31

THURSDAY

The cab rolls down our short tree-lined driveway. A couple of large blue tarps cover one and a half bays of our garage. Gutsy move by the hooligans to trespass through our decorative wrought iron gate, which we never close, and another fifty feet to our home, nestled among elms and hemlocks. Perhaps it was the old growth that gave them the cover they needed.

Clint and I decided, when the craze hit, not to pepper our house with surveillance. We don't even have a Ring doorbell, popular along our street. Maybe the police can see if anyone else caught a strange vehicle last night on video.

I tap my card against the cab's credit machine and leave a hefty tip in appreciation of the clean, fresh-smelling car. Artificial pine is better than the stench of unwashed bodies and fetid deep-fried food that can perfume my ride in the city.

I walk up and peek under the plastic tarps. In letters as tall as a schoolkid, one word is scrawled in bloodred paint. Is this retaliation for the video Erika posted? My blood boils at the thought of someone saying this about my baby girl.

Or is this about me?

Betsey knows where I live. Not only was she here last weekend, she's been an invited guest a few times, including last Christmas. I distinctly remember sipping a mulled cider while talking about the neighborhood and our decision not to spy on ourselves with cameras. Not so much from the fear of someone hacking into the feed, like many have concerns about, but just one more bit of technology to manage. Betsey had familiarity, opportunity, but what would be her motive? Not a smart way to compel me to cooperate.

The front door opens, and Clint stands in the warm light from the house. His scruff is more salt than pepper. Probably why he's almost always clean-shaven these days. He's wearing a black T-shirt with a stretch that hugs his biceps. I got him that shirt months ago, but this is the first time I've seen him wear it.

He's so handsome, but he's stopped believing me when I say it.

"Admiring our new paint job?" He walks across the front flagstone pavers toward me.

I wanted to add a basic front porch to our Tudor-style home when we bought it five years ago, but the architect we hired to design the renovation said that would be like mixing metaphors. He suggested this low-slung almost patio nestled within the landscaping. It has become one of my favorite parts of the house. If they had defaced those stones or my mahogany rockers, I'd likely be in tears right now. The garage can be seen from the street, but it is not the heart of our home.

"Have the police been here?" I ask.

"They just left. They're going to canvass the neighbors and do a little digging. They weren't happy with our lackluster security."

"Door locks not enough?" I pick up my bag.

"Especially when we don't use them." He tugs my bag out of my hand and places it behind him.

"What do you mean?"

"Follow me."

He leads me around the corner of the garage to the side door. The potted wisterias flanking the small threshold have been kicked over. Did no one think to right them? I wrestle with the terra-cotta pot to the left of the jamb, which has rolled onto the collection stones that serve as a catch basin for our gutter.

"Take a look." Clint opens the simple white door, painted to match the siding on this side of the garage.

I upturn the pot and spin it in place. While fingering the light-purple blossoms, I glance into the garage.

My breath whooshes out of me.

I drop my hand and stumble through the door, pushing up against Clint. His arm moves automatically around me.

"Has she seen this?" I whisper.

"She was the one to find it."

^ ^ ^

An hour later, we're sitting at the kitchen table. Light dances over the table strewn with the remains of a blueberry pancake breakfast. Clint's instinct had been the right one. Back two days ago—had it really been only two days? Not even forty-eight hours?—he suggested ice cream and then lunch yesterday. Kind of brilliant. Whether it was anger fueling our appetites or the desire to delay the family discussion we were soon to have, this time we all ate. Heartily. Now the three of us sit back in our seats, satiated. A drip of maple syrup runs down Clint's mason jar of boiled liquid gold—the only sign that something is radically amiss.

My husband never lets sticky messes go unwiped.

I tossed my baseball cap in the mudroom and unwound my elastic when we came inside. My hair has dried into a limp mess. I'm trying to not let it distract me, as I tuck loose strands behind my ears. The fact that my hair is even a blip on my radar indicates how much I don't want to have this conversation.

I clear my throat, and Erika jumps up with her and Clint's plates.

"I'll do the dishes, but then I need to get on my physics. We have a quarter test on Monday." She turns on the water in the sink and opens the dishwasher.

Clint grabs my plate and the platter of remaining pancakes. "Honey, why don't you take a seat? We don't have to do this right now." He sets the dishes on the counter.

"You're always on me about chores. I'd think—"

"Come on." He tugs lightly at her sweatshirt to get her to return to her chair. "The police are coming back. They're going to want a fuller story."

Fat tears roll down her bloodless cheeks. Her blue eyes shine. Both Clint and I have hazel eyes, though different shades. When Erika was born with deep-blue eyes, everyone said they'd darken to a color similar to ours, but they didn't. They lightened. In times of stress or in streams of sunlight, her irises look like the sky on a perfect summer day. I swallow a sob and then bite down on my lips. Just now, I see how identical in color and brightness they are to Lucas's.

"Do you know who might have done this?" Clint asks.

I flinch as Erika shrugs.

"We need more than that. Maybe start from the beginning." Clint sits back down.

"I don't know how," she whispers, hunched over in her chair.

"Is this about that terrible substitute?" I ask. My heart clunks behind my ribs. Secrets really are prisons.

"No. But I don't know." She exhales a huge sigh that catches.

I tip back in my chair to grab the tissues on the kitchen desk behind me. I place the box in the middle of the table. When I was a financial advisor, we had a grief counselor visit our office. In that line of work, you are often talking to clients through some of their worst and best times—family deaths, long-awaited weddings, and confounding seasons of career retirement. I remember many things from her presentation, but two things in particular: Don't rush a person to tell you what they need to tell you, and never hand them tissues. The second one only made sense after she explained that giving someone a tissue may imply that you are uncomfortable with their tears and you wish them to stop. That may, in fact, be the case, but better to have boxes of tissues within reach. They can decide when to use them.

Our daughter might need to cry. And we're here for it.

Clint fidgets in his seat. Not getting answers is likely killing him. "You met him at a party and didn't see him again until he showed up at your school. Anything more to that?"

"I met someone else at the party." She picks at the polish on one of her fingers.

"Who?"

"Just a guy. My age." She bites down on the last two words. "I sent some messages—"

"That picture." Clint bolts straight up in his seat.

"No! No." Erika shakes her head hard. "See, I don't know how to talk to you about this."

"Well, it's either us or the police," Clint spits out.

I lay my hand on his leg under the round table. Doesn't he remember I'm usually bad cop? As hard as this is to go through, I'm not sad about our reversed roles. But I do need him to calm down if we are going to make progress with her.

Erika lowers her chin to her chest and is crying now. It takes everything in me not to go to her, wrap her in my arms, and bring us both back to beating on drums in Mommy and Me music class. When the biggest concern was another child snagging the bongo with the leopard-print strap. But now, I know if I go over to her, we'll lose her.

She grabs a tissue and mops her face. Shaking her head at both of us, she begins again. "I started talking to a guy online. He'd been at the, uh, you know, party, and he stood up to Danny, who we all now know to be Mr. Doward." She sighs. "I know he couldn't have anything to do with this. Never mind."

"What's his name? Does he go to your school? Who is this boy?" Clint asks in rapid succession.

Our daughter tucks her head in like she is trying to escape down her own neck.

The muscles in Clint's jaw pulse.

I remember the first time I saw what protective Clint looked like. His long strides through the ranger station as he discovered that my roommate and I'd been left alone on the side of a mountain without proper equipment.

"Honey." I try to speak as gently as possible. "Why don't you think the garage is him?"

"Because he's great. He would never do anything like this. That's not what . . . It's just that we haven't snapped since this weekend, and then Dad took my phone—"

"A phone you never should have had. Did he give you that phone?" Clint can only see the paint. I need him to see our daughter.

Erika's eyes widen for a moment. "No. I got it from you."

"What?"

"It's your old phone. New cover. I've had it for months." She looks almost pleased with herself.

"You took my phone," Clint snarls.

"You gave it to me, Dad. Remember? When we were diagnosing what was up with the Wi-Fi?" She rolls her eyes like a champ. "You never asked for it back. Can I have it now, maybe if . . ."

"No," Clint roars. Obviously she's asked many times before.

I say a silent plea for peace as they glare across the table at each other.

"Okay, thanks for telling us about this boy. If you don't think he did this, but you mentioned him for a reason . . ." I soften my face and try smiling with my eyes, although I've never understood the description. Instead, I look at her with all the love that often overwhelms me. "Is it possible this isn't about you at all?"

Clint starts to talk, but I continue. I want to speak to what I'm hoping. "No, hear me out. Could someone have gotten the wrong house? I know things have been weird for Erika, but maybe this is not anything to do with her." I sit straighter in my seat. This could not be about either one of us. Just some stupid kids who tagged the wrong house.

"Mom." Erika leans forward. "Dad showed you what was spray-painted inside the garage."

I nod. The words have seared a brand on my brain. I yearn to scratch them out.

"Buttercup is what he calls me," Erika says.

"Buttercup?" My voice falters.

"*Times up bc*—the words written on the Range Rover." Erika rounds her eyes like I'm a bit slow.

"Why *time's up*?" Clint barks. "Blast it, Erika. What is going on?"

"I don't know!" Erika shouts.

Clint leans across the table. "It must mean something to you. Someone pressuring you. Some deadline for you to do something else stupid."

"Clint!" I roar.

We stare at each other, my heart pounding. Clint scrubs his face with his hands, as Erika quietly sobs. Silence descends on our table.

I roll *Buttercup* around in my brain. Someone I had no idea existed is calling our daughter Buttercup? Who has Erika gotten herself mixed up with?

And is that even the truth?

32

"HOW LONG HAVE YOU KNOWN HIM?" I again try to reach our daughter with my soft tone. Whether or not *bc* refers to Buttercup, our daughter is mixed up with some guy we didn't even know existed. Is he even her age?

"We just celebrated five weeks." She waves her hand at us. "I know it doesn't sound long, but we text all the time. He listens. I know all about him. Weeks for us is like months, or more."

I smile and nod without glancing over at Clint. We just need to keep her talking.

"So, who is he?" I feel like a sagging balloon with a slow leak. "Does he go to your school?"

"He's a freshman at Gatwich."

Clint leans over his elbows on the table. "He's in college. In Vermont?"

"Vermont?" I sputter. Not sure why it's the Vermont part and not the college age that is pressing on my chest. Perhaps because we're on thin ice focusing on the age difference.

"Only four hours away. He was getting a ride this weekend. He wanted to meet me in Poughkeepsie."

Clint booms, "Meet you in Poughkeepsie. Have you lost your ever-loving mind? I don't understand—"

I loop my arm around my husband's taut bicep and tug. "I think we may be getting a bit off course."

Clint sits back in his seat and nods, not at me, but I assume he appreciates me yanking him back from whatever edge he was about to careen over. Again.

"The police are coming back. We are still not sure if *bc* refers to you. Do you have any idea of the time being up? Your dad's right. It sounds like a threat. Maybe this is about that terrible substitute?"

A banging at the door has all three of us jumping in our seats.

"Probably the police. I'll check." Clint wobbles up from his chair. This conversation has taken a toll. He looks every day of his sixty-one years.

Clint ushers the police into our formal sitting room, and we all take seats. Do I want to know what these men will say? They're too early. We needed more time with our daughter. I feel unprepared for this conversation—a very queasy sensation. I run my hand down the plush arm of the sofa. We haven't done much with the room since we moved in. My mother helped me pick the two conversation chairs that face the curved leather sofa. Our coffee table sits between. In its center a squat candle labeled *Sea Spray*, which has never been lit, is surrounded by a stack of coasters on one side and dated magazines on the other.

Maybe if I keep noticing the room, they won't bring it all down around us.

The taller officer, with a dramatically receding hairline, flips through his notebook. "I'm Officer Gary Komoroski." He hands each one of us a card. "We've canvassed a few of your neighbors. No one noticed a strange vehicle or anyone suspicious since last night around eleven when"—he traces his finger down the page—"when you, Mr. Hansel, said you were outside, and the garage doors were fine."

Eleven? What was Clint doing out so late? I glance at him around Erika, but he's trained on the officers. The three of us are spaced on the long sofa, with Clint and me hugging the arms, and Erika in the middle. Two of the throw pillows are pressed against her stomach.

The officer gives a few more details about the neighbors he spoke to and the surveillance film they will be getting, but based on the layout of the private driveways, most don't have views of the road. "Any more thoughts on what was written on your vehicle?"

"We think it might be related to an incident Erika had at school with a substitute." I go on to explain about Danny Doward and the video. Before they ask any questions, Clint interrupts.

"I think it's related to someone else our daughter met at that party." Clint flips the officer's card back and forth in his fingers, almost ripping it. "He's a student at Gatwich University. He, uh, he calls her Buttercup, so *bc* could be short for that."

Erika glares at her father. Ripples of betrayal emanate from her like heat off hot asphalt.

"Tell us about this person, Ms. Hansel. Name? Age?"

"Marcus Jamal. Eighteen. Look, I can tell you what I know about MJ, but I know he didn't do this. Maybe it was Danny . . . I don't know. But it wasn't MJ."

"That's fine. We understand. They can both be starting points." They continue to ask her questions about the substitute, of whom she has almost no information. Her responses change when they start asking about this other boy, about where he lives when not at school and how he communicates with her.

I listen and lap up all the details. These officers get to information much faster than we ever could. An impulsive sob rises up in my throat. I swallow repeatedly to try to dislodge it. We are learning about our daughter's first boyfriend from the police.

"Any recent changes? I mean, you've only known him for a few weeks, but anything out of the ordinary?" The shorter officer, with rounded cheeks and a ruddy nose, speaks up. He introduced himself earlier, but I can't remember his name.

"I don't know. Maybe. But again, I just don't think . . ." She squeezes the brocade pillows hard against her.

We all sit in silence with only a faint ticking from Oma's German wall clock.

"It's just . . ." Erika picks at one of the loose threads in the corner of the pillow.

I want to stop her before she unravels the embroidered flower, but I want more for her to continue speaking.

"He had military maneuvers on Sunday. I, uh, I don't think they went well."

"What makes you say that?"

The thread loosens from the pillow and a petal on one of the flowers dissolves. "Oh, sorry, Mom."

Shrugging, I smile, but I gently tug the pillow away from her. I shouldn't care about a silly decor item. It's just that I remember the fun my mom and I had picking them out. She risked life and limb as she dove headfirst into a massive bin, convinced she could find the mate. I clutched her legs so I wouldn't lose her. We hadn't laughed like that since before Dad died. Very uncharacteristic of my mom to involve herself with throw pillows.

Erika clutches the matching pillow squarely across her lap. "MJ's been under a lot of stress. You know, college and ROTC."

"Sure, can be very stressful." Officer Komoroski nods.

Erika makes a strangled noise and then bears down on the pillow.

"I haven't heard from him since Sunday afternoon. I got worried, and I, uh, took a picture."

As if all the air has been sucked from not only my lungs but the whole room, I stop breathing. I knew that picture was wrapped up in this new relationship. I close my eyes. I can't watch the officers watching my daughter. She's still a child. Someone to be loved and protected from all the predators out there. I blink and slide toward her. Reaching around her shoulders, my hand bumps into my husband, who has done the same. I let out a deep sigh.

"And you sent it?" the officer gently asks.

Erika's tense muscles begin to relax. "Just one. He never asked me to. He was having such a hard time. I just wanted to be closer." She stares down at the crushed pillow. "He never responded."

"So, the message on the car about time being up?" the officer asks.

"Doesn't make any sense. Calling me a—and then the car. I don't get it." Erika presses her hands to her face.

The officers stand in unison, perhaps some silent communication I missed. "We'll look into this. If you hear from him let us know."

"Officers." I pull Erika close to me. "Maybe there's another way to look at this? The wrong house, or it was meant for one of us?"

"We'll look into all the possibilities. Be thankful no one was hurt, and nothing was stolen. We'll stay on it. The damage will likely be covered by homeowners' but that cost and the implied threat makes this a priority for us." Officer Komoroski moves toward the door.

"Unless there's something else you need to tell us." The other one steps in front of me. I lower my gaze to make eye contact with Officer Colby. I'd forgotten his name, but his lanyard badge is now clearly visible.

"We're learning right alongside you, Officer." My voice is strong, not at all reflecting the storm inside me.

Clint opens our front door, and the officers step out.

I clamp down on my lips, not ready to tell them about my chaos at Garman Straub. I slip in behind Clint as he shakes both their hands.

After running a hand down my husband's back, I head to the garage door off the kitchen. Now that the shock has worn off, I need to take another look.

Under the fluorescent light, specks of what looks like mica sparkle in the SUV's gray paint. The Range Rover looks perfect from this side. My steps slow as I move around the front grille. Drips of bloody red paint begin to appear.

I stare at the words. Maybe this is about Erika. But the longer I stand here, the less any of this makes sense.

times up bc

It's not yet Friday. I still have a day, but the defacement is looking more and more like Betsey Comarsh telling me it's time to act.

33

I PULL THE DOOR CLOSED BEHIND ME as I enter the kitchen. The house is eerily quiet, as if even the refrigerator dares not hum in the aftermath of such upheaval. With the appliances on high alert, I hear no one wandering about. Erika has likely evaporated up into her room.

"Clint?" I call out as I place the rest of the white dishes, sticky with syrup, into the dishwasher and grab the reusable bamboo-fiber square from its hook. We now hide the paper towels. I run the replacement cloth with the twin pears under running water to soften it up and then scrub the counters. At first it felt good to be saving the planet one rip of the roll at a time; now it is somehow anticlimactic. I realize I miss the satisfaction of dropping the mess into the trash at the end, but I don't miss it enough to endure the guilt of melting polar caps.

"I think we should go to the Poconos."

I startle. "I thought you went upstairs."

Clint grabs a length of paper towel from a roll stashed under the sink, wets a large corner of it, and attacks the table.

A bloom of jealousy erupts in my chest. I breathlessly watch as he then stomps on the trash pedal and drops the wad in the trash. My eyes shut tight. How can I have emotional bandwidth to waste on disposable cleaning supplies? I bite back a laugh and realize I want to laugh more. Maybe this trip to the Poconos is what we need. Maybe we can leave this all behind and just enjoy each other. Everything, everyone can wait. We need to get at the business of being a family. I need an escape.

"Maybe we can get checked in, and then I can come back tomorrow, or we all can, to pick up Reid." Clint settles in the farthest kitchen chair pulled a couple feet back from the damp table.

I dry my hands on the blueberry tea towel hanging from the stove and take a chair opposite him. "With all that's going on for us, I'm so thankful for our family."

Clint cocks his head.

"Doesn't it overwhelm you sometimes, the love? Especially today."

Clint's eyes, which are usually squinted with tiny lines in starburst formations, grow round. "You remembered."

My heart clunks in my chest as I reach both arms across the table, ignoring the wetness.

He squeezes my hands.

"I don't, but I want to," I whisper. I decide in the moment to only speak full truths to this man I desperately love.

His fingers stiffen, but he doesn't pull back. "Today's my mom's birthday and, uh, the day she passed."

I yank back before I can stop myself. My hands shoot to my mouth. "Today is October fifth? Oh, Clint."

Clint nods. "She'd have been eighty today. Sounds so old, especially since she was younger than you when she died."

"Why didn't you say something? What about Maine this weekend? We haven't even talked about it." I scramble to find the right thing to say.

"Seemed not the year. I thought I could move past it, but when you started talking about family, I thought maybe you . . . It's strange being alone in the world."

"How can you say that?" I jump up from my chair and go to him. Wrapping my arms around his shoulders, I lay my head on his. "You have me."

"Do I?" His words are pure.

I yank the empty chair next to him and sit with our shoulders touching. I wiggle my fingers to interlace with his. "Tell me about her." Even with everything going on at work and with Erika, this seems the most important thing to do right now—speak of the woman who both nurtured and damaged my husband.

"I've told you."

"Tell me . . . tell me something that would make her laugh." I squeeze his hand.

"Oh, Mer."

"Come on, tell me for her. For her birthday," I say as softly as I can without whispering.

"I, uh, what do you want to hear?" Clint suddenly stops fidgeting and then slouches back into his chair. "Okay. She'd laugh every time she told the story of the box turtle."

"What box turtle? You never told me you had a turtle." I cuddle in closer.

He shakes his head. "Not mine. Mom's either. She must have been in maybe fourth grade on her way home from school. Walking all by herself. A silver-white car was coming toward her on Windham Center Road, driving a bit too fast. I, uh, like to imagine it as one of those Chrysler Thunderbolts with the sleek encased bodies. Know what I mean?"

I say nothing but smile big.

"Anyways, a huge box turtle was in the middle of the road. Without thinking, she ran to it and waved her arms. The car came to a screeching halt right in front of her. From the first time she told it, I'd squawk about her getting taken out, but she'd wave me off. She'd only say that the turtle would have been crushed. With the car waiting, she tried to encourage the beast to move, but at this point the turtle had retracted its whole body into the shell. So, she picked it up and ran to the side of the road. Just as she was about to place it in the stream, it poked its prehistoric head out and blinked at her. She tossed the turtle into the water as quick as a flash—her words—and then her whole body shook like her Aunt Bea's tambourine. She turned around, and the man driving that cool car was laughing, not just chuckling but full open-mouthed, let-it-loose hysterics. Of course, she was mortified and grabbed her book bag and ran home."

I giggle into Clint's arm as I hear the huge smile in his words.

"When she'd share that story, she'd always try to shake like she did that day when that crazy turtle head looked at her. She said she could never make her body move that way again."

"Can't believe you never told me about the turtle." I shove against his shoulder.

"Yeah." He holds me tighter. "She was amazing. That's why it's so hard to fathom what my brother did."

"I know."

This is where we go every year. The unfinished anger that lingers and sprouts up on this day like the green nub of a bulb that's been sleeping all winter.

"He killed her, you know."

He's never put it so bluntly. I squeeze his hand. "You were both still kids. He was only four years older than Erika is now."

He pulls his hand back and stands.

Is that comparison as startling to him as it is to me?

"Every year I tell myself to let it go," he mumbles.

"Maybe it's time to see him. Talk it out. Maybe he can—"

"He left us, Meredith." He turns on me with as much emotion as he did twenty years ago when he first told me the story. "We lost the house. She lost all hope. And in the end, all she wanted was him."

I stand. "I know. I just wonder if it might help."

His face hardens. "I know this day is unfair to you. I'll do my best to snap out of it. I know we have bigger issues than something that happened decades ago."

"I didn't mean it wasn't important. In fact, the opposite. I've been—"

Clint's phone rings. He slides it out of his pocket and looks at it. His eyebrows knit together.

"Wait, I don't want to leave talking about your mother."

"No worries. I've got to take this." He strolls from the kitchen.

I strangle the rail posts of my chair. I begin to let myself feel hope, and then, again, I'm dashed on the rocks of our crumbling marriage.

I park each of the chairs squarely under the table and then fetch an insulated bag. We'll need to take some food to the cabin. I'm sure there are good take-out restaurants in the Poconos, but it would be nice to have solid snacks and breakfast supplies. I grab a couple freezer packs and then study the full refrigerator.

Everything will be all right. If I can nab the right food, keep it precisely cold enough, and serve it before anyone realizes they're hungry, all the rest of the disasters will work themselves out. When all else fails, I just need to be the perfect wife and mom.

34

I FLIP THE LIGHT SWITCH in my home office and immediately shudder when I notice the lily wilting in the corner. I hate plants. Correction: I hate plants in my home. I love them in other people's homes. Rubbing their silky leaves, I find myself agreeing to cuttings and listening to watering and fertilizing schedules as if I'll intuitively comply. A big part of me knows, even from the first conversation, that I will regret accepting the new pot. But a small part of me is unreasonably optimistic. It's not all my fault. Seems my friends ought to have discovered my murderous bent. They should've banned me from ever accepting another green baby. Now, I live with the knowledge that at any moment I could be asked, *Meredith, where's the gorgeous Boston fern that used to be in your front window?* Or *Meredith, where are you hiding the parlor palm Cathy gave you?*

As opposed to my previous green office dwellers, who seemed to thrive for weeks and then inexplicably shrivel up into a brown tangle,

I appreciate how the peace lily wilts after only a few days, as if calling out to me, *Hey, lady, I'm as dry as one of your mother's store-bought biscotti.*

I empty the half-full glass of water from my desk into its white-speckled soil. Promising us both future hydration, I open my inbox. As I scan and reply to a few congratulatory and follow-up emails, I see it. Phil has responded.

From: Phil Langford (Phil.Langford@garmanstraub.com)
To: Meredith Hansel (Meredith.Hansel@garmanstraub.com)

Your slides look excellent for Monday. Expect some good conversation following your pitch. Joanne will have ideas. Probably a few of the others as well. Run the task force by Hardwin.

Phil

I read the five sentences twice to tease out the true meaning. His first sentence translates to—after a cursory glance at my pitch document, he skimmed the slides and will likely send me last-minute notes on Sunday. *Good conversation* means the trustees are ruffled. Joanne Ketter's addition to the board has likely disrupted the testosterone status quo. She has new ideas around governance, which means the men, who talk of accountability but shrug off the yoke themselves, are raising bureaucratic concerns. I need to be prepared for difficult feedback that will look like pushback but is actually posturing.

His last sentence, six words on the task force, is where I focus all my hard-fought political acumen. My effort to put together a task force seems like overkill, but he doesn't want to be priced out of the market we created. Yellow light. I will need Hardwin's go-ahead, which is, of course, a nonstarter. The questions of what Phil knows about there being a separate securities lending agreement and if he knows the data is likely legitimate, remain unanswered.

And I won't speculate. Not today.

Instead, I hit reply and type.

From: Meredith Hansel (Meredith.Hansel@garmanstraub.com)
To: Phil Langford (Phil.Langford@garmanstraub.com)

Phil,

Thanks for the heads-up. I'm out of the office until Monday, but let me know if there's anything else I can do to prepare for the board meeting. I recently realized I don't have the fully executed custodial agreement including securities lending. Can you have one of your admins send it over or let me know where I can track it down?

Thanks again,
Meredith

Each word was hard to type. I press send before I rethink how I'm exposing my own flank. If he knows about possible lending issues, this is a clear shot across his bow. I scrub my cheeks with my stiff fingers.

Distracting myself, I read a message from Alyssa. She's looked into the new funds and wants to know if she should set up meetings for me next week. I tell her yes, not for me but for her and Temor. Why don't they take the lead on exploring the right index partner? As soon as I press send, an email from Phil hits my inbox. I've never heard back from him this quickly.

From: Phil Langford (Phil.Langford@garmanstraub.com)
To: Meredith Hansel (Meredith.Hansel@garmanstraub.com)

Will have contract and board notes sent. Hope they're helpful.

Phil

He's letting them be sent without hesitation. This should relieve me, but his speed makes my stomach clench. He's also sending me notes, likely the minutes, from a past board meeting. I dig the base of my cross necklace into my chest. The pain exposes my frustration. I should have been the one to ask for the minutes when I asked for the contract. I can't forget these details if I'm going to figure this all out. The notes will likely tell me what was said about the custodial agreement including the securities lending policy for the ETFs. I've only been to a few board meetings, when particular milestones have been reached, like the ETFs' launch and getting on the Meymack platform. I was so proud. I guess I still am; it's hard to tell.

There must have been something discussed about the contract in a board meeting that he thinks I will find helpful. Maybe the board agreed to the stand-alone contract, although I can't see how. The word *helpful* keeps drawing my gaze. It's often batted about with sarcasm, like when someone lectures in a meeting when a single sentence would've sufficed. *Well, that was helpful.* Or when someone needs a time-consuming task or goes off topic, the other might respond, *I'd like to be helpful but . . .*

I push back in my seat still staring at the email. "Helpful."

"What?" Erika stands on one foot in my open doorway, her pretty head cocked to one side.

"Oh, hey." I smile up at her.

"I'm going to make a smoothie. Want one?" she asks.

What time is it? I check my computer clock. Almost two o'clock. How is that possible? Didn't we just finish breakfast? We were on our way to the Poconos.

"Lost track of time again?" Erika smirks.

"Yeah. I thought I just sat down."

"My European history teacher says that's a sign you're doing what you love, when the time flies by." She glances around the room. "Hey, your plant is green."

"So surprised?"

"A living houseplant hits different inside this house." Erika pinches one of the petals.

I partially rise from my desk chair. "Are you making sure it's real?"

"Legitimate question." She turns around toward me with a small smile, and I'm hit by the maturity etching her features. Her shapely eyebrows frame her large eyes, which look almost violet in the lower light of the room. Her mouth, not as prominent as mine, has full lips that are naturally a warm shade of pink.

"I can still picture you as a baby grabbing at my necklace."

"That was a long time ago, Mom. Smoothie?" She turns.

"Sure." Spell broken, I stretch and feel for the thin gold chain at my neck. Not the same gold chain as sixteen years ago but bearing the same petite cross from my grandmother. She gave it to me when we arrived home from the hospital with Erika. The first gift I opened. With her hand covering mine, Oma spoke of resting in the truth of God's love. I so easily agreed. Growing up, I paid only passing attention to her devout Catholicism—more of a quirky personality trait than an invitation to any real faith. Her daughter, my mother, believes only in what she can see and what she can affect, which made sense to my logical mind. I've worn the religious symbol off and on during my parenting years, but it's become a habit over the last few months. Holding on to it now makes me yearn for something lost, or maybe something I've never truly found.

35

THE BLENDER CHEWS UP BERRIES, protein powder, and almond milk with grating sounds I've come to associate with Erika.

"Looks yummy." I perch on a stool at the island and brace myself for what I'm about to tell her. "We're all going to the Poconos for a few days."

"I know."

"You do?" How is this not a fight?

"Dad mentioned it. Sounds good."

It does? I slide back to get a good look at my daughter, and my elbow wedges itself in the wrought iron back of my stool. I tip backward and then try to catch my foot around one of the bars. Right before smashing forward, I grab the edge of the granite island and wobble precariously back into place.

"You okay?" Erika raises a perfectly arched eyebrow at me.

I straighten. "Yes. Great. Glad it's all set." My heart sorts itself in my chest. For a moment there, I pictured busting out my two front teeth on the island edge simply because my teen daughter agreed with a family plan.

"Are we still thinking of leaving today? It's getting late. We have to find this place, right?"

"Excellent point." My voice seems overly gleeful. I clear my throat. "Seen Dad?"

She pours the thick spotted slurry into two mason jars. "He was talking to some guy in the garage."

"Oh." I glance toward the door. A clean house, a full refrigerator, and Clint has probably already arranged to have the car fixed up. Remarkable how well it all runs without me. And I have trouble remembering to water the lily.

"What do you think?"

I start to say, *I think I've let go more than I realized and that my husband has silently slipped on both our shoes, and I wonder if he resents me for it,* when I glance up and see Erika lifting her glass toward me.

"Delicious," I say after a quick sip.

"Pasture-raised goat whey." Erika slumps on the island across from me.

"Wow. Protein powders were just for bodybuilders when I was growing up."

"And you weren't allowed potato chips or other processed foods. I've heard it." She takes another sip and leaves the room.

An hour later, I'm upstairs when my phone pings with a text from Terrence.

Running between meetings. All set on the slides on my end. Expect a few thoughts from Phil this weekend. We've got a packed agenda with all the funds to review. Thanks for being mindful.

As expected, Phil has already signaled a few thoughts to Terrence, but I'll probably need to wait until the last minute to get them. Terrence is also concerned that excitement over my new ideas will overshadow his desire to talk, at length, about our mutual funds. If consistent with each of my previous appearances, Phil and Hardwin will both ask me to take all the time I need and then will stir up a lengthy discussion with the trustees. It's never too early for that, but I'll feel Terrence's heat to keep the focus on the bulk of our business. The heat is more like flames from a campfire than a raging inferno, but in either case, burns are possible.

I respond with appreciation and then notice the battery life on my phone. Emails will have to wait. I plug in my phone on my bedside table and then am digging in my camping bin when my fingers close around something I haven't felt in a very long time. The scratchy fibers are unmistakable. I lower my overnight duffel from the bench at the end of my bed and sit. Unfurling the sock pair, I raise the wool to my nose and mouth and breathe in. Earthy winter air smells locked inside the weave.

My roommate and I went missing on a hike in late spring of my sophomore year at Boston College. We'd been enticed to join a trip by a couple of upperclassmen outdoor club guys in our economics class. Wasn't until we loaded the car that we realized there were only four of us. While Boston was in bloom, Katahdin, Maine's highest peak, was still in snowpack. Wet, cold, and without even an extra pair of socks, Katie and I got separated from the guys. As night fell, and it got darker, we had no choice but to both climb inside my orange safety tent. Earlier that morning, I'd bought it on a whim from a Walmart endcap. The guys had laughed when I'd pulled out the folded instruction sheet in the car.

The next morning, as we huddled together inside the reflective material, we heard the voices of wardens. With our bare feet shoved inside one of our backpacks, we hollered back. Katie's insistence that we peel off our sopping-wet cotton socks had saved our toes from frostbite.

I squeeze the thick wool of the socks. Clint brought this pair in his Appalachian Trail rescue pack. The coarse material felt luxurious, once I could feel anything at all.

"Where'd you find those?" Clint asks as he steps into our bedroom.

"Do you remember?" My throat floods with warmth as tears prick my eyes.

"How can you ask me that?" He pulls open the top drawer of his highboy.

"I want to talk about something real."

"Something real," he mumbles.

"Thank you for sharing the turtle story, but it seems lately we only dance around our conversations, avoiding anything that stings. We used to share it all." I suck in my top lip and then lean forward. "I want to stop the pretense. I want to—"

He swivels toward me. "You're having an affair."

I've shot to my feet even before I fully comprehend his words. "No!"

His face is blank, as if the act of saying the words has stripped all the emotion from his body.

"Never." I lurch toward him. He can't honestly think this of me.

He holds up his hand. "Stop. Don't."

"Why?" I sag but my knees knock, keeping me from pooling onto the carpet. "Why won't you let me close?"

He slams the drawer shut. "Why won't I? You're the one. You've shut me out. You've so many secrets, you're in knots around me." Anger flies with each of his words. Only a weariness remains. "I knew I was too old for you."

Tears flow freely down my cheeks. The platitudes I've used so many times before bounce through my mind. Words of love and assurance. The inconsequence of our age difference. Phrases that speak to who he is and how lucky I am that he wanted to be my husband. No matter how I try to say it, my pleading always falls on deafness. My efforts rebuked, I often walk away in disgust over my inability to get him to believe me.

This time I can't. I won't.

This time I try something new. "You're right."

His body sags, like he's crossed the marathon's finish line. "I knew it."

"Not about our ages. Irrelevant. And certainly not about an affair. But you're right about me. I've kept too many secrets."

His chin slowly rises and the muscles in his jaw pull his skin taut. "Tell me."

36

I GRAPPLE WITH HOW TO HELP the love of my life understand me better. "As you know, these past few years have been incredible. I mean, beyond the obvious success, I've learned a ton."

Clint rests his shoulder against his chest of drawers. He knows I'm circling the building trying to find my way into what needs to be said. Instead of pounding on the front door, I decide to climb up to an attic window and squeeze inside.

"I always thought sales was about getting someone to buy from you or do something you really needed. Like the guy at the car lot that needs to get rid of the clunker that's been sitting by the back dumpsters for too long. Not the case at Garman Straub. I've learned a whole new side of sales. In mutual funds and ETFs, it's about building relationships."

Clint sucks in his lips as if waiting for me to get to the point—for me to finally say that I've betrayed him. And maybe I have, but not in the way that he thinks.

"Sure, there's banter, but with few exceptions, sales is professional and mutually beneficial." I rub my upper arm remembering a late night a month ago.

"With few exceptions?" Clint asks this clear-eyed, like he really wants to know.

"I've been propositioned, of course. And had moments of awkwardness, occasionally, but I've never been overpowered." I taste the word *overpowered* only after it has left my tongue. Unfortunate phrasing.

"I would hope not!" He furrows his brow at me.

He will never truly know what it is like to be a woman in the career I love. Most days it's worth every hassle. Some days, those hassles are harder to shake free from. I was coming back from a late dinner at the Impact Conference when, in the hotel lobby, an advisor with a loose tie and even looser tongue grabbed my arm and playfully dragged me to his table to introduce me to his very drunk colleagues. He held me there, asking questions about my childhood, my husband, and the color of panties I was wearing. At that point I yanked and spun. The pressure on my arm increased. His eyes grew dark. I would not be the one to decide when our conversation was over. I gritted my teeth and pulled away. It came right up to the moment when he would've had to physically and obviously force me to stay. He burst out laughing instead. The table joined him. I marched off. Late nights, flowing alcohol, and lack of diversity are bad combinations.

Clint walks to the bed and partially sits, partially droops up against the headboard.

I join him but keep space between us. "I'm known for being able to take care of myself." I wonder if this is true. "Anyway, relationships. We—quote, unquote—*sell* our new funds to advisors, who are organized into teams, at firms like Meymack, and are managed by Wealth Management leaders. Forming a partnership is key. If I can get Wealth Management excited about our funds, maybe even before their competitors, doors open to the advisor teams. That's what happened with Lucas. He was my doorman."

Clint shifts toward me with his shoulder against the headboard. "Lucas?"

"He's on Meymack's senior leadership team, head of Wealth Management. He's been there for a couple of years after spending the last decade out in San Diego at a large independent broker-dealer, doing about the same job. He has a wife, no kids, but does a lot of work with St. Jude Children's Hospital."

"Meredith, why are we talking about this Lucas guy?"

"Because he's your Lucas," I say.

Clint stares at me. He doesn't move a muscle.

"Lucas Anderson. He changed his name from Hansel years ago. He's a good—"

"No." He lurches off the bed. "Better if you were having an affair."

"Don't say that." As I crawl across the comforter to try to get closer to him, my foot gets caught in a fold, and I wrestle for a moment to free myself. This was not how I planned to tell Clint about his brother.

But that's not true. I never did have a plan. Which has been the problem all along.

"This is the ultimate betrayal." Clint glares at me. "You know what Lucas did to me, to my mother."

"I know. I know." I finally shake myself free and stand. "But, honey, she had pancreatic cancer. Back then, all the money in the world wouldn't—"

"No. You don't get to defend him. I was seventeen years old. Who had to figure out Medicaid and get doctors to accept her? I did. Lucas abandoned us. More than that. He took everything." Clint glares at the ceiling. "I was forced to move out of the house while she was in the hospital." His fingers claw at his face.

I want so badly to pull his fingers away, to absorb the hurt.

Instead, I watch my husband suffer.

"I've told you how she had to come home to that dirty, ugly apartment to die." He shakes his head slowly as if he's back there. "And she still asked for him."

I stand in front of him. The kindest, cleverest, coolest man I've ever met, but I've never been able to help him heal these wounds that he reopens every year. How can we finally suture him up? I've tried so many ways. He has to be the one to hold the needle.

He speaks slowly. "I don't want that man within a mile of you, of my family. I'll get a restraining order if that's what it takes."

Another thing I haven't told him. The suffocating "protection" that urged me to sign the legal order against Betsey continues to constrict.

I've strangled my family in the same way.

Without knowing the truth of what I've hidden, the invisible weight must have been bearing down on Clint. I take a deep breath and try one more time. "He wants to apologize. He wants to explain."

"How, Meredith? How can you take his side?" The sadness in his eyes pulls at the sorrow consuming my chest.

"Not for him. For you. I want this for you." I force myself not to reach out to him. "Your pain is eating you alive. You've chained yourself to unforgiveness."

He blinks at me, but the misery remains.

The doorbell rings.

We both take a step back like we've been roused from delirium. We stand for what feels like hours but is maybe only minutes—caught in the space between his past and two desperate futures. Only one of which will allow us to heal.

"I'll go," he finally grumbles as he opens our bedroom door.

Erika shuffles down the hall, sliding in her stocking feet. "Delivery for Mom."

I eye the white and blue bubble mailer in her hands as I stumble back against the bed.

Clint takes the package. "You know what this is?" He eyes me with suspicion.

"No, and I don't think now is the right time to—"

"Open it," Clint almost barks.

I glance toward Erika, and she must see the fear in my face because she charges forward. "What's going on?"

"Everything's fine," I say automatically.

"No, it's not," she fires back. "I want to know what's happening. I heard you guys yelling. You never yell." She crosses her arms over her chest. "Is this about me? It's about me. I'm not leaving."

Clint folds his arms too. They look the same. Both glaring at me but also, almost comically exasperated. Suddenly I feel a giggle bubbling inside me. Probably insanity. I'm losing my mind.

No more hiding. No more protection. "Hand me the scissors from the hall closet."

As Erika leaves, I check the return address. DCP from the Bronx.

I know it's from Betsey. Tomorrow is Friday. It's more than just instructions on where to meet her. It's a threat. But what more can she have over me? Lucas and I met only a handful of times. The last few to talk about Clint and his mom and for him to try to explain.

"Here." Erika hands me the scissors as I'm palpating the package. Feels like a small thin book.

I cut off the top of the mailer and slide out a white envelope with *Dranker Clive Photography* embossed on the flap.

Air empties from my lungs.

DCP, of course. These are the proofs from the bell ringing. I forgot. They told me they would overnight me the images. They wanted me to see the quality of their prints so I can decide on framed images as gifts. My knees quiver. I want to crumple onto my bed in relief.

"What is it?" Erika asks, leaning around her dad's arm.

"Pictures." The crackle in my voice sounds like a ligature around my neck has loosened, because of course it has. But the invisible noose hangs stiffly down my chest. "They're from the closing bell." I slide out the images.

"Oh, cool." Erika's tone indicates the opposite.

I turn and, after smoothing the comforter, start laying out the glossies. Suddenly, I desperately want to see our celebration, to be reminded of the joy. There's one with me clapping next to Phil as he presses down on the controller. There's also one of us after we switched—he's smiling at me as I look down at the podium with a huge grin on my own face. I love this image. I will definitely be ordering a larger print for my office. Hard to see my features, but the joy on everyone's faces is unmistakable.

I pick up the next one. I must have just noticed Betsey. My face betrays me. I thought I'd kept up the facade, but it's easy to tell in my tight smile that something is very wrong.

Clint suddenly bolts forward and swears.

"Dad." Erika swats at his arm.

Clint's face is white as he points to the final image.

37

"WHAT?" I stare at the posed picture of a few of the folks who hadn't been able to be on the balcony for the bell ringing but wanted their picture taken at the lower-level podium. They look happy.

"Candy?" Clint squints down at the image in his hands.

"What are you talking about?" Erika and I both strain to look around his shoulder.

"Is that Candy Thibeault?" Clint whispers more to himself than to us.

My stomach drops. "That's Candace Anderson, our head of security."

"No, I'll never forget her wide-set eyes and that pointy chin. That's Candy." His Adam's apple bobs up and down. "I grew up with her."

"Honey, that's your brother's—I mean, Lucas's wife. She's your sister-in-law." As I say the words, my mind starts to tick like the spinner on the Life game tucked away in the basement. If Candace has history with Clint, then what Lucas told me about how he met her was a lie.

"Lucas married Candy." Clint staggers back.

"Who's Lucas and who's Candy?" Erika tugs the picture from Clint. "You have family, Dad? I thought there was no one."

"There is no one." He yanks open his shirt drawer and throws a few tees in his bag.

"I don't understand. Why are you so upset? What did this woman do?" Erika walks over and stands next to him. "You tell me to talk to you. You say it's bad to keep it all bottled up. Take your own medicine. Talk to me." She looks over her shoulder. "Talk to us."

He sighs.

I hold my breath.

Clint's shoulders edge down as he looks at both of us. He blinks and then nods. A gossamer of fear begins to wrap itself around my heart.

We decide to go downstairs. I'm thankful we won't be having this conversation in our bedroom. Echoes of difficult conversations already crowd the space.

Erika pours us each an ice water. I can see the bounce in her step. To be included, to be trusted, gives a powerful sense of belonging. But I hope Clint knows what he is doing.

Clint takes a long swallow and then sets his glass on the side table. "Candy grew up in Maine too, in our neighborhood in Windham. She was Lucas's age." He gives Erika a sad smile. "Lucas was my brother. I don't remember a time of not knowing her as one of us. In the summer, we'd play outside all the time. The summer I turned ten was tough for my mom." Clint swallows hard but plows ahead. "Dad had left years before, but he still sent a monthly check. That summer they stopped. She always made excuses. I could barely remember our father, but Lucas, he remembered, and it made him angry." Clint stops talking, like he's back in his two-bedroom shotgun house watching his family crumble.

"Must have been so hard on your mom, so young and raising both of you," I say.

Clint sucks in his upper lip and then nods. "She refused any assistance and instead took another waitressing job. This one in the evenings. She always hated leaving us. And that night she was supposed to be home. We were outside. Before the porch lights even came on, my whistle blew. I was so mad. We hadn't even started playing. And then as I was trudging home, my brother's whistle blew."

Erika's brows furrow.

"That was how your dad's mom told them to come in at night. She blew a whistle. Two short puffs for your dad. One long for his brother. Your dad was younger, so he'd usually have to come in much earlier . . ." I let my words fall away as I feel the intensity of Clint's eyes on me.

He knows where I learned those details, because in all our years together, October fifth has been his day of remembrance but also his day of silence. He's only shared select details of his early years and never told me about the whistles.

"But . . . that night you both had to come home early?" Erika's words pick up the pace as if rushing her dad through a story with which she's losing patience.

"Yeah." He takes another sip. "Mom had been called into work. She left and Candy came over. She pulled on drawers and opened cupboards in the kitchen. Lucas marked her movements from the living room, but I confronted her. I pleaded for her to stop. She chucked me against the sink, and I dropped to the floor, my ankle twisting under me. Candy was only two years older than me, but she was bigger, and she was a bully. Her dad was a Marine, and she'd been taught how to fight."

He takes a large gulp of his water. "I later figured out she'd been looking for alcohol. She'd recently developed a taste."

"Hold up. You were ten. She was drinking at twelve?" Erika is back on the edge of her seat.

"She was the youngest. A girl with three older brothers. She was growing up fast. Anyway, instead of drink, she found my mom's cash. I didn't even know my mom kept cash. She'd probably been saving her tips. Candy took it. All of it. And left the old beat-up Folgers can in the cupboard. She threatened to kill me if I told. She was specific in her process, and I believed her." Deep furrows line his forehead. "Worst thing I could have done."

"Not tell your mom?" Erika eyes him over her glass.

"Believe Candy. Let her control me. She grew up rotten. I slipped away from her, but Lucas, he became her pet." Clint stares across the room at nothing, but everything from his past.

"Her pet?" Erika wrinkles her nose.

Clint's eyes find mine. "She's the reason."

I cock my head at him without dropping my gaze.

"She's the reason Lucas left us when Mom got sick. Why he emptied her account."

My arm automatically wraps around his shoulder. Oh no. He'll never reconcile with his brother. Probably why Candace, or Candy, has been so distant and defensive with me. She probably thought I knew. I thought she was just giving Lucas space to figure out his family.

Erika makes a small growling noise in the back of her throat. "What is her name again?"

"Candy Thibeault."

"I know her as Candace Anderson." I pull the pillow with the unstitched flower onto my lap. "She came onboard about a year ago. Highly decorated Air Force veteran. A few stints in Iraq, including

Desert Storm. Lucas recommended her. Phil hired her after our last head of security retired. She's never been very friendly."

"Why do you need a head of security, anyway? It's not like you work with actual money." Erika's face is bent low over her laptop, which she'd left on the coffee table. Does she have messaging apps on her computer? We probably should have checked. These devices are given out by the school, and we have no access or any reporting on what the kids are doing on them.

I sigh. "You're right, I don't deal in cash. Security isn't for that."

Erika doesn't press the matter.

"How long have Lucas and Candy been married?" Clint asks. His face looks like it pains him to continue to talk about them.

"I think just a few years, but he never told me he knew her from when you were kids. Made it sound like they met out in San Diego."

"Yeah, not surprising."

"I found something." Erika slides to the floor with her laptop on the coffee table in front of her face.

"What is it, honey?" Clint seems to be crawling back into dad mode. This day has taken a toll.

"An article in the *Windham Eagle*."

"Our local newspaper." Clint smirks. "Usually stories about the Rotary Club and tree lightings."

"This one is different. It's about Candy Thibeault. It's about how she got into some fight at a bar in Arizona while in the Air Force. She avoided a court-martial, but her brothers did time." Erika whistles. "This article is fierce."

"In the *Windham Eagle*? Doesn't sound like their usual." Clint leans over to look at the screen. "Who wrote it?"

"Kim Rourke."

Clint slowly nods. "Not surprising. Another victim of Candy's. She was a year above me in high school." Clint suddenly stands. "I think we should get out of here. I need new walls. Actually, I need no walls. Who's with me?"

Erika and I both rise to our feet.

I almost cry in relief at the resolve etched into my family's faces and then realize we will likely need every ounce.

38

CLINT CHECKS HIS WATCH AND SCOWLS.

"It's getting late; we still need to pack and probably think about dinner." I glance toward the kitchen.

"We could still leave tonight and likely drive around in the dark looking for this cabin. But how about if instead we eat dinner, pack things up, and then we can pick up Reid on our way to the cabin in the morning?" He looks back and forth between us both.

"Fine with me." Erika scoops up her laptop. "Not like we're on the run or anything."

Her words make me freeze. My fingers go instantly cold. I make fists, tucking them under my thumbs, trying to warm them. No, we're not on the run, but should we be?

"We've got that chili in the freezer." Clint walks toward the kitchen.

"I'll, uh, whip up some corn muffins, so why don't we eat in about half an hour?" I can't let irrational fear take over.

Erika nods and then shuffles from the room, her laptop hugged to her chest. "Back in a sec."

Alone in the kitchen with Clint, I can't help but press on his memory of Candy. "I had no idea someone else was involved in your brother abandoning you and your mom."

"And stealing from her." He then shrugs as he digs in the freezer. "Actually, I really don't know how much she was involved. But Candy was all my brother could talk about. He was always trying to impress her. I guess not so shocking they married, but you said it was recent?"

"Yeah. Military came first, I think. Did you know she joined up?"

He walks to the microwave. "I guess again, not surprising. She never talked about college. Her dad wasn't active duty when they moved to Windham, but the whole family breathed military. I think at least two of the older brothers were Marines."

"Interesting she went Air Force." I arrange cheese slices on a small platter of crackers to give Clint and me something to nibble on while I make the corn bread.

"Her version of defying her father?" Clint shrugs.

As I continue to ask him basic questions about Candy but avoid any more talk of Lucas, my mind is whirring on Betsey. Is there a connection between these two women that I missed? Maybe there's a reason no sign of Betsey was ever found at the New York Stock Exchange. My arm aches as I beat the gritty cornmeal. I open my mouth and then close it. I avoid telling Clint about the mess at Garman Straub only because we all need to eat. This is what I tell myself.

After dinner, we volunteer Erika to clean the dishes.

"You heading to your office?" Clint says almost over his shoulder as he heads upstairs.

Is that his way of telling me he still needs space?

"I'd like to talk for a bit." I try to keep my tone light.

"I've got nothing more to say about Candy." He plods up the stairs.

"Not her." I remain on the landing.

"Or Lucas," he says.

"Something else." I shove my hair behind my ears.

"I want to finish packing."

I bite the inside of my cheek. It's like we can act like we're going to be okay for only so long. The rubber band stretches and stretches. Then, like now, it releases and slaps back into my face.

"Come up, let's talk," he says but doesn't turn, just continues up the steps.

I stifle a sigh. I've become a wife who waits for an invite from her husband to come to her own bedroom.

"Do I need to sit down for this?" Clint says as we walk into our room.

Without the light from the large windows overlooking the huge oaks in the backyard, the room feels cold. "Maybe."

He nods slowly as he sits in our white upholstered chair with faint blue lines. I perch opposite him on the bed bench.

"I signed a restraining order against Betsey on Monday."

"Betsey, your sales manager?" His face looks like I've gone a bit mad.

"Yes. She was confronted here on Sunday, when we were . . . well, when we were supposed to be hiking."

"But you shot up to Rhode Island instead," he spits out and then takes a breath. He still hasn't forgiven me for fleeing.

We'd never argued with venom like that before. I panicked at who we were—a husband and wife who tore into each other. But I never should have given him the space he said he wanted.

"What do you mean she was confronted? By the police? Why didn't you tell me?" He waves his hands in obvious frustration.

"No police. Firm wanted to keep it in-house."

"In-house. Whatever. Why didn't you tell the officers that were here today? Did she have anything to do with the garage and car?" Clint runs his hands through his hair.

"I don't know. I don't think so. I mean, you know her. Seem like something she would do?"

"No, but I also wouldn't think you'd file a restraining order against her. What happened?"

I sigh. He's right, and he's not going to like any of this. "Candace and the team came to talk to Betsey. Calls were made. Garman Straub thought Betsey could be reasoned with. Like maybe firing her would settle her down."

"But I don't understand why she was here, and how they knew." Clint scowls at me.

"She'd been acting erratically all week. She'd blown off a conference she was supposed to speak at and stirred up the sales team by visiting advisors, unannounced. Apparently, while she was waiting for me to get home, she made calls to others on my team. A couple of them got alarmed by how desperate she seemed, and the security team was asked to swing by. They called me Sunday night after we got back."

Clint nods. "The night I didn't come home."

This fact has burrowed deep inside me, and then to hear he was out so late last night . . . have I lost him? I open my mouth to finally ask where he went on Sunday.

"Let's swing back to Betsey. What are we dealing with, Mer?"

I bite down on my lips and then answer him. "When I finally got back here to my phone—can't believe I left it on the kitchen counter—Hardwin asked me to let it lie for the night. They had me block her. Anyway, things escalated fast. At one point I thought she trashed my office. Hardwin had me sign the order Monday morning."

"Wow. You have to tell the police."

"There's more." I take a breath. "Betsey defied the order and came to the bell ringing. She had a package delivered to me. Client data no one should have."

"Why would she do that?"

"That's the question. She's given me until Friday to turn over information about our securities lending agreement or she'll come at you about Lucas." Simmering it all down to the basics, I wonder: *What if her demand is a distraction to keep me from discovering what she's really up to?*

"She's extorting you." The pain on Clint's face makes me look away. "That's why you told me about Lucas."

"Not the only reason, but yes." I spin my wedding ring around on my finger. The diamond catches the light, and a rainbow dances across the parquet floor.

"I'm going to put a pin in all the secrets you've been keeping from me—"

"To protect you. I needed to figure—"

"No." He slams up from his chair. "No. We're partners. You don't get to decide not to tell me what threatens you and our family. Because . . . oh." He slowly sits.

"What?"

"On the car—*times up bc*." Clint squints at me. "That could be Betsey Comarsh. She's telling you time's up to give her what she wants."

"I thought of that, but the timing is off."

"Of course, you thought of it but kept it to yourself. You never even mentioned it to the police. There could be a significant threat to our family out there, and you neglected to tell any of us."

I hang my head. How ridiculous everything I've done sounds when it comes out of his mouth. "I'm sorry. It just didn't seem like something Betsey would do. I wanted them to focus on the Danny guy and now this MJ. I've been more worried about Erika. The timing of all this has been excruciating."

He slumps back into his chair, staring past me.

"I needed time to tell you."

We sit in silence until he finally leans forward.

His lips I've kissed a thousand times are set in a hard line. We vowed to do this life together. I've made so many mistakes, including not trusting him with the truth, and he's disappointed me—refusing to believe my love for him and harboring all this pain of the past. We both have to be willing to forgive. Something he refuses to offer his brother.

Maybe he has nothing left for me either.

He holds out his hands.

I stare at them like they might be a trap.

"It's okay," he says.

I slide my cold fingers onto his warm palms.

"Do you want me?" His eyes find mine.

"Yes," I say without hesitation.

"No more secrets. No more deciding what I can or can't handle."

"Yes. I promise." The ease of the words masks the complexity of willingly opening myself up to what he might not want to see. "I love you."

He drops one of my hands and reaches toward my face. His fingers brush my temple as he wipes a lock of hair that has fallen in front of my eye. "You're so beautiful, so smart. I just don't see why—"

I drop to my knees and grip his face, placing my fingertips against the lines extending from his troubled eyes. "You have to believe me. We won't survive without your trust in my love. Twenty years . . . they will always separate us. I will never catch up. But I love the man you are and who you will become." I take a small breath. "Don't let the years divide us. We made vows knowing we'd never bridge the gap, so we promised to always celebrate it. You have to stop questioning."

Clint sucks in his lips as he leans his face into my hands. "Why do you never age?"

I press up and snuggle into his lap. "You complain because you have a younger wife who adores you?"

His arms wrap me as I feel the rumble of laughter in his chest. "A beautiful wife who loves the old man."

I kiss his neck. "I do love you. We will both continue to get older together." I whisper up into his ear, "Enjoy me."

His eyes widen as he pulls back to look into mine.

I wiggle my eyebrows. "Want to—"

"Oh yes." He scoops me under my legs, bolts from the chair, and tosses me on the bed.

39

FRIDAY

A ringing jars me from sleep. Blinking open my eyes, I see only gray light filling our bedroom. I pat my bedside table for my phone. I come fully awake as I say hello, but I hadn't even made the decision to answer.

My throat tightens as I realize it's Friday. It's probably Betsey. Time to confront it.

"Mrs. Meredith Hansel?"

"Yes?" I can't place the clipped male voice.

"This is Curt Stevens from WFBC News. Can you tell us about the graffiti on your garage? Do you fear for your daughter?"

I panic, not sure how to respond. He's asking me about my garage and my daughter. Who is this guy? "No comment." I poke at my phone three times to finally end the call.

My phone immediately rings. As I'm about to decline the call, our neighbor's name appears.

"Oh, my dear, they're swarming your house." The older woman's voice is almost breathless.

"What's that, Mrs. Varnella?" I silently slip from the bed and grab my robe from the hook in the bathroom.

"The reporters are everywhere." She makes shushing noises. "Napoleon's scared. Poor boy." She continues addressing the dog.

I walk to the front window and peer out. There, on our well-manicured lawn, stands a small army of news vans. A few reporters spill from the vehicles with cameras poised and microphones in hand. Why are they coming for us? Why is a house with a large blue tarp a target? Slow news day in Scarsdale. Ridiculous.

"I see them, Mrs. Varnella. Thanks for calling."

"I hope you can get rid of them. We don't have this kind of thing here." Her tone implies we have brought this with us. We've been in the house for over five years, but according to many of our neighbors who live in legacy family homes, we're brand new.

I know I should ask her if she's feeling all right or if there is anything she needs. The poor woman lives alone. Her only daughter rarely visits. "Thanks again. We'll talk soon." I hang up and put my phone on silent, pushing aside my abrupt dismissal of a woman who holds grudges.

Clint's tousled gray-streaked hair frames his peaceful face. Overnight stubble blurs his strong jawline. I run my finger from his perfect ear to his chin. His eyes slowly open.

"Good morning."

He hooks me around my waist and pulls me toward him, his hands at the ties of my robe.

"We have visitors." I say the words with as much nonchalance as I can muster.

"Someone's here?" He fists the plush straps instead of tugging at them.

"A bunch of reporters outside. Probably need to get dressed." I screw up my face.

My husband groans and then gently hauls me down until our lips meet.

Fifteen minutes later, showered and shaved, Clint decides to address the contingent on the lawn. He asks me if I want to join him. No. I prefer not to get my picture taken outside my house under some dodgy headline about defacement of affluent suburbia. He kisses me on my forehead and heads out. As soon as he's gone, I question if we should have called someone for advice. Are reporters like raccoons? If you feed them, do they just keep coming back?

I head to the kitchen to finish packing the perishables for the cabin. We can never have enough yogurt in our family. I throw in smoothie ingredients, including the goat whey stuff.

Within minutes, Clint is sauntering to the coffee maker.

"Went well?"

"I confirmed our garage had been spray-painted. Didn't know by who." He pours the coffee into a large insulated travel mug. "They knew about the car in the garage. That was a surprise. I told them the police were handling it and left."

"They were satisfied?"

"Definitely not," he scoffs.

"Then why do you look so smug?"

"Because I love my wife." He says it as if it ends all other matters.

Something releases in my chest. "You're a goof."

"I'm your goof." He takes a sip from his mug.

The thought of black coffee on an empty stomach makes my belly churn.

"I'm definitely peeved about the police leak though." Clint sets his mug down a bit hard on the granite. "Having all these reporters show up like this is ridiculous. But I just can't be bothered to care much." He leans up against the counter, looking very much like Erika yesterday. "I'd convinced myself you'd stepped out on me."

I finish zipping the insulated pack and straighten. I don't want to go back to this, but I'm here for it if it keeps him talking.

"Maybe not a full-blown affair," he says. "I refused to allow those thoughts, but the idea of an emotional affair has haunted me. I've been in protection mode for so long I forgot how to . . . how to see us."

"Weeks of therapy. Why didn't you say something?" I frown. So much wasted time.

"Didn't want the answer," he says with a frankness that looks good on him.

I nod. "How do we protect our marriage? How do we not find ourselves right back here?"

"I was wrong."

"I don't understand."

"I was wrong that talking to Lucas was worse than having an affair." His dark lashes close over his soft eyes.

I slide up next to him.

He speaks into my loose hair. "I do not want that man in our lives, but I do understand why you thought it would help me heal."

"Maybe we can find another way." I kiss that soft spot behind his ear.

"Gross," Erika calls from the living room.

"Hey, you're up." I squeeze Clint and then head to the pantry to grab oatmeal.

"You said early start." Erika slumps onto one of the stools. "And I'm missing the little bug."

We eat fast. Seems all of us are missing Reid. As I'm wiping down the counters, the doorbell rings. Erika is getting ready, and Clint is messaging a guy about picking up the Range Rover. I peek through the peephole at the two officers.

"Good morning, gentlemen." I open the door wide.

"Looks like you've had the pleasure of some of our local news teams." Officer Komoroski glances behind him.

One station-emblazoned SUV is backing up in our driveway, and another van is still parked on the street. No sign of reporters milling around. Perhaps they recognized the lack of story. With the police visiting, I wonder if they'll be back.

"You know anything about our yard party?" Clint's voice is both hard and loud as he steps into the foyer.

"Just what we observed as we drove up." Officer Colby's voice is flat.

"You make it a habit to share with the local news?" Clint is not backing down.

"Mr. Hansel, whatever you are dealing with here didn't come from us." The officer's voice remains calm, but there is a warning shaping his words.

"Can I offer you both a coffee?" I reach out my arm to usher them further into our home.

"No, thank you, ma'am." They both shake their heads.

"Let's head back into the living room." Clint turns and we follow.

As we all take our assumed seats, Officer Komoroski opens his notebook. No pleasantries. Clint looks annoyed instead of conciliatory. I lay my hand on his thigh and feel his quadriceps loosen.

"Danny Doward is out of town at his parents'. Seems unlikely he was involved, but we're keeping tabs." He pauses and then looks back and forth at Clint and me. "We also have an update on Marcus Anthony Jamal."

My heart stutters. The first time I hear my daughter's boyfriend's full name is from the mouth of a police officer.

"As you know, Marcus, or MJ, as he's called, is a freshman at Gatwich University. He is in the ROTC program and began military maneuvers on Sunday night. He's been with his platoon since then."

"So, he couldn't have been our artist?" I ask.

"Marcus has a solid alibi. Also, his phone has been in a secured locker since Sunday at two p.m. He won't have access until noon today." The officer reads the details from his notebook. "We've put in a request to gain access to his phone, as any images your daughter sent would constitute child pornography." The officer's mouth is tight as if he has more to say but isn't willing to share with us. "We'd also like to have access to your daughter's phone and the other one you saw her using."

Clint and I glance at each other. I'm confident he's reading the officer's tone the same way I am.

"If you do find a picture or pictures, exactly who could be in trouble?" Clint says his words slowly and carefully.

"At this point, if it is as you say, no one will be in trouble. Erika is free to take and possess the pictures she wants to take." The officer turns his gaze to me.

I begin to stand, but Clint lays a hand on my knee.

The officer raises his palm toward Clint, as if to make a concession. "Look, we're not trying to get a couple of kids in trouble; on the contrary we want to keep them and their personal information safe. We just need to know if there's anything on the phones that can explain the threats. After what was written on your garage and car, we may be missing a part of her story."

Words to defend the integrity of our daughter slam against the back of my teeth, but I keep them trapped, because I also know she's not telling the whole truth. Yet it's one thing for me to think it, and a very different gut punch to hear it from the police.

Clint nods, and I shove myself up from the sofa. "I'll grab the one I have."

As I pass the stairs, I slow my pace. Erika stands at the top. Tears flow freely down her face.

I grab the railing, my first foot on the step.

She thrusts her hand out, her face hard. Silence speaking. *Do not come.*

Bearing the weight of my inability to make any of this better for her, I proceed to my study and locate her device still in my bag.

As I walk back into the room, Clint is handing over the phone he confiscated from Erika. "The code is 4662. It'll need to be charged."

I hand the iPhone over to the officer, give him the code, and then clamp my jaws together. If I speak of work, the officers will start digging around. We'll lose the advantage of me knowing the data is real. Although at this point that's all there is. I have no theory. "Do you have other ideas on who could have defaced our property?" I ask.

"We do."

40

THE OFFICERS DECLINE TO SHARE THEIR THEORIES and I decline to hint at the craziness at work, because I really don't see anyone at my job doing something as bizarre and frankly sloppy as spray-painting my garage and car.

Clint and I return from the foyer after ushering the officers out.

Erika's muffled footfalls skid down the stairs.

"I knew MJ couldn't have been involved." Her voice is slightly husky as she drops her duffel bag at the bottom of the steps. Confident nonchalance exudes from her but is only a thin veneer over something else. Fear?

I want to wrap her in my arms, but Clint steps in front of me and shifts her old gymnastics bag to the side of the stairs and out of the way. "Sounds that way. Also seems like the police have another theory. Any thoughts on that?"

"I don't know. If you'd let me look at my phone before you gave it to the police, maybe I could have put together a theory." Her eyes shine out from a face that is freshly scrubbed and devoid of her usual makeup.

"Which phone? Which phone would have helped you determine who defaced our property?" Clint's eyes flare in similar fashion to our daughter's.

Instead of assuming my new normal posture of calming their storms, I lean toward Erika and bluff. "Come on now, you've been messaging on your computer this whole time. You don't need your phone."

Erika flinches.

I straighten before my shoulders can sag. She is hiding something. I take a tiny step forward, crowding her. "Tell us. Is it about this substitute or someone he's gotten involved? What's going on, Erika?"

She shifts her gaze between us. "I have been able to message on my computer."

Clint groans.

Our wily daughter continues. "What did you expect? I've had clients to reschedule, but none of my friends or anyone they know had any idea about the spray-painting. I mean, until the local news covered it."

"And this Danny Doward?" I press again.

"I have no idea. I've never contacted him online and Snapchat is blocked on my computer. Even if it wasn't, I agree with that officer, I don't think it was him. He was just a bully, and I was so stressed out." Erika sucks in her top lip and then glances up the stairs, like there's somewhere else she needs to be.

"Stressed about MJ?" I ask softly.

Erika hesitates and then nods.

Clint sighs heavily, likely thinking the same thing I am: she's still hiding something. Might not have anything to do with the garage or car, but we're done with the lying. "Erika, we need you to think long and hard about what you have and have not told us. It's not a matter of pride or preference; it's the safety of our family." He reaches for my hand and grasps it firmly in his. "Fortunately we've got a bit of time to get into all this. I mean, we're going to a cabin, and you don't have a phone." He scowls. "Or phones. Fifteen minutes, and we're leaving."

41

I RUSH INTO MY OFFICE to pack my computer and the files I need. My other laptop is already in my bag. Before I slide my work one in next to it, I boot it up to check my inbox. Maybe Phil has sent the information for the funds. Betsey will try and find me today, and I need to understand why she set all of this in motion. Of course, I've eliminated her threat, so this will be on my terms.

There's an email from Phil's assistant. I open it and notice two attachments.

From: Nonie Jenkins (Nonie.Jenkins@garmanstraub.com)
To: Meredith Hansel (Meredith.Hansel@garmanstraub.com)

Hi Meredith,

Good morning. Hope you are well and enjoying a few days of rest. Phil asked me to chase down both attachments for you: the securities lending agreement and an extract of

Q1 board minutes from almost two years ago. Please let him know if you need anything else.

We'll see you on Monday.

Best,
Nonie

Chase down is an interesting way of putting it. I shake my head as if trying to free myself from an annoying mosquito. I've gotten where I see conspiracy everywhere. She probably meant that neither of the documents was simply hanging out on her desktop ready to be sent off. But it did mean she probably had to ask someone for them, maybe Hardwin or someone on his staff?

I scan my inbox. No emails from Hardwin. That is suspicious in and of itself. On the two previous occasions I've been invited to board meetings, I've gotten flurries of emails from Hardwin, Dave, and Terrence prepping me for what to expect.

Everyone is so quiet.

I click on the first pdf, an electronically executed contract through our digital document management system, Remotesign. The agreement I had Alyssa and Temor review was just a few pages; this one is with our custodial bank and is over eighty with signature pages. It not only contains the lending agreement but all the custodial services for Garman Straub funds. This is what I expected.

The sound of Clint's boots slapping the steps has me scanning the document for an understanding of the agreement and anything odd. The first thing that stands out is a reference to an appendix of funds. I scroll to the end, but the addendum doesn't list the new ETFs. They must be catalogued somewhere else. I make a note and move forward. There is also language around the investor documents including the fund prospectus. Which all sounds appropriate. Investors need to be aware of both the risk and return. Another section is all the service agreements. This also sounds appropriate.

I check the date of the agreement. It was updated as we were launching. The ETFs should have been included, and we get regular reporting on the revenue we receive. I've seen the payments summarized in fund accounting. I continue scanning, and then I stop.

The room falls away. I no longer hear Clint and Erika moving around in the other room. Only the document exists. I lean closer and blink twice.

My name.

Clearly written into the management section of the contract. I've rarely seen a corporate contract at Garman Straub that names someone who is not an officer of the company. Maybe a title. But even more revealing is that there is no named counterparty at the custodial bank listed. Have I been hung out to dry alone? I send the file to my printer and open the other attachment. Although it's quite easy to guess what it contains.

I find the text. They officially recorded my name in the management of contract. A contract I've never seen until now. Did no one think this was odd? And if the ETFs are not included in the master contract with the custodian, then the contract Alyssa and Temor analyzed could have been drafted to make unsanctioned side deals. That's a big *if*.

"Hey, Meredith, you almost ready?" Clint pauses in my doorway.

I smile. I should draw him over and show him, but I don't. Ingrained habits die hard. "I need another ten minutes."

He cocks his head at me. I see him trying to be supportive and not paranoid. "You got it. Anything else you need me to pack?"

"Maybe a couple of games or puzzles we got last Christmas that we haven't cracked."

He nods and turns away.

I only skim the words surrounding my name in the board minutes—minutes for a meeting I never attended. Pages begin to spit out of my printer.

Today is Friday, Betsey's deadline for turning over the securities lending agreement. But beyond the obvious—the master document doesn't include the ETFs—something else doesn't sit right with what she's asking.

If I do hand over the custodial contract, I'm incriminating myself. She's asking me to deliver documentation that names me responsible for excluding my ETFs from an ongoing lending program with our custodial bank. An agreement different from what is written into the investor prospectus documentation, which makes it a crime.

But we *are* lending our securities. We're getting the income. I see the reports. We use it to offset our expenses. So, where is that money coming from?

I scrub the sides of my face with my hands. The recent income reports should tell us if the custodial bank is actually paying us. Alyssa and Temor can dissect them. I pinch the bridge of my nose. Maybe I have this all wrong, but something tells me someone is setting me and the ETFs up to take a big hit.

I quickly bang out another email.

From: Meredith Hansel (Meredith.Hansel@garmanstraub.com)
To: Alyssa Grant (Alyssa.Grant@garmanstraub.com)

Hi Alyssa,

Can you track down recent investment income reports we have received from Compliance for our ETFs? I'm not sure what I'm looking for. Anything that looks odd or may be missing from what we report as an offset to expenses in the prospectus. And while you're at it, see if you can locate the dividend replacement confirmations. We sign off on these, but I think they run through fund accounting. Legal set up the fee split. Please don't bother Hardwin or Terrence. If you have a friendly on their teams, maybe make some inquiries, but keep it quiet. Everyone is working hard, and I don't want to call attention until I'm back in the office. Use Temor as needed.

Best,
Meredith

I stare at the email. Should I draw Alyssa and Temor into this without giving them a heads-up that something may be very wrong? At this point, I don't think I have a choice. I have to know how I'm being framed.

But I delete the email and pick up my phone.

No paper trail.

"Hey, Alyssa." I ignore the niggle that I am still not entirely sure Alyssa doesn't know more than she's saying. I guess I'll find out. "I've got a project for you." I continue to draw her into the web that was spun for me.

Ten minutes later as I'm finishing packing my bag, something sticks as I try to position my notebook along the two computers. I pull out the envelope Betsey gave me in the Grand Central bathroom. My hand hovers above my trash can when I remember she said she wrote something on the back, maybe a number. I slide out the photograph and stare at the image, remembering the minutes after it was taken, after I left Lucas. As I rushed to the train station, Clint called. I didn't fumble for why I was late. The lie spilled freely from my lips.

"We really have to go, hon." Clint holds out his watch as he approaches.

I immediately flip the picture and read the number.

"What is that?" Clint comes around the side of my desk.

"Before we go, I need to make one call."

"To who?"

"Why don't you take a seat? I'd like you to listen. I can explain more in the car."

He scowls but sits on my office sofa. It pulls out to a surprisingly comfortable bed. I would know.

I lay my cell phone on the desk and dial the number, putting the call on speaker.

"You have reached the Securities and Exchange Commission. If you know your party's four-digit extension—" I blanch. My finger disconnects the call. The trembling starts in my hand.

"You're calling the SEC?"

I shake my head. Each number is clearly legible on the back of the photograph. I must have misdialed. Taking my time, I peck out the numbers again.

"You have reached the Securities and Exchange—"

I slam my index finger down on the red icon like I've just been bitten.

"I don't understand." Clint leans forward.

"I don't either." I take a huge breath and point to the back of the picture. "This is the number Betsey gave me to get in touch with her."

"And this is the first time you're calling it?"

"Yeah." I stare down at the numbers, trying to make sense of it.

"Call it again. Ask for her."

I don't respond. That's either the most foolish idea or perfectly brilliant. Something scratches at my memory of the Grand Central bathroom. She might have told me to do just that when she tried to give me the envelope. Either way, maybe we'll finally get some answers. Together.

"You haven't done anything wrong." Clint squeezes my quivering knee. "Talk to them."

"Might not be that simple. I think someone at Garman Straub has set me up. Maybe even Phil himself." And the SEC is not an organization to take investor fraud lightly. Their enforcement division isn't going to assume the portfolio manager of the funds didn't know what was going on under her nose. They won't hesitate to charge me with misconduct, at the very least.

"All the more reason. Everyone's made their trek and strung their tents. Time you at least took a look at the trail map."

A small smile curls my lip. I do need a map.

"We're in this together." He nods encouragingly.

I press redial, and we listen to the greeting again. I press zero to be connected to reception.

"How can I direct your call?"

I widen my eyes. "May I speak to Betsey Comarsh?"

Sounds of keys clicking come over the line. "One moment please. I'll connect you."

"Betsey works for the SEC?" I whisper but it feels more like a hiss.

Clint shrugs. My eyes are probably as wide as his.

"Meredith Hansel, is that you?" an older man's voice asks.

"Who is this?" I ask.

"Gaven Newal. Enforcement Division chief. Are you ready to come in?"

I stare at Clint. Am I? I can share what I've found, which all points to me perpetrating a crime against our investors.

His tone softens. "We just want to talk."

"Where's Betsey?" Not exactly the question I had planned to ask, but I'm not ready to answer his.

"One of the questions we have for you."

I suck in a yelp.

Clint flies up from the couch and disconnects the phone.

I stare at him like he's lost his mind. That was the SEC.

"Enough. We need to figure out what the—" He gnaws his lips and then breathes deeply, his body rigid. "We need to get our son."

I drop my phone in my bag and follow my husband to the car. Fear propels my feet.

42

ALMOST AN HOUR LATER than we originally planned, we scramble into Clint's beat-up Tacoma. I've kept my head down. I don't want Erika to see the panic in my eyes. We need to get to Reid. I yank on the seat belt, but it won't budge. I force myself to slow down and gently pull. After three tries, I'm able to click in.

Erika grumbles but doesn't complain as she climbs up into the cracked gray leather bench of the extended cab. Nothing luxurious about the smell of greasy metal and used basketball socks.

Clint slams the door behind him. "I've got the tarp slid back. Everybody good?"

"All set, honey," I say with false breeziness.

Erika makes a noise from the back seat that somehow means she's also ready to go.

Without discussing it, Clint and I decide to sit with our own thoughts. I've got lots of theories but none of them are good.

Ten minutes later as Stevie Nicks croons on the Tacoma's surprisingly good stereo system, Erika speaks up as if we've been talking the whole time.

"I can't believe I've been beating myself up for being such a bad judge of character when it wasn't even him."

Clint taps his thumb against the down volume button on his steering wheel.

"You really thought he spray-painted our garage and car?" I shift slightly in my seat as I can barely see her in my periphery.

"No. Never. But I thought he told." Her halting voice belongs to her much younger self.

A weight settles on my chest. "Told what?"

"But they said he hasn't had his phone since Sunday afternoon. So, he couldn't have," she mumbles. "We've been using tests we shouldn't have." Erika's voice shakes. "For tutoring."

"What do you mean? Tests you shouldn't have?" I stare out the front windshield.

"Stolen tests." Her voice is soft, but it's as if each word burns a brand into my brain. Having a daughter who started, with her friends, a tutoring business that helps other students is like a monument to my success as a mother. When my self-recrimination gets too harsh, I buff this statue of mothering achievement. If my teenager could be part of something so altruistic and, frankly, profitable, I was doing something right. But they have been doing it with stolen tests?

Clint squeezes hard, but my hand goes limp.

"Did you hear me? Your perfect daughter is a cheat." Erika's voice is caught between ages—immature but resolute, feisty but fragile.

"Oh, Aery." Her toddler name, which is more like a moan, slips from my lips.

"What tests?" Clint asks.

"I didn't know. I promise. I thought it was from a previous year, and I used it for all my one-on-ones." A sob makes her stutter. "I-I messed up."

"It's not your fault if you didn't know." We can fix this. She just needs to explain. We can help her get back on track.

"But then I did," Erika says with a drop-the-mic tone that makes my stomach churn.

"Someone found out?" Clint's tone matches his daughter's. He's put this together. Before me. Has someone been threatening her?

"I got a snap that MJ said we were stealing tests. Which is bull—anyway, they said he was laughing about it Sunday night at an off-campus party. But he couldn't have." She takes a deep breath. "Then these randos said I had to come forward and admit to cheating, but I didn't know. I mean, none of us knew." Her voice breaks and then she continues in a whisper, "At first."

"What do you mean—at first?" Clint grips the steering wheel with both hands.

"If I don't admit to it, they're going to ruin all of us. They're going to make it seem like . . . It was only a few tests . . . and when we really knew . . . But they'll make it seem like . . ."

I wring my sweaty fingers in my lap. "Why would you not tell us any of this before?"

"I thought I could fix it. I mean, this is so much more than some paint. This is my future. And I . . . I thought MJ told someone after I sent him the picture." Sounds of her crying fill the cab, and then she sniffs hard. "I need a tissue."

"Should we stop?" Clint asks me but then glances toward the back seat.

"No. Please," Erika utters between sobs. "I want Reid." She wheezes and then snuffles. "And I really need a tissue."

I pull my purse onto my lap and dig around inside, remembering I pulled the pack out while I was at my desk.

"Check the glove compartment," Clint mumbles.

I pop open the surprisingly disciplined glove box.

"I organized it last weekend before our, uh . . . well, for Sunday." Clint raises an eyebrow at me.

I nod as I pull out a small pack of tissues and hand it back to Erika.

"Do you want to tell us why you kept this from us? Even after what happened to our garage and car?" Clint's words are so tight, as if he strangled them as they left his mouth. Feeling obliged to ask the questions and wanting to know the answers are two entirely different things.

Silence from the back seat.

"Just tell us—did you send the picture over Snapchat? And only the one?" I suck in my lips.

"Erika?" Clint prompts.

"Yes, Dad. And just the one. Can we drop it? You guys know everything."

"Hardly." Clint slaps at the blinker. "Where did these tests come from and who have you been talking to?"

My fingers itch to pull out my phone to contact the police. And say what? That my daughter is being threatened online by someone who knows she profited from stolen tests and that they might have that picture she took? My head pounds. I guess they'll see the threats on her phone. They've likely not stopped since we took the phones away.

"This is *not* how we communicate as a family, Erika." Clint is frustrated, and I get it. Erika throws out shocking revelations and then clams up.

"Oh, really?" Erika blows her nose. "What happened on Sunday?"

I look out the window and wait for Clint to answer.

"I mean, no one communicated on that day. Not that I was overly disappointed not to have to go hiking, but then we were driving to see Grandma. Who definitely hates surprises." Erika's voice has rediscovered her teenage brawn.

I squirm in my seat. "She was happy to see us." Eventually. My mother's face when I showed up with the kids, unannounced, on her doorstep in Narragansett . . . She recovered well. She always does.

"Mom." Erika's eye rolling has a tone. "She stood in her doorway and wouldn't let us pass for a full minute. She was like the Praetorian Guard."

"What do you know about Roman bodyguards?" I scrunch up my eyebrows and swivel in my seat to look at her.

"Don't deflect." She sniffles. "Why did you bring Reid and me to Rhode Island when we were supposed to be hiking with Dad?"

The pot calling the kettle. My clever one is currently deflecting from talking about stolen tests. We need to get back to who might be threatening her online, but I want to do that sitting face-to-face, not awkwardly in the car. I sigh. "The weather wasn't great, and I just wanted to see my mom. It'd been too long."

Clint stays silent. Apparently, neither of us wants to step back through the minefield of insecurities and hidden truths that got us to our blowup on Sunday.

I glance up at my husband's face as he stares out the front windshield.

43

THE CAVERNOUS PACE UNIVERSITY GYMNASIUM has been transformed into a bustling showground of creativity and innovation. Playing host to a bunch of middle schoolers obsessed with robotics is no small or tidy undertaking. Crumbled Doritos and Cheez-It baggies litter the ground. I am struck by how many middle school kids were willing to give up their fall break and the rest of the school week to participate.

Most of the bleachers, usually occupied by cheering fans, are now collapsed, and the space is lined with tables adorned with laptops, wires, and a myriad of mechanical parts. Banners displaying the names of competing schools flutter overhead, adding splashes of color to the otherwise industrial setting.

In the center of the gymnasium floor, an elevated makeshift arena has been erected, complete with a maze of obstacles and challenges for the robots to navigate. Based on the stooped postures and splayed bodies huddling around their creations, the teams are making articulation adjustments and fine-tuning their programming.

Erika steps forward. "There he is." She points toward the arena.

At that moment, scratches boom from a central announcement system. "Good morning, parents. If you are just joining us, we are running a bit late this morning. We've had quite the battle to the final three. Instead of formal presentations, we're inviting you to just wander the space. Every team has a flag. Ask them about their experiences this week, what they've learned, and the amazing maneuvers they've learned to perform. In the center ring, Peekskill Junior High, Scarsdale Middle, and Pinepoint Academy are currently competing for the top prize. Enjoy your explorations."

"He did it." Erika claps. "Made it to the end. Little stinker. Head to the middle?" She strides forward.

A bumping sound over the speakers, and then the voice continues. "Your students should be ready to leave in about ninety minutes. We will make announcements then. Thank you."

"An hour and a half?" Erika abruptly stops walking, and I bump up behind her, taking the opportunity to give her a quick hug.

Clint and I glance at each other over her head. The tightness around his eyes says it all. "Yeah, we won't be waiting that long. I'll go talk to the coach."

Reid's dark hair, spiky in the crown, is about all we can see of him as he bends low over a thick laptop. Erika and I find a few metal chairs off to the side. The rest of his team is doing assembly, but as Reid is one of their strongest programmers, they probably know to leave him alone.

Erika suddenly straightens. "I'll be right back." She stalks away.

My eyes follow her. Two teen girls in identical wide-legged jeans and huge hooded sweatshirts stand about thirty feet behind us. They look familiar, but no names come to mind.

I shift back to watching Reid. He hasn't moved. So focused. I imagine him designing some elaborate air and space control system. He's always chatting about how plane travel will look so different in twenty years. I swallow the lump forming in my throat. We need to get us all out of here. I glance back at Erika and then pull out my phone to take a picture of Reid. A couple missed texts from Alyssa glare up from my screen.

We found something.

Call me.

44

I PULL MY BACK AWAY from the cold metal and perch on the edge of the folding chair. What if someone has actually committed fraud and set me up to take the fall? But why? There's no reason to take me or the new ETFs down. We've been so successful. Maybe the answer hides in our achievement. Could it be someone from outside the firm? A competitor? But they'd never have access.

The picture of Candace at the bell ringing pops to mind. She certainly has access, but it makes no sense that she, or Lucas, or even Meymack would want to see Garman Straub fail.

But would they want to see me fail?

Reid is still head down, but now another kid from his team, a small girl with braids the color of fresh habaneros, has pulled up a chair next to him and is also attacking her laptop. Reid takes notice and says something to her. She points to her screen, and he drags his chair around to sit close. Must be Bobby. I know the other programmer is new, quite brilliant, and has shockingly red hair. But I thought Bobby was a boy.

Reid must have wanted us to think so too.

No longer able to see either of their keen faces, I stare back down at my phone. Secrets are killing me. I make the call.

"Glad you rang. Some weirdness." Alyssa's voice is low, like she's someplace she doesn't want to be overheard.

"Tell me." My voice doesn't sound like my own.

"I think we may be acting as our own lending agent. Like perhaps someone at Garman Straub is negotiating directly with borrowers." Her words tumble out quickly over the line.

"Do you know who?" I ask.

"No. But based on some analysis, I think the rates may be quite favorable."

"Why would anyone cheat the funds?" I ask, not really expecting an answer.

"Maybe there's another way we're being paid."

"Like an illegal side deal or kickback?" As soon as I say the words, I want to claw them back. "What do you know about the borrower?"

"Enjoying your time away?" Alyssa's tone changes, all fake cheer. "I hope you're able to get in some good walks."

"Can't talk?"

"Not yet but hoping to. Thanks for encouraging me to enjoy what will be a beautiful weekend. I'm planning on leaving a little early today."

I rarely say anything about anyone taking time. Being surrounded by professionals makes it easy to rely on them to set their own hours. If they need to cut out, I don't micromanage. Of course, it usually has the opposite effect, and we all work late.

"Good. You should leave early."

"I'm on it."

"You're leaving now?" I pull the phone away and check the time. It's ten minutes after eleven.

"I know, Mom. I heard back from Aunt May. I hadn't realized she'd switched retirement homes down in Florida." Her pattern of speech slows as if she is plucking each word from a list. "The return address was new, but she hadn't mentioned anything in her letter."

A man's voice says something about Hardwin needing her in his office.

My heart pounds in my chest. "Just leave, Alyssa. Follow your gut. I think—"

"Look, Mom, I got to go. Oh, and Aunt Mackie wants to borrow your rose dishes. Love you."

The call ends.

I quickly flip to my Notes app and jot down what she said.

Aunt May

Retirement home in Florida

New return address

Nothing in letter

Aunt Mackie wants to borrow rose dishes

My breath releases in a squeal from my tight chest. I call Alyssa back, but it goes right to voicemail.

May and Mackie. She's such a bright one. I shake my head as I sit back down. All of this has something to do with Meymack. Of course it does. We got the ETFs on their platform in record time. What about the reference to Florida? Was that just to throw off anyone who was listening? But no. Meymack has a huge operations center in central Florida. If she got ahold of the investment income reports, maybe something about one of them referenced Meymack's ops center? *New return address.* Makes sense.

Except it doesn't.

Securities lending of even the hardest-to-source funds can't be that lucrative. Our individual positions are not that huge, and only some of them are valuable. Could it really be worth all this effort? It can't be about the money. Or it can't only be about the money.

I try Alyssa back again, and it again goes to voicemail. I send her a text to go home.

Maybe I should just call Phil and admit what I know. If he's in on this deception, do I even have a chance of getting out unscathed?

I know a lot of facts, but none of them fit. It's like I have pieces to a few different puzzles and no boxes to show me the pictures I'm creating.

45

A CALL FROM OFFICER KOMOROSKI lights up my screen. Perfect. He's the one I need to talk to. I quickly answer.

"We found something troubling." No niceties, just a gruff voice on the other end.

"Give me a second." My voice is surprisingly steady.

I grab my purse from the floor and walk toward the other side of the flattened bleachers. I realize if someone has been watching me, I might have looked rather distressed on my phone. As I tuck myself behind some storage canisters, I search for Erika. She is still talking to the two girls. They all seem to be smiling. More than that, their body language seems to indicate they are very interested in whatever Erika is saying. Her stunt with that awful substitute has likely given her some star power at school.

"Okay. I'm ready. What did you find?" My throat constricts on the word *find*.

"A tracker on Erika's phone. Quite a sophisticated one. We didn't even see it right away."

"A tracker?" The word inside my mouth is like a warm oyster. I almost gag. "Like, so, what, someone can track what she's doing on her phone or, um, does it show where she's going or what?"

"Both. We found it in the Messenger app and also tied to her location services."

I shut my eyes and then immediately blink them open. "Which phone?"

"Her iPhone. The other one she was using is clean."

My baby is being stalked. Oh, and the picture Erika sent. Who has it? My heart tumbles in my chest. It's as if someone is explicitly trying to destroy my family.

"What can you tell us, Meredith?"

"About what part?" I spit out. This is outrageous. Someone is coming after our daughter. I glance around the folded bleachers. She's still talking with those girls. Can they be trusted?

"You tell us. Maybe about the tracker? What do you know?"

"I don't know anything about a tracker. Someone is after her. How do we keep her safe?" My heart pounds in my chest. Is this related to the stolen tests?

Erika hasn't moved. She looks relaxed. Her head is slightly cocked to the side.

My palm is suddenly damp. I switch my hold and wipe my hand down my khakis.

"Meredith, we have reason to believe you're keeping something from us." The officer's aggressive tone feels like a shove. I keep getting shoved. Not the best way to gain my trust.

"What reason is that?" I feel the chill in my words as they leave my mouth.

"You asked for our help. Your home has been breached. Your daughter has been threatened. Help us put the pieces together."

He's right, of course. "I filed a restraining order against an employee on Monday. She'd been fired, but the firm felt I needed protection. Her name is Betsey Comarsh." I provide spelling of her name and agree to send full contact information after we get off the phone. My clanging heart begins to slow. Sharing this information with people who can help keep our daughter, our whole family safe, feels right.

"Where was it filed?"

"New York. Lafayette Street. Preliminary order was filed by Hardwin Donovan."

"And who is Hardwin D-O-N-O-V-A-N?" He barks the question more than asks it. His anger is not misplaced.

"Chief legal counsel at Garman Straub, where I work."

"We'll track down the order of protection. Why am I just hearing this now?"

"I thought this was all about Erika. This secret boyfriend and the trouble at school. I didn't think any of this had to do with me." I massage my left temple. "You said you had reason to believe I knew something. Why would you say that?"

"After a lucky break, we were able to trace the tracker. Meredith, we pinged a server in your office building in Manhattan."

I freeze. Erika's phone. Someone from my building is stalking Erika. From my company? No. These guys can be tough, greedy, and even mean, but they wouldn't threaten a child. There has to be a mistake. What did he say about a lucky break? Maybe it was just meant to look like it came from Garman Straub.

"Now whoever is tracking your daughter knows we have it. Maybe this Betsey Comarsh. Do you want to come in?"

"No. We're at our son's robotics tournament. We're fine." But we're not fine. The best thing to do might be to go to the station.

"Let us send someone to escort you back here. We can review the reasons for the protective order."

If I go in now, whoever set me up has won. Even if I can prove I had nothing to do with it, which is a huge *if*, they'll have time to clean this up. The board meeting is on Monday. I can't let this be resolved without me.

"Soon, but not yet. I'll be in touch. I need—"

"Actually, Mrs. Hansel, I'm going to have to insist. You said you are at a robotics tournament?"

"We'll come in soon." I rush the words and hang up the phone before he can tell me what *insist* means. I shiver as I turn off the ringer.

"Mom?" Erika stands behind me.

I slowly turn.

"Are you okay?"

I force a smile and shove my phone into my purse. "Did you see some girls you know?"

"Yeah. I came over to ask if we could walk over to the quad, but obviously something's wrong. Tell me."

"They found a tracking app on your phone," I blurt.

"A tracking app?" She yells it and then clamps her hands over her mouth. "The police found it?"

"Yes." I bite the inside of my cheek. I've just told a sixteen-year-old child that she's being stalked.

Tears rush into her eyes, making them appear as sapphires. They do look so much like Lucas's. From what I know, he inherited them from his mother, but Clint has never mentioned any resemblance. Has he hidden the hurt of looking into our daughter's eyes?

She wipes under her eyes, but only a few tears have fallen. "Do you know how long they've been tracking me?"

"No. I didn't ask." Should have. Such a smart girl. "But they traced the tracking device on your iPhone back to my office building."

"You're kidding. Someone at your work." She shakes her head. "Well, my phone has been with yours since Wednesday. And I was in the office twice recently. Once last week. Do you think whoever was tracking me is also tracking you?"

"Hey." Clint suddenly appears, and he's panting.

"You okay?" Erika squints at him. "Both of you are scaring me."

"I'm fine." He lowers his voice and leans toward me. "Did you tell anyone at work you were coming here today?"

I shake my head.

"I just saw Candy outside."

"Candace is outside?" I glance across the huge gym toward the closed wall of doors. No windows to the lobby. From this spot, we have no idea what threats lurk on the other side.

"Yeah, I went to the lobby to talk to Coach and saw her. She's got two big dudes with her. Doesn't look like she's here to watch the robotics final."

She knows it's Friday. Does she also know I'm getting closer to figuring out how they set me up?

"She's probably tracking Mom's phone." Erika roughly crosses her arms across her chest.

Clint steps back like he's been slapped.

"Yeah, Mom just found out my phone's been hacked. Hers probably too. At least now we know who's behind it."

"Let's not jump to conclusions."

Erika rolls her eyes like I need to keep up.

"But we should get out of here." I glance toward Reid, still huddled.

"Maybe we should just call the police?" Clint also glances toward the center arena.

"We could. I was just talking to Komoroski. He offered for us to come in."

Clint slowly shakes his head. "To tell them what?"

I love this man.

He'll do the hard thing with me. He won't give in without a fight.

"Exactly," I say. "We need to figure out who to trust."

"Well, I can tell you with certainty it's not Candy." Clint puts his hand on my lower back.

"Then let's go," I say.

All three of us look over at Reid, who is now standing behind his teammates as they finalize the staging for whatever task their bot needs to run.

"You grab him, and I'll pull the truck to the back entrance." Clint pushes me slightly.

"Wait." Erika grabs both our arms.

"We don't have time to argue about this," Clint almost shouts then lowers his voice to a whisper as a few of the parents look over at us. We're being watched.

"Mom's phone is likely being tracked and your truck is probably also. Whoever broke in and spray-painted the Range Rover had access."

Clint stills.

"Maybe that's even why they did it." She shrugs. "I watch a lot of true crime shows."

Clint and I look at each other. This whole thing may be well beyond us. I sigh in surrender. "Maybe the college has security or even police? I can call Komoroski back."

"I have another idea. Dad, give me your keys."

Clint shakes his head. "I'm not risking—"

"No. I'll get Ella to give us her Accord. We'll leave the truck here. She can bring it home later."

"She'll give you her car?"

"I've become a minor celebrity. I got this." She reaches out and takes the key ring Clint offers.

I glance over at our intensely focused son. "Reid's not going to be happy."

"I'll get Reid. I know the other coaches." Clint glances across the gym.

"And I'll stash my phone in one of the school's robotics bins. We can at least try not to be tracked. But what about all our stuff?"

"Candy just walked in. She's still on her phone." Clint keeps his gaze on her. "Let's leave the stuff in the truck. One of her guys didn't come in with her."

"Maybe watching the front or coming around back," Erika murmurs.

"Okay, have Ella go alone and bring her car to the exit by the bathrooms. Leave the Accord running, but don't have her take the truck. Keep it parked here. I don't want her followed. You both head to that side entrance." He points to the exit signs. "I'll meet you there with Reid."

Erika turns and sprints toward Ella.

Clint opens his mouth to call out, but then only mutters, "I'll get the keys later."

Candace, or Candy—hard to think of her by any other name—is still on the phone. I haven't even seen her look up. Her goon is standing behind her. They haven't moved from the entrance, but in moments they could be across the gymnasium.

Clint is now talking to Reid's coach, his back to the observers. Good man. One of the assistants is dispatched to talk to Reid. He's going to be so upset. Poor guy. At least he's got his programming done. He nods and then grabs one of the guys on his team and talks urgently before being led away. Suddenly I realize I haven't moved. Candace is off the phone and moving in my direction. I slip behind some of the motivational banners, careful not to trip over any of the power cords.

Clint and Reid are already at the mouth of the restrooms. Clint takes a brief glance behind him and double-takes when he sees me still making my way.

I'm sorry, I mouth. *Just go.*

Clint pushes Reid toward Erika, but I lose them as they run down the hallway. My husband's eyes widen as he looks behind me.

I run. As I make it to him, I spy a fire alarm on the wall. I flip up the plastic protector and yank on the red lever. The gym roars with a blaring alarm and flashing lights. I barely lose stride as Clint presses me toward the exit.

We round the side of the building behind a line of dumpsters.

Just as I am throwing my body into the old sedan, Clint freezes on his side of the car.

46

"WHAT IS HE DOING?" I yell to no one in particular.

"Pop the trunk, Mom." Erika shoves at my shoulder from the back seat. "Ella brought our bags from the truck."

Throwing myself across the front seat, I fumble around at the door and then along the floor. I have no idea where the button for the trunk is. I growl in frustration. I don't care about our bags. I just want to get out of here. Candace is not someone I want to trifle with, especially not with my family here. They represent a lot of leverage to get me to cooperate.

"RIP me, I have the keys." Erika taps my back. "It's okay—I've popped the trunk, Mom. Dad's got it."

As soon as I sit up, Clint slides in and starts the car.

I take one quick look around. All I see is Ella and the other friend nonchalantly joining the crowd of people leaving the gym. These girls are good at evasion and camouflaging in plain sight. I park the concern of how they've learned these protective skills.

As Clint pulls out of the campus, I reach back between the seats and squeeze both Erika's and Reid's knees.

Reid smiles, but his tawny eyes are huge behind his flurry of lashes. Women would pay big money for those.

"How are you, buddy?" I ask.

"Who died?" Reid's voice is quiet and teary.

"No one died, lil' maggot," Erika says.

Not the first time she's called him a maggot, an egghead, even a turd, but can we all try to be kind, especially today?

"Fart face," Reid shoots back.

I rear up to scold, but Reid continues to talk. "Dad said someone died. Why did I have to leave early?"

"I said *family emergency*." Clint keeps glancing in the rearview mirror. "Anyone following?"

I kept watch out my side mirror as Clint made the last few turns. "Don't think so."

Reid tries to spin around in his seat belt. "Who would be following us?" he asks with something like glee in his voice. "And why are we in Ella's car? Are we being chased? Like for real?"

"How do you know we're in Ella's car?" I don't know how to answer his other questions.

"Erika said when we got in." Reid hops up and down in his seat. "We are being chased. What did we do?"

"We didn't do anything," Clint barks. "Now I need—"

"Then what is going on? Why did I have to leave?" Reid's voice matches Clint's intensity.

"Hold on, Reid." I turn back to him. "I know this is confusing. First, we've got to help your dad." I put my hand on Clint's tense arm. "What can I do?"

"Where am I going?"

Oh, right. Good question. We can't go home. Definitely not to the Poconos. We need to get somewhere safe for a few hours so we can figure out who to trust. Someone at Garman Straub has set me up to take a pretty big fall. Who knows what else they've done to cover their tracks?

The sign for Taconic State Parkway looms ahead. "I don't know. I think you're doing the right thing. Driving until we figure it out."

"Like most teen cars, the gas is on less than a quarter," Clint grumbles.

"I have some cash if we have to stop." I dig into my purse.

"Can we go back to Grandma's?" Reid pushes his face between the seats. "She said I could take the boat out next time."

"That's one of the first places they'll look, doofus," Erika says.

"Who's looking? Someone tell me something," Reid moans from the back seat, his frustration palpable.

As Erika begins to explain about bad actors at my job, I lean over to Clint. "What do you want to do? Hotel? Do you think they're tracking our cards?"

"If they're tracking phones and maybe my truck, I don't think we can trust our cards." Clint rubs his hand down my thigh.

Suddenly, I'm very cold. I lean into him. "I'm not sure who I can even call."

"Mom, maybe if you just explained to your boss about how you didn't do anything wrong. Maybe you can help get them caught," Reid says.

"Good idea, bud. We just need to figure out who to explain what to." I dig around in my computer bag, unsure what I'm looking for. I pull out a fresh pack of wet wipes.

"Do not clean Ella's car," Erika growls from the back seat. "Seriously, Mom."

"I wasn't going to." But maybe I was. I don't even know. I shove the packet back in my bag. "When we give the car back, maybe we can have it detailed for her."

"Not a bad idea," Erika mumbles.

"Still not sure where I'm driving." Clint glances over at me.

I take a quick breath. "You're the only one with a phone. I don't have anyone's number memorized. Maybe we can just show up at someone's house within a quarter-tank radius?"

"Hate to bring this to anyone's doorstep." The muscles in Clint's jaw pulse.

"True." I wilt back against my seat. "Maybe a vacation place. Who has one close?" I squint as I can think of a few folks who have unused ski places this time of year in Vermont and Maine.

"Can you call Rob on my phone?" Clint switches lanes without a blinker.

"I think a black SUV is following us," Erika pipes up from the back seat.

47

I CHECK THE SIDE MIRROR and then spin around in my seat. What SUV? I finally see it three cars back. "How long has it been there?"

"I think Dad's last two turns." Erika's voice is soft.

"I'm taking the 134."

The exit is in two miles. Not like we can evade them. Best to try to figure out where we're going. At this point the police station is better than Candace and her guys. I snag Clint's phone from the cup holder in the center console and find Rob's contact. After pressing it, I hand it to Clint.

"Hey, wondering if you're using the cabin today."

I replay Clint's words, delivered with Oscar-worthy ease. Rob has a cabin? Since he moved back to the Hudson Valley from Georgia, he's been trying to find his way. He sold a specialized backpack business. His expertise as an outfitter for the Appalachian Trail served him well with the kind of gear hardcore hikers needed. Rob is full of ideas, but I didn't think he'd really decided to settle.

"And Mer and the kids. Maybe through the weekend." Clint responds to something Rob has said with a part grunt, part chuckle. I'm not sure Rob is my biggest fan, so probably smart not to put it on speaker. My career has never sat well with Rob's notion of a well-lived life.

"I know you say that. I don't want to overstep." Clint lowers his voice. "Look, mention to no one that we're heading there." He chews on his lips. "Yeah, nobody."

I point to the exit he said he was going to take.

Clint shakes his head. "Thanks, buddy. Yeah, of course." He says his goodbyes and then hands me the phone.

"Are we going to Uncle Robbie's cabin? Do you think the raccoon babies are grown?"

"You've been to Rob's cabin?" I spin around again, taking in the faces of all my family.

"I've only been once. It smells like a hamster cage," Erika says. "Hey, that was the SUV I thought was following us."

I glance over at the car beside us. A woman in a ball cap is driving alone, talking animatedly.

"I've been watching it catch up from the passing lane. I think we're in the clear." Clint pulls off onto the Bryant Pond Road exit.

"So, Erika has been to this cabin once. What about you guys? How many times? And where is it?" I keep my tone light, but I'm a bit shook at not knowing anything about this place.

"Dad and I've gone a few times after school, but we've never spent the night. Can we?"

"Probably, buddy," Clint says. "We're only about twenty minutes away."

"You already knew we were coming here?" Tall pines hug both sides of the road.

"Strong possibility. Unless you had another idea." Clint pats my leg. "Look, Rob's only had it for a few months. I've helped him fix it up. It was a disaster."

"Who knows you've been up here?" Certainly not me.

"Don't think many, if any, even know of it. Much less that I've been there."

"Is it decent?" I ask but it hardly matters at this point. It gets us off the road without putting any of our friends in whatever danger we're in.

"It's cool," Reid says. "Raccoons live in the woodpile by the bathroom, and you have to eat on the floor."

At least there's a floor, but an outhouse? I'm not a big fan of spiders, and I imagine an outdoor toilet room is exactly where they live. I try to refocus on the fact that we have a place to go. Something crawls up the back of my arm. Stifling a yelp, I grab at the imaginary tickle.

"It's not the Waldorf." Clint swerves around a fallen branch as the road grows dodgier. "But it's off the grid and will give us some time to figure out our next steps."

"Maybe we should just go to the police." I watch the trees rush by my window.

"I agree, maybe we should," Clint mutters.

I suck in my lips. The police can protect us, but they also won't give us time to figure this out. How deep is the setup against me? Pretty sure it's well beyond me losing my job if the SEC wants me to come in. A federal indictment could follow.

None of that matters if my family is in danger.

"The cabin will give us time. I think we should take it." Clint squeezes my thigh.

I put my hand on top of his. "Making a call."

I grab Clint's phone, enter the number from the card, and get Officer Komoroski's voicemail. "Hi. This is Meredith Hansel. Clint, our two kids, and I are headed to a friend's cabin. I'll text you the address. We'll be in touch soon."

"You didn't tell them about Candy." Clint's hand turns up and I lay my palm in his.

"Who's Candy?" Reid's voice sounds excited again, like this is all an interesting puzzle to solve.

"I didn't get through all the details," Erika says. "And scoot over. Stop jumping on me. You stink. Did you shower?"

"They didn't make us," he says with so much joy I almost laugh. Almost. Because it wasn't clear from the description if the cabin has a shower.

"Well, let's get you cleaned up first thing when we get to the cabin," I say hopefully.

Reid grumbles back at his sister.

I ignore the back seat and speak to Clint. "How do I summarize all the ways I've been set up at work? I don't even get it yet. I think as long as Komoroski knows where we are . . ." Not sure how to finish the thought. As long as he knows where we are, he can have someone pick us up and arrest us. Or he can more easily pull together the crime scene if something happens to us? I look in the side mirror for any dark SUVs.

"We're only a few minutes away." Clint holds on tight. "We'll be fine."

48

THE TIRES BUMP AND CHAFE along the deep grooves of another dirt road. The sedan feels lower to the ground than before we made that last left. I grit my teeth as I anticipate gouging our undercarriage. Ella's undercarriage. We keep going deeper into an old-growth pine wood.

Finally, nestled among dozens of tall trunks with what look like Christmas trees sprouting out their tops, we pull up to an old cabin.

Like many, many decades old.

A knot of apprehension tightens in my stomach. Dark, uneven siding is frosted with green moss, and the roof over the porch, running the length of the low-slung building, looks ready to crumble. I glance back at Clint, but he's already stepped out. I open the door and take a deep breath of earthy crispness. It's cooler here. I stare down the long drive. A tiny wave of relief like a stray breeze washes over me. No one has followed. Yet.

With cautious steps, I approach the weather-beaten porch

planking. I want to cry out to the kids to be careful where they're walking, but the wood is surprisingly firm under my feet.

"Isn't it cool, Mom?" Reid twirls around. "It was built like a hundred years ago."

"Sixty." Clint grabs the bags from the trunk.

"I'm going to check on the raccoons." Reid disappears around the side of the cabin.

Clint and I both call after him, but Erika says she'll stay with him.

From a small zippered pocket of his day pack, Clint fishes out a ring of keys.

He has keys to Rob's place. I swallow my hurt.

Clint unlocks and pushes open the larger-than-normal hardwood door. "We've got some shingles and siding to replace, but the bones are solid."

Leaving the crisp forest aroma of pine, the cedar scent of new wood fills the air. My breath catches in my throat. Gentle shadows are crossed by shards of sunlight that dance across a wide-planked floor, partially covered by a round woven rug. Its fibers are a symphony of earthy tones and a subtle leafy pattern. A stone fireplace stands proudly against one wall. Beside it, a collection of weathered logs anticipates a flame. A cozy nook is nestled in the corner, beckoning with its bookshelf of novels and other books.

I trail my fingertips along the smooth surface of the cedar paneling, marveling at the craftsmanship that has gone into its creation. My eyes immediately seek my husband, but he's back outside, probably checking on the kids. I take in the quaint furnishings and simple yet homey decor.

Anger erupts inside me.

"We'll make this work," Clint says as he steps up behind me.

"Whose cabin is this, really?" I whirl around and shove my hand at his chest, eager to feel the beat of his heart as he answers me.

To his credit, he doesn't lose eye contact, and his heart stays steady. "Rob knows a guy. His late father built it. It needed a lot of work."

"And who owns it?" I flail my aching arms around, taking in the gleaming rough-sawn mantel and concrete waterfall island.

"Rob is the only one on the deed." Clint swallows. "But he's preparing papers to give me half ownership." His words tumble over each other. "Rob bought it for next to nothing. After selling, the old guy just wanted a place he could still come and fish a couple times a year. There's a great pond out back. He hasn't made it up yet, but I can't imagine him taking too many weekends."

"I'm not worried about the vacation schedule, Clint." My words shoot out from between my clenched teeth. "Why is Rob putting you on the deed?"

"We've both made significant investments of labor and materials."

"When?" I ask, with my breath leaking out of me.

"You work a lot, Mer."

Reid runs up and hugs his dad around his waist. "The baby raccoons are gone. Erika said they're on their own now. But can we try and feed them tonight?"

"Hey, Reid. Why don't we go check out that hidey-hole in the bedroom where we put those old games?" Erika tugs at his arm.

Reid crushes his face against his father's side, looks up at him with devotion, and then allows Erika to drag him away.

I quickly mouth thanks to our daughter and then glare back at my husband.

"You lied to me," I whisper.

"Huh, ditto, babe." Clint's sheepish look is changing into brazenness. "I think we stopped telling each other about our lives many months ago, if not years." He's in for it, if I want to go there.

Righteous anger burns inside me, tempting me to give it oxygen and fall into the pattern of a failing marriage. The urge potent and the words juicy across my tongue.

Except he is right. I fully realize how righteous my anger is not. We have patently stopped confiding in each other. Not only the stuff that would set each other off, but we've hidden our dreams.

Clint has wanted a cabin in the woods for longer than I've known him. We've taken trips back to Maine exploring seashores, lakesides, and remote forests. We've vacationed in Vermont, New Hampshire, and even up into Canada. Our imagination spooling out between us. Before Clint, I figured vacations were just warmer or less congested versions of real life.

Clint introduced adventure.

The cabin is beautiful.

"I knew as soon as I saw the cedar shiplap." My voice is still low.

"You remembered?"

"I'd almost let myself forget." Tears dampen my lashes, but my heart beats steady. "Show me."

"Do we need to—"

"Show me quick?" A little laugh bubbles out of me. Underneath what I now know is hurt is tremendous pride in all that my husband can do.

"Rob and I basically rebuilt the interior this summer. If you can believe it, it was in far worse shape than the roof and siding." Clint's eyes widen. "There's a small solar array on the back side of the roof, which we reshingled, and another one in a little clearing just behind us. We also have a generator if needed. We can come up in the winter, but we'll see how much of that we actually do."

"When did he buy it?"

"April."

I think about the last six months as he takes me through the open-plan kitchen and living space. He shows me the new windows they got at a Habitat for Humanity reclaim store. Never has he hinted about an entire property he was renovating. A property he will own. We will own, I suppose.

But did he really never tell me?

A conversation last Mother's Day itches the back of my mind.

"You did try to tell me about this place. We were playing—well, getting our paddles handed to us at pickleball. My mom's latest guy friend . . ."

"Howard."

"Yeah. Howard, 'your most successful real estate partner in all of Narragansett,'" I parrot. "He interrupted your question about buying properties with friends. He never let you finish."

Clint closes the electrical panel and turns toward me. "That wasn't the only time I tried to tell you. I've actually said out loud to you that I was going up to the cabin." His eyes stay on mine as I sift through a summer of memories that revolve around fund sales and work calls.

An ache pulses in the back of my throat, and I swallow. He tried telling me earlier in the week—something about Rob and a grant. We got interrupted, and I never asked him a thing about it.

"Is this where you came last Sunday? After our fight?" I ask. Until now, I've not wanted to know the answer.

He nods.

"I'm sorry, Clint." I step toward him and pull him toward me.

"Hey, Dad, is there Wi-Fi? I want to see if our team won." Reid creeps back into the main room.

"No cell service or Wi-Fi, and as much as this feels like family vacation, your mom and I have some things to figure out. We're going to need some time to do that."

My stomach clenches. Definitely off the grid. Are we safe, or did we back ourselves into a cedar-walled corner?

Reid moans.

Clint interlaces his fingers with mine. "We do have a satellite phone we can hot-spot, but . . ."

"How about some food?" Staying off the grid sounds good, for now. I pull out options for sandwiches and lots of fruit that I start to cut up.

As we are finishing up our early dinner, I comment on the changing of the light outside. It looks like filtered gold.

"Can we go to the pond?" Reid twists around and sprints to the window.

As much as I want everyone to stay inside, stay safe, I also need a moment to think. I've gotten so obsessed with work, I've not paid nearly enough attention to Erika, who has barely eaten. I wonder if she is thinking about her tracker being linked back to Garman Straub and about whoever is threatening her over these tests . . . "I think there is just enough daylight left. Why don't you and Dad go check it out?"

I ignore Clint's confusion as Reid whines, "But you're the only one who hasn't seen it. You have to come."

"Thanks for thinking of me, honey, but I'll see it later. Erika and I need to talk." Feeling Erika stiffen in my periphery, I keep my eyes on Clint's. "Erika, please take your brother back to the bedroom to help him get ready for the pond."

Turning my back on the kids, I hear them shuffle from the room.

"Meredith, I think—" Clint begins.

"I have to figure out this connection with the tracker and Garman Straub." I keep my voice low, but an urgency threads my words. "Erika's not going to talk to you about the picture. You're her dad and you've seen it. I haven't, and we need to figure out what she knows. How the picture and tests might be related. I mean, it doesn't have to be the pond." Suddenly the idea of Clint more than ten feet from us feels like a bad idea.

"All right, you win, but only because I can see the approach to the cabin from the shore. I'll leave the satellite phone here. Any car comes down that road, call the police. There's a sheriff's office right over the ridge."

While tamping down the panic fluttering in my chest, I nod.

Minutes later, Clint leads Reid, with an old tackle box banging against his knees, down a pine-needle path to the left of the cabin.

I've split us up.

During every horror movie I've ever watched, this is the moment I yell at the screen.

49

"ERIKA, I WANT TO TALK ABOUT the police finding the tracker on your phone." I place an optimistic bowl of Parmesan crisps on the island between us.

"Did they say more about who or when they did it?" She settles onto a wooden stool, but her hands remain in her lap.

"No, but do you think it's simply a coincidence—the picture your dad found, the tests, and now this tracker on your phone?" I stifle a shiver. "We need to figure this out, Erika, and I need your help." I grab a chip and run my thumb along the gnarly edge. "What haven't you told us?"

She strangles the hem of her T-shirt in her hands.

I pop the snack in my mouth but forget to taste it. I try the therapist's counting technique, but Erika remains silent. Impatience gets the best of me. "Come on, sweetheart, we all have to be on the same side."

"I need to unpack." She slides off the stool and trudges to the bedroom she's sharing with Reid.

I cover my mouth with both hands. We used to play the silent game when Erika was in grade school. I'd just want a few moments of quiet in the car. Erika would be prattling along about a Blow Pop she had stashed at home, her teacher's new haircut, or the fact that horses can't burp because the air only goes one way. I'd challenge her to silently sing an absurd tune like "Rudolph the Red-Nosed Tiger" without a mistake and then tell me when she'd done it. The rule was she'd have to start over if she sang *reindeer*. While my hands unclenched the steering wheel, Reid would intently watch his sister's knotted-up face from his car seat. I needed a few moments of peace so I could think, but about what? Did I wish away her words?

Please talk to me, sweetheart.

I walk to her room and lean against the doorjamb. She turns away and shoves a handful of clothes into an old dresser. The wood scrapes and buckles as she tries to push the drawer back in place. Blowing out an exasperated moan, she slumps against the dresser, her back still to me. "I don't know where to start."

Responses crowd my mouth, but I stay silent.

"It has nothing to do with the picture."

I open my mouth.

Erika glowers. "Stop. I know parents freak out about this. It was stupid. I shouldn't have done it. But it was only one picture." She throws her hip into the drawer. It finally closes. "I even tried to tell you."

I think back on her quietly crying on the phone. I nod.

"When the snaps started on Monday about the tests, I couldn't believe MJ had told. I mean, it was like rejection and betrayal all crumpled up and thrown in my face. I hadn't told anyone else about the tests. It had to be him. Dylan was still so upset, and we hadn't even admitted it to Sophie." Her knees look about to buckle.

"So, maybe they figured it out by the tracker on your phone?" Monday was after Betsey was removed from our lawn and I reluctantly filed the restraining order. The tracker had already been set on Erika's phone, and they decided to go after my family. Heat broils me from the inside.

I risk approaching her. She allows me to lead her to sit next to me.

"That first test was dropped into my lap by a new kid." Her face in anguish turns to me. "He was having trouble in geometry, and I didn't question it. I didn't even think to. Then his friends started bringing in other tests, and I went with it. We raised our rates to tailor our approach. Dylan is a master at this cash app, Hippa, and was using the social component to broadcast our success. Even people who'd turned off the feature were seeing our growth. He could see trends on Hippa that matched all the requests we were getting. He's kind of a genius. But I've stopped even going into Hippa. I just can't use the money."

The food trucks—why she asked Clint for cash. The heaviness in my chest turns cold. They were cashing in on stolen tests. A deep desire to escape the words I have to hear makes my muscles tense. "When did you know?"

She tents her hands over her face and then lifts her gaze to the ceiling. "A student we helped last semester brought in her graded test to try to figure out what she did wrong. She was upset because it was hard, but a bunch of kids did well, so she was left at the bottom of the curve. It was the same test. I knew, but I waited to say anything."

"Why?" I whisper.

"Because I had no idea how these kids got their hands on current tests, and by then we had gathered a handful. It could ruin us. We needed a new policy or something. No one would believe we didn't know."

"Erika, we would have believed you."

"That's what MJ said. He was helping me figure out what to do. How to make it stop. He was also jammed up about maneuvers this week. I sent the picture and then I heard nothing." She wipes hard at her wet cheeks. "Until the weird messages." Her voice breaks. "And then the threats."

"When? When did the actual threats start?" I whisper.

"Monday night."

After I told Candace about Betsey's thumb drive.

"All on Snapchat. I'm sorry, Mom." Erika curves her back and raises the bottom of her sweatshirt to bury her face. She makes herself small.

No. Oh, Erika, you are not small, or weak, or a victim to be taken advantage of.

I pour everything into my words to my daughter. "We will not let them hurt us. I will protect you with everything I have."

"How, Mom?" Erika's eyes are red, but they are no longer buried in her shirt.

"First, by trusting each other, including Dad." I glance toward the window. "No more secrets."

She nods.

"And second, by going on attack. We're going to figure this out, and we're not going to let anyone control us." I grab her ice-cold hand and squeeze. "I think they were watching what you were doing on your phone—"

Erika starts to get angry again.

"I know. It's diabolical." I take a deep breath. "Did these snaps ever mention the picture?"

"No. Just the tests. Since the tracker was on Messenger, they wouldn't have seen it. Right?" Erika's earnest face makes my eyes sting.

I hug her to me and then quickly release. "Exactly, and I'm thankful for that. But it feels like these scumbags are using your test issue to get to me. I need to figure out who's trying to ruin us both."

"I have to help." Erika's back straightens, and her eyes level with mine.

^ ^ ^

Half an hour later, we hear Reid's voice as he and Clint traipse down the path to the cabin. Erika and I'd gotten so absorbed in the thumb drive data, I'd forgotten about being vigilant. If someone had slowly approached the cabin from the drive, would I have even heard them? I clench my fist in my lap.

"We're fine, Mom." Erika lays a hand on my tense arm.

I nod as I study the data tables on the screen. After I told her about the data that Betsey gave me, she wanted to see if she could help determine who created it. She's come up with some good ideas for looking at the client data, suggesting maybe there were connections between the coded investors like age or investment experience, but none of the analyses have panned out.

I need to find a way out of the noose that has been discreetly winding its way around my throat and our daughter's.

Clint and Reid enter the cabin, and Reid immediately starts telling us about the fish they almost caught. How he really wanted to go out in the canoe, but Dad made them stay on the dock. As he's rambling, Clint catches my eye and mouths, *Heard something.*

Worry apparently washes over my face because Clint shakes his head and speaks over his son. "Hey, why don't you guys show Mom all the games in your closet. Maybe we can play one. I'll be right back."

I want to scream at him not to leave. It was a mistake before. We just need to hole up inside or maybe leave together. We can't take these chances. Our strength is in staying together.

But then I see Reid's knitted brow and pursing bottom lip. "Yeah. I'd love to see what you guys have up here. Dad'll be right back." I drag my eyes away from watching Clint shut the door behind him.

After perusing the options, Reid and Erika decide to set up a card table between the two single beds and tackle a puzzle called The 1990s. I got it for Clint a few Christmases ago. I thought we might have fun. The nineties were my growing-up years. I started high school in ninety-eight, the same year Clint was moving back to Maine to join the game wardens after a decade in Virginia as an EMT.

Erika flips up the cover and examines the patchwork of small images.

My head swivels again toward the front door. Clint has been gone too long. I can't leave the kids to look for him. He has to return soon. I drag my eyes back to the kids as they dig through the pieces looking for the edges. Something worms into my memory.

I was so excited to see his face when he opened the puzzle that Christmas morning.

"The rise of Teletubbies, Mariah Carey, and Bill Clinton. Oh, the memories." Clint chuckled at the cover.

"What's the cast of *Friends* doing on there?" Erika pointed to the upper left corner of the box.

"*Friends* first aired in the mid-nineties. Way before you were born." I began to hum "I'll Be There for You" badly.

"No way." Erika's horrified face had us all laughing.

"First time I voted for an Independent in a presidential election. Ross Perot was my guy. Twice. Wasted votes." Clint shook his head.

At the same time Erika asked about the blue Beanie Baby, Reid spoke up. "We voted in school to name Mr. Whiskers." Reid got up close to the cover, looking at where he saw his dad point. "This guy has funny ears. Mommy, who did you vote for?"

If I'd only answered Erika instead.

The front door opens, and I startle.

Clint walks in and sets the lock before turning toward me. The tension has melted from his shoulders, signaling we're safe for now. And yet I still feel the deadly squeeze. Should I make some excuse to scoop up the puzzle pieces? But Clint was the one to bring it.

Clint joins me in the kids' room and whispers in my ear, "They're good. We should talk."

I nod my head and allow him to tug me away from the view of all I could lose.

"How was your time with Erika? Anything I need to know?" The pained expression on his face juxtaposes itself against the lingering image of his ruined face that Christmas two years ago as his daughter, leaning over the puzzle, interrogated him about his age and mine.

Was the puzzle the beginning of Clint's insecurity with his age? How had I never seen the connection?

I look away and give him the basic outline of what she shared with me. "She's hurting, Clint. But the best we can do for her is to try to figure out who is terrorizing our family and why, because I'm convinced it's all related."

"I agree. Thoughts on how to start?"

We settle at the island with files and both computers at the ready. "As an analyst, I'd start by asking and answering as many questions as I could and see where it led us."

"Solid plan. That guy at the SEC said he doesn't know where Betsey is. Is it time to unblock her and give her a call?"

"Probably, if I had my phone."

"Right." Clint sighs. "An email maybe?"

Not a bad idea, but I still don't trust her. "Not sure I love the paper trail. I think we should figure out more first. I'm not sure who she knows. The SEC could be a setup."

"Maybe." Clint shrugs.

"Probably not, but they've got to have people looking for her if she's truly missing. Perhaps she's just off the grid like us." I never imagined anyone at work sending us into hiding like this. Inconceivable.

Clint squints at me like he wants to believe the best about Betsey's safety but needs to ready himself for the worst. His lifesaving skills are showing themselves.

"Let's look at what she gave me." I open the Excel spreadsheet I'd started at the office. "A thumb drive of data that I copied before handing it over."

"Why is it significant? Why would she give it to you?"

"Good questions. It's data we shouldn't have. We've elected not to pay for any data, and even if we did, we'd never be supplied with all this. So much of this is confidential."

"Are you sure it's authentic?"

"No, but I also don't necessarily think it's fake, as I've been told to believe." Dave theorized Betsey created it just to spook me. Had he seen the hard evidence that the data was bogus? Hardwin was right: I hadn't asked one question. Certainly a sign of my own self-delusion or, worse, incompetence.

"Don't do it." Clint takes my hands and holds them in both of his.

"I'm not doing anything."

"You are. You're second-guessing. I see it all over your beautiful face." He brushes my unruly hair from my forehead. "I love every brain cell. And stick with me. I'm going to continue to say dumb things like *Use your phone* when you've left it behind. We're going to stumble through this, but together we're going to figure it out."

"Yes. We will." I love this man.

"Let's move on to what Betsey wants."

"She said she wants the securities lending agreement for the funds." I pick through a folder containing a printout of the documents Phil had sent to me as well as the stand-alone agreement Alyssa and Temor found.

"Do we need to get into the nitty-gritty? Would that help?"

"No. Basically there's a standard agreement that all the funds *should* share. What's crazy is that my name is on the master agreement and in the board minutes when it was discussed, but the ETFs are missing." I hand him the printouts I haven't had time yet to scrutinize. "I think Betsey knew, or suspected, and wanted me to find it."

"Your name? Because you presented this agreement to the board?" He looks down briefly at the papers and then up at me.

"No. I never saw this version. Total idiocy. I never knew my name was inside any legal document." I bite the inside of my lip and mutter, "Especially one from two years ago."

"Someone has been at this for two years?" He flips through more of the pages.

"Someone anticipated it might be a problem. Or *I* might be a problem." How could someone I know and work alongside make me a scapegoat? Underneath all my anger and confusion is a deep well of hurt. I stare up at the open roof trusses above me. The rough-sawn boards are stained a dark brown, almost black. I imagine coming back here during Christmas, wrapping the rafters with twinkling lights. "Don't we lose a lot of heat without any insulation up there?"

"Yeah. Do we care right now?" He gently pinches my chin.

"No, sorry." I close my eyes. My mind is spinning and not about the right things. "I think someone—or multiple someones—set me up because they figured out a quick way to get what they wanted—money, information . . . I don't know, something. Could the ETFs not being included in the securities lending contract with our custodian be one of many ways our ETFs have been excluded from better arrangements?" Dave and his reluctance to help us with sales should have tipped me off.

"I put my money on money."

"Probably, but there's not a lot of it to be made. Payments based on actual securities being lent out from the ETFs have still been received. Alyssa thinks we have falsified reports that indicate we are making deals outside of our custodian. The rates may not be optimal, but we're getting some revenue. So, there's got to be more than just money, some other advantages. I think they got greedy. I just don't know for what. I also don't think they expected this to go on so long."

"Why would you think that? Are there other proposed agreements?" He picks up the draft agreement Alyssa and Temor analyzed.

"Not that I've found. It's just a sense, I guess. When I was an advisor, I'd see clients hang on to positions way past when they should have sold. The risk far outweighed the reward, but they'd get greedy or unwilling to drop a loser." I make a few notes in my spreadsheet.

Clint puts all the papers back down on the polished concrete. "Doesn't the board hold some responsibility in not following up with you on any of what you were supposedly doing with the securities you were lending?"

"Yes, they should have asked. I wonder if whoever set this up is counting on them being focused on our success. But when Betsey got close . . . they started tracking me and Erika as insurance. Then they fired Betsey and used me to keep her away. Maybe they didn't count on her determination to get to me."

"Ready to contact her? She might know who's behind this. Who Candy is really working for."

"Maybe."

"Mom, I'm hungry," Reid whines as he stalks into the main room.

I open my arms, and he slides in. I kiss the top of his head.

"At camp, we had a good-night snack before bed." He starts to pull away.

"Hmm. Yes, I can see how you could get used to that."

Clint walks to the farthest cupboard. "I think I have some of that fun popcorn that you can heat right over the stove, and it puffs up."

"Cool. And I want to know who won. Can I check?"

"Sure, honey." I slide off my stool. "I'll help you make the popcorn, and Dad can see if he can get us some Wi-Fi. But first"—I give Reid another squeeze—"I'm going to change into my pajamas. Seriously, Ella is my hero for giving us her car and grabbing our bags."

Erika walks into the room. "Enjoy the perks. My status will be dirt by next week." She grabs a novel from the corner bookcase and curls up in the nook.

My heart thuds. Even if, or when, we figure this all out, Erika is still going to have to account for those tests.

Accountable. I press my hand against my chest and my finger automatically seeks the chain at my neck. Although none of us deserve to be targeted, we all did things for which we're accountable. Sliding the gold fastener to the back of my neck, I fist my cross, and Oma's warm home floods my mind. Twice in two days. I used to think about her all the time, but now one afternoon stands out. I'd just clicked shut her heavy oak front door when I heard her call out to me. The smell of vanilla and cinnamon had me licking my lips as I slid open the pocket doors to her dining room.

"*Liebchen*, join me." Oma patted the seat next to her as I eyed the plate of *Zimtsterne* between us—the icing dripping off each point. "You may have one after."

My backpack slid from my shoulders as I ran my thumb along a deep gouge in the old walnut table.

"You won an award today?" Oma asked.

"Yes. For getting the most pledges." I straightened in the hard-back chair, my eyes still darting to the star cookies, each as big as my hand and almost too warm to retain the icing.

"Your paper. Let me see."

I sucked in my top lip as I dug between my brown-paper-bag-covered textbooks.

She silently read my stapled packet and then looked directly into my rounded eyes. "Tell me."

"We're jumping rope for—"

"*Nein*. Tell me."

I lowered my head and tucked both hands in my lap. "I asked our neighbors for pledges," I said, each word feeling as if it were being gouged out of my flesh.

She flattened the last page on the table. "Here."

I had tried to write the last dozen pledges in different handwriting, but as I looked past her knobby knuckles, I could see how similar they all looked.

"Meredith Martina, how many?"

Martina was her name. My mother's homage.

"Fourteen," I mumbled.

"How many for prize?"

"Twenty-five," I said. My shoulders slumped toward the table.

She placed two fingers under my chin and lifted. "You know word *accountable*?"

I shook my head. It sounded familiar, but I would not be able to define it, especially if I hoped not to pee in my pants as I struggled.

"You will look it up and then write me a paper about what it means."

I nodded and rose from my seat.

"Wait. I explain other word. *Forgiven*."

I slinked back down.

"You know you did wrong?"

I nodded.

"You not do it again?"

I nodded again.

"You will correct the form and tell your teacher, but *Liebling*, you are forgiven. I forgive. God forgives." She pushed the plate of cookies toward me and waited until I chose one. "God always forgives. People, not always. Even Oma can be stubborn. But God—no matter what. No matter how long. He waits. He forgives." She picked up a *Zimtstern*, tapped one of the frosted points against mine, and took a bite. I learned about accountability that day, but I also learned the simplicity of forgiveness. And yet after all this time, I've given little thought to the trust required to admit my need for forgiveness. Because when it comes down to all the lies, the hurts, and the selfish moments of pride, I don't trust that I'll always be invited back to the worn walnut table.

I walk into the primary bedroom and run my hand down the old lighthouse quilt from our early days in Kennebunk. Like so many things, I just didn't notice. I didn't notice it was missing from our downstairs linen closet. It looks perfect in the room. The black, blue, and gold fabric is warmed by the copper light fixtures on either side of the queen bed. I sit, slide off my boat shoes, and stare at an unframed map above the small desk. The New York portion of the Appalachian Trail takes up most of the pine paneling opposite the bed.

I step up to the printed map laced with tidy notes in both Clint's and Rob's hands and notice the intertwined *T* logo in the lower right corner of the map. Odd. Same logo as the New York AT map in Dave's office. But on this version, it's bigger and the organization's name is printed.

As I read the familiar two words, all the air leaves my lungs.

50

"CLINT." My voice gets stuck in my chest. I cough and try again. "Clint, can you come here?"

Clint strolls into the room. "Our son is going to be a successful leader one day. He got me talking about Jiffy Pop, and somehow, I was making his popcorn. You better grab a handful if you want any. Unfortunately, we only had the one foil pan left."

"We?" I spin around.

"Oui oui." Clint laughs.

"No." I close my eyes. I don't want to fight. Just the opposite. I want to congratulate the love of my life on launching his dream.

Tru-ly is the song of the eastern bluebird. The New York state bird is known to roost in flocks of up to fifty, hiding together at night to stay warm. They are the reason Clint and Rob met, when both answered a Brownie troop's distress call that ended up being about a bluebird flock in Hiawassee, Georgia, caught up in some aggressive mating ritual. After assuring the spooked campers they were in no danger, the guys had a good laugh, and a friendship was born. When, years later, they both wound up in the New York Hudson Valley, they blamed it on the call of the New York state bird. Tru-ly Trails was inspired.

I open my eyes and place both my hands on my husband's chest. "You launched."

His gaze flicks over to the wall. "Oh, not entirely. Not really. You know, we've just been knocking around the nonprofit idea for years."

"I recognize the logo."

Clint cocks his head.

"Dave Alliston has a trail map with that exact logo in his office." I run my fingers over the logo. "I saw it this week." A shiver runs down my back.

"Right." Clint shifts his gaze away from my face. "Dave has been a supporter and has opened some amazing doors locally. Beyond the maps and experiences, he's had great ideas on structuring a nonprofit while also being able to sell outfitting supplies."

"Dave?" I want to shake my husband or maybe punch him. My fists clench at my sides. "We've been debating who could do this to our family, and you never thought to mention your relationship with Dave? Clint, I don't—"

"It's not a relationship. Calm down, Meredith." Clint swiftly shuts the door.

"No. I will not calm down. Is he after us? Are you blind? This could all be part of taking me down." My hands reach toward the door. "Does he know where we are?"

"He knows there's a cabin, but he's never been here. We've only met—"

"Would Rob tell him?" I push past Clint to get to my kids.

"No." Clint holds on to both my arms. "When I told Rob to tell no one, he even mentioned Dave. We need to connect about the grant. I explicitly told Rob not to tell him."

I remember the call from the car. We have to be able to trust Rob. Right?

Clint tries to tug me toward him, but I resist.

I want to rail at him about why he hasn't told me about Dave, but I feel like both a broken record and a hypocrite. Exhaustion steals over me. "Is this another thing you tried to tell me, but I didn't listen?"

"No." He runs his fingers up my arm. "I haven't said anything."

"Why?" I whisper. Dave has been so difficult. Never an ally. I still remember him grabbing me at the bell ringing reception. His hands were where Clint's are now. The bruises fainter but still there.

"He asked me not to."

"And you took his side?" I pull away.

"I didn't know there were sides to take."

I stare at the trail map. The path through is never the most direct. "You know who he's been to me at work. I've complained about that man." But not often, I now realize. Another protective measure, I guess. Keeping the ugliness at work out of my home. "I did tell you that he wouldn't help me with sales, and he's *head of sales*." My voice goes a little screechy. I swallow.

"Yes. I think that's why he asked me not to mention anything. I told him I'd never lie. If you asked me or it came up, so be it, but I agreed not to volunteer his name."

"I don't understand." I finally look into my husband's eyes.

"From what I've gathered, he hasn't been proud of the way he's treated you. Competition gets the best of him. He's told me more than once that he's wanted to start over with you, but then he experiences another slight or rebuff, and he's right back to where he started."

I didn't invite him to ring the closing bell.

There is no doubt he felt my slight, but I have felt far more from him.

He is not an ally.

Clint pulls my hand toward him. "He's wanted to make amends, but not because he helped me. He didn't want your sense of duty to bridge a gap he should have paved over."

"You guys have really talked a lot about this." A sticky chill creeps up my back.

"Some. You know me and wanting to talk about my feelings and relationships." He chuckles and I tug my fingers from his.

This conversation just feels wrong.

Clint's face loses its mirth.

"I think you should steer clear. He's . . . unpredictable." The least of his worst attributes that I can muster.

Clint breathes out a heaviness and something else, like sadness.

"Is there more?"

He glances back at the map. "I thought I'd be happier about Truly, but our issues . . ." His words fade away, and I feel him studying much more than the map.

He's right; there are so many issues. Are they because we don't fully trust each other?

Because I do worry that his patience and forgiveness will dry up. I will run out of chances.

I wrap my arms around his waist and crush him against me. "*We* need help."

He doesn't stiffen. Perhaps he is resigned. "More counseling?"

"Maybe, or maybe something different this time." I speak into his chest. "I've been thinking a lot about Oma lately."

"Wise woman." His chest vibrates as he chuckles. "Remember that first Easter when she stayed with us and then woke us up clanging those pots and pans, singing at the top of her lungs? We shot straight out of bed, still tangled in our sheets." He pauses. "But her prayer as the sun rose above the ocean was beautiful. You miss her."

"I do." I want to say more, but perilous emotions strapped down inside me threaten to burst free.

He seems to feel my need to process. "Well, the popcorn is probably all gone." He looks down at me with eyes attempting to be playful. "Are you hungry?"

"Strange, but yes."

"Let's get my woman something to eat."

We walk back into the main room. Reid's head is in Erika's lap, the empty popcorn bowl on the coffee table.

"He fell asleep talking," Erika says as she tries to smooth his still-spiky hair down on his head. "I forgot to make him take a shower."

"In the morning." I glance over at the basic bathroom with a beautiful regular toilet and magnificent pint-size stand-up shower. One of the first renovations Clint said they did. The outhouse with a toilet plumbed to the same septic tank and leach field is still operational, but I'm thankful for the indoor variety. I can rough it, but only if I must.

I dig into Reid's backpack to find his toothbrush and paste while Clint rouses him from his nest on the couch.

"Come on, buddy." Clint pulls him to his feet.

"I want to check who won." Reid yawns.

"Tomorrow." Clint pushes him toward the bathroom.

"Oh, please, Dad. You said I could." He wrenches his head around, suddenly wide-awake. "I can't sleep without knowing."

"All evidence to the contrary," Erika grumbles, her face still in the novel she picked up earlier. When Erika got her first iPhone, she stopped reading. She used to always be tucked into a story.

"It's too late, buddy. It's already . . ." Clint looks at his watch. "Eight thirty?"

"What?" I pull out Reid's brush from his bag. "But it feels like midnight."

"I forget about the time vortex in the woods." Clint squints at the blackened windows.

"Please, Dad." Reid jumps, jangling his body up and down.

"Sure, buddy. I'll crank up the sat phone." He walks back into the bedroom.

"Now come here and brush those teeth—thoroughly." I kiss Reid's forehead.

"And wash your face and pits," Erika yells over from the couch.

"Do I have to?" Reid picks up his toothbrush.

"I'll find you a washcloth, and you can give yourself a little sponge bath before you put your pajamas on. When you're done, maybe your dad will be ready." I find a few towels, reserving a couple for Clint and me, and shut the bathroom door as I walk out.

"Did you figure out why they're after us?" Erika asks as if she's asking what I'm going to fix for breakfast.

"Getting closer. Still not sure who." I ignore the kitchen. Work has a way of killing my appetite.

"Dad's a really good judge of character." Erika's nose is still pressed into the old romance novel.

I freeze as I pick up one of the files. Strange thing for our teen daughter to say.

Erika turns and slides her elbow over the top of the blue corduroy couch. "No, really." She lowers her voice, glancing at the bedroom as if she'd hate for him to overhear. "At school, he always knows the parents to avoid and has a sense of my friends right away. I usually blow it off, but he's almost always right."

"I'm not sure your dad knows any of these folks well enough to render a judgment." I pick up another page of my notes, Dave's face swimming into view.

"You might be surprised. He pays attention." Erika says and then curls back around to continue reading.

51

CLINT WALKS BACK into the main room with only his cell phone.

"Did you get the hot spot running?" I ask.

"Not a problem. Ready for Reid when he's done." Clint lays his phone on the island. "You find a snack?"

"No. I don't need it." I glance around the cabin. It's starting to feel very small. We've looked at the data and the contracts every which way. We're not going to solve this tucked away in the woods. Maybe Clint is right about an email to Betsey. I can just ask her to call me on the sat phone. If I need to show her the contracts, I will. Maybe we can get to the bottom of what she and I both know.

"It's not about need."

"What?" I shake my head, realizing he's still talking about food.

Clint opens a cupboard above the refrigerator. "A snack is not about need."

"Did you check? Do you know who won?" Erika pops her head back over the couch.

"Nope. I'll let Reid do the honors." Clint shifts what looks like a first aid kit and then a small tool bag inside the cabinet.

"You have too much willpower." Erika flops back down.

"Hardly," he says and then spins around. "Here you are, my lady."

"Dark chocolate?" I scowl at the bar in his hand.

"Amano seventy percent." He hands me the bar with a beautiful rendering of a cacao tree on the wrapper. "Thought you'd be more pleased."

"I am. Sorry. How do you have this?" I peel open the wrapper, and the thin foil knocks something loose in my brain. My taste buds tingle.

"Actually, Dave." Clint busies himself in the sink. "He gave us some goodies when we shared our latest business plan."

I break off a square, not letting its provenance ruin my bite. I slump on the stool and let my eyes close as I savor the smooth bittersweetness.

The bathroom door bangs open. "I'm ready," Reid announces. "How do I get Wi-Fi?"

"I've pulled up your coach's email to the team and parents, but I haven't looked." Clint hands Reid his phone.

Reid should never play poker. His face explodes with glee and then turmoil and then delight again. His eyes scan, and occasionally his mouth moves with silent words, but he doesn't make a sound.

"Did you win, maggot?" Erika calls out from the couch.

"Erika." My words come automatically in the parental tone I've perfected. "Give him a minute."

As the seconds bleed into minutes, I too become anxious to hear the outcome, but since I corrected Erika, I can hardly jump in. I look to Clint, but he seems content to give Reid time.

So annoying.

Finally, Reid looks up. "We won on speed and agility, but the

Pinepoint team won on creativity and efficiency. Which is totally wrong, because I wrote the code, and it was clean and logical."

"So, you tied?" I ask. "That's great. Right?" I look around the room. My family hates to tie. Every sport, every game, even an empty wager is met with a fight to the finish. I understand because I'm one of them.

"They don't allow ties. A team has to win. They had to do a speed round. Just us and Pinepoint. Bobby was our lead programmer, and I wasn't there to do any of it." His face falls.

"Sorry, buddy. I wish you could've been there for your team." Clint hugs Reid around his shoulders, jostling him against his hip.

"You're irreplaceable." I walk over to hug my little guy.

"No, I'm not." Reid scrunches up his nose. "We won."

Clint pulls Reid away and holds him by his arms. "Way to fake us out. Congratulations!"

"Yeah." Reid smiles but with only half his face.

Erika flops over the back of the couch. "Sucks they didn't need you."

"Of course they needed him." I swat at my daughter. "He got them to the finals and is an absolutely brilliant robotics kid."

Reid wiggles away from his dad and walks right into Erika. Her arms wrap around his still-small body. She gets him.

Clint slides in next to me. Sometimes you just need someone to understand. The encouragement, even the celebration, can come later.

The sentiment surrounding the hug they shared doesn't last long. Insults skewer the air as they settle into their twin beds. Exhaustion clear as they both curl onto their sides, Erika looking younger and Reid older, their age difference almost immaterial.

"Stop staring at me," Erika grumbles from behind closed eyes.

I stumble away from the doorway.

At just after nine thirty, Clint and I are back at the island.

"Maybe it's time to contact Betsey," I say.

"Okay?" Clint pours us each a glass of water.

"Betsey said she found the sales data."

"And Dave told you it was fake. So did Hardwin and Terrence, but then you overheard Hardwin and Terrence saying they lied." Clint smiles as if he is proud of his ability to remember.

"Maybe the data was the insurance policy and not the payment." I look up from my current list of what I know.

"You've lost me."

"I've been thinking about the data as partial payment or perk for whatever securities were being lent, and what if . . ." I flip through the pages to find my notes from Alyssa.

Aunt May

Retirement home in Florida

New return address

Nothing in letter

Aunt Mackie wants to borrow rose dishes

"Alyssa only had moments to come up with this. Incredible. She was scouring the income reports from our custodial bank, which should have been coming from Minneapolis. What if someone was scrubbing those reports so they only looked like they were coming from there? What if they were coming from the Meymack ops center in Florida?"

"She also said *nothing in letter*?" Clint points to my scribbled words on the note.

"Yeah, I can't quite remember her exact words, but it could mean that there was nothing strange about the reports themselves—just an address she found on one or more of them?"

"So, backing up. Someone is collecting revenue from Meymack but making it look like it's coming from the bank in Minneapolis. For what purpose?"

"Exactly. Someone, probably from within Garman Straub, could be acting as an independent lending agent."

"But couldn't Meymack just borrow the securities from your custodian?"

"Maybe we offer subpar rates? The funds are still getting paid. Maybe it's not the entire fee but something. I'm still missing the motivation. Why would someone risk it?" I slam both my hands down on the pile of papers and folders.

"You'll figure it out."

"But in the meantime, is Alyssa all right? Where's Betsey? And why is Candace after us?"

"Maybe we need to sleep on it. Store all these bits away and take them out to examine them in the morning. If we can't figure it out, we'll contact Komoroski."

"Oh! I forgot to text him our address."

Clint's eyes drill into mine.

"I know. He insisted I come into the station, and then I didn't message him." I tent my hands over my mouth and blow hard. "I'm done with all of this, Clint." I dig into my bag and hand him the officer's card. "Can you just text him the address?"

Clint nods and starts typing. "What about Betsey?"

I keep thinking about those pictures of Lucas and me. Threats of something she didn't understand. She was desperate, and I don't trust her. "No more hiding. First light, we are out of here. We'll connect with Komoroski, and then we're finding Betsey. And I'll lay all of this on the table. Someone is going to answer for it."

"Everything we have has your name or fingerprints on it. You sure?" Clint glances up from the phone.

"Absolutely. The truth has to be enough." I just wish I was sure that it would be.

52

SOMETHING WAKES ME. I try to glance around the room, but no light filters through the twin dark curtains. It must still be night. Beyond my husband's heavy breaths, the cabin is silent. All I can hear is my heart pounding in my chest. So strange. I shrug up against the paneled wall and listen.

A light flashes near the rod at the top of the back window.

I gasp. Then, barely able to move, I creep my hand along the bed to push against Clint. "Honey," I whisper, my voice scarcely above a breath. "Wake up. There's someone outside."

Clint groans softly, rolling onto his back. His eyes flutter as he blinks away sleep. "What'd you say?"

I swallow hard, still pressed up against the wall. What if Candace has found us? She's come in the middle of the night to . . . do what? "I saw a light, like from a flashlight, and I think I heard something." My voice trembles. "Someone's out there."

Clint's eyes snap open. "Stay here," he says quietly, but his tone is firm as he reaches for his flashlight in the bedside table.

As he heads for the front door, I slip into the kids' room. Erika is sound asleep, her hair fanned out on the pillow. I glance over at Reid. I try to make out the bumps of his body but it's as if my mind is playing tricks on me. I stumble forward as I try to sprint around Erika's bed. I desperately pat the blanket but don't feel him. Reaching across, I shake Erika's shoulder. "Where's your brother?"

"What?" she mumbles.

I race out of the room to check the bathroom. "Your brother. Where is he?" I call to her.

"I don't know. He was sleeping."

The bathroom is dark. I flip the light switch. No Reid. My heart slams against my ribs. Where is our son?

The front door bangs open, and Clint calls out, his words tumbling over each other. "It was Reid. He was behind the outhouse."

"I was looking for the raccoons. I thought maybe in the dark—"

I run to him, drop to my knees, and wrap my arms around his thin frame. "You scared me." My face is wet as I kiss his cheek.

"I'm sorry, Mom."

I straighten, taking gulps of air to try to calm my reaction. He's fine. Everyone is fine.

"Let's get our raccoon hunter back to bed." Clint gently shoves Reid toward where Erika stands in the doorway of their room.

"I wasn't hunting them," Reid whines.

"Come on, goober. Back to sleep." Erika slips back under her own sheets.

I slump against Clint as we walk to our room. "Not sure I can remember being that frightened," I mumble. With someone coming after Erika online, I thought for sure someone had grabbed our boy. I don't care about the agreements or the client data, I just want this all to end.

Clint turns off the light and hugs me to him. I lay my head on his shoulder thinking there is no way I am going to fall asleep.

Three sharp raps at the door fracture the quiet of the cabin.

My eyes shoot open. What was that?

Clint bolts upright. "I think someone's here."

Clint slips from the bed, his movements fluid and purposeful. He pauses and glances at his phone. "It's probably the police."

"In the middle of the night?"

"It's only eleven." Clint is already striding toward the front door.

Something instinctive stops me as I walk around the bed. I pull the door mostly shut and grab the sat phone from the closet. I don't have time to figure out the hot spot, so I pray Clint has contacts saved. I scroll until I find the one I need. I click on it.

Voices boom from the front of the cabin.

I was right, not the police.

Two voices that sound eerily similar.

I quickly write out a text that's far more confident and assured than I feel.

This is Meredith. I was given data on a thumb drive. It is real and troubling. Someone other than our custodian is lending securities from the new ETFs. The data might be an assurance that if they are caught, I will be blamed. I urge you to keep this confidential, but if you don't hear from me by noon on Saturday, call Officer Komoroski in Scarsdale and Newal at the SEC. Be careful.

I try to read over my hasty text. I sound paranoid but I don't know how to fix the tone. The shouts from the other room continue. Clint keeps insisting Lucas be quiet. Lucas insists I show myself so we can all talk. The voices grow strangely quiet, and then Lucas shouts at Clint to get over himself and how the past needs to stay in the past.

My head pounds. How are the kids not awake?

I focus back on the phone. There is so much more I should say in the text. The part about keeping confidential is eerily similar to the words used by Betsey in her note, and look how well I took that direction. If I had, we might not be here. What if something has happened to her? I shake my head. I have to trust that the SEC has put their full weight behind finding her.

I press Send.

As I go to power down the phone, Erika's words about Clint wiggle into my consciousness. *Dad's a really good judge of character.*

My icy fingers copy the previous message and send it to the other contact in the phone. I've either begun construction for the new bridge or bulldozed my career.

53

BOTH MEN STAND IN SILENCE at the entrance of the cabin. Although the front door is shut behind them, Lucas has barely stepped inside.

"How did you find us?" I speak smoothly although all my insides are trembling.

Lucas tries to step around his younger brother, but Clint doesn't let him get any closer. "We need to talk."

"How'd you find us?" I repeat, my voice icy. I have to know how he tracked us to a cabin I've never been to and Clint doesn't own.

Lucas squinches up his lips, full like his brother's, and seems to make a decision. "Candace slipped a GPS tag into your bag." His eyes scan the room. "You were distracted on the phone, maybe."

Another tracker. My head pounds. Must have been that call with Clint when I asked her to excuse me, but I ended up leaving her alone in my office. I glare at Lucas.

"My idea. I'm sorry. We lost the signal earlier but got a ping a couple hours ago. I couldn't wait."

When we turned on the hot spot for Reid's results.

"But it was for your own protection." Lucas tries again to move toward me. "We needed to know you'd be safe."

Clint swears and sidesteps in front of him. "Don't treat us like we're stupid. You've never done anything for anyone else's good or protection in your life." He gets into Lucas's face, baiting him to hit him.

I want to squeeze between them but know if I do, it's over. Clint will force me to choose. He'll think I'm choosing between him and his brother, but what he'd really be asking me to do is to defend his self-inflicted cage over his possible healing.

Instead, I stay calm. "Who is *we*?"

Lucas pulls his focus from Clint and looks blankly at me.

"You said, *We needed to know you'd be safe*. Who exactly is *we*?"

"Candace and I."

"Candy." Clint snorts. "Where is she? Off terrorizing someone else at Garman Straub? Betsey is missing. She have anything to do with that?"

"What? No." Lucas cocks his head to the side and sucks in his lips as if he might make some confession if he's not careful. Instead, he levels his gaze at Clint. "I admit you and my wife have bad blood."

My jaw clenches. *Not conciliatory enough, Lucas. You must try harder.*

"Bad blood! I have bad blood with you, brother." He spits the last word and then shoves his index finger into Lucas's chest.

"Dad?" Erika's voice pierces the air behind us.

I spin around and pitch toward our daughter. "Go back to bed, honey. Sorry we woke you."

"Is he Dad's brother, my uncle?" She scoots away from me.

"Yes, I'm your uncle Lucas." A huge smile on his face, he tries to step around Clint.

"Don't you dare," Clint hisses.

I hold on to Erika's shoulders and whisper to her, "I need you to be with your brother. I don't know if this man is safe. Your father needs to know you and Reid are together."

She raises her chin.

Don't do this. Please.

"I understand." She begins to turn.

I clutch her wrist. "Grab the sat phone from our closet. Call 911 if I yell to you."

She nods while rounding her eyes at the men, who are still locked in a tangle of wills.

I walk to within five feet of them and lean back against the couch with an air of dispassion. "Lucas, why don't you take that seat?" I point to the scuffed leather chair. "We can discuss whatever you felt you needed to protect me from."

"Good idea." Lucas steps around Clint, who glares as he passes.

"Where's Candace?" I say casually as I take a seat on the couch.

"Yeah, Lucas. Where's your wife?" Clint snarls his words as he perches on the couch beside me, his body almost vibrating with tension.

"She really is a different woman. Combat changed her. In a good way. When she got back and got into private security—"

"Cut the crap, Lucas. We know about her court-martial." Clint shakes his head.

Lucas's eyes blaze as he almost levitates from his chair, ready to fly across the coffee table at his brother. "There was never a court-martial. She was only defending—"

"Don't lie to my face!" Clint spits out.

"Please. Both of you." I extend my hands to each of them. They are forcing me to the middle. "Tell us why you've come, Lucas."

"We came to warn you."

We. My spine straightens. "What do you need to warn us about?"

I hold up my palm to him. "And before you say anything, you have to know that I've already sent a message about everything I know. The investment data, which is real. The borrowing from our funds. The falsified reports. There's no more hiding."

Lucas sits back in his seat, his face blank. A switch has been pulled. He says nothing.

For the first time since the pounding on the door, I am truly afraid. My breathing accelerates. Maybe I should call out to Erika to dial 911.

Maybe this has all gone too far.

54

"WHAT DO YOU MEAN, *falsified reports*?" Lucas asks without moving, without any disruption to the space around him.

"The reports coming from Meymack that spell out the subpar rates—those falsified reports." I watch for the explosion. The denial.

"Does Betsey have these reports?" Lucas still hasn't moved or shown any emotion.

My stomach churns. Completely different reaction to the court-martial that we all know didn't end up happening.

Clint is silent beside me. Like me, he's probably aware—this is when we learn the truth.

"She gave me data from your advisor offices about our sales. How did Betsey get that, Lucas?"

"I can't tell you that." Tiny beads of sweat break out across his hairline.

"Of course you can't. You're up to your eyeballs in this, and you're setting up my wife to take the fall for your greed." Clint begins to rise, but I clamp a hand down on his thigh.

"No. Nothing like that." Lucas blows out a breath as his face falls. "Betsey came at me about someone working against the funds. I can tell you, it's the opposite. Our advisors have been impressed with the investment opportunity. You can see it in the sales."

"Yes." I lean forward. "But what about the reports?"

"I haven't seen them. I assume we send reports regularly. I haven't heard anything troubling about that business. Certainly nothing falsified." His face is tight. There is more there. Clint senses it too. I clamp his leg harder. I need him to let me do this.

"But Meymack is going through an independent lending agent, not our custodian." I speak slowly and clearly to the man who's been using me. Pretending to want a relationship with his brother, just to keep me in line for whatever scam he's been running.

He holds up his hands in mock surrender. "I don't know anything—"

"Give it up." My words are coarse. I'm losing patience. "You know what our prospectus says, what we've reported to our investors—what we report to the SEC! We have the same deal as the mutual funds. Securities lending runs through our custodian."

"Couldn't you just let it go until Monday?" Lucas finally breaks, rubbing his face hard. "Honestly, it's not a big deal. We arranged to borrow some of your fund's on-specials to cover some positions we'd become overextended on."

"What's on-special?" Clint's voice is low but also without any more patience.

"Securities that we own but are hard to acquire on the open market." I shake my head at Lucas. "You couldn't unwind. You've sat on them for two years?" My tone has gone acidic.

"No! Only for a few weeks." His eyebrows crunch together while he rapidly shakes his head.

"No, I saw the agreement. It was executed before launch." What I really saw was a draft of the agreement without any borrower listed or signatures.

"Impossible." His face animates. "You saw wrong, Meredith. We've only needed to cover those positions for a few weeks, maybe a couple months. The board is getting updated. On Monday."

"And the client data? I know you supplied it to get a better rate."

"It wasn't like that. I thought I was helping. We talked about selling Garman Straub the data, and I provided a sample. It was—"

"Wrong again." This side of Lucas is very troubling. "It was much more detailed than anything we could pay for."

"It was what I had access to." He hangs his head. Finally, some truth.

"What else did you give up?" I ask from between clenched teeth.

"Honestly, Meredith, I don't know all the details. With our firms' growing relationship, I know there were meetings about the positioning of your mutual funds. That's all I know."

Waves of anger almost overwhelm me, but I believe him. His posture, his fluid words. He's not tripping over himself. He's been played for the fool. For what, better rates and to be the man at the center of the deals? He's implicated himself in shady idiocy.

"Lucas, you have to tell me who's behind all this at Garman Straub. If you care about me at all, I have to know. My family has been threatened. My career is likely finished." As I lean forward, Clint flinches as if he'll throw himself in front of me if I move from the couch.

Lucas glances toward the door. "Candace saw your fear. As you were running from the gym. It gutted both of us. She and I were on the phone together. Meredith, she came to help you."

Clint snorts. "Give it up, Lucas. I've heard enough. I need you to leave."

I lean into my husband. "Please, Clint, I want to hear this."

"You believe him?" The hurt on his face skewers me.

"Erika told me tonight that you're one of the best judges of character she knows. Our teenage daughter said this." I lean closer to him and hold both his hands in mine. "I need you to listen without the hurt and pain clouding everything you hear. I need your partnership in finding the truth."

Clint stares hard at me.

I keep one of Clint's hands and then shift back on the couch. "Lucas, tell us who is behind all this."

Lucas shakes his head. "I want to, but Candace knows more than I do. She's in the car."

My head whips toward the unlocked door.

"She wants to explain. Can I invite her in?"

"No." Clint must've had the same thought about the door because he bullets from the couch and sets the lock. "She's not coming anywhere near my family."

Lucas stands. "I think she can fill in the missing pieces. None of us know the full picture. That's the insidious nature of what we're trapped in."

"Trying to make us believe you two are not behind all of this. No." Clint stalks back to Lucas but then looks over at me.

Lucas shakes his head. "I think we've all been used."

Clint stares at up at the open ceiling. "I can tell you that woman is not setting foot in this cabin with my kids in the other room."

I slip my arm around my husband's. "Please let us finish this. Maybe—"

"No." Clint's voice isn't loud, but it's made entirely of steel.

55

SATURDAY

Eight hours later, I slip my hand around my coffee mug. The inch or so of cool brown liquid ripples inside. I shouldn't have drunk the acidic brew on an empty stomach and certainly shouldn't have had two refills. But I have no appetite. None of us do. My fingers itch to pick up Clint's phone, lying on the Formica table next to me. I'll check it again soon.

"So, you're certain Dave had nothing to do with this?" I ask across the booth.

"Dave is in the dark. You have to understand, I never intended for any of this to happen." Candace speaks just above a whisper.

"We don't have to understand anything about you, Candy." Clint spits his words.

We agreed to meet this morning. The four of us. Clint seems to keep forgetting that we just need to get the information and leave.

"Please, call me Candace." This is not the first time she's made this request. Each time with the same measure of patience.

Clint scoffs.

Candace tries something different this time. "I know, Clint. I was a wounded creature when we knew each other. I won't pile it on, but my home was not a safe place for a small girl. I learned quickly to eat or be eaten. My dad and brothers were proud of the rough, take-no-prisoners young woman I grew into. My one rebellion was joining the Air Force instead of the Marines."

Clint's face is hard, but he's not interrupting her.

"Remember that mutt that followed me around the end of our senior year?"

Clint's eyes squint as if he's looking deep into his past. "Squirrel?"

"Yeah, Squirrel. Stupid name for a dog, but he was a stupid dog. I told my dad that I did everything I could to get rid of him, but I was secretly feeding him behind the old Chevy. When I got home from graduation, Squirrel failed to meet me at the end of the drive. No one had come to see me toss my square hat and now, not even my stupid dog wanted me. As I got closer to the house, I could somehow hear her cries through all the shouting. They'd set up a dogfight in the backyard. Squirrel was a pit bull with as much aggression as a stuffed koala. I shoved those idiots out of my way, scooped her up, and walked her to the animal hospital on Ward, near the high school."

Lucas murmurs something, but Candace continues.

"I knew the vet thought I'd sanctioned the fight. I also knew nothing I could say would change his mind. He saw the person he wanted to see, but he also saved my dog. Anyway, I told him to adopt her out. I enlisted in the Air Force and was on a bus to San Antonio before the ink was dry. I've been back home only once since then."

"Got more joe for y'all." Our waitress, her hair scraped back into a bun, fills up our coffees yet again. "Still able to resist the call of the bacon and the smell of the sausage?"

"Can I get an ice water?" I slide my mug away.

"You know, I will take an egg, bacon, and toast platter," Clint announces as if proposing a peace deal with a rogue nation. Perhaps that's what it is.

"I'll have the same." Lucas shuts the menu he snagged from the wire holder in front of the window.

Candace and I order as well.

The waitress nods as she scribbles on her pad. "Back in a jiff."

"Honestly, Candy, Candace, whatever, you can tell us anything you want. I'm always going to remember the girl who stole Kimmie's new lunch box, the only new thing we ever saw her with. And when you were forced to return it, you set it on fire with a Roman candle."

Candace's eyes glisten in the harsh fluorescent lighting.

"I don't care if you've become a Missionary of Charity; I need to know how to keep my family safe from online predators, nasty people with spray paint, and bad actors at Garman Straub. So, unless you can tell us more about what is happening and how you're involved, I'm not interested in either one of you." A ropy vein pulses down the left side of my husband's temple. As sure as he sounds, this meeting with the two of them is taking a toll.

"I want to tell you everything I know, but I'm certain you don't trust me." Candace leans over her crossed arms on the table.

Clint widens his eyes at her blunt logic.

"Lucas mentioned that you know about my arrest in the Air Force—"

"I. Don't. Care." Clint glances toward his phone and then at me. He's ready to leave.

I lean back in the booth and find Clint's hand with mine.

"Two more minutes, and then I'll answer anything. First, you saw the article in the *Windham Eagle*?" Candace asks.

"Erika found it," I say.

Candace winces.

"I never lied to you, Meredith. The story I told at dinner was the truth. But the other story is that my brothers came to visit when I got back, and I ended up defending those drunk imbeciles. A couple of civilians got hurt, and there was damage to a local bar. The investigation dragged on, and I went home. Kimmie wrote that article before I was cleared. Clint was right, blowing up her lunch box was a boneheaded thing to do, and she's never forgotten it.

"The Air Force taught me a lot of things. Most good. I learned the importance of truth. I learned chain of command. And I thought I learned discernment in the lending of my power."

In barely a whisper, I repeat her last words: *"Discernment in the lending of my power."*

"Yeah, I learned we all have a currency. What motivates us and how we want to be paid. People say it's money, but it rarely is. It's often what money can procure—power, safety, appearance, fame . . . My commanding officer worked with me to harness my ability to lead and set me free from my more caustic traits that you remember, Clint."

"Then tell me this." Clint lets go of my hand and leans both his arms on the table. "Why'd you get involved in all of this? If you learned all these amazing things and turned your life around, why did you do it? To my wife."

"I . . . I thought I could reinvent myself. Lucas recommended me for the head of security job at Garman Straub." She looks over at me with such sadness. "I—we—didn't initially know you worked there. When I met you, I was stunned. At first, I thought maybe this would be our way back into Clint's life. Lucas was excited when he reached out to you." She smiles tightly at me.

"How's that for fast? These plates are hot." Our waitress slides our breakfasts in front of us. "Syrups, ketchup, and hot sauce are in the wire holder at the window. Anything else I can get you?"

We all glance around and then murmur our thanks.

I breathe in the smell. I would have sworn I wasn't hungry, but my stomach growls for the thick slices of sweet cinnamon French toast and crispy slabs of bacon.

In between delicious bites, I flip over the phone and check for any word from Rob. He came out to the cabin, armed with both a gun and donuts, at six this morning. We woke the kids briefly to tell them goodbye, but I asked Rob to let us know when they got out of bed. It's 8:15, and Rob has once again confirmed that they're still sleeping. He's been nothing but patient with my frequent check-ins.

Lucas scrapes his fork across his plate. "I changed my name to Anderson a couple decades ago. The creditors had gotten bad, and I just needed a fresh start."

I don't look over at Clint, but in my periphery I can see he's stopped eating.

"Candace had reinvented herself as well when we met up again. We've been married for five years. And it has been over a decade since she left the Air Force." Lucas is trying, but Clint won't be willing to hear it until he knows his family is safe.

As if she senses the same, Candace uses her fork to cut off the end of her breakfast sausage but doesn't eat it. "I was protecting you."

"Me," I say. This is when we will find out if the four of us have a way back from this, because *me* also means *us*.

Candace moves her napkin from her lap onto her plate. "I'd never do anything to harm or—"

"What about our daughter? What did you do to her?" The anger in Clint's questions has not dissipated.

"Nothing." She glances at Clint and then back to me. "I had nothing to do with—"

"With what? What do you know?" Clint asks.

Lucas almost imperceptibly moves closer to his wife. "We know something happened at school. We know Erika was harassed online. And we know about your car and garage."

"And how do you know these things?" Clint almost spits the question.

Candace glances at me. "I meant to watch over you. Make sure you were safe. Betsey had lost it. She was stalking you and . . ." She speaks steadily. "I'd never do anything to harm any of you."

"You keep saying that." Clint leans back hard in the booth, and it creaks. "Means nothing."

"Are you thinking about reporting this to the police?" Lucas asks me.

"For certain," I say. "They're waiting to hear from us this morning."

"But why our family? Erika was threatened." Clint's jaw turns to granite.

"We know. Any way we can help, we will." Lucas nudges Candace, who is pecking out something on her phone. "We're on your side. Both of us. We thought we had the chance to start new with our relationships and our careers." Lucas puts down his fork and knife on the side of his plate. "But he found out about Candace's trouble in Arizona. She hadn't disclosed the arrest, and even though she was completely cleared, it was a fireable offense. Instead of letting her go, she was *encouraged* to take side jobs. Nothing illegal. Nothing like that."

Candace jumps in. "Some scouting jobs, private security. Occasionally an interesting character that needed to be picked up or dropped off. I was always paid through this app—off-the-books, of course." I stop chewing. Suddenly I know who. Of course he found out. His expertise is reading people. He made up the story of my office trashing at the perfect time to make me sign the restraining order. When Betsey showed up at our house desperate on Sunday, he must have unleashed his hounds on Erika. My heart slams against my ribs.

"The only thing is—right now, we don't have anything concrete tying anyone criminally to the things that have happened to your family." Lucas's cheeks grow round as he blows air out. "I just wonder if there might be another way."

"No." Clint's voice is raised, his body rigid. "We aren't getting sucked into your messed-up schemes."

The older guys in the booth behind Lucas and Candace peer over at us. They wait a few beats before continuing their conversation, probably now lending one ear to ours.

Lucas's eyes, so blue, so reminiscent of Erika's, blink a few times. "Just hear me out. We probably have enough for the SEC to show how our firm was misled into leveraging those securities against the prospectus, but we don't know if there are other firms involved."

While they chat about how much we still don't know, I pick up Clint's phone and text Rob a question for Erika, asking him to wake her up.

"That's enough. We're going to the police, and we'll let the SEC investigate the rest. I'm protecting my family," Clint growls.

Lucas shakes his head. "We need more."

Clint starts to argue.

But I talk over him. "Clint is right—we need to protect our family—but hear me out. I might have an idea."

56

"I WAS THINKING ABOUT something Erika told me yesterday," I say, glancing up from Erika's response to the question I texted.

Over the next few minutes, I explain about the social networking connection of payment apps. If you use one of these services, you can let your friends or even the whole world know you've gifted or paid someone. If you get your nails done with your girlfriends, you can put a little polish bottle in the transaction feed. I go on to explain how Erika's tutoring partner has been able to track the trends in the notifications and see the details. "If we knew how everyone was being paid, we might be able to track it."

"Actually, I think I have someone who could help." Candace scrolls on her phone. "If we knew Hippa would be used again—"

"That's the same app," I say. "Can we track it even if the user has turned off the social announcement setting?"

"Yes. I think we can." Candace continues to explain about a friend of hers who's a genius at these kinds of things.

Clint makes a noise that sounds like a growl. "I don't like this. I don't like using anyone's shady friends to hack into apps. We need to get back to our kids and then meet up with the police. None of this is convincing me to delay."

"Sorry," Candace says in a small voice, having gotten quite animated in her description.

Her apology hits me. She hasn't actually apologized for getting herself embedded in all this. Instead, she's said a lot about how it wasn't her fault.

As if she also recognizes her lack of accountability, she doubles down. "I am truly sorry. Each time I was paid for a security task, I was paid using the same app by the same username. I think Meredith is onto something."

"Honey." I shift toward Clint. "If someone was paid to harass our daughter online and spray-paint our garage and car, we can trap them."

"*If* the same app was used to pay everyone," Clint says.

"Candace. Can your friend put a tickler on the account that was used? If it's used again, we can get a ping on the account." I glance at Clint.

"A lot of what-ifs you're relying on," he says.

"True," says Lucas. "But we could get evidence."

"Evidence of criminal payoffs to the people who went after our family." I squeeze Clint's hand again.

"But we can't just wait around for him to come up with another way to harass us." Clint leans forward, the gears ticking in his head.

"We could set up a fake meet at our house. Maybe I make it known that I'm going to try to talk to Betsey." A sick feeling crawls up my chest. "But maybe not. What if this is bigger? What if she's in trouble? The SEC said they didn't know where she was."

"She's fine," Lucas says with an assurance that makes all his previous sentiments sound fragile.

"How do you know?" Clint asks, bits of the wariness and anger edging back into his voice.

"Because I'm here."

I gasp. The woman I want to both hug and pummel stands at the end of our booth.

Betsey's hair is pulled back into a ponytail and her face is freshly scrubbed. She looks like she's slept. "Thanks for texting me. Can I sit?"

Candace scoots in next to Lucas.

My dilemma of whether to welcome her or grab my husband and flee must be obvious on my face.

"I know, Meredith." She speaks quickly as if peppering me with her words will tie me to my seat. "I wish I'd come to you much earlier. I thought I could assemble a full picture of how our ETFs were being manipulated and the mutual funds given advantage. But I was stymied on every approach. I got desperate. There was only the—"

"You threatened me with pictures." Anger at her deception and relief over her safety war inside me.

"Bad judgment. I don't know what made me take them. I guess at that point I didn't know if you were behind all this. My boss and head of wealth at Meymack—something was not right. I wouldn't have actually done anything with them." Her eyes dart to Clint.

"Right, well, I'm glad you're okay." I believe my own words, but there's no joy in them. "For now, I think we need to focus on our next step." I summarize where we are with the planning to set up the fake meet at the house and watch the app. If someone is paid to go watch our house, or worse, we'll have the proof.

"We should do this." Betsey glances around the table.

"Candace, do you think your friend will be able to set the trap on the app?" I bite down on the inside of my lip. This is a pivot. Are we making a mistake? Now that I see them sitting all together across from us, how can we possibly trust these people?

Candace nods as she pecks at her phone.

"No one will be at the house. It's worth the risk," Lucas says. His Meymack executive posture has returned. I want to warn him to approach carefully, but if the brothers have any chance of mending their relationship, I'll need to stay far away from the middle.

"I hope our house is left standing. This is a desperate situation." Clint's hand grips mine again. I look up at his surprisingly untroubled eyes. It's more than resignation. He wants to bring on this fight and get the evidence we need to end strong.

"Anything else we're missing?" I ask.

Lucas leans forward. "Stay at the cabin—"

"Don't tell me where my family will be." The heat of Clint's glare falls on all three of the adults pressed together on the other side of the booth. "I don't trust any of you."

At least the two of us are on the same page, as this uneasy alliance could shatter at any moment.

"I didn't mean . . . I meant just stay away from the house until you hear from us. I promise, we're done tracking you," Lucas says.

"Don't promise me anything. None of this is as simple as you say." Clint shakes his head as if we've all been duped. "I'll take care of my family."

Lucas swallows and then nods. "Fair enough. We won't ask. There's enough disinformation swirling around. I mean, the things we were told about Betsey . . ."

I stare at Betsey's hands, folded and trembling on the table.

No one says anything for a full minute, perhaps each imagining a very different way this all could end.

I look hard into Clint's eyes. "All right. We'll head somewhere."

Lucas nods. "And we'll contact you when we have proof."

A half hour later, we're on our way back to the cabin. Rob texts that Reid is still sleeping, curled up around his stuffed dog, Henry, who came with him to camp but spent the week in the bottom of his bag, as apparently no one else brought their stuffies. I finally make Rob go in and let him know breakfast, boxed in to-go containers, is on the way.

We sit in silence for a couple more miles before Clint says, "I'm going to ask Rob to return Ella's Accord."

"Gassed and with some cash?" I ask. Not enough time to get it washed and detailed, but she'll probably prefer the cash anyway.

"Sure thing, and we'll take Rob's F-250 for the day."

"We'll take his truck?" This sounds like the least sure part of the plan. Rob and his Ford are more inseparable than Clint and his Tacoma, and that's saying a lot.

"I'm going to ask him to head over and pick up the Range Rover. He'll love being decoy man. I just need to sell him on the danger. If he thinks he might be able to break a tail, he'll be all in."

I chuckle. Good to find some humor in all this darkness. "Are you going to ask him to try to find the tracker on both cars?"

"Even more fun for him." Clint stares out the windshield as if all these logistics are the most important things to be talking about, but I can see the pain in the etched grooves across his forehead. His home is not safe. His family is on the run. And his brother, who robbed his mother of comfort in her dying days, is back in his life.

57

MONDAY

My heels click to the beat of "Eye of the Tiger." The lyrics remarkably appropriate as I stride through the hall of Garman Straub early Monday morning. There's no way I'm walking away from the thrill of this fight. We've gotten almost enough to ensure both a criminal conviction and a ban from the industry. Almost. If I can harness the tiger, we might get it all. We ended up staying at the cabin over the weekend. Reid was so excited to show me the pond, we didn't have the heart to leave until last night when we checked into an Embassy Suites my mom reserved for us. This morning, I woke up ready.

I stride into the C-suite wing. As my Louboutins hit the plush carpet of the hall leading to Phil's office, silence shrouds my steps. A panoramic view of a bright and sunny sky stretching over the city fills the floor-to-ceiling windows.

In the waiting area outside Phil's office, Terrence sits in one of the nutmeg-brown club chairs, his ankle crossed over his knee. He glances up from his phone. His eyes widen and a flicker of surprise at my sudden appearance crosses his small neat features, but a ready smile plumps his cheeks.

"Meredith, good morning. Have a seat?" He indicates the other leather chair and then goes back to poking at his phone.

"Waiting for Phil?" I ask, trying to restart the internal humming that sustained me on my march from the elevator. All I hear is static.

"A few clarifications ahead of the board meeting. You know how it is." He shrugs. "Well, maybe not. This is your second meeting with the fund trustees?"

"Third," I say, swallowing but not fidgeting. How long do I have before Phil opens his door and all this hits the street?

"I hope we get a chance to chat after the board meeting. I've taken a look at the new funds you're proposing, and I'm looking forward to working with you on them." Terrence speaks more to his phone than to me.

"I appreciate that, but I need to take into account what's best for my family. That's why I'm in early." I glance at the door. "Recently I've had to consider resigning from my position and focusing my energy at home."

Terrence slowly makes eye contact. "Meredith, I'm speechless. Why?"

"As you know, this has been a rough week. Not only the ugly business with Betsey, but my daughter has been trolled online and our home threatened." I say more than I intend, and I force a swallow before I ramble. When is the door going to open?

"How terrible. I've read about these things happening to teens. So sorry to hear your family got caught up in it. Must be scary and unsettling."

"You understand. Yes, terrifying." We had a long talk with Erika last night. Clint and I tried to find comfort in her desire to make things right with the tutoring business and talk directly to the teachers whose tests were compromised. She's home from school again today.

"I, well . . ." He straightens as if a load's been lifted from his shoulders. "We'll be sorry to lose you, Meredith. Your innovation has been a spark to our mutual fund legacy. A good run. I hope you catch this predator soon." He looks back down at his phone.

I sit forward. "Oh, they've already caught him."

The creases between his eyes grow deeper. "What a relief for you. Some unhinged teen?"

I frown and nod my head. "That was who the police identified."

He raises his phone and shakes it. "I tell you, these devices—the bane of our existence." He smiles with all his teeth. "I am sorry to see you go, but you must excuse me, I've got—"

I stand. "We figured that the online harassment and vandalism at the house were part of an overall campaign to distract me from the data that Betsey found."

Terrence looks curiously at me.

"The heat needed to be turned up. When Betsey showed up at my house and then I brought in the data and started asking for the securities lending agreement, we got too close. The statements run through your department—in fact you specifically." I see Clint's face and the faces of our children urging me to take back the power. "Don't you find that odd? And then they come out cleansed with—"

"Meredith." Terrence stands, puffing out his scrawny chest. "You're sounding paranoid. I do not cleanse reports. If there are any alarming reports, they're the client data reports you've been receiving from Meymack. That's what I am here to discuss with Phil. We've been quite concerned—"

"Oh, you mean data you collected to frame me. Yes, let's talk about the data you assured Hardwin was fake." I'm spitballing here, but I assume Terrence is the origin of the data being called fake. Perhaps he thought if he could discredit Betsey and distract me with Erika's troubles, he could clean this all up without it going nuclear. Regardless, I'm certain he'd have found a way to get rid of me too. Perhaps, in this, he'll end up succeeding.

Terrence sputters but pulls back his shoulders and finds his next gear. "Well, maybe I should have my team take another look. I mean, after all, your sales practices have been highly successful. Perhaps you had some unsanctioned help?"

The anger inside me threatens to turn into mutinous tears. I grind my heels into my shoes. The pain biting at my ankles serves to focus me. I will speak truth to this man. "That was your plan all along, wasn't it? If I caused waves, you had this over me."

"I have no idea what you're talking about. But I am sure Phil will be understanding when you tender your resignation to spend time with your family. We can just let your little cheat be our little secret. Because, Meredith, the business of Garman Straub is mutual funds."

"Another thing you twisted out of your subpar lending arrangements—more favorable placement of your precious funds."

His mouth slackens for a brief moment, but then he recovers. "Your fleeting success is over. We need to get back to the work at hand."

"That's the thing. I'm tired of secrets, and I'm not going anywhere."

"Oh, but we know you. Once Phil finds out what you've been up to, there's no future for you. I mean the things you didn't tell the board. Tut, tut, Meredith." He shakes his head like I'm a puppy who messed the carpet. "Because in the end, it's men like me that ensure the foundations of this company are not eroded by the next cheap, shiny thing."

My breathing has accelerated, and a nerve burns between my shoulder blades, but I refuse to fidget. I've never been spoken to this way. Perhaps I've been lucky to have mentors who've shielded me. Sure, I've been on the receiving end of opportunities that evaporated in favor of guys in clubhouse networks who have known each other for ages. I've been asked to get the coffee at meetings I presided over. I've been followed into bathrooms so that a male colleague can get his last word, as well as his last lecture. I've been propositioned while laying out a business opportunity. But each time, I considered my long game. This time, I'm playing to win.

Terrence continues with self-assurance born of privilege. "Phil understands how this business runs. He's been my mentor since my days at Villanova. We are both Tau Zetas—a decade apart, but fraternity brothers with vision. He knows I'm next in line. He needs me to carry his legacy."

Terrence turns his back to me and stalks toward Phil's door.

Terrence appears clear on his future and my demise. He may be right; I may not survive this. But I'm not going down without a fight. I know I'm good for this firm, and I'm great at what I do. The steady bass line of the Survivor anthem breaks through the static and pulses through me, just a woman and her will to survive.

58

THE SOLID OAK DOOR OPENS and Phil strides out. "Good morning, Terrence and Meredith, I trust you both had a good weekend. Are we ready to impress the trustees?"

Terrence picks invisible lint from the sleeve of his dark suit jacket. "I came by to inquire if there was anything you needed."

"Appreciate that." Phil smiles.

"But now, I'm going to need to bring you up to speed." Terrence sighs almost theatrically. "There's been some unethical conduct—I might even say criminal—I've been made aware of. I'm sorry to say, but Meredith has gotten herself mixed up in some very troubling behaviors."

Phil's mouth opens, but he doesn't speak, while I simply can't. Although nothing that Terrence is saying is any surprise at this point, the surreal shock in hearing his condemnation in the executive suite, in front of our CEO, skewers a rod straight through me.

Terrence spins toward me. "She has obtained confidential sales data to boost the success of her ETFs. Simply unconscionable."

Phil finds his voice. "Terrence, that is quite an accusation, and right before our board meeting. I don't understand. Meredith was the one to bring the data to our attention. I can hardly believe she's behind it."

"Oh, she's crafty. As you know, I've had Candace track her movements with Betsey, and I have proof of her accepting the data." Terrence shakes his head, stepping closer to Phil.

Phil begins to talk, but Terrence continues. "We might never know how she was able to convince Meymack to comply with her fraud, but we can assume it has to do with how she's been able to rise so quickly in this industry."

Something cracks deep within me. I thought I could sit by and watch this play out, that Terrence would say more to incriminate himself. But I want to slap the smugness from his face.

"At least I wasn't idiotic enough to pay all the minions using the same account, traced right back to the source." My lip curls into a sneer of its own accord.

Terrence also appears like he wants to hit someone. Probably me.

Phil must sense this as he steps forward. "We need to deal with this right now." He turns slightly and extends his hand toward his door as a tall, trim Black man strides from his office. "Terrence, have you met Gaven Newal? He is the SEC Enforcement Division chief. Gaven, this is my chief of compliance, whom I've just finished telling you all about."

59

THE CONFERENCE ROOM IS DEAD QUIET, the kind of silence that builds like layers of ice before the roof caves in. I take a deep breath, will my nerves to settle, and then place the thumb drive on the polished mahogany table. Twelve pairs of eyes dart down and then back up to me. At the head of the table, Phil—the presiding chair and, for the moment, my only ally—looks at me with an intensity that makes my throat ache. But the board deserves the truth, no matter how tainted it is.

"This . . . this won't be easy to hear," I begin, pushing back a wave of nausea. I can already feel my carefully rehearsed words slipping away, scattering like marbles spilled across a wooden floor. These men and one woman hold the future of the firm and my career in their hands. I force myself to continue. "The funds I manage have been used for unsanctioned securities lending and in at least one case, subpar rates given to benefit the mutual funds."

Clearing of throats, narrowed eyes, a few furrowed brows meet my swinging gaze.

"This happened through our custodian?" asks Barry Eiten, the board member who, at our last two encounters, treated me as if I were an annoying intern. He's a year away from the mandatory retirement age of seventy-five and seems to take it out on those younger for pushing him toward the end of the plank.

"The custodian was not the lending agent. The transactions were orchestrated directly by Terrence." I don't yet add that he used my name to do it. Phil didn't think it necessary to give all the details up front. I tense the muscles in my arms and hands to keep from fidgeting.

The group looks around, registering the absence of our chief compliance officer at the table.

"And worse, he didn't stop at the funds. After he managed to get my sales manager fired, she delivered this thumb drive to me. She had been putting together the . . . his plan." I can't bring myself to use the word *fraud* in this room. "Then he went after my family."

"Meredith, you're saying Terrence targeted your family?" Barry's voice is low, but it cuts through the stunned silence, demanding an explanation, an answer I'm not sure I can give without breaking.

"Yes, he did. He—" My voice catches. I can't let them see the tears gathering. "He paid people to harass my teenage daughter, playing on her biggest fears. He defaced my home. He drove me away from my job. And then he hid his transactions in the system, buried under layers of altered reports. He used stolen data to make it look as though I was the one—"

"Terrence did all this? Why?" Barry interrupts.

Phil begins to speak, perhaps to show his support, but Barry won't allow a united front.

"I'd like to hear from our portfolio manager. Meredith, why?" Barry keeps his gaze locked on me.

"Because the success of our ETFs threatens Terrence's legacy. He knows the business is changing and his compliance process needs to modernize. Terrence is no longer the man people ask about the future. He's the one with the stories of the past."

Something flashes in Barry's eyes. I've reminded him of all that threatens his place of power too.

Did I go too far?

"And yet, you knew nothing?" Another board member speaks up.

"We trusted the altered reports. He gave some of the revenue back to the ETFs but used the rest for his purposes." My voice hardens as confidence replaces the fear. "He made sure I wouldn't find out. He exploited the system and my trust, and when my team got close to uncovering it, he put a tracker on my daughter's phone, harassed her, and diverted my attention."

"So, you're the victim here?" Joanne Ketter, our newest board member, speaks up. "You're also supposed to be the one in charge."

I meet her gaze, heat spreading through my chest. Is she using this moment to establish herself? To be seen as the one not swayed by emotion but leading by power? With so much disappointment swirling around, I won't let her rebuff settle into me.

"I *am* in charge. I'm standing here, risking my career, my reputation, and exposing the truth. The truth is that Terrence abused his power, undermined this company, and deliberately went after me and my family when he realized I would get in his way. I trusted him, and he weaponized that trust against me, against all of us. He leveraged income meant for the ETFs and used it to curry favors for his legacy funds."

For a moment, the room is silent. And in that silence, the weight of what this job demands of me crashes onto my shoulders. Flickers of skepticism dart between the faces around the table. But I'm not going down without a fight.

"He extorted Candace, our head of security, to make her do his bidding. Many of you know her. She had some trouble in her past. He found out. No way would he allow her to remain working for Garman Straub, but then he delayed taking action and instead asked her to do things. Nothing illegal or unethical, just not her normal duties. She drove by a few of your homes, ensuring security was tight. Then he told her she was protecting me."

Board members take furtive glances at Phil, the one who insisted on hiring Candace.

Phil speaks up, tentatively at first and then with growing power. "Meredith put this all together. Terrence was desperate to get to the board meeting today. Her sales manager knew this and waged her own campaign to figure everything out. Terrence's plan, as we've been able to piece together, was to expose Meredith for leveraging unsanctioned sales data, maybe more, and make it impossible to go forward with new ETFs. At least until he was the one in charge." Phil catches my eye and nods, almost imperceptibly.

This is the hardest part. I swallow and then open my mouth to explain how the SEC has already gotten involved.

Barry speaks first. "Meredith, I am sorry on behalf of the board for what you and your family have gone through. It is incomprehensible that anyone, especially someone we have all trusted, would do something like this and put all of us at risk. You have my deepest concern for your teen's well-being. Let us not stand in your way of supporting her."

I see a father and grandfather in the warmth of his gaze. His kindness almost breaks me. But the last thing he said—was I just fired? I was certainly dismissed. My lungs feel as though they've been rubbed raw. My breath catches on each inhale. Is this the way it will end, with me being excused from my own future? I struggle against the urge to roar.

"Phil, we have a few questions for you, and then we will need to go into executive session. Independent trustees only." Barry flips open the document in front of him.

Hardwin, who remained silent during the board meeting, flanks me as I leave the room. "Meredith, would you join me in Phil's office?"

I nod my head, not trusting my ability to speak. All that just transpired tussles in my mind to be rehashed and examined. Was it as bad as it felt?

The two of us sit opposite each other at a smaller chrome and glass conference table.

"How are you holding up?" Hardwin's eyes are clear and wide as he searches my face. "I'm sorry, Meredith. Anything else you wanted to say?"

So much more, but the heat is dissipating, as if leaving the room has deflated me. I do wish I'd gotten to talk about the SEC and then been able to help them understand. I glance up at Hardwin's kind eyes. "I keep thinking I should've met with our custodial bank. Specifically on the lending piece. I knew I had securities that were on-special. I kick myself for taking those reports at face value." Not what I had planned to say, but it has worn on my conscience.

"You did meet with the bank. Multiple times on multiple topics," Hardwin says.

"Maybe if I'd asked more questions?"

"You're not the only one," Phil says as he waltzes in with a handful of papers. "If we're taking responsibility. Had I insisted that Dave manage all the sales, you'd have had a spare moment to look around."

Quite altruistic of him, but my gaze resettles on the small stack he holds. Is that my separation agreement? I knew it was a strong possibility when Clint and I talked last night. Even if I came entirely clean, I was still a tremendous liability to the firm. The buck stops with me. I'm the portfolio manager.

Hardwin nods at the table. "When I started in this industry, we were on the phones getting the deed done. I've caught boys setting up front-running schemes. I've escorted off nasty floor traders. I've called hedge funds on their unbridled use of leverage. But I didn't even see this coming. Terrence was trying to recruit me. Dave said the same." He points to the papers. "This is what we both know. Printed out for the authorities to see how we were duped into complacency."

My shoulders drop an inch. So, they're not firing me. Yet.

"Thank goodness for Betsey," I say to test the waters. Will reminding Hardwin of his role in silencing her raise his hackles? I need to know. "Thinking back through her desperate search for the nexus of the issues, I wish she'd found another way to tell us what she suspected. But I can understand her concern—from her perspective it could have been any one of us involved."

I've had only one short conversation with Betsey since the diner. She's been fully cooperating with the SEC but went off-grid when I failed to contact her and Candace was breathing down both our necks. She has whistleblower status and could come into a significant monetary award for her efforts.

"I'm dropping the restraining order this afternoon. Our official statement, only if we're asked, is also included in those pages." Hardwin's massive hand points across the table.

"I spoke to Vern over at Meymack," Phil says. "They're fully cooperating with the SEC. Lucas Anderson had already gone to him. He's going to lose his job and may get more than blowback from the SEC. Depends on how much they need him to make their case against Terrence." Phil shakes his head at me. "Terrible how your family got caught up in all this. I hope you take all the time you need to make sure everyone is good." He bites down on his bottom lip.

I've never seen him do that before. He's probably nervous he may not be able to protect his firm. There's no doubt, he may be forced to fire me. I'm sure he also wonders about Lucas being my brother-in-law. Something everyone now knows. I have nothing to say about Lucas. Although I do have my beliefs about his integrity, Clint is less conflicted; having witnessed his brother keep his word, he still doesn't want the man, or his wife, in our lives.

"Candace resigned this morning." As Hardwin shakes his head slowly, a few stray hairs wave on the crown of his freckled scalp. "We'll need to find a new head of security. Perhaps this time without a past that makes them vulnerable. She did put in a solid structure and plugged a lot of holes."

Phil nods. "Hardwin is also going to help the SEC. We're working on ensuring full cooperation in exchange for immunity, but in the end, we'll do the right thing for our investors." Phil taps the papers beside him. "The board has a copy."

I rest my back against the buttery leather of my chair. They both might not survive this either. It happened on their watch as well. I also see what they're doing. They're stalling. They have something to tell me and have been laying the tracks.

Phil and Hardwin look at each other across the smudgeless glass table. Phil finally rotates his chair toward me. "The board is likely going to come back with a strong recommendation."

I swallow hard. Since we got word that Terrence had taken the bait and engaged his payment app, I've been fixated on this executive session.

I fold my hands in my lap and let Phil tell me what else will happen.

"We think there might be a fairly good chance that the board will push for your firing." Phil takes a quick breath but plunges ahead. "Although their recommendation will be read into the minutes, we will have time to assess. We've retained outside counsel to advise us. We do not want to see you go, Meredith. You are talented." He glances at the ceiling. "Mercy, you're a rainmaker. We would be foolish to let you go. We just might not have a choice."

And if they push me out, even if they allow me to resign, I'll be tainted. Other firms will smell the stink on me. No one wants someone who, at best, allowed this to happen to such successful funds—and, at worst, was complicit. "I hear you. I've also retained counsel."

"I see." Phil lowers his face for a moment. "I assume this means you are considering taking action if you are let go."

"Please assume nothing." I glance to my other side. "Working so closely with Hardwin and his team has taught me the wisdom of seeking smart and capable legal advice. I adore working for Garman Straub. I hope we can work through this." A queasiness snakes through my stomach.

There's a small knock on Phil's door, and then Nonie sticks her head in. "They're out of executive session. Phil, they'd like you, only you, to join them."

60

ELEVEN MONTHS LATER

MarketSite is simply a Times Square soundstage, but I feel every bit of the excitement I did almost a year ago when I stood on that thin white balcony at NYSE and rang the bell. The rhythms are the same. Each exchange offers a fresh start every trading day, and six and a half hours later, the gavel bangs. This morning, we all move toward the right of the floor, allowing others to file in after us. Cameras will catch every angle of the opening bell.

This time I watch from the shadows.

Carrie Scovill steps up to the wide white podium and accepts a cylindrical Lucite plaque from the head of listings at Nasdaq. I pull out my phone and catch the moment along with almost sixty other people in the room. The diverse senior leadership team of Wilson Outdoors joins her at the podium for more pictures. On their beaming faces, both pride and gratitude are obvious. Somehow it feels like innocent enthusiasm, but I know every company has their secrets—cultures that are not quite as empowering as they advertise or leadership that serves itself.

I shake off my cynicism and give Clint a shove. This is the part he dreads. He loves both ideation and execution, but can't stand the applause of the masses. I shove him again. We've talked about this. He groans, kisses me on the cheek, and stumbles forward.

There is so much more room on the Nasdaq podium than there was at the NYSE. Clint immediately goes to the back, as is his plan. He stands at least a half a head taller than many around him. Carrie twists back and pulls him forward. They're proud of the investment they've made in Tru-ly Trails. Largest grant winner in the company's history.

The cheering begins. The countdown is on. Moments later, Carrie jabs her finger on the screen built into the podium, and the pealing of the bell fills the room. She then tugs on Clint's shoulder to give him the opportunity to press the screen and ring the bell. This was not part of the plan. Clint cringes and messes up his face. Next to me, Reid points and snorts out a laugh. I grab his arm and yank it down, but I'm chuckling as well. I remember Phil pulling me up from behind Dave and Terrence, the satisfaction of being seen and promoted.

Clint probably has no such thoughts.

"He looks good up there."

I startle at Betsey's voice. Even with all the commotion and noise in the room, her presence rattles me.

I turn toward her, my arm automatically tugging Reid close.

"Didn't expect to see you here," I say.

"Probably the same words that rang through your head almost a year ago—at a very different bell ringing."

No, not quite the same words.

"Dave invited me." Betsey tips her porcelain chin to her right. Her hair is shorter. I'm not sure it suits her round face.

Dave is tucked behind a group of employees invited to watch and cheer. He raises his hand.

I return the wave. Interesting he's not pushing himself into the limelight, but I resist the urge to read too much into it. The din of the room recedes as the opening celebration winds down. Reid runs to hug his dad as Clint tries to make it back to us but is pulled into introductions. It's a shame Rob couldn't make it. The networking here would be priceless, but that is not their way. He called last night from Kilimanjaro, grateful Clint was taking the monkey-suit bullet.

"I've been wanting to connect." Betsey shifts into my line of vision. "I applaud your move to Dyverse Funds. I have to say, I was surprised. Dave said Phil fought to keep you."

Although her query is masked in observation, her question is clear. After working so hard to preserve my job, how could I have left?

But I don't owe her or anyone an explanation of my career choices.

"So, Dave?" I cock my head but keep a small smile in place.

She nibbles on her lip as she glances over at him. "Dave's a good guy. All that time we spent with the forensic accountants and with the SEC . . ."

I suppose my face indicates my doubts as she rolls her eyes.

"I know," she says. "I wouldn't have guessed it either."

"Clint agrees with you. We wish you both well." Limited to the contacts saved in Clint's sat phone, after Rob, Dave had been the one I texted as Lucas showed up at the cabin. I trusted my husband's instincts. Apparently surprising only me, Dave proved himself a potent ally through the SEC investigation.

I continue to keep my distance.

"We're just dating. His wife divorced him a few years ago. He's still hurting. Figuring it out." She looks at the floor and then back at me. "I'm happy for you. That you landed on your feet. You know none of what happened—"

"Betsey, we're all good," I say.

The SEC doesn't take kindly to ignorance. I had to prove that even though we were all deceived by Terrence, for me it was not a sign of incompetence. My capacity for trust took quite a hit as everything went down. I'm still working on opening myself up again.

I finally smile. "Look, I love it at Dyverse. A pure ETF company. Assets are growing. We just launched another thematic." The team is younger, eager for success with innovative ideas without the concerns of a legacy business. I'm not sure if it's a long-term career move for me, but I have a lot of flexibility. Some days, I miss the dynamic creativity born through the roots of history entwining with a confidence in the future, like I found at Garman Straub. For now, I am content and leaving any forecasting to my portfolio choices and not my career.

"Yeah, I saw your new fund launch. It's just I hope you—"

"I'm fine." Maybe not fully healed, but I'm working on it. My marriage is on solid ground. I appreciate my family and recognize the contentedness we've found.

"I've wondered, since you haven't wanted to get together."

I step closer to her, giving her my undivided attention. "It's not you. I appreciate what you did. Not how you went about it." I hold up my hand when she opens her mouth to probably try to explain again. She's used the same words in a handful of voicemails over the past year. I appreciate her need to say them, but I need her to appreciate my need to not get caught up again. "I'm happy for you. You deserve every dollar of the whistleblower settlement. And you're right; I could have stuck it out at Garman Straub, but I was ready to move on. I've also found better balance." I glance over at Erika and MJ pointing at the podium. Erika fought hard to get her boyfriend here—one of the many things I love about our daughter, her loyalty and perseverance.

"Good to hear it. You let me know if you find the time." Betsey holds out her hand.

Instead of shaking her hand, my fingers itch to grasp my necklace. Oma would urge simple forgiveness. She would whisper about the path of healing for us both. I hesitate. I don't feel ready. But Clint and I found our something different, and our new pastor would say it's not about feeling. It's about seeking freedom by unshackling ourselves from the anger and the hurt. Clint and I have started going to church with the kids. It's new. The people are very kind. Erika thinks they're too friendly, and although I admonish her comments, I kind of agree. It's hard to trust, but that's the point: we need to learn. And we are. We're finding that trusting in a God who knows us and created us is a whole lot easier than in the people who've hurt us.

I look down at Betsey's hand and grasp it. "All is forgiven." Although I still don't feel it, something shifts inside me, and I gently draw her into an embrace.

Betsey's stiff shoulders slacken against me. A tiny sob escapes her. She covers it with a cough and pulls back, her smile soft. "I learned so much from you. I'm so grateful."

"We made a powerful team. I wish you the best, Betsey."

Half an hour later, we're all ushered outside and onto Broadway to look up at the MarketSite tower. Massive Times Square screens surround us, and as Clint hugs me to him, we watch the thirty-second commercial for Wilson Outdoors. Applause begins spontaneously as seven-story-tall images of the opening bell cycle through. The kids cheer when an image of our family flashes on the screen. Erika takes a picture. Reid's enthusiasm turns to boos. His face is missing. A number of square windows Swiss-cheese the picture, looking like random missing puzzle pieces. He got robbed and lets everyone around us know it.

"We'll frame the full picture when we get it, buddy." Clint roughs his hair. "Who's ready for brunch at the Knickerbocker?" He points down the bustling walkway of Times Square.

"Can we really see where they drop the ball?" Reid's disappointment is already forgotten. His ability to bounce back and find pure joy in the next opportunity is something I aspire to emulate. I'm growing weary of my stifling reluctance to trust anyone outside my tight circle.

"Even better, from the roof we can check out the actual crystal orb sittin' at the bottom of the New Year's pole," MJ says with more words than I usually hear him string together.

Reid gazes up at Erika's boyfriend with a huge smile. Obvious adoration from the start. But MJ isn't who I'd have chosen for Erika, not at first. Too quiet, too measured, like he was holding something back. My hackles were always twitching. Over time I've come to see that's just who he is—unflustered, dependable, and never one to make promises he can't keep. He's good to her, I'll give him that.

My phone vibrates in my suit jacket. "Just a sec." I glance down at a text from Alyssa about the rough opening. When she found out I was leaving Garman Straub, she made no secret of her desire to follow. She's one of the reasons I enjoy my new position so much. She's brilliant and insightful. I tab over to her email and open one of the earnings reports she attached. Dismal, but as she knows, opportunities abound, no matter which way the market points.

Clint squeezes my left hand. "You have to go? We understand, sweetheart. Don't we, guys?"

The kids' faces say differently. Only MJ appears neutral—smart young man. My heart tugs at our small group. Lucas and Candace have tried their best to get close, but Clint remains steadfast in his refusal to welcome them into our lives. Regardless of his repeated brush-offs, they've asked to see us up in Maine while we're there next month. Clint won't confirm what our plans are for the fifth, but he's talking more about his mom with me and the kids, which I take as a win.

"Nope. I'm in." I shove my phone in my bag. "Work can wait. Let's go eat our body weight in scrambled eggs and waffles."

I thread my fingers through Clint's, and he squeezes back—steady, certain. Our eyes meet, a quiet promise passing between us. Then, together, we step forward, hand in hand.

crazy4
fiction
.com

A Note from the Author

DEAR READER, I felt a deep calling to write the kind of novel I longed to read—one that captures the relentless push and pull between ambition and devotion, the high-stakes pressure of making the right call, and the razor-thin line between success and disaster. At its heart, this story is also about the love of family—the truth that anchors us even when the world spins out of control. I hope you've been gripped by the storyline as much as I was while writing it. Please also let me assure you that while this novel is full of deception, betrayal, and financial foul play, you shouldn't let it shake your confidence in the markets. The reality is that while sometimes things like what Meredith encounters in the story *do* happen, it doesn't mean they are widely occurring. For every scheme or scandal that makes headlines (or, in this case, the pages of a novel), there are thousands of professionals working every day to keep our markets strong, transparent, and accessible. Instead, I imagined what could theoretically happen as a way to take Meredith on a journey of discovering not only what it means to have courage and stand up for what is right in the face of adversity, but also to help her see what the most important things are—family, faith, and relationships.

So, you may be wondering how much of this story is based on my own experience on Wall Street. I have had the opportunity to ring a few bells, attend a number of town halls, and I have been detained by others on higher rungs in order for them to make their particular points clear. This novel was loosely inspired by my own career as well as those I interview on the *We Talk Careers* podcast, but in the end is a completely fictionalized story of the exciting world of high finance. I hope you enjoyed the twists and turns—but remember, the real markets aren't a rigged game. Play smart, stay informed, and may all your investments trend upward.

Acknowledgments

How can I possibly thank all the people who inspired this novel—including over twelve thousand accomplished professionals in the Women in ETFs community? A spreadsheet with color-coded appreciation levels? A diversified gratitude portfolio overweighted in your collective brilliance? Every day, you challenge and motivate me—whether through the incredible stories you share on our podcast, *We Talk Careers*, or the insightful (and sometimes brutally honest) conversations we have. I'm honored to sit on the global board, even if keeping up with all of you sometimes feels like a full-contact sport: Laura Morrison, Jillian DelSignore, Michelle Shanley, Emily Meyer, Janel Jackson, Kara Pagliuca, Christine Berg, Elisabeth Kashner, Deborah Fuhr, Joy Yang, Enid Lal, Fiona Bassett, Tanya Rowntree, and Deborah Yang, as well as past board members Allison Fumai, Joanne Hill, Jill Mavro, Michelle Mikos, Sue Thompson, Diana Tidd, Linda Zhang. A big shout-out to Sharon French, mentor extraordinaire in guiding and supporting me through my first book launch.

To Lynette Eason, bestselling author and my agent, thank you for responding to a random message on Kate Angelo's Discord channel. Lynette, you gave me my first *yes*.

To Elizabeth Jackson, who said *no*. Incredibly hard to hear, but I'm thankful you did, because a week later you unexpectedly asked,

"What else?" and I got to write this novel. You took a chance on a writer with passion to bring light and excitement to the opaque world of high finance. Enter in Sarah Rische, and I won big—a powerhouse editorial duo. To the entire team at Tyndale, I am so thankful to be able to work with all of you.

To Genevieve, Miranda, and Zach, you have each believed in my dream before I could even articulate it. That's some serious early-stage investing. You, along with your amazing dad, have prayed for me, supported me, and cheered me on. I am blessed. You know how much I love you all.

To my mom, Ruth (all the emojis), and sisters, Bobo and Becca, and my entire family, thank you for the encouragement and the love. You are all gifts. And to my cousins Betsey and Clint, thank you for the unsanctioned lending of your names.

To my lifelong friends Nicole, Kim, and Colleen—we've weathered marriages, motherhood, and the occasional bear market of life's toughest moments. Thank you for being my ride-or-die investors in this journey.

To my church family and friends, including Kati, Abby, Kim, Lorraine, Marissa, Jenna, Mindy, Sara, and so many others, your prayers and excitement for this journey have been unwavering and undoubtedly powerful.

To Katie Milazzo (@katiearnoldphotography), thank you for taking my very first author photos—your joy is contagious, your friendship so sweet. And to the selfless Young Life leaders who continue to honor me with the sharing of your lives: I am here for you always.

To Jamie Ogle, Christy Award winner and the best writing buddy. You've shown unshakable confidence in my writing. Thank you for inviting me into your home and family. I am so grateful for our brainstorming, our page critiques, and our friendship. And to Chris Posti for bringing us and Diane Samson into a powerful writing group, my first.

To my writing community: Leslie (x2), Sarah, Sherry, Jessica, Ruth, Natalie, Heather, Courtney, Kristi, and so many incredible others, we all run our own amazing races. Thank you for playing such a pivotal role in mine, whether offering bullish encouragement when my confidence wavers or pulling me back when I'm about to over-leverage an idea; your talents and perseverance encourage me every day.

I thank God for you, reader, and for the calling to write stories that bring light to the unseen, hope to the unbalanced, and a bit of fictional fraud and greed to the chaos.

Thank you for reading.

Discussion Questions

1. *The Lies We Trade* offers an inside look at the world of Wall Street and is full of twists and turns. Which were the biggest surprises to you? What did you learn about the industry that you didn't know before?

2. What was your initial perception of Meredith? Of Betsey? How did those perceptions change as the story unfolded?

3. Meredith begins to feel like every area of her life is unraveling at once, and she's torn between focusing on the problems at work and those at home. Were there moments when you felt she made the wrong call? Have you faced a similar time of multiple stresses colliding at once? How did you handle it?

4. Clint and Meredith are at a crisis point in their marriage due to unresolved tensions, hurts, and misunderstandings that have gone unaddressed, and important revelations they've kept from each other. Did you find yourself siding with one of them over the other? Did that change as the story went on?

5. As a woman in the finance industry, Meredith has faced many obstacles and even outright discrimination and abusive

behavior. She thinks of herself as "a master of the long game." How does that prove to be, as she says, both her advantage and her Achilles' heel?

6. Meredith and Clint face multiple revelations about what's happening in their teenage daughter Erika's life. How do they respond—both helpfully and not? What would you have done in their shoes?
7. Phil Langford advises Meredith that *time is the valued currency of a wise life.* What do you think he means by this? Do you agree with his philosophy?
8. Why does Clint respond so strongly when Meredith tells him the truth about Lucas? Did you sympathize with his reaction? Are there events and relationships in your own past that still feel unresolved, even in adulthood?
9. Meredith remembers her grandmother's devout faith, in contrast to her mother, who "believes only in what she can see and what she can affect." Which perspective is more like your own? Where does Meredith land on the question of faith?
10. After all that has happened to her and her family, Meredith struggles with trust and forgiveness. How is she trying to move forward? What next steps would you recommend for her?

About the Author

KRISTINE DELANO spent over twenty years navigating a career on Wall Street before trading her panoramic city view for her standing writer's desk. A lifelong fiction lover, she now crafts thriller novels set in the high-stakes finance world, exploring the emotional tension of work-life balance.

In pursuit of compelling stories, Kristine hosts the popular podcast *We Talk Careers*, where she interviews the voices of Wall Street on leadership, growth, and purpose. She is also a board member, speaker, and strategic advisor for businesses, schools, and parachurch organizations. Her faith fuels her passion for helping women navigate their calling.

Kristine's work has been recognized in fiction-focused writing competitions and with the ACFW Crown Award. She also loves the chance to stay connected with fellow authors and readers on Instagram and LinkedIn and through her membership in writers' groups.

When she's not writing, Kristine enjoys playing games with friends, scuba diving, and chasing her husband and children down the snowy ski slopes of western Maine—never does she catch them, but with joy she tries. Connect with her online at kristinedelano.com.

CONNECT WITH KRISTINE ONLINE AT

kristinedelano.com

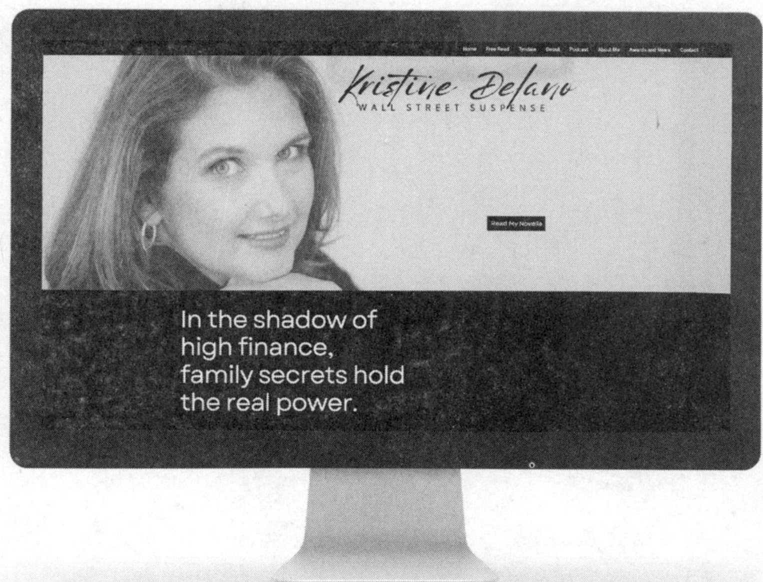

OR FOLLOW HER ON

KristineDelano.Writer

kristine.delano.writer

kristinedelano

CP2079